P9-DNZ-944

A Fireproof Home for the Bride

Also by Amy Scheibe

What Do You Do All Day?

A Fireproof Home for the Bride

Amy Scheibe

St. Martin's Press
New York

This is a work of fiction. All of the characters, organizations, and events portrayed in this novel are either products of the author's imagination or are used fictitiously.

www.stmartins.com

Frontispiece photograph from *Ladies' Home Journal* circa 1920

Designed by Kathryn Parise

The Library of Congress Cataloging-in-Publication Data
is available upon request.

ISBN 978-1-250-04967-4 (hardcover)
ISBN 978-1-4668-6970-7 (e-book)

St. Martin's Press books may be purchased for educational, business, or promotional use. For information on bulk purchases, please contact the Macmillan Corporate and Premium Sales Department at 1-800-221-7945, extension 5442, or write to specialmarkets@macmillan.com.

First Edition: March 2015

10 9 8 7 6 5 4 3 2 1

For Catherine, Ann, and Hedda,
the glittering points of my triangle

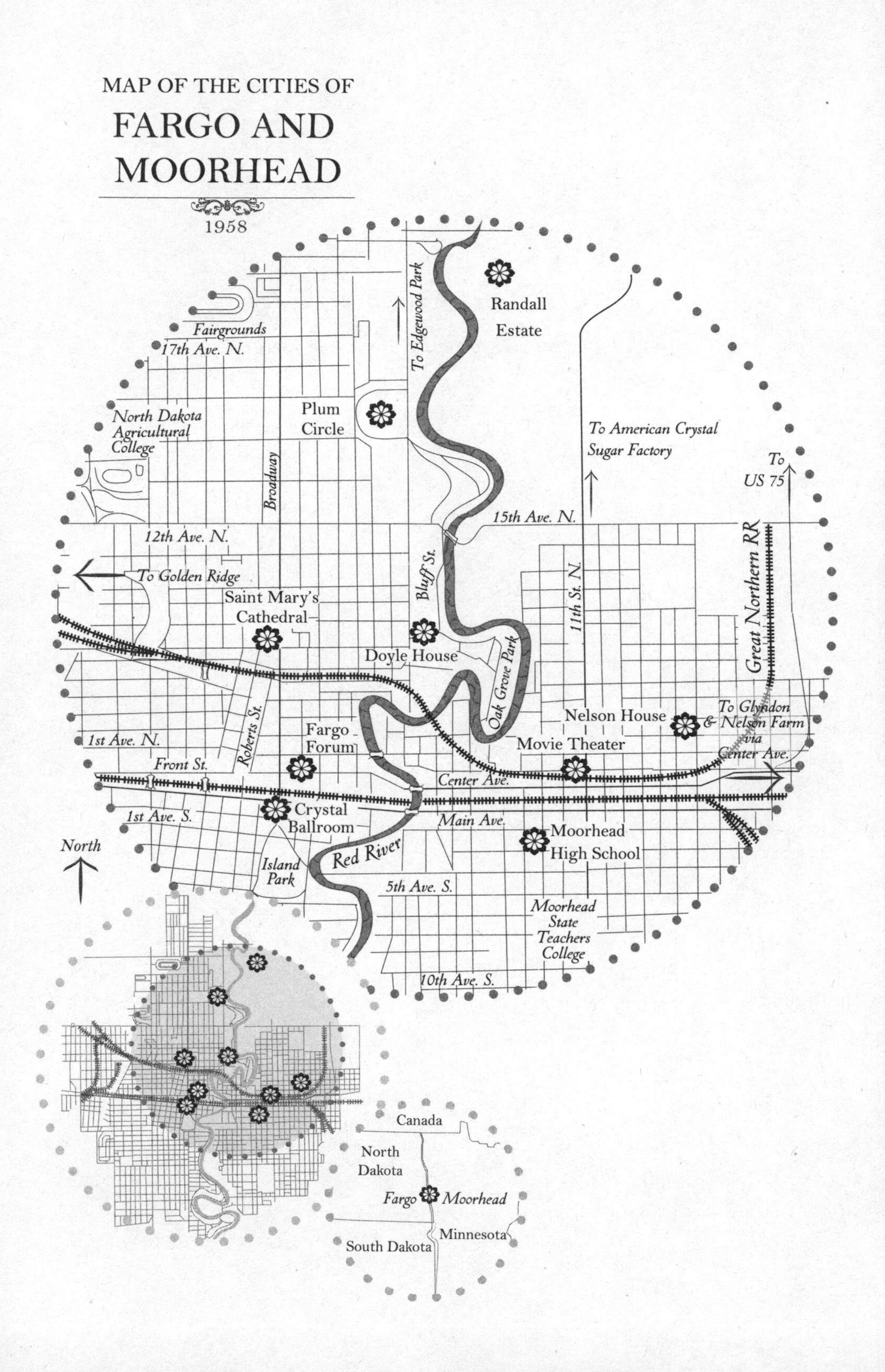
MAP OF THE CITIES OF
FARGO AND MOORHEAD
1958
Fairgrounds
17th Ave. N.
To Edgewood Park
Randall Estate
Plum Circle
North Dakota Agricultural College
Broadway
To American Crystal Sugar Factory
To US 75
15th Ave. N.
12th Ave. N.
Bluff St.
11th St. N.
Great Northern RR
To Golden Ridge
Saint Mary's Cathedral
Doyle House
Oak Grove Park
Roberts St.
Nelson House
To Glyndon & Nelson Farm via Center Ave.
Fargo Forum
Movie Theater
1st Ave. N.
Front St.
Center Ave.
Crystal Ballroom
1st Ave. S.
Main Ave.
Moorhead High School
North
Island Park
Red River
5th Ave. S.
Moorhead State Teachers College
10th Ave. S.
Canada
North Dakota
Fargo
Moorhead
Minnesota
South Dakota

Contents

Part III
A Child of Solitude

What shall I do, if all my love,
My hopes, my toil, are cast away,
And if there be no God above,
To hear and bless me when I pray?

—Anne Brontë,
"The Doubter's Prayer"

Prologue

His Wonders to Perform

October 1952

A hazy dawn broke over a small lean-to of weathered gray planks and multicolored leafy branches that had been meticulously assembled the day before, the work completed mostly between the morning chores and those dispatched in the afternoon. Emmy looked up at the speckled yellow covering of boughs that she had carefully chosen from the row of shrubs and smaller trees that edged the barren late-autumn field of sheared cornstalks, their papery remains bent toward the earth, waiting for the punishment of the long Minnesota winter to grind them into dust.

Emmy exhaled into the frisky air of late autumn, gauging the temperature by how quickly the cloud of visible breath dissipated. She'd been quiet for the better part of an hour, too excited to long for the fitful sleep that had been disrupted by her mother's insistent "get up and out, he's here, go on," as though the girl needed more encouragement. Her heart had felt as though a small, tremulous rabbit had somehow gotten down inside of her and wanted desperately to be out in the field, in the shelter, waiting. Emmy had been given a cup of black coffee from Ambrose's thermos when they had first arrived, and the sweet, bitter taste of it now lingered in the pockets of her cheeks, where her tongue kept poking in an attempt to keep her voice still. All summer, she'd waited for this day to arrive, for Ambrose to return from college in Michigan and make good on his promise to take her on her first deer hunt. When he'd gone off to school four years before, she'd been only eight—old enough to shoot a BB gun, but too small to keep a rifle from bruising her shoulder. Since then, determined not to fail when the time came, she'd carried endless pails of milk and loaded countless hay bales onto flatbeds until her shoulders were high and square like those of a young man.

It should have been her grandfather next to her in the blind. He'd always told her that when the time came, when he felt she was ready, he would take her out into the shelter belt of trees next to the strip of land they planted every year with feed corn in order to draw the big and small game for hunting. Instead she waited with the neighbor boy—now a man—who had served as the third point of their triangle: the replacement grandson, the respectful and diligent student of the outdoors. The three of them had trapped gophers and fox, caught walleyes and northerns, and on lazy afternoons sat in a row, whittling objects out of soft wood, the careless soapy shavings drifting across the porch at their feet. It didn't seem right that the old man wasn't present, but at least his gun was there, cradled in Emmy's lap. The rifle was exactly like the one he had used in the army—not ideal for a young girl, but its familiar length of walnut wood and the satisfying throw of the cold metal bolt felt right to Emmy. When her grandfather died quick-slow from a thing gone wrong in his head, this rifle was promised to her, and she was promised to Ambrose. That had been when she was ten. Now Emmy was twelve, and with each passing year, her understanding of the world grew by inches to where she was almost a woman, certainly no longer content to be a child.

The first orange ray of sun split through the slot they'd carved in the screening plank, and a sharp stripe of light illuminated the skim of grassy green behind Ambrose's blue eyes. He'd gone away to college a lanky, quiet boy and come back a sturdy but no more voluble man. Emmy looked at his nose in profile, surprised by how it had taken on the prominently pointed shape of an arrowhead, the kind chipped from opaque flint that her grandfather had taught her to find, brown against the windblown black soil of spring. Once they had found bones as well, and not far from where she currently sat, a jawbone that retained long, sharp, glossy yellowed teeth.

At the crunch of rustled leaves in the distance, Ambrose moved from his squat into a creeping crawl, picking up his shotgun as he squinted into the piercing daylight. A slight nod of his head brought her gaze level alongside of his. The deer was small and tentative, its spindled legs lifting as though recoiling from the singe of a hot frying pan; the animal's velvety nose lowering and stretching toward the mound of shucked corn Emmy had piled a respectable distance from the blind. From instinct, she bit off her right mitten—the rough red wool of it lingering on her bottom lip—and raised the smooth wooden flank of the gun to the point of her high cheekbone, letting the stock settle into its groove against her shoulder, just as she had done hundreds of times since her father had allowed her to take ownership of the gun in January, her twelfth birthday. Most girls would treat a baby doll as well as Emmy had polished and cleaned that Springfield, meticulously running the oiled rags over, around, and through the elegant length of it.

"Go," Ambrose said so minutely above a whisper that she might have imagined the word. Emmy silently righted the tiny ladder sight atop the gun's metal and lined it up with the notch at the end of the barrel. She recalled her grandfather's scorn of men who had come back from the war and affixed fancy scopes to their hunting rifles, as though this gave them an advantage over the animal that they didn't deserve. Emmy inhaled deeply and began counting as she waited for the deer to finish feeding. It raised its head in Emmy's direction—a mistaken benediction—the tufted white ears pointing forward and then back, a hasty indication of something ill on the wind, which caused the deer to lift its nose higher. Emmy opened her left eye on the number sixty and then pinched it shut again. Though she had tossed on her pillow the night before, her nerves were now absent as she slipped her finger into the trigger guard on the next inhale and gently squeezed. The crack of the shot echoed beyond the small makeshift room and out into the field, where it ripped through the flurrying sound of many wings ascendant, and Emmy couldn't help sitting back on her heels, defeated, knowing that this was the one shot of the day, certain that she'd acted in haste. His low, soft whistle told her otherwise.

"Well, I never," Ambrose said, lifting the earflap of his winter cap with a finger and scratching at his scalp before picking up a leather haversack that she knew had been given to Ambrose by her grandfather, who had used it during the First World War. "Let's go dress her."

"Is that all?" she asked, the gun only one bullet lighter in her hands but bearing the same weight as a length of folded cloth for all it meant to her in the order of the morning.

He took his hat off completely and struck his thigh with it. "All? You kill your first deer in the first hour of the first day with your first shot?" She fought down a prideful smile as she looked up into his reserved face, though she could sense a glint of ownership flicker deep in his eyes. He broke open his shotgun, slipping the unspent cartridge into his coat pocket before bending the gun in the crook of his arm and muttering, "Is that all." He shook his head and walked away from the blind. She followed, her legs unsteady in the warmth of the sun. They'd had a good number of Indian summer days, and the heavy field coat she'd chosen in the cold kitchen was now smothering. She shrugged it off and let it drop to the inky dirt as she took two steps to each of his in order to reach the prostrate animal in stride. He lifted the doe's head and turned the snout skyward. The eyes were wide open and seemed to Emmy as if they hinted at a more complicated purpose than simple life or death. As she leaned closer, Emmy's tight white braids brushed the deer's cheek, and Emmy caught her own beveled reflection in the glassy eye. Under the muzzle, at the base of the velvet tan neck, Ambrose pointed at a muddy-colored dot where the bullet had entered.

"I did that," she said, reaching a bare finger to the hole.

"Heart shot," he replied. "Cleanest I ever seen." With a quick flick of his wrist, he shifted the deer onto its back. "Yearling. She's small, but pretty fattened up."

Emmy stayed in her crouch next to the doe's head as Ambrose unrolled a length of leather he'd pulled from the haversack, revealing an assortment of knives and a small saw. He anchored his knees between the upended hind legs of the doe, then picked up the largest knife, slipped it from its leather sheath, and pointed the serrated tip into the lowest part of the doe's belly. "Give me your hand," he said, and Emmy complied, feeling the bumpy calluses that dotted his palm scrape across her knuckles as they grasped the smooth white handle of the heavy knife. He drew her hand quickly and with precision up the tender front of the animal until the blade reached the rib cage, at which point Ambrose gripped her hand tightly enough to make her wince as he forced the knife through the hard sternum. The cracking sound their effort produced caused Emmy to shift her eyes elsewhere, taking in the rising steam from the gaping incision, the milky sack of odd-shaped organs pressing out of the animal and jiggling with the pull of Ambrose's intent. Where is all the blood? Emmy wondered. Where is proof that a living thing is now dead? She slouched back onto her heels as he released her and reached into the cavity, drawing into the daylight a bright red misshapen ball still connected to the interior of the animal by snarly cords. Emmy flinched slightly as she imagined the heart beating in his large bloodstained hand; saw the tear of metal into flesh where he pressed his thumb and glanced at her with more reserved approval. He handed it to her, richly warm with the last unpumped, unspilled fluid. Here was the evidence she had sought, the warrant for her crime. Ambrose cut free the veins and arteries, and her hand jolted away from the deer, sending the bloody orb into the air.

"Pay attention," he said, sticking a curved knife into the cavity with a practiced twist.

This is not me, she told herself as the resolve to be like them abandoned her and she stood up. A dozen yards away in the trees something moved. The girl stumbled blindly toward the sound, feeling a burning need to relieve herself of the coffee and all else it had washed down. So much of her life had been like this: slow until it was fast, right until it was wrong. She would cautiously pad forward on kitten feet only to find the milk pail overturned and empty. This is how it felt—the anticipation of joy shifted in a moment to regret. As she neared the edge of the field, a resettled brace of pheasants flushed at her feet and caught her up in their swirling ascent. She spun away from the towering line of elms and waved her hands above her head, shooing the lifted birds in an empathetic panic, tired of the world proving her place was not where she thought it to be.

"Stop playing," he shouted, the deer now draped over his shoulders, the entrails mounded next to the darkened patch of ground where the animal had bled out. Ambrose held two twiggy legs in each hand, and his arms were speckled a rusty red up to the elbows, where he'd pushed his jacket sleeves out of the way. "We need to get her skinned before church."

"Of course," Emmy whispered, her voice an empty honeycomb, brittle in the cooling wind. She would be more cautious, she resolved as she watched his deer-slung figure move away, more patient and careful. She followed him slowly, gathering her coat, the guns, and the haversack as she went, hoping that this thing now done—this deer now dead—would be the last by her own hand.

Part I

Disinheritance

January 1958

One

Faith Alone

The day after her eighteenth birthday, Emmaline Nelson sat with her spine hovering a good two inches away from the straight, cold back of an oaken pew, her feet planted next to each other on the pine floor, knees pressed together as she'd been taught. Her wool serge skirt should have been cozy, but the nylon slip her mother had insisted she wear crackled like electric ice against her dark stockings from its contact with the charged January air. Her coat hung cold and useless out in the makeshift foyer, where her mother had made her leave it, even though the inside of the church was not much warmer than the air outdoors.

Emmy worked hard at achieving what she hoped would look like a good Christian demeanor—eyes focused on the front of the church, Bible open to the day's scripture reading on her lap, hands folded on the Good Book, mouth slightly open and whispering along with the Nicene Creed. She knew these words so well she no longer had to parse their meaning. She knew the service so well that she barely kept her thoughts on God. No, Emmy's mind was quite understandably drawn over her right shoulder, pondering instead the man who would soon officially become her betrothed.

The prayer over, Emmy cocked her head to the left and turned it just enough to steal a glance of Ambrose Brann. She could feel his steady gaze warm on her neck, even as the congregation stood to sing another hymn. It seemed as though Ambrose had always been there, somewhere, in and out of her memories of youth. They had played together when she was small, endless indulgent games of hide-and-seek at one farm or the other on Sunday afternoons while the grown-ups visited over coffee and her sister toyed with dolls on a flannel blanket stretched out in the grassy sunshine. At times inseparable, Emmy and Ambrose had walked through muddy spring-dense fields of ankle-deep black soil in order to place a penny on the railroad track down at the end of the farm's quarter section, returning later in the day to find the bright copper disc pressed flat and smooth. He had taught her how to hunt, to clean a gun, to shave a piece of soft wood into a palm-sized cross, and after Grandfather Nelson died when she was ten, Ambrose's economy of words had made her feel her loss less keenly, even though the few things he did share revealed little of his heart.

Ambrose was a good deal older—nearly ten years—and yet he never seemed to mind his young companion, always extending to Emmy a level of familial love that promised to keep her comfortable the rest of her life. She tried to imagine what the weight of his silence might feel like in the stretch of time about to be set before them, and an unexpected feeling rose against it, a slight hiccup of concern.

The Brann family's status was considered a significant step up from her family, with Delmar Brann's vast acreage of sugar beet fields and hundred head of fine beef cattle comprising the largest farm in the township. Unlike her Norwegian-born grandfather, Mr. Brann was second-generation American—a fact he frequently worked into conversation. Still, the two men had been the kind of friends who were more often seen together than apart, and it had been Grandfather Nelson's dying wish for Emmy to marry Ambrose. She could learn to live in a quiet house, she supposed, or fill it with the noise of children by and by.

Emmy waited to join in the singing a moment too long and felt a quick, sharp pinch delivered with dogged expertise to her upper left arm by her mother. As Emmy slowly stood, she took quiet note of the increase of her stature, for she recently had cleared the brim of her mother's hat by a solid three inches. Emmy's life up to now had been constrained by her mother's views, her instructions, her limits. Yet somehow, a strange miracle had happened in September: Her father moved them from a shack on her grandmother's farm near the sleepy town of Glyndon and into a small, tidy house in the much bigger city of Moorhead, Minnesota, across the Red River and in the shadow of Fargo, North Dakota. Emmy had entered her final year of high school surrounded by the kinds of ideas and knowledge that unfolded a crumpled sheet of possibility inside of her, and Karin's influence had started to pull away from Emmy like warm taffy. The move had revealed tiny windows that were now opening onto new opportunities.

On Emmy's right the bright singing of her sister, Birdie, cut through Emmy's preoccupations. Birdie had burst into the Nelson household three years after Emmy, a gift of uncomplicated grace and laughter among a previously glum trio. Sometimes Emmy wondered what would have become of them if Birdie hadn't been born. Emmy's own arrival had been less auspicious, coming as it had three months after their brother, Daniel, had died. With so much grief in such a small house how could anyone joyfully greet a red-faced, colicky girl? Instead, Emmy had slept in her grandmother's bed, fed from a bottle and carried around on the older woman's hip until Emmy was big enough to walk. When Karin had come home with Birdie, three-year-old Emmy eagerly accepted the role of mother's helper, happy to be useful and wanted. She couldn't remember much from those early years, and besides, she had quickly learned to appreciate the feeling of being needed more than loved. Now that she was eighteen, Emmy was ever more mindful of what kind of wife and mother she wanted to be, itching to cook meals the way she preferred, keep her own house, and create for her children a pocket of happiness that no one would fill with the pebbles of grim self-sacrifice. Marriage to Ambrose was not merely a promise to be fulfilled, it also seemed the only way forward, a destination she knew as well as any other, a place she could feel finally at home.

Once the blessing was given, Karin quickly slipped past Emmy's father in order to join the women serving coffee in the basement, and gave him a look that suggested he keep a close eye on the girls. Christian frequently deferred to Karin, even after their own small farm had failed when Emmy was ten, and they'd had no choice but to move into a three-room shack on Grandfather Nelson's farm. It had once been used by the *betabeleros* who took the trains north every spring to plant sugar beets and back down south to the Texas border once the harvest was completed late in the fall. The interior walls of the outhouse ten feet behind the shack were still papered in Mexican movie magazines featuring Rita Hayworth's toothy smile.

As much as she had wondered why they couldn't just live in the farmhouse with her grandmother, Emmy knew that there was some strength behind Christian's quiet pride. Rather than replace his newly dead father as head of the farm, Christian took a mechanic's job at the sugar factory. It took seven long years of taxing work, but Emmy could tell that Christian was never happier than when he unloaded their possessions into the small house in Moorhead that fall. Even so, they all continued to help Grandmother Nelson maintain what little was left of her enterprise: a handful of milking cows, a half-blind hunting dog, a dozen laying hens, and an old inedible hog named Sausage. Lida wouldn't hear of selling one feather of the place, and it had been made plain to Emmy that the farm would be given to her and Ambrose, finally joining the two families as Grandfather Nelson had desired.

Task-driven blood in her veins, Karin Nelson looped her arm through Grandmother Nelson's, helping the much older woman out of the pew and down the short aisle toward the stairs. Lida Nelson was the center of the church's universe. She had left her family early in order to create her own place in this loop of the river, and she took on the history of every parishioner as though it were her own. The Nelsons had all been baptized in this room, they would all be married here, and God willing at the end of their lives receive the blessing of rejoining their relatives in the attached graveyard of good Lutherans. Emmy touched the smooth pew, finding the slight dent where she'd cut her first tooth. She imagined what the low-shouldered country church must have looked like from the sky, set back from the meandering creek just far enough to stay high in flood years, close enough to hold picnic suppers in the late afternoon shade of early September harvests. Since she was very small, she'd been told stories about the great Norwegian settlers who had staked out this land and constructed a sod lean-to from the densely packed soil, slicked the sides with paint made from quicklime and chalk, and retained the services of a traveling preacher until they could afford a full-time recruit. Soon after, a suitable wooden building was constructed.

All that hard work was swept up into the spinning maw of a tornado in 1929, leaving only the organ untouched. Twice more, twisters had descended on them, the most recent coming late on a cloudless day the past June, when the deadliest cluster ever seen had ripped its way through a speckled swath of the county. One tremendous funnel that looked like an upside-down birthday cake had flattened areas of Fargo, while a group of three smaller spirals barely missed the little church as the storm made its devastating way into their valley, leaving pieces of houses from as far away as North Fargo scattered about the farm. Emmy had found a dollar bill, the wheel from a child's wagon, and the cracked head of a porcelain doll, among other displaced treasures. Even now, in the dead of winter, when the sky turned black, a shiver of trepidation would come over Emmy, reminding her of how scared she had been as they huddled in the disused coal bin, listening to the howling winds encompass her grandmother's home.

Emmy rubbed the gooseflesh from her arms as she stood between her father and Birdie in the crowded aisle. She gazed up at the stained-glass depiction of Christ ascendant, wondering what He thought of the poor souls from the Golden Ridge area of Fargo who had been killed in the storm. Had He opened his arms to the five Acevedo children taken alongside their mother? Did it make sense that God chose to leave behind the father and one son? She'd read their stories in the local paper, and had wept over the picture of the baby of the family being carried away from the wreckage by a fireman who had either lost or discarded his hat—his limp slant of bangs obscured the horror he must have felt—until her heart couldn't stand any more of it.

The feel of her father's hand on the middle of her back brought Emmy's thoughts around to the sturdy brick church, and she let her questioning melt away, as she often had when the wall of God's reason seemed too high for her to scale. Christian roped his other arm around Birdie's shoulders and engaged Ambrose's father as he moved out of his own pew.

"Good morning, Del," her father said, offering his hand to the dark-suited gentleman. Delmar Brann, reed thin and yet a good head taller than Christian, took the slighter man's hand in both of his as he grunted a greeting.

An older, squatter, and unfamiliar man moved out of the pew, nodding solicitously at them as he slid past and broke into the line waiting to greet the pastor at the door. Emmy noticed her father's look of irritated surprise before she cast her eyes to the floor, while Birdie used the moment to sprint out from under her father's arm and rush off to join her friends at the back of the church. There was something in Mr. Brann's stature that always made Emmy feel small, insignificant: almost breakable. He was closer in age to her grandfather than to Christian, and had been married late, but widowed early, to a woman rumored to have come from a wealthy Chicago family.

"Good morning," Mr. Brann said, and moved in a lanky shuffle along the aisle. "What are you hearing in town about Burdick's attempts to get into Congress?"

"I prefer not to talk politics in church," Christian said, forcing a friendly enough laugh, but Emmy sensed discomfort in her father as he tipped his head in her direction.

Mr. Brann turned brusquely to Emmy, sliding a rough knuckle under her chin. She resisted taking a step back. "How's our girl?" He leaned closely enough for her to see a fleck of pepper between his top teeth. "The winter cold enough for you?"

"Oh, you bet," Emmy replied, an embarrassed shade of red prickling her skin. Karin had told her that after Sunday dinner at the Branns', matters would be discussed between the two families, and from Mr. Brann's solicitous smile, Emmy could tell that her position in his favor had risen. The obvious downside of a marriage to Ambrose was the eventual, continual proximity to his father, though Emmy knew that there was no fairness in comparing Ambrose to Mr. Brann. She was nothing like her mother, and Emmy's blush began to rise up to her ears with the notion of Ambrose setting them in the same frame. Her mother was cold and firm, hardworking and driven, serving Jesus with her every breath. Emmy loved Jesus but found less of her soul compelled to model his mission. She wanted to do good works in her life, but she also wanted to look up and out at the world, rather than stare deeply into a pair of prayer-folded hands, whispering words of devotion and salvation. What was the point of being saved if she never did anything that required the risk of being lost? Her mother lived within the limits of this room, even when she was outside of it. Emmy's view was drawn to the horizon, and whatever might lie beyond. How she would incorporate this yearning into a marriage to the farm boy next door she had no clue, but she hoped her brand of faith would lend more guidance than her mother's had.

Emmy gave her head a little shake to clear the muddling thought and quickened her step to leave the older men behind. She slipped her hand into the crook of Ambrose's arm. He smiled down at her.

"How's the farm?" Emmy asked, feeling the heat of his body through the layers of clothing, hot like an ember in the grate. Beads of sweat stood out on his brow and Emmy had to quietly wonder whether he might be ill. Clearly she wasn't the only one nervous about what the day would hold for their future.

"A dozen hens are off their lay," he said.

Emmy laughed, then darkened her tone. "That sounds serious."

"You'll see," he said, a small smile pulling at one corner of his mouth.

"Yes, I suppose I will," she said, her attempt at merriment waning as they approached Pastor Erickson where he stood in the entryway, shaking hands and listening to the needs of his flock with a look of either deep sympathy or abject senility. He was a perfectly square man with straight, feeble lines of white hair laced atop a face that was always bright pink, regardless of the weather or circumstance. Emmy had loved the pastor when she was a small girl, but as she'd filled out her Sunday dresses over time, his lingering eyes had made her increasingly uncomfortable to the point of slouching.

"Good morning, Emmaline," he said as he took both hands and held them out to her sides. His touch was oddly damp and dry at the same time, like washing taken in from the line five minutes too early. "You're looking especially pretty today." Emmy broke her own sweat, which she could feel collect at her temples and underneath her gray wool hat, where her scalp began to itch.

"Thank you, Pastor. You're very kind to say so," she said as Ambrose stepped between them, saving her from further discomfort.

"Yes, she's a pretty one, sir," Ambrose said as he shook the pastor's hand. "Wonderful sermon, I especially enjoyed your thoughts on Nadab and Abihu. I had never considered how their punishment related to the great flood, or Gilgamesh." Emmy looked at Ambrose, surprised by how much he had to say, as though the coal of Isaiah had touched his lips when she wasn't looking.

Pastor Erickson narrowed one eye. "You're a great study, Ambrose. You should consider taking the cloth yourself, you know. We could use more men like you."

"So you always say." Ambrose bowed his head. "But I serve the Lord through faith alone."

"His Grace be with you," Pastor Erickson replied, turning back to Emmy and casting a rheumy glance down the length of her frame.

"And with you," Ambrose said, moving Emmy along toward the basement stairs. The smell of percolating coffee and the clattering of the church women setting out cups pointed up the silence that rested between the young couple. In the few moments it took them to descend, Emmy sought a topic of conversation to begin, but nothing came to mind. She certainly hadn't listened closely enough to the sermon to engage him on the topic of divine retribution—or whatever it was the pastor had spent so much time talking about. If it wasn't damnation, it was likely wrath or some other brimstone subject. The gamut Pastor Erickson ran was as small as that of a penned-up rooster, and nearly as nonsensical, but she knew better than to speak her mind on to Ambrose. It seemed to her at times that she was the only person who noticed the paucity of words and ideas coming from the pulpit, so eager were the parishioners to have Pastor Erickson's holy approval.

"School's going well," Emmy said, feeling the awkwardness in Ambrose's lack of response. She wanted to tell him all about her new life in Moorhead, and what an adjustment it had been for her, going from the immigrant shack her father had improved as much as he could, to the slightly larger, faintly more comfortable two-bedroom house situated in what Emmy had quickly learned was the poor side of the big town, on the lesser bank of the Red River. To the west across that river lay Fargo, which, in the early days of both settlements, had claimed a much bigger stake with the railroads than its little twin sister, Moorhead. Emmy was only beginning to understand the myriad effects of this dynamic, though, and worried that if she tried to express her impressions of it Ambrose would wave away her insights like slow-moving attic flies.

When they reached the wide, warm basement the young couple wordlessly parted ways, Ambrose to join the men gathered around the coffee table, and Emmy to the kitchen and a sink of soapy water. Her mother passed with a plate of her homemade doughnuts, which were always hard and dry but somehow the most popular Sunday-morning hospitality item. Emmy slipped into the bustling kitchen, quietly past the women swarming there, and out the back cellar door.

Once outside in the cement-lined structure at the foot of the stairs, Emmy let out a long sigh and climbed to the top, where she sat hugging her knees for warmth. She found an instant comfort in the solitude of the moment. Behind the church a number of young boys ran around in the snow, impervious to their reddening hands and dripping noses. Emmy smiled at their predictability—boys had been like this when she was young, and they would be like this when she was old. One of them stole another's cap, and the shock of white-blond hair made Emmy wonder if her son would look like so many of the children who had passed through this yard. Her own hair still held its childhood brilliance—a gift from her grandfather, along with the blushing skin—while Birdie's had darkened to a tawny brown.

The basement door opened and out popped Svenja Sorenson, her russet-colored looped braids catching the morning sunshine and her pale blue eyes slicing up to meet Emmy's in a squinted, freckle-splattered smile.

"Oh, Emmy! Here you are!" Svenja dashed up the steps and squeezed into the smaller space to Emmy's left, rather than take the two feet of empty stair to her right. Emmy scooted over.

Emmy turned one palm up. "Here I am."

"Tell me *everything*—what's happening in the real world?" Svenja asked, smelling of strawberry jam. "Oh, how I would die to live in Moorhead, away from the gophers and milk cows and hay-smelling boys." She propped her dreamy, round face in one hand. "What are the boys like in your school? Have you made a new best friend?" Svenja was an only child with poor prospects who, Emmy imagined, would choose a life like so many of the women in the basement below, settling down with a local farm boy and losing her beauty slowly over time to successive babies and the layers of flesh they'd drape around her ample figure. Emmy had watched this progression plump the older girls in Glyndon, and she couldn't deny that marrying Ambrose might seal for her a similar fate. Emmy felt a sliver of solidarity as Svenja pulled her into a confidential hug. "You know, when we graduate this spring, I might just join you there," Svenja whispered.

"Oh, I don't plan on being in town for that long," Emmy said. "I'll be back around here for good before you know it."

Svenja shrugged, playing with a loose button on her threadbare cotton coat. "Don't you ever wish there was more than this?"

"Sometimes." Emmy looked Svenja in the eye. They had been baptized on the same day and confirmed together fourteen years later, but had very little else in common other than parallel time lines pointing forward from the step on which they were huddled. "Of course there's more out there, but there's plenty here as well. Do you?"

"Me?" Svenja shook her head with a light laugh before a cloud passed over her expression. "Can you keep a secret?"

"I'd rather not."

Svenja took her hand and leaned closer, though Emmy hardly thought that possible. "My mother says that I should marry John Hansen. Apparently he's been asking about me."

"That's good, right?" Emmy said, trying to sound cheerful. John was even older than Ambrose, and a longtime bachelor who lived with his aging parents on a disheveled sheep farm that smelled in a way that made Emmy roll up the window of the car on a hot day whenever they drove past. It didn't smell much better in the winter with them closed.

"They do have quite a few acres of beets. Enough to afford a field hand, who comes all the way from Texas every spring." Svenja attempted a hopeful aspect.

Out of kindness, Emmy chose not to speak the obvious—everyone knew John to be slow of thought, and beyond hiring himself out to work with the Branns' cows, his prospects were slim.

"I know he's not as worldly as Ambrose." Svenja sprang to her feet. "But I suppose there are far worse fates. I'm going in. You?"

"It's quiet out here, and too hot in there," Emmy said, pointing at the door.

"Okay, then. You know where to find me." Svenja sat on the iron handrail and slid down the length of it, just as they had done over and over again when they were small.

"God be with you," Emmy said as Svenja slipped through the cellar door. Soon enough Emmy would have to follow, tie on her apron, and clear cups, as she did every Sunday. Then they would all get into the car and drive the half mile to the Brann farm, make the polite small talk, eat the overdone roast, and wait for the details of her fate to be decided. How could she not at least try to take a step in another direction, one small step to know what she might be missing? Emmy found great comfort in her life with her family, but she felt as she sat and looked out on the graves of people she had known, and people who had known her whom she didn't even remember, that the distance between where she sat and the rectangle of earth awaiting her had precipitously shortened. Her foot itched and her stomach growled. The inertia of passive solitude stretched within her as a deep shiver began to rack her body. A scrim of dread descended as she imagined the next ten minutes: rejoining Ambrose, having another chat about the weather with Mr. Brann, and saying a ten-minute good-bye to the pastor as he slowly worked his hot, damp hand from her elbow up to her shoulder while he talked about the Apostle Paul. The one time Emmy had tried to evade his lavender-smelling breath, Karin had lectured her for no less than a week on the shame of having a daughter who couldn't show respect to a man of the cloth in God's own house.

The door below her opened again, and Ambrose stuck his head into the cold, smiling tightly up at her. "You're blue," he stated. "Come in."

Hearing his reined impatience, Emmy was startled to see that the Ambrose who stood at the bottom of the staircase was no longer the maypole that her childish imagination had wound itself around. Where once was a companion running, fishing, and hunting alongside of her, now there was a partner of a new sort: one whose lead expected a follow. His expression softened and he extended his hand with a coax of his fingers, a gesture whose familiarity pulled her away from Svenja's romantic whisperings of *more out there.* Emmy turned the wheel of doubt back one click in Ambrose's favor, took up the braces of her expected routine, and let the capricious notions of youth drift behind her in their gathering cloud.

❧

"Are you nervous?" Birdie whispered to Emmy in the backseat of their father's old Coronet. The seats were threadbare, and the heat was so paltry that the girls had to spread horse blankets both under themselves and across their shared lap, causing a prickling sort of nonheat that they suffered without complaint. Emmy slipped her gloved hand into Birdie's and nodded.

"Terribly," Emmy said, looking out the window at the bleached monotony of the barren sugar beet fields. She swallowed hard against the dryness in her throat and took a deep, purposeful inhale, as though she were preparing to go underwater for an undetermined amount of time. Her parents sat on either side of her grandmother on the wide front bench seat, three bobbing heads in three different hats. As usual, Grandmother Nelson's tiny frame was draped in layers of black fashion from the late 1940s, the absence of color or style marking her desire to be deep in the ground, next to her husband of fifty years. Emmy tried to imagine what that amount of time would feel like, how she would look at her grandmother's age. Would she likewise shrink down like an apple-headed doll left for days in the sun? It was very possible that Emmy would outlive Ambrose, that she too would mete out her days in the middle of a son and daughter-in-law, being driven from one day to the next, and left to wander the rooms of an overlarge house with only the ghost of her dear dead husband to comfort her.

A forlorn smile pulled at Emmy's lips and she immediately fought it down as the car turned off the main road and onto the long, narrow drive edged with plowed banks of gravel-studded snow that led into the Brann farm. Towering skeletal oak trees marked the property on four corners, connected by stands of bushy spruce planted as protection from the relentless year-round winds that would aspirate fine layers of topsoil straight into any open window, impervious to screens and sometimes even silting its way right through solid windowpanes.

At the top of the drive, the path curved into a circle around two tangled box elder trees, the spot where Emmy had spent many a warm Sunday afternoon, either on a sturdy, gnarled limb or in the shady grass below. She could almost picture her own children up in these trees, spying on pirates or Indians, or maybe even little green men from Mars. This thought helped with the notion that she might someday be the lady of the enormous white Victorian house looming before them, the neatly trimmed green shutters and bare front porch giving Emmy the same old feeling of a thing untouched by love. Christian stopped the car in front of the big white slope-shouldered barn across the circle from the house, and Emmy crossed her fingers and made a quick wish: Please let me be happy here.

They were greeted at the door by Maria Gonzales, who had been both housekeeper and cook for the two men since Mrs. Emmaline Brann had died from consumption the summer before Emmy was born. It was from this tragedy that Emmy got her name—a sign of respect for the dead woman who had been Grandmother Nelson's best friend. Maria was the smallest grown woman Emmy had ever seen, and the tightly wound bun of hair at the crown of her head had gone completely white in the years since Emmy had first looked up at it, and then gazed down on it, fascinated by its pristine roundness. Before Emmy was born, Maria had been a *betabelero* alongside her husband and five sons, splitting the beet roots in the muddy spring fields and thinning the rows by hand, stooped to the ground for hours on end. Moving out of the field and into the house was a rare but fortunate event for a migrant, and Maria's cooking for the Branns bore none of the spice or color that Emmy had on occasion seen her take to the team of Mexican laborers who worked under Pedro on the immense Brann acreage.

Emmy removed her coat and slipped out of her snow boots, replacing them with the low-heeled church shoes that she had worn once a week, in every season, since her feet had reached their full size. The tight little group of Nelsons moved together into the formal dining room, where the table was set and Mr. Brann spoke in excited tones to the unfamiliar man Emmy had seen at church. She glanced at Ambrose, who stood behind a chair, ready to pull it out for her.

With the delicacy of a china teacup, Lida walked over to where the two older men sat, her arms extended in a warm welcome. "Why, I can't believe my eyes," she exclaimed, a childlike look of wonder brightening her face. "I didn't notice you at church."

The man stood and gently took her hand. "Dear Lida, you haven't aged a minute."

"Mr. Davidson was sitting in our pew," Mr. Brann said, a proud smile of ownership on his narrow face.

"Please everyone, call me Curtis," the stranger said, looking in particular at Lida, who seemed confused by his request. "With God's help, I've begun my mission anew." Emmy had never been invited to call a man of Mr. Davidson's age by his first name, and certainly knew better than to do so in front of her mother. His teeth gleamed in a way that nearly glowed, small in size, but straight and neat between his thin, moist lips. Emmy assumed they were false.

"We're glad to have you back with us," Lida said, looking as though she might topple over. "God knows your heart." She lifted one hand out to the room while holding fast to Mr. Davidson with the other. "You know my son, Christian, and his wife, Karin, of course. These are their girls." A small sound clipped her speech and she pressed her smile into a frown for a brief moment, the ghost of some lost memory haunting her face. "If you will excuse me, we'll go see what we can do to help Maria."

"Naturally," Mr. Davidson said, turning to Ambrose. "Which of these young ladies is Emmaline?"

Ambrose extended his arm toward Emmy, and she moved to his side. "Emmaline, I'd like you to meet Mr. Curtis Davidson," he said. "A good friend of our family."

Emmy glanced at her father, who stood watching from the foyer doorway, hat turning slowly in his hands. She felt coltish and clumsy as she walked closer to Mr. Davidson. He was slightly taller than Emmy, with a puffy face and deep-set eyes under thick brows, and thinning gray hair streaked with an unnatural yellow that he had combed back in slick rows. His suit was made from a brushed wool fabric that was fine and well fitted to his oddly shaped frame. As he lifted her hand in his powerful grip, a thick silver ring of diamonds set in a small cross shape on its flat surface flashed.

"Hello," she said, and he brushed the back of her hand with his lips, a gesture that drew a bright shock of carpet light between them. "Oh," she said, rubbing her fingers. She hadn't expected such strength from a man who had to have been almost as old as her grandmother, even though his corpulence gave him the features of a well-fed babe.

"You favor her," he said with a nod to the kitchen door. This surprised Emmy, as she had never been told that she looked like anyone in particular, and certainly never her grandmother, whose complexion and hair had been dark, like Birdie's. Perplexed, Emmy moved to her chair on the other side of Ambrose and smoothed her skirt across her lap, feeling the warmth of the heating grate under the table begin to melt her icy feet. She wondered why this man in particular would be invited on a day that had been intended for her and Ambrose. The stranger captivated the men, and Emmy couldn't help wondering if his cursory glances at her were some sort of measurement that she would somehow fail, or if he had the kind of influence over the Branns that would result in her having to prove herself worthy in ways she couldn't begin to attempt. If only the wedding could happen this May instead of next, then her feelings of being on uneasy ground might lessen. That kind of thinking was useless in the face of her mother-ordered schedule. Karin deemed a year-long engagement the most appropriate; abandoning any part of the plan was unthinkable.

The conversation among the men shuffled through Mr. Davidson's assessment of how the county had changed in the years he'd been away—apparently very little—which made Emmy wonder where he had been and why he seemed so curious about their family's small piece of Moland Township. Eventually, the topic turned to the usual Sunday dinner speculation of when the earth would thaw and the beet seeds would be sown, what the *Farmer's Almanac* had to say on the matter, and just how many cows on both farms were likely to give birth soon. Emmy fought the itchy sleepiness that comes from wearing layers of wool in an overheated house, drifting into the middle of the very important subject of calving.

"I've got a good deal of them here," Ambrose said. "We're going to be busy."

"We've only got the two, the dam and the heifer," Christian said, speaking for the first time since they'd arrived and causing Emmy to take careful note of the way he leaned back in his chair, while the three other men leaned forward. He picked a piece of lint from the tablecloth and rolled it between his fingers as though he found it more interesting than anything being said.

Lida entered on the tail of his words, her hands in quilted potholders carrying an oblong dish. "He's been after me to sell that heifer," she said to Mr. Davidson in a lilting voice, setting the steaming yams pooled with butter beside Christian's plate and speaking over his head. "But I tell him she's our fortune, the first piece of rebuilding our herd. We'll fatten up that calf and sell it for two older dams." Christian lifted his milk glass, but instead of drinking from it, he turned it slowly in the air.

"You always did know your cattle," Mr. Davidson said, drawing a finger across the edge of his chin. He looked at Emmy and then at Christian, who set down the glass without further comment as Lida patted at the back of her tightly braided and wound hair, as though she were wishing it had been set and combed for the occasion. Something about Christian's demeanor hung heavily in Emmy's mind, a subtle aloofness in his aspect that she hadn't specifically noticed before but felt quite certain had always been there, like a doily on the radio, or a layer of fine dust on a high shelf. It was almost as though he disliked the very idea of farming, and yet here he sat, pretending that its dissection was worthy of his consideration.

"Well, I think she's already showing signs of discomfort," Emmy said, attempting to assert a standing modeled after her grandmother's. If Emmy were to be the wife of this household, she wanted her voice to be heard. Her father met her gaze and raised an eyebrow in what looked like mild amusement. Mr. Brann cleared his throat.

"What have you heard about the new leadership in Indiana?" he asked Mr. Davidson. "Will you be heading down there?"

"Ah, yes," he replied, aligning his fork and knife. "They've got some fine ideas." He watched Lida disappear into the kitchen. "But I think the Lord needs me to tend his flock here, begin again."

Mr. Brann rubbed his hands together. "God willing, your voice will reach many eager ears," he said, and picked up a small silver bell, ringing it sharply. It was the first time Emmy had seen him do such a thing, and it made her wonder what else might happen in the course of dinner. He set down the bell. "Until then, please make our home your own."

"I thank you for the kind offer, brother," Mr. Davidson said, looking around the room as though he'd already unpacked his bags in the main bedroom upstairs. "I've always felt at peace in Minnesota."

Emmy cleared her throat. "I've never been to Indiana," she said, only to find her second attempt at entering the conversation treated with the same maddening silence from the men, and a discreet tap on the knee from Ambrose that caused embarrassed heat to flow into her cheeks.

Karin hurried into the room with a platter of roast beef, carved and ladled with thick brown gravy. She went directly to Mr. Davidson and served him first, treating him with the kind of reverence that made Emmy wonder whether Mr. Davidson might be a minister of some sort. Emmy looked at her father, who was tracing a faint pattern on the tablecloth with his fork. The other women bustled in with an assortment of side dishes, then retreated to the kitchen to fetch more. When Emmy stood to help, Ambrose placed a firm hand on her shoulder and guided her back into her seat without stopping the flow of detailed information regarding the scientific timing of animal insemination that he was in the process of imparting. She sat and clenched her teeth, filling her plate with whatever food was passed her way. If she wasn't going to be allowed to talk like an adult or help like a child, she could at least occupy her mouth with something that might keep her from spitting in frustration.

"Curtis, you will honor us with a devotion?" Mr. Brann asked once all the food had been dispersed, the women seated, and hands folded in practiced anticipation of a blessing.

Mr. Davidson stood and motioned for the rest of the table to do the same, grasping a hand on either side of him. An awkward moment passed as the Branns and the Nelsons took up hands. Emmy closed her eyes and bowed her head, Ambrose's palm moist on one side, Karin's cold and dry on the other.

"Our Dear Lord," Mr. Davidson broke the silence with a sonorous voice that sent a chord humming in Emmy's chest. "When King David prayed for You to 'wash him whiter than snow,' he knew that he had to first come to You with the cleanliness of repentance and hope of forgiveness for his multitude of sins. For we are all sinners in Your eyes until we know what we have done and repented for it. Show these Thy children in this loving home how to be whiter than snow on the inside as You wash them in the purity of Your love and in the Life Everlasting. For without Your glory and the promise of Your home in Heaven, we are but ants in the field. Bless this food we are about to enjoy through Your bounty, and the bread that we break in the name of Your Son, through Whom we are promised the Divine Retribution at the end of our days. Please let us be thankful for this great country in which we live, founded on Your behalf, and protected by our tireless patriots. Let us not take for granted our roles as protectors of God, country, women, and our religion, for there are those who would want us to cast aside Your mercy and Your ways for their own selfish needs. In Christ's name we pray. Amen."

Though she was used to far longer devotions, when Emmy opened her eyes she had to blink against the sudden brightness of the white tablecloth set with white dishes and napkins, the good silver, and the crystal glassware filled with fresh milk. She took her seat and watched her own hand lift the glass and felt the cool liquid as it passed her lips, but for the rest of the meal she neither relished the food nor attempted to interject her thoughts on the rumbling conversation, which centered mostly on the sugar beet harvest that had only just wound down from its early winter frenzy. How they could enjoy such endless minutiae on an annual topic—yield gains, soil astringency, labor contracts, upgrading of the discs and drills and tractors—bewildered Emmy, but it also made it easier for her to concentrate her efforts on chewing and swallowing. It became increasingly clear to her that the strange visitor's arrival had taken precedence over her own affairs, and as the ticking of the clock became ever louder in her mind, she felt a curdled mixture of relief and dismay that the day was no longer about her betrothal. The minute the last bite of food was eaten, three of the men stood and moved off into the parlor, which Maria went toward, carrying a tray of coffee and biscuits. Christian lagged behind and turned to the foyer, pulled on his coat and walked out the front door. As the other women took the food into the kitchen, Emmy stood, stretched the nerves in the small of her back, and held still for a moment, trying to hear the men's conversation drifting through the open parlor doors, wondering what they were talking about instead of her and Ambrose.

"This new mayor over in Fargo," Mr. Davidson said in a deeper, less polite tone than he'd used at the dinner table. "Is it true that he's a Semite?"

Emmy stilled further, the tone of Mr. Davidson's voice raising the flesh on her arms.

"It is," said Mr. Brann. "We always said it would happen, but no one would listen."

"Emmaline!" Karin said, grabbing Emmy's arm hard and spinning her around. "You're needed in the kitchen."

Emmy's hands shook as she quickly lifted the emptied plates and utensils and retreated to the overheated kitchen with a well-practiced resignation settling over the uneasiness that was simmering in her soul.

Two

The Bloom of Youth

Pay attention, girls. Today we will be learning about the various cuts of beef." Mrs. Hagen stood at the front of the home economics room, a roll-down map of dissected cow draped behind her. "This is the rump." She tapped on the lower right portion of the drawing with a long wooden pointer, the snaking silver rivulets of her permanent wave clawing at the peaks of her pale pink horn-rimmed glasses. Her dress was nipped in at her nonexistent waist to a degree that made Emmy worry for the metal teeth of the zipper that strained to hold everything together. "You can cook this wonderful section many creative ways, most commonly in the densely flavored German sauerbraten, but the best, to my mind, is the classic Sunday roast."

The words made Emmy slowly close her eyes, sleepy with the memory of how tediously the day before had stuttered to an end, punctuated with a chaste kiss on the forehead from Ambrose: an apologetic promise. Now that she was back in the routine of school, the idea of marriage paled.

"Wake up," Bev Langer whispered under Mrs. Hagen's lecture. "Don't let old Brillo catch you napping." The girls sat two to a table and worked on their projects in pairs. Bev was everything Svenja Sorenson was not: sophisticated, sharp, and attractive in a way that was almost handsome. Her jet green eyes were framed with a tight cap of tamed curls, a chestnut shade of brown that she combed as smoothly as mink on the crown. Sometimes it was hard for Emmy to look at Bev directly without a spike of unwelcome envy rising up and threatening their curious bond. Bev's constant kindness had set her apart from the other city girls that Emmy had met, and it had taken her a good four months to trust its sincerity. Most town kids regarded anyone from outside the city limits as a hick or a hayseed, words that had kept Emmy from pursuing other friendships. Bev was different.

"Thanks," Emmy whispered back, slipping into another near doze.

"Emmaline Nelson," Mrs. Hagen snapped, rapping the stick against her desk. Emmy stretched her eyes against their droop and stood.

"Yes, Mrs. Hagen," she said.

"Would you care to tell the class the difference between Swiss and Salisbury steaks?" The older woman balled her plump hands into fists and propped them on a tightly girdled roll of doughy midsection.

Emmy took a deep breath and tried to ignore the girls giggling behind her, or the sharp turn of Bev's head as she glared at them.

"Salisbury steaks aren't actually steak, but cheaper cuts ground up and filled with pork or bread to resemble a steak," Emmy said. She heard a girl in the back whisper, "She should know," but ignored the insult. No matter how much the home economics class taught them budgets and sewing, Emmy already knew her skirt was cut from noticeably coarser fabric. She pressed on. "Swiss style is made from the lesser cuts as well, but pounded and scored and then braised with peppers and onions until tender."

Mrs. Hagen nodded approval without lowering her nose, and Emmy stopped listening to the lecture. Though they had been living in town for a few months, they were still scraping aspects of their pastoral life off their boots, and it didn't surprise Emmy that Mrs. Hagen would single her out as an expert in the area of cheap steaks.

Emmy glanced at Bev, who mouthed the word *witch* while raising one eyebrow in a delicate arc. After graduation Bev was going to summer in New York with some distant cousins and then fly on to Paris, to live with an uncle for a year and study at a college called the Sorbonne. Bev was the first person Emmy had met who actually had dreams and the means to make them come true already purchased in the shape of a one-way ticket tucked away in her father's desk. Cooking lessons were simply Bev's way of marking time until the final day of high school.

Bev pretended to take a note, then scooted her tablet across the table for Emmy to read.

Come out with me tonite.

It's Monday. Emmy scribbled back. *What's to do?*

Be young, have fun.

Can't.

Bring Birdie, your mom won't mind.

She will mind. Emmy wrote, longing to say yes. Though she wasn't fond of her mother's severe daily schedule, she didn't have the nerve to challenge it.

Movie Saturday?

Maybe. This she thought she could attempt. Maybe there was a way for her to escape the Saturday evening routine of listening to the radio after a long day of cleaning and mending, baking the bread for the coming week. She could always back out if she failed to convince her parents.

Pick you up at 5:30.

Okay.

Okay?

Let's hope.

❧

"Dad," Emmy said the second her father walked through the door. It was Friday night, his most exhausted moment, but also the time at which he was the most agreeable. "I made Swiss steak for dinner. It's still hot." Christian Nelson gave his daughter a weak but warm smile. She'd raced home after school and pounded the scant pieces of round she could find into four small slabs of meat. The recipe called for green peppers, but onions and canned tomatoes were all Emmy had—that and the never-ending bounty of potatoes. The steaks had simmered for a full three hours and now were as tender as veal. She and Birdie had eaten egg-salad sandwiches, saving the meat for their father.

"I've had a long day," he said, and went to the kitchen sink to wash his grime-weathered hands. His sloped posture indicated that she wouldn't have to prattle about her school or his work. Not that they had lengthy conversations on a typical day, even when it was just the two of them. Emmy had set the small kitchen table with a pretty cloth and had buttered the last of the week's bread for her father to sop up the gravy. Karin wouldn't be home from prayer circle for another hour, and Birdie was listening to *Gunsmoke* on the radio in the other room. This was Emmy's moment. As her head began to buzz, she sat down across from her father and noted how small his blue eyes were set above his graying stubble. He was getting old, she couldn't deny it—at least forty, probably older. The girls' birthdays were marked without fanfare, and Emmy had no idea when her father was born. Reaching out to touch his hand, she tried to summon her will to ask permission for the movie, but a lump took over her throat and she tapped his knuckles lightly instead. He turned his hand over and caught hers before she could slip it away.

"Why don't you ever want anything?" he asked. Emmy stood and glanced through the open doorway at her sister, who seemingly hadn't heard Christian's question.

"I do," Emmy said, bringing Christian's warm plate of food to the table and sitting back down. She hadn't known she was allowed to want something, and his simple query sent her thoughts flying through a list of stanched desires, rolling up to the edge of wanting one thing very badly: to go to that movie.

"You're eighteen now, Emmy," he replied without picking up his fork. "Your mother's kept a tight rein on you, and I reckon that's all right." He paused and Emmy waited as he stared at her, hard. "You need to speak your mind."

Emmy cleared her throat, but a small gurgle came out when she tried to speak. She cleared it again. "Well, my friend, Bev Langer, is going to a movie tomorrow night—*The Ten Commandments,* the one with Charlton Heston?" she began, then stalled. He nodded for her to continue, so she took a deeper breath. "I was wondering if maybe . . . I could go with?" She exhaled. Picked at a stain on the tablecloth, making a mental note to rub some baking soda into it before washing it in the morning.

Christian smiled slightly and continued eating. Emmy wondered what he might be thinking, if he was trying to come up with a way to square it with Karin, whether he'd wait the half hour until she came home to give an answer. Emmy forced herself to not look at either the clock or her Bulova, playing instead with the stretchy metal band as it pinched at the skin on her wrist. She focused all her energy on keeping her eyes on her father. She knew that if he looked up and met her gaze he would never say no.

"I'd be back right after the movie," Emmy offered, not sure how to read her father's silence. "I can get all the chores done, I'll get up extra early, and I can teach Birdie to help bake the bread."

"Movies cost money, Emmy," Christian replied without looking up.

"Bev said it would be her treat, for my birthday. Oh, please, can I go, please?" She sprang up from the table and went to the icebox to get a bottle of milk. Her birthday had just passed and, as usual, they had done nothing to mark it. Mentioning it to her father made her feel ungrateful, and her hand shook a little as she carefully poured half a glass, keeping the rest for the morning's porridge. The price of milk had recently dropped and they needed to sell most of the farm's production to keep things going. There was a time when they'd had so much fresh milk that Emmy couldn't stand the sight of it, particularly the thick layer of cream that would float on the top of the pitcher and would have to be either scooped off or pierced to release the milk below. Now that it was dear, she licked her lips at the thought of the small glassful that she set in front of Christian. She hovered over his right shoulder, swaying with the keen excitement of having asked for something, feeling as though she didn't deserve it. She shifted from foot to foot. Her father had fallen into a steady rhythm eating his meal, and not until the last drop of gravy had been cleaned from the plate, the final boiled potato speared and chewed, the bottom sip of milk consumed did he look directly at her.

"I'll want to meet this . . ."

"Oh, thank you thank you thank you, yes, of course, I'll have Bev come in before we go. Oh, you're the best!" She hugged him so hard he choked and laughed, clasping her around the waist, then pushing her gently away.

"Okay."

"Okay I can?" she asked, picking up a dishrag.

"Okay I'll ask your mother, but you'd better make sure the kitchen is clean. Don't give her a reason to say no."

Saturday broke with a distinct chill in the air. Emmy rose at five to get an early start on her chores. She hadn't really slept at all with the potential excitement of an evening away from the small house and its Saturday night airing of the *Good News Broadcast* on the radio and the smell of frying doughnuts in the kitchen. Sure, she'd gone out before, but not once without her parents and never to a function that wasn't church sponsored. She had taken quite a chance asking this small liberty, and as she crept down the stairs she couldn't still her pulse from throbbing at her temples.

The kitchen light was on. Emmy slowed her step, clasped her hands together. She saw her mother standing at the sink, wrist deep in dark water.

"Once the sun rises we'll hang these out," Karin said, pulling a long black dress from the murk and feeding it through the wringer of the white enamel washtub. Emmy took over the task without comment and found the dye bath to be as cold as the kitchen. These were her grandmother's winter dresses, threadbare, heavy, and widow-worn. Usually they redyed and mended them in the spring before packing them away until the fall, a chore that could take many hours. Emmy didn't dare ask why they were doing this now, in the dead of January, and instead tried to predict how much time sodden wool would need to dry in cold weather. She handed her mother another heavy dress, then crossed to the cupboard, drawing out the flour tin and proofing bowls. The kitchen would need to be warmer than this to properly raise the dough, but Emmy didn't start the gas on the range until her mother told her to do so. Her plans began to slip away.

The women worked in silence for more than an hour, dying, wringing, rinsing, wringing again, and then hanging the dresses on the clothesline behind their house, the thickly fleeced garments flapping and freezing in the cold wind. Emmy didn't care what the neighbors might think about this solemn process, as their activities often were equally as odd. Old man Luders across the alley had filled his backyard so completely with junk he collected from garbage cans that he had created a maze only he could find his way through. Every day he would load a wheelbarrow full of items for sale, push it around the neighborhood and return not having sold anything but with a clearly increased pile of discards. No one ever saw Mrs. Luders, except for Karin when she would go over and pray with the old woman, who had grown so large that it was unthinkable for her to leave the house at all. There was also an assortment of farm animals to be found in the backyards around them, from laying hens to a couple of goats and even, she had heard but never seen, a milk cow. Having animals in proximity made Emmy miss the rhythm of the farm less, and she was happy to dispatch her chores to the merry crowing of a rooster a few yards away.

The kitchen eventually warmed a few degrees due to the heat of the two women bent to their work. Karin took the brown crock of cultured yeast from the icebox and handed it to her daughter. Sometimes when Emmy was kneading the Herman mixture into dough she could sense her mother watching her, swelling a bit with the knowledge that she had taught Emmy well. These were the rare times she actually felt that her mother loved her, yet if Emmy ever looked at Karin directly in those moments, the glimmer of warmth would always be doused like a hand-trapped lightning bug brought too quickly into a bright room.

At six Birdie and Christian appeared in the kitchen, just as Karin set the table with a platter of scrambled eggs and a pot of porridge. Eggs were the one food they always had plenty of, since the farm's hens produced too many for Karin to sell to local grocers. The larger chicken farms down around Fergus Falls were beginning to undersell her in the new supermarkets and there were those who believed that when the new four-lane highway was built up to Moorhead, trucks would start bringing all sorts of things from farther and farther away. Progress, they called it, but for Emmy's family it already foretold the opposite.

"Oh, Mother," Birdie said as she quickly ate her bowl of porridge, blowing on each steaming bite, "you'll never guess what happened at choir this week." Her sapphire-colored eyes held the kind of depth that Emmy imagined an ocean might contain; Birdie's wavy hair was silky and more black than brown. She favored her father, even as their mother favored Birdie. "I was chosen to sing a solo for the spring concert!"

"That is a good thing," Christian said, considerably brighter after his night's rest.

"It's God's gift, Birdie, not yours. Remember that," Karin said, punctuating her words with a sharp look at Christian. She got up from the table and began to clean up the breakfast dishes.

"Yes, of course you're right," Birdie said, clearing her own bowl and washing it quickly at the sink, her shoulders slightly slumped as though she was trying not to cry. Emmy swallowed the last mouthful of eggs and went to her sister.

"I'm proud of you," Emmy whispered to Birdie. "I know how hard it must have been to stand up in front of all those kids and sing."

"Thanks," Birdie said, her small smile of joy rekindling. "I thought I would die, right there."

"But you didn't." Emmy wrung out the dishrag and wiped down the oilcloth as Birdie and Christian pulled coats on over their coveralls, ready to head east to the work awaiting them on the farm. The Nelsons paid Maria Gonzales's oldest son, Pedro, to help with the morning milking, but Christian took care of everything else—the weekly mucking, moving six day's worth of corn silage from where it was packed into a hole dug in the ground to an old truck bed behind the shed, and whatever else Grandmother Nelson needed done. During the week, Emmy's parents made the seven-mile trip every morning to do the milking before Christian went on to work at the sugar beet plant and Karin at the Glyndon school lunchroom, returning to the farm for evening chores and then home to eat whatever Emmy had made for dinner. Sometimes she wondered why they all worked so hard on a farm that wasn't theirs, but then she would simply reason that the fifth commandment rang strongly in Christian, and until his mother was dead and buried he would expect his family to lean toward the homestead as obediently as he had for forty-some years. Karin herded him and Birdie to the kitchen door.

"Have her home in time to go out with Emmy," Karin said, pulling on a sweater and following them out into the yard.

As the door closed with a jerked-up shudder, Emmy sank her hands into the lukewarm dishwater, calculating how long she could indulge her disappointment. She had figured her mother would find a way to polish the shine off her very first night out, but Emmy hadn't considered this possibility, nor could she imagine asking Bev to pay for the extra ticket. Emmy didn't even know whether there would be room in the car or who else was invited. Maybe Bev would think this presumptuous of Emmy and change her mind about their friendship. But hadn't Bev already suggested that Birdie come? She was a good companion, and incapable of being disliked by anyone she met. At least Karin had said yes. Emmy picked up her pace with fresh energy. She was going out on the town on a Saturday night. So what if she wasn't going solo—there were far worse chaperones than Birdie. Besides, Emmy secretly liked the way the girl looked up to her, even if at times Birdie seemed to forget that she was only fifteen, and not eighteen like Emmy.

❧

At four that afternoon, Emmy set down the last of the dress mending and tapped a wet fingertip to the bottom of the iron. It sizzled. Her mother had finally given her a moment of peace, taking a pot of chicken broth down the street to Mrs. Lavold after a quick lunch of coffee with a slice of freshly baked bread. It was a ritual Emmy shared with her mother, to sit down in the middle of their housework and break the first loaf together—a ten-minute repast punctuated with a heavy sigh from Karin as she pressed herself up from the table and back into duty. Though Emmy could think of many things she wanted to share with her mother, it was hard to begin a conversation knowing that Karin wouldn't sit still long enough to form an opinion. Today was no better than usual, and silence had once again ruled, pressing forward Emmy's determination not to live like this, not be who her mother was. She would talk to her children, not be a shadow in her own house, cooling the rooms with her presence, giving herself so completely to God that she couldn't see His creatures around her.

Emmy shook her head, attempting to clear her thoughts and quell the burst of nervous energy that always accompanied her cup of afternoon coffee as she ironed the pile of dresses.

"I wonder if we'll get popcorn," she said aloud, startling herself. She'd been to the pictures only a handful of times, and there was never money for treats or snacks. They had once, a long time ago, gone to see a movie called *The Robe* at the Fargo Theatre and there was a popcorn vendor on the sidewalk outside as well as a candy counter inside. The proximity of the forbidden treat had been endless torture for Emmy, who knew better than to ask for a penny to buy a bag, and now these many years later she could not remember the details of the movie but she could still almost smell the popcorn.

As she worked the heavy iron, steam rose out of the cloth and warmed her through for the first time that long, cold day. She looked around the tiny living room, which was the only space large enough to set up the ironing board, and wondered why her parents couldn't have moved them into a slightly larger house, if they were bothering to move them at all. She had learned not to complain, though, as Karin would only conjure stories of her own childhood and how they had lived little better than the sodbusters before them. There was never a hint of fondness when she told these tales, and whenever Birdie or Emmy would sigh over the coldness of the house, Karin was quick to remind them that they could have scant heat or no indoor water whatsoever. She also told them about using rags for personal hygiene or putting milk and meat in pails down the cistern in the summer to keep them from spoiling. But through these tales, Emmy learned very little about Karin's family, beyond the somewhat surprising mentions of a deceased mother and drunken father. There might have been other children, but Karin never spoke of them. Eventually the girls preferred to meet their small disappointments with silent forbearance, rather than be told the same three stories that no matter how hard they pressed, never revealed Karin's interior.

Tithing took part of their family income, and certainly all the missions that her mother supported with small change here and there didn't help their situation. But where did the rest go? Not to this shabby furniture and cold bare linoleum floors. There was a small rag rug in the middle of the room, woven from old clothes and dishcloths; Emmy recognized a sliver of brown- and yellow-flecked calico from a play dress she wore as a girl. She missed the warmth of her grandmother's farmhouse and the respite it had provided her on cold winter days after school, doing her homework in the kitchen before her mother would come home and, after supper, take them all back into the shack that was hardly an improvement over Karin's own childhood home.

The light outside had fallen as Emmy worked, and she switched on a small lamp. It suddenly occurred to her that Bev would have to come in to meet her parents. The Langer house was one of the biggest in Moorhead; what would she think of how the Nelsons lived? Emmy had met a few other girls since September, but because she was never allowed to use the phone or join a potluck group, Bev was the closest thing she had to a best friend. She wasn't even sure what the term meant, but Bev bandied it about in a way that appealed to Emmy. She supposed that Birdie occupied the role for her by default and proximity, although since Emmy had met Bev, Emmy realized that having a sister was far different from having a friend.

In the fall Emmy had worried that Birdie wouldn't be able to find her way in the big school, but she had more friends than her older sister, and seemed to draw boys around her as though she were dipped in honey. She was instantly expert about playing down her popularity at home—Emmy had heard about it through Bev, mostly, and seen some evidence in the hallway as sophomores, juniors, and even some seniors hovered around beautiful, tiny Birdie. It was almost as though Emmy didn't know who her sister was at school, but the minute they walked into the house together at the end of the day she became her familiar reserved self, and settled in to study next to the radio. Emmy felt more like an aunt than a sister in these moments, and knew that she needed to be generous with Birdie, to share whatever she had with her. This Emmy would do, whether it made her feel some of the excitement of the evening waning at the prospect of a tagalong or not.

❧

The dresses now hung in a somber row on the wooden curtain rod that Christian had installed in the double doorway between the living room and entry. During the winter, a heavy gray wool blanket was strung on the rod to keep the small gusts of heat produced by the oil-burning furnace from escaping up the stairs and into the profoundly cold bedrooms and bath. The thermostat was routinely turned down to forty-five degrees when the house sat empty during the day, and Emmy cooked supper wearing her mittens the first hour home after school while the place slowly warmed to sixty. They all took hot water bottles to bed at night and slept in flannel nightgowns with thermal long johns underneath. Oh, how she *hated* the winter. Someday she would escape this cold and either live someplace hot or at the very least, with heat. Emmy stood in front of the neatly arrayed garments and smiled at the precision of the knife pleats she had pressed into the seams. It was five o'clock and in half an hour she would be on her way someplace. She heard her mother's step on the front walk and went to open the door.

"Good work, Emmy," Karin said as she inspected the dresses. Emmy knew better than to show how proud she was, so instead she took the empty pot from her mother as Karin hung her coat in the small closet under the stairs.

"I've started dinner," Emmy said, taking the kettle into the kitchen, which was filled with the subtle smell of carrots simmering, and the sharp overscent of lutefisk bubbling away in a glass baking dish.

"I see you're going to miss your favorite meal," Karin said with a slight smile. Hers was the last generation to embrace the lye-cured cod with its pungent taste and slightly viscous texture. Neither Emmy nor Birdie could get it down without much restraint and even more water. "I'm sure your sister will approve."

"I thought it might be a good night to get it out of the way," Emmy said, enjoying the moment of mirth. "How was Mrs. Lavold?"

Karin sat down at the table and deftly rearranged the hair that had loosened when she removed her hat. Emmy noticed her mother hesitate slightly in her movements, as though her joints hurt.

"I'm quite sure she's got cancer, but she won't go to the doctor," Karin said. "She puts her faith in God, not science, she says, and how can I argue with that? If God wants her, He's going to take her in His time. I just wish she'd get something for the pain and to release the amount of fluid trapped in her poor body. Her soul is strong, though, so I can't presume to say what's right." She looked off into the distance, past Emmy's shoulder. "Where's your father?"

"I don't know," Emmy said, suddenly realizing how the time had slipped past. "I need to get ready." She ran up the stairs, changed out of her scratchy woolen work pants and pulled on her new dungarees, fastening the small button at the side and zipping them closed. She'd wanted a pair of Blue Bell Jeanies—just like the ones Bev had shown her in *Seventeen* magazine—with deep pockets topstitched with orange thread, but Karin had taken one look at the page Emmy had brought home and made her a more modest version. They hung from the snug waistband in an unflattering and somewhat uncomfortable way, but at least they were approaching what the other kids would be wearing. She carefully folded the hems up two inches in an attempt at improving the overall look, and chose the least pilled of her sweaters to go with them. Emmy rushed to the bathroom and tried to gauge her outfit in the small, cracked mirror over the sink, but even jumping didn't give her enough perspective. She sighed and brushed her corn-silk hair into a tight ponytail that pulled her cheekbones a bit higher and made her eyes look rounder. Pinching at her lips for a little more color, Emmy didn't mind what she saw in the mirror, though she also knew better than to get caught smiling.

The doorbell rang and Emmy raced down the stairs to find her mother holding out her coat and hat. "I don't know what could be keeping those two. You'll have to go without Birdie. No alcohol, no dancing, and no card playing. Be home by ten." Karin took Emmy's hand in hers, slipped a bill into her palm, and smiled. "Just in case." Karin's hand was warmer than usual, and Emmy held still there for a moment, then grabbed her things and went out the door.

Three

A Single Comma

The first surprise of the evening came after Bev and Emmy dashed together up the Nelsons' sidewalk and toward a sleek black car rumbling at the curb. Emmy had never seen an automobile look so brand-new, with its shiny black sides and glowing white top and fins. She briefly imagined plunging into the sea in this creature and driving out the other side dry and safe. As they got to the car the passenger door swung open and a jet-haired boy who looked as though he'd been born inside of his car leaned across the seat, smiling up at them.

"I thought it was girls' night," Emmy said, stopping on the walk and glancing back to see if her mother was watching. Bev turned and gave Emmy a dazzling smile, her arm reaching into the car and her black-gloved hand ruffling the boy's thick wave of upswept bangs.

"Never mind Howard. He's my cousin. Right, Howie?"

"Sure thing, Sophie, whatever you say." Howie nodded to the backseat and looked at Emmy. "Get in."

"Sophie?" Emmy asked, but Bev just giggled and shook her short curls. Emmy slid across the smooth leather as Howie put the car into gear and jerked it an inch forward before gliding away from the curb.

"Like Sophia," Howie said. "As in *Loren.*"

"Oh," Emmy said, surprised by how low the car sat on the road; it was almost like sinking into a plush, comfortable couch. The space was warm, friendly.

"It sure is a beautiful night to be out, Emmy, don't you think?" Bev asked, and then answered herself without waiting for Emmy's response. "Yeah, just beautiful. We're going to get an early spring this year. At least by Easter." They drove down Eighth Street, and at Main Avenue Howie put on the signal to turn left.

"Isn't *Ten Commandments* at the Fargo Theatre?" Emmy asked, attempting to sit forward on the seat in order to be heard.

"Oh, sure, kid," Howie said. "We're just going to pick up some more gals before going over to the Bison for a bite."

Emmy reached into her pocket and pulled out the slip of paper her mother had given her. It was a two-dollar bill. Karin must have taken it from her egg money, and meant for the girls to share it. Emmy would do what she could to spend only her half.

Bev and Howie chatted away in the front seat as Emmy watched Moorhead fly past. So this is what it's like to be a regular teenager, she thought, and felt a sudden nervous thrill. The air around her body took on a charge as the car started to go faster, and though she wanted to tell Howie to slow down, something about the way he gripped the steering wheel suggested he never would. Before she knew it, they had turned onto Highway 75, leaving the city limits behind. Emmy scooted to the middle of the wide seat in an effort to balance her increasing vertigo and could see in the near distance the winter-darkened arrow of the White Spot Drive-in. She'd heard about this burger joint for years and had driven past it once, but her family had never eaten there. In fact, they had never eaten out at a restaurant of any kind, only Sunday dinners at the church, where everyone brought a hot dish to pass.

In class Emmy thought Bev looked up to her, admired her even. But in this large car so far out of her element, Emmy felt again like a child, her legs barely touching the floor, as though the two in the front seat were parents about to take her out for ice cream. If it wasn't already more than apparent that Howie was not Bev's cousin, on the sharp corner turn into the drive-in Bev slid across the seat and curled up under Howie's arm, causing Emmy to feel more keenly her solitary place in this equation.

Her loneliness didn't last, though, as two girls from Emmy's school burst into the car on either side of her. She recognized them instantly—Donna Kratz was in her English composition course and her younger sister Paula was in choir with Birdie.

"By golly, Bev, it's about time," Donna exclaimed, dropping onto the seat on Emmy's left. Her soft blond hair fell in enviable waves from the edge of her thickly knit woolen hat to her shoulders. "Heya, Howie," she said, then looked sidelong at Emmy for a moment. "Emmy, right?" she asked. Emmy nodded. Donna's bright red wool coat was thick and fluffy, cutting the draft the girls had brought into the car. She removed her hat and worked at smoothing her hair back into place.

"Hey, aren't you Birgitta's sister?" Paula asked, pulling shut the other door and mirroring her sister's grooming.

"Yes," Emmy said. Birdie had taken to using her formal name around school, it seemed. The sight of Donna with her little sister caused in Emmy a feeling of regret that she had been so quick to jump into the car without even hesitating to wait a few minutes longer for her own.

"We were about to freeze out there, you know," Donna said to Bev. "The keeper dropped us off centuries ago."

"Centuries," Paula agreed, fixing her lipstick in a small mirror. Though also gifted with thick tresses, she wasn't as pretty as Donna—her small brown eyes were hidden behind heavy-rimmed glasses—but Paula had an air about her that promised something unexpected, something fun.

"So sorry!" Bev yelled over the grinding sound of the car backing up and tearing out of the lot. "We had to pick up Emmy." Howie revved and then gunned the engine, flying down the few miles back to Moorhead. Emmy held on to her cute little crocheted cap, even though it was tied under her chin. Donna scooted Emmy aside so she could lean over the seat and talk to Howie and Bev.

"How about that drag last night?" she asked. Howie barely moved, but Donna didn't seem to notice. "Crazy! Two Fargo South hotties blew out over at Hector Airport. Wish I could have seen the patch they laid on the tarmac." She leaned all the way into the front seat and switched the radio station, turning to a song about a girl named Peggy Sue. "Buddy Holly just kills me!" Donna exclaimed. The hitch in the singer's voice sounded to Emmy like a boy in stuttering love, his urgency causing her to feel just the slightest bit light-headed.

"Ix-nay on the ag-dray," Bev said to Donna. "Howie wasn't there, were you, darling?"

"Well," Paula's voice squeaked from Emmy's other side. "Karla Kindlespire told Frannie Peterson that you were one of the rods."

"This car?" Donna purred, stroking the top of the seat as she whispered something in Bev's ear. The two girls giggled and Bev slapped at Donna's hand playfully. Emmy suddenly realized that "best" did not mean *only* when it came to friendship.

They reached the Fargo side of the river, sailed onto Broadway, and joined a stream of cars that were slow moving and beautiful. An array of chrome-bright boats passed them as they looped around a parking lot in the middle of Broadway and started making their way north on the strip, past Herbst's, Woolworth's, and the Hotel Donaldson. When they reached the Bison Hotel, Howie eased the car into a recently vacated parking spot right in front of the building. He jumped out of the car and ran around to open Bev's door, offering her a hand up to the curb. They walked into the café in front of the other two girls, and Emmy lagged a step behind, pulled by the seductive magnetism of these beautifully confident people. This was not at all what she had been expecting from the evening and she began to feel anxious with the swirl of possibility around her. She'd never felt this free or this scared in her life.

Passing through the door and smelling the hot fryer oil, hearing the clinking of silver against china, the chatter of a dozen or so happy voices—all of it made Emmy question her sense of reality. She knew her hunger was real, though, and as she sat down at the table, she found she couldn't summon a single word. There was a piece of paper in front of her with letters and numbers, and slowly it dawned on her that it was a menu, but her eyes were too jumpy to make out anything on it other than the prices. Howie took the laminated cards away from the girls and insisted on ordering something called a "buck-nine" for everyone. The Kratz sisters giggled and Bev smiled with benevolent pride. The four friends chattered away about people Emmy didn't know and about events that had transpired either before she moved into town or outside of her purview. She didn't mind being left out of the jokes, and instead smiled and laughed along with a genuine spirit of belonging—a feeling she couldn't remember having felt anywhere before.

"Oh, my Lord," Donna sputtered as the plates of food were swiftly dealt to each place. "Did you hear about that girl who's gone on a murder spree in Nebraska?"

"Caril Ann Fugate," Paula answered, her long lashes nearly brushing the lenses that framed them. "She's only fifteen, but she fell in love with a boy who's older and he murdered her parents and baby sister. With a knife. Starkweather something." She leaned in closer, her voice hushed for effect. "The radio says they're on the road, headed north."

"It's crazy," Howie said, one arm slung over the back of his chair, chewing a fried potato with his white teeth. "What if they're headed up here?" He raised his eyebrows in mock horror, and Bev swatted his arm.

"Stop," she said. "It's not funny when people are scared."

"That's right," Donna said. "They've been on the lam for three days. That's long enough to drive here from Lincoln if you don't stop."

Paula dabbed at a spot of ketchup on her chin. "Can you imagine, the girl's a whole year younger than me. They say it's like Romeo and Juliet meets Bonnie and Clyde."

Howie shook his head. "You all have some imagination." He turned to Emmy. "What about you, kid. You scared?"

Emmy chewed and swallowed the bite of meat in her mouth and wiped her lips carefully while everyone looked at her. "It's the first I've heard of it," she said, trying not to sound stupid. "I can't begin to imagine taking another life, much less what you're saying."

Bev's eyes sparkled as she looked at Emmy. "You are by far the sweetest person I've ever met," she said. "But you really do need to start living in this world, Emmy. I'm afraid of what it might do to you if you don't."

Emmy blushed and fell back to eating, chewing every bite carefully, as she'd been taught. The buck-nine was the best steak she'd ever had—small, about the size of a flattened baseball, and probably taken from the sirloin of the cow, but she couldn't be entirely sure. She attempted to tune out the continued banter about the young murderous lovers, but the sordid details of one person stuffed into an outhouse and the baby sister being stabbed to death grabbed Emmy's imagination and she hung on every horrible word.

When the waitress slapped a small slip of paper on the table, Emmy panicked. She didn't see how she could possibly afford food this good. Her heart quickened and she drew the two-dollar bill out of her pocket, fumbled, dropped it on the floor, bent over to pick it up. She sat up in her chair as Howie pulled a long wallet attached to a chain from his back pocket and walked over to the till with cash in his hand. The other girls continued their conversation as though this was the natural order of things. They rose from the table and drew on their coats, collected their purses, and headed to the door like a flock of birds driven to casual coordination by instinct. Emmy remained in her chair, watching Howie pay a man at the counter. Howie began to leave, and then suddenly looked back at the table as if he had forgotten something. He slowly grinned and tipped his head toward the door, regarding Emmy as though she were a newly discovered species. Emmy leaped to her feat, ducked her head, and walked under his arm as he propped open the door. Catching a whiff of his earthy leather jacket and hair pomade, she closed her eyes against the draw of it and stumbled over the threshold. He caught her, the same hungry grin now one foot away from her face. Beads of sweat collected at her collar as she ran to the open door of the car, where she scooted into her place behind Bev and patted away the moisture, out of breath.

Howie moved the car onto Broadway, and just as quickly swerved out of the way of a pickup truck that had swung around the corner from Fourth Avenue. Emmy yelped as the brakes shuddered and she saw that the other vehicle was the Branns' truck. Emmy caught a glimpse of Ambrose and the long dark hair of a girl sitting next to him. Some other girl out on the town, in a place that was meant to be Emmy's. It seemed so casual and normal for young people to be out on a Saturday night, and yet her mother had kept their courting to parlors and the church basement. Even so, Ambrose was brazenly ignoring the customs of their courtship. Emmy felt as though she might be sick as the car swayed back into traffic.

"Get bent, Clyde!" Howie yelled out his window. At the next stoplight, Emmy watched the truck pull away as the girl's head leaned closer toward Ambrose. Emmy coughed to try to quell her confusion.

"You okay, kid?" Donna asked, slapping her gently on the back. *Kid* had become Emmy's name in this new crowd and she didn't really mind its connotations of naïveté. She *was* naïve—about everything and everyone.

"I'm fine," she said, smoothing her lap as the car bumped onto the highway.

"What a nosebleed," Howie said, shaking a cigarette out of a pack, then handing it off to Bev. "Did you gals see that? Goddamn bumpkin." Howie's cutting assessment made Emmy slouch into her coat. She had to admit that from this swell car, Ambrose's pickup truck looked rustic and mud splattered, his checked flannel cap a thing out of pace with the hatless boys with slicked-back hair who prowled the road in their showboats.

The cigarette pack made it to Emmy and she took one without pause. This seemed like the kind of thing that would move her forward into the company in which she rode, and besides, her parents had never prohibited her from smoking. Emmy tried to hold the dry white paper between her index and middle finger, the way she'd seen her father hold his, as she waited for the lighter to pop in the dash. Bev held the red coil to Howie's as he drove; he inhaled and blew an enormous stream of smoke out of the window. She then lit the girls in the back and stuck the lighter in the dash to reheat it for herself. Emmy drew slightly on the smoke, holding it in her mouth and blowing out with the fear of looking useless. Nobody seemed to take much notice of her in any case, so she slowly began taking deeper and deeper inhales, the sweet tobacco scratching her throat in a way that made her want to pull in more.

The smell in the car was increasingly foreign—the combination of perfumes and Howie's scent mixed with the smoke made Emmy's head expand until she felt bigger than the girl she'd been two hours earlier, a girl who had been preparing to commit herself to marrying a man she clearly hardly knew. The ease with which the evening was unfolding lifted her thoughts to a higher plane. It would only be fair to give Ambrose a chance to explain his actions, but until he did, Emmy felt free to enjoy her evening as a grown-up woman without promises to be kept or made. If he was outside the limits set forth by their tiny society, so was she.

As Howie parked the car in front of the Imperial Theater, Emmy looked at the marquee. It wasn't *The Ten Commandments*, but something called *Smiles of a Summer Night*. Just one more thing she wouldn't be able to tell her mother. Emmy joined the ticket line, a soft thrill passing through her when she slid her two-dollar bill to the girl in the box, as though Thomas Jefferson himself were winking up at Emmy's secret disobedience.

❧

The minute the movie was over the group left the theater and piled back into Howie's car. Emmy went from feeling like a third wheel at the beginning of the evening to a slightly flat fifth one. The movie had peeled away at Emmy's exhilaration, casting her out into the cold night with even less emotional protection than she'd had at six o'clock. For one thing, it was in Swedish and she had to read along with the odd-sounding words, but more directly because Emmy couldn't stop thinking about whether she should confront Ambrose. She'd tried to imagine what such a conversation would entail but couldn't get past the idea of his laughing at her, having a reasonable answer, or some other outcome that showed her to be as foolish as she felt. Nor could she imagine what she was going to tell her mother when Karin asked about the movie's content, which certainly had not come from the Bible.

Donna and Paula slipped into the backseat next to each other and no one bothered to address Emmy directly, nor did she attempt to join in with their constant babble. She was still pleased to be out of the house, though, and happy that Bev kept looking at her with the protective glances and smiles of a worldly chaperone. As they pulled back into traffic, Emmy gazed out her window and saw car after car pass them, some honking, others silently floating, all of them festooned with beautifully polished chrome and brightly colored paint. When they would pass a glossy black car Howie would give the horn a couple of quick taps. It was all like watching a parade of sorts, but one decorated with gorgeous young faces and bright laughter. As they passed neon signs for everything from Royal Jewelers to Red Owl groceries to Kinney's shoes and the Mary Elizabeth Frock Shop, the commercial lights of Broadway glowed around all this extravagant youth, and the hum inside the car exploded into rolled-down windows and shouts of "Later, gater!" and "Moorhead Spuds!" At least Glyndon had the respectable Lion mascot. Whoever cheered for a root vegetable to win a game?

"Did you bring them?" Bev yelled over the din to Howie.

"Nope, we need to slide by Frank's," he roared back.

"Bring what?" Emmy said, though no one could hear her over Donna's loud whistles and Paula's high-pitched prattle. The next thing Emmy knew there was a small, flat, clear glass bottle in her hand. She paused, considering her mother's admonishment, but then a swirl of repressed opportunities boiled up inside of her and she hastily tipped it back and coughed hoarsely before looking at the label, which she read as a streetlight flickered through the window: EVERCLEAR. She took a more cautious sip and found the alcohol slightly less biting, but equally oily and pungent. A steady, unfamiliar warmth seeped up through her, softening the frigid air of the open windows. She knew that her foot had surely slipped out of her family's protective circle and into someplace fiendish. No one drank alcohol and lived long enough to regret it.

In the front seat Bev presided like the homecoming queen she had been last fall, royal. Splendid. Everything blurred with a friendlier glow, and Emmy tossed aside all churchy thoughts while she took a more convincing swig and passed the bottle over the seat to Howie.

"Hey, kookie, keep that down," he barked, grabbing the bottle and spilling some on the seat. Bev tilted her head and stroked Howie's arm. "Sorry, kid," he said to Emmy before ducking down by the steering wheel to take a drink. "A little goes a long way, right?"

"Yes," Emmy replied, boldly making eye contact with him in the rearview mirror. He was much more handsome than Ambrose, with thick wavy hair that slicked upward in the back, and deeply set black eyes under his sulky brow. Howie held the gaze and gave her a little smirk. A rash of goose bumps shivered over her skin, so she adjusted her view out the window as they pulled up in front of a very large house with carefully painted trimmed porches and a three-story turret. Even Emmy knew who lived in this house. Howie blasted the horn and out ran Frank Halsey, scion to the richest family in Moorhead. His father was the county attorney, and his grandfather had been a prominent preacher in Grand Forks. Emmy was surprised to realize that they had crossed back over the river; the time was passing so quickly. She glanced at her watch, relieved to see that it was only nine.

Howie got out of the car and helped Frank carry two burlap sacks across the snow-encrusted yard to the trunk. The radio announcer introduced "Roll Over, Beethoven," by Chuck Berry, and Bev turned up the volume.

"I can't be*lieve* we're actually, finally going to do this!" Donna shrieked over the music, passing a fresh bottle to Emmy.

"Do what, Donna, do what?" Paula said, tugging on the older girl's sleeve. A couple of loud thuds came from the trunk, and as Emmy sipped, she felt the vibrations in her legs, which were otherwise somewhat numb.

"What, are you writing a book or something?" Donna said to her sister before taking an extra swig.

"Hush, Paula. We'll tell you when we get there," Bev said more kindly, winking at Emmy. "You've never had a bash like this one, have you, kid?"

"No, I—" Emmy started to say, but almost fell out of the car as her door opened and Frank caught her and nudged her across the seat and into Paula.

"Look out!" Paula squealed, crawling over Emmy to sit next to Frank.

"Hey, Howie," Frank shouted over the music as the other boy returned to the driver's seat. "Can you turn that jungle bunny down?" Frank set his lips on Paula's and kept them there until they had once again reached the Red River. Emmy suppressed the urge to ask Howie to stop the car at the bridge. It wasn't that far to her house, and she suddenly had the feeling that if she didn't bolt now, she wouldn't be home for curfew. A panicky jolt shook through her as they made their way into South Fargo, but still she didn't open her mouth against the direction the night was taking.

Emmy pretended not to notice Frank's hand moving steadily and urgently on top of Paula's coat, pretended that every Saturday night meant smoking, drinking, and petting in the back of a brand-new car. Emmy had never been kissed, much less fondled by a boy, and it took more than a lot of effort for her to keep from gawking. When her eyes would flit onto the rearview, though, Howie's were right there, flashing back at her. Emmy wondered whether Ambrose was the type of boy who would be steaming up his pickup truck with the unknown girl out in the dark prairie night. Emmy unbuttoned the top of her coat and pulled at her scarf, wishing the windows were open. She was used to close spaces, but not ones filled with people who actually touched one another. In fact, the only person who ever kissed her was Grandmother Nelson, and that was only on the cheek. Emmy always had to fight the desire to wipe the kiss away, so foreign a feeling it was to her.

When the car finally stopped, they were outside a looming brick building. In front of it a small stone announcement board read: FARGO CENTRAL HIGH SCHOOL. Howie killed the engine and turned around to address everyone in the car, the cool ambient light from a nearby streetlamp making his toothy smile glow. The lovers untangled, Paula smoothing her hair and Frank adjusting in his seat, glancing at Emmy briefly, then grinning at Howie. A bottle from Frank was making the rounds, this one full of a thick, dark, syrupy liquid that tasted like blackberries in August. Its smooth, sweet velvet eased Emmy's anxiety as the fruity smell in the car rose around her and tilted the contents of her head into a mild spin.

"Okay, here's the gig," Howie said. "Frank, Bev, and Paula, you take one bag and start on that side of the sign, Donna and you, kid, you're with me. We need to line them up quickly and carefully so you can see it from the road."

"See what?" Paula said while reapplying her lipstick in a small mirror, bored and interested at the same time.

"The *M*," Bev replied, smiling wickedly. "We're writing the letter *M* in potatoes—get it? Spuds?" She looked at Howie. "You're a genius!"

Emmy mused at the cleverness of writing the school's initial with the school's mascot and for the first time thought the Spud was an okay thing to cheer. She watched her own hand pass the bottle to Paula, who held it to Frank's lips. Howie checked the mirrors.

"Okay, I'm going to get out and place the two bags next to the car, one in front of each wheel. When I give the signal—three taps on the roof—everyone get out. Me and Frank'll carry the bags, and you girls grab the spuds and line them up. This should take about four minutes, tops."

Emmy felt a surge of slurry energy shoot through her veins as Howie got out of the car, Bev holding her hat over the interior dome light. Donna pulled a cigarette from her clutch and put it to her lips, striking the wheel of a Zippo lighter.

"Hey!" Bev blew out the flame. "Are you trying to get us arrested?" Donna held her hands up in apology and let the offending objects fall back into the open bag on her lap. Just as she did, the trunk closed, and the taps came. Everyone tumbled quietly out of the car and set to their mission. Emmy felt the sudden sharp cold on her neck, but waited to button her coat until she had grabbed an armful of potatoes and laid them out according to plan. She dusted the rich valley dirt from the front of her coat as she raced back to Howie, who was steadily placing spuds of his own. Stifled giggles and shushing broke louder than firecrackers, and Emmy held her breath. She had never done anything like this before and didn't stop to worry about how much she enjoyed it. They were collectively finishing at the point of the *M* when they heard a siren off in the distance.

"Put an egg in your shoe," Frank yelled to Howie and caught the near-empty sack midair. Everyone raced to the car, even as the flashing lights swiftly approached. Bringing up the rear, Emmy tripped over a potato and fell face-first into the snow at the bottom of the slope. The others were already in the car; the doors slammed and Howie drove off into the street and around the corner just as the police rounded the block. The cop car started to slow—this was Emmy's one chance to flee. She popped up and raced off behind the stone sign, leaning against it and steadying her breath. A floodlight illuminated the glory of their handiwork, and Emmy suppressed laughter with her hand against her mouth. The dark brown potatoes etched the snow, even with their many footprints in between. The light passed above her and the car picked up speed, following in the direction of the Chevy. Emmy exhaled and laughed out loud. She realized she was happy to be alone, even though she had no idea where exactly she was or how she would get home. She looked at her watch and stopped laughing. It was almost ten o'clock. No way to beat curfew, she thought, brushing her clothes of powdery snow and more potato dirt. Fresh flakes began to fall and Emmy gazed heavenward and uttered, "Whatever next?"

❧

When Emmy got to Sixth Street she headed toward Broadway, hoping that she could find the kids still cruising and catch a ride home. They hadn't come looking for her, and her momentary relief of being out of the car had frozen into frustrated anger—something Emmy was not accustomed to feeling and caused her to stamp her feet with each step forward. It burned in her that these well-heeled kids wouldn't even give her a second thought, and she imagined them laughing at her situation as they celebrated their own cleverness in the warm, boozy car.

A block before Broadway she turned left onto Roberts Street, which seemed more like an alley as she continued walking. It was darker than she had expected and her heart rattled as she moved quickly past garbage cans and a stray dog. Donna's nonsense about the murderous fugitives bobbed to the surface of Emmy's mind, making her breath come shallow and fast, her eyes widen. In the near distance she saw a tall white steeple, still in the swirl of drifting snow falling against the dark night sky—that's where she would go. As she passed over train tracks and neared the end of Roberts Street, she was startled into a yelp by the sound of a woman's moaning: a couple leaned against a Dumpster, entwined and writhing. With the last bit of her nerve effervescing, Emmy swiftly crossed the street and ran toward the church, relieved to see lights on in a small vestibule off to the side of the enormous building.

As she reached the double door, she looked up at a cross positioned above it and said a little prayer as she grasped the door handle. The lights from inside went off and the door swung open, yanking her body into the darkened entryway, where the figure of a man in shadows stood before her.

"Pardon me, may I please use a phone?" Emmy said, hoping she didn't reek of her night's transgressions. On the verge of tears now, she assumed she was talking to the pastor, but when the light came suddenly back on, she saw instead a beautiful golden-haired boy about her age and somewhat taller, wearing a crimson athletic jacket with the large white letters *SH* linked over the right breast. Emmy couldn't think of a school with those letters, which only added to the mysterious draw she suddenly felt. The boy's translucent blue eyes held hers for a moment, until shyness forced her to look instead at his forehead, where his hair was combed back except for a single comma of a curl that had shook free.

"You okay?" he asked, moving back into a slightly larger room and switching on another light. "I'm Bobby Doyle, and this is my friend Pete Chaklis, and this here is Jesse." Emmy held out her hand to Pete, who was taller than Bobby, and had an easy smile and sandy brown hair—a grown-out flattop falling nearly into his eyes, where a spark of familiarity glinted.

"Hello, I'm Emmy Nelson," she said, turning next to Jesse, who was no more than ten years old. His slender form and caramel skin struck something distant in her memory. She held his small hand for a second, sensing in him the fragility of a broken-winged robin. His face was slack, and when she took her hand away, he slipped silently behind Pete.

"Don't mind him," Pete said, leading her into the warm parish hall. "He hasn't talked much since the tornado."

Bobby touched Emmy's sleeve. "Lost his mother," he said, as though the boy had also lost his hearing. "Siblings. All but his dad."

A coolness spread through Emmy as she realized where she'd seen Pete's face before: the newspaper picture of a fireman carrying the limp body of a child from the harrowing wreckage of the storm, the same shock of bangs obscuring half his face. "Jesse Acevedo?" she asked. "That Jesse?"

"His dad works for my dad," Bobby said. "I mean he did, or he will, when he gets better."

"How awful," Emmy said, striking a sympathetic tone. "Is his father ill?"

"You look lost," Pete drawled, abruptly changing the subject in a way that made Emmy feel ashamed for having asked such an openly voyeuristic question. He dropped a shoulder and hooked one thumb through a belt loop. "Not from Fargo, are you?"

Emmy tried to hide her discomfort by turning back to Bobby. "My friends, and their car, well, you see . . ."

Pete took a step closer to her and she caught sight of the tip of a toothpick that was tucked into his cheek. "You need a ride someplace?"

"Oh, no," Emmy said, swallowing around the lump in her throat. "If I could use a phone, my parents are just over in Moorhead and they'll . . ."

"We just finished cleaning up after CYO," Pete interrupted. The way his smile turned down on the sliver of wood put Emmy on her guard. He turned his head slowly. "I'm the youth coordinator, and Bobby's a junior mentor. We don't bite."

"Of course you don't," Emmy faltered, her voice on the edge of cracking.

"Cut it out, Pete." Bobby pushed his hand into the pocket of his coat and pulled out a key. "If it's okay with you, I'd be happy to drive you. Pete can drop Jesse."

Emmy looked up at the ceiling in relief. "I guess that would be all right," she said, letting the last of the cold air leave her lungs.

"You run right along, Bob," Pete said, crossing his arms and not moving. "I'll get the lights."

"Thanks," Bobby said, and ushered Emmy through the door. "It's all settled." He pulled the door closed, and laid a hand on the small of her back, guiding her toward a cream and red pickup truck down the street. His palm felt hot through her coat, and when he moved his hand to open the cab door, the spot where he had touched her stayed warm for a very long time.

Four

Clad in the Cloth

By the time Bobby drove his Sweptside up to the curb outside the Nelson house, Emmy had said little, but learned much: His father was in the concrete business; he was the oldest of eight children; he drove with one hand on the wheel, the other tapping on the seat between them to "Wake Up Little Susie"; he was mad for the Everly Brothers; and he played basketball for Shanley High School, which turned out to be an all boys' Catholic school in North Fargo.

"Well, I hope I haven't talked your ear off," he said, swinging the gearshift into park and switching off the engine. "Gee, you haven't told me anything about you. I guess when you have so many kids around all the time it's a relief to hear your own voice. I hope you don't mind."

"I don't mind," she replied, nervously taking in the stillness of the nearly dark house, wondering if Karin lay awake, listening for the door to creak open. At least Emmy hadn't spent all the money, and it really wasn't her fault that she had been left behind. "I'd better go." Emmy opened the door and the light in the middle of the cab came on, firing Bobby's wavy combback and making his eyes nearly glow. She inhaled sharply, and then put her foot out into the cold.

"Hey, let me help," he said, and was out of the truck and running around the front before she could stop him. She said a silent prayer that no one was watching them as she ran her hand over the fine cream-colored leather of the seat, new smelling and soft to the touch. It was a far cry from the beaten old Coronet her family drove. Bobby took hold of the door and swung it open. She reached for his hand and he met her grasp midway. Their eyes locked again and this time she didn't break the gaze and so missed the curb as she stepped down. He caught her in his arms and they stayed that way for a moment before she broke free, clumsily, and uttered a hoarse "Thank you very much" as he let go of her. She backed up the sidewalk, pushing her hat an inch higher up her brow.

"Sorry if Pete was rude," Bobby said. "He's kind of like everyone's big brother. He runs the CYO and makes sure we don't all turn into delinquents."

"He wasn't rude," Emmy said quietly, glancing at the house and relieved to see no other lights had come on. "It's not every day a strange girl walks into a church, after all."

"You're welcome to walk in again any time." Bobby turned halfway and stopped. "I guess this is good night, Emmy Nelson."

"Good night, Bobby Doyle." She stood there, her body midway between the street and the house, shoulders squared and head turned toward the boy as he walked to his truck, jumped into the cab, and drove away. Floating now, Emmy sprinted to the house, abuzz with the sparkling stillness in the air, as if the sky had become a net of crystals arrayed for the first time just for her. She opened the door as noiselessly as possible and then leaned against the closed door, completely incapable of slowing her breath. She pressed a hand to her heart, holding it in her chest as best she could, her ears ringing with the silence of the house. It was too quiet.

Looking around, she saw a small light on in the kitchen and moved quickly toward it. There was a note for her on the table. Her grandmother was in the hospital; they were all there with her. Emmy glanced at the clock; it was nearing midnight. The phone jangled in the front hall and Emmy shrieked at the noise before dashing to it and grabbing the receiver.

"Hello," she whispered hoarsely. "Mother?"

"Oh, thank God, Emmy, you're home," Bev said. "We kept circling and looking and I feel just terrible that you got left. We didn't realize until we were a block away, but we went right back to get you and you were nowhere to be found."

"It's all right," Emmy said, pulling off her coat and hanging it in the hall closet. "I'm just happy you care."

"Care!" Bev said. "I would have killed myself if anything had happened to you."

Emmy smiled in relief. "Thanks, Bev. I'll see you at school."

"See you later, alligator," Bev said, and the line went dead in Emmy's hand.

How about that, she thought, my first phone call from my first friend. She shook her head and sat down with the note, reading it more slowly this time. Her instructions were to make the doughnuts for church, and she set to this assignment, feeling a mix of relief and worry settle over the strange excitements of the evening. Grandmother Nelson had these spells; she'd be fine, Emmy told herself, even as she couldn't explain away the fact that her father and sister were required at her grandmother's side, too. She hurried with the doughnuts, anticipating with each moment that someone would return home and figure out her ill timing. Once the job was completed and the doughnuts were cooling on the counter, the clock ticked past two and Emmy fell asleep on the couch, fully dressed, prepared for the worst.

❧

A ray of weak light shone against Emmy's closed eyes, and she awoke to find the house still. She rolled over, thinking about all the colorful, exciting, shifting people and cars and images of the night before. She sighed, remembering the brown slice of Ambrose's truck, his scowl at Howie, her sickening response as she sighted another girl next to her supposed beau. But then came Bobby Doyle and how absolutely perfect he seemed, and how completely forbidden he would be in the eyes of her parents. Catholics were unwelcome in the minds of some Lutherans, and her grandmother had told her that marrying one was a sin against God. Her grandmother. Still no word. Emmy tossed over to her side and sat up. Might as well get dressed for church, she thought. Nothing stops the car from pointing east on Sunday morning, especially when prayer was going to be needed.

By the time Emmy was washed and dressed and had the doughnuts in their tin, she heard the old car crunch up the drive. She ran to the window. There they were, her family. It was as though she had never been with them on the other side of the glass. She could already feel the pull away from these small gray-shaded people. Even Birdie looked pinched and drawn, as though she had fallen in line with the family history of slope-shouldered farm women overnight. Emmy sighed and opened the door.

"How bad is it?" she asked her mother as she took Karin's hat and coat.

"Bad. But she's home now, and resting. Ambrose is sitting with her," Karin said, going to the kitchen and inspecting the doughnuts. "Thank you, Emmy. It's a great relief not to fall short this morning. I need to pack." Christian followed her up the stairs, smoothing a few hairs on his head and turning left toward the bathroom at the top landing. Birdie clutched her sister's arm and dragged her into the kitchen.

"Oh, it was grim," she whispered, looking over Emmy's shoulder as she talked. "She was just fine one minute, and then that man came to the house while Dad and I were unloading the silage, saying he needed to see her."

"Which man?" Emmy asked.

"You know, the strange one who came to dinner after church." Birdie trembled. "Mr. Davidson. He went in the front door and came out the back, shouting that she had fallen. By the time we got to the kitchen, she was just lying there on the cold floor, crumpled up. They say it was a stroke, but she isn't crippled. She's been awake and talking this morning, weak as a kitten." Emmy poured her sister a cup of coffee and they huddled at the kitchen table.

"The strange thing was, that man didn't wait for the doctor to arrive," Birdie continued, leaning in closer. "Said he'd get help, and that he'd be back. I had to help Dad carry her to the couch, she really doesn't weigh more than a feather. Next thing you know, Ambrose showed up with the doctor, so I guess Mr. Davidson told him."

"Maybe he's still staying at the Branns'," Emmy guessed, feeling that her sister was paying closest attention to the details that mattered the least. "The important thing is that she's going to be okay."

Birdie drank down her cup of coffee in one long swallow. "Ambrose and I tried to find you, but you weren't at the movie. We waited outside for it to end, but you didn't come out."

A shock of guilt unfolded inside Emmy. All of her rebellious actions had been based in vain suspicion and nothing else. Bobby's face appeared in her imagination, and she covered her eyes for the shame of how she'd let herself be so childish when her grandmother lay in the hospital, ill.

"They've worked it all out," Birdie said, grabbing both of Emmy's hands. A knot tucked upward in the middle of the girl's delicate forehead. "I'm to help Mother at the farm during the week, and you're to stay with Grandmother Nelson on the weekends."

Emmy felt her sister's hands tremble and she squeezed them, hard.

"But what about school, Birdie, and choir?" Emmy asked, and her sister burst into silent tears, her mouth opening and closing in small round *O*s. Emmy had never seen Birdie too distraught to cry. "Oh there, there, dear, it won't be for very long. And I'll ask Mother if I can take the weekdays instead. I can always finish my studies at summer school." She said these things knowing that what she and Birdie decided between them wouldn't matter in the least. They heard the toilet flush upstairs and moments later their father's footsteps heavy down the risers.

"Don't tell him I told you, please, Emmy." Birdie took the cups to the sink. "Especially about Mr. Davidson being there. I don't think Dad likes him much."

"I promise," Emmy said, and she went to help her father with the coat he had shed minutes before. There was a small red cut on his jaw where he'd done a hasty job of shaving. Emmy pulled the sleeve of her woolen dress over her thumb and dabbed at the blood. Christian gingerly caught her wrist and held it to his cheek.

"Let's get a move on," he said. He turned up his collar and went out the door to where the car sat, idling its plume of blue exhaust into the frosty air.

❧

Before Emmy could count the days it was already Friday, her first night to spend alone in the old groaning farmhouse with her grandmother tucked into the big bed upstairs. She had tried to convince Karin to switch the schedule, and was not surprised when the idea was met with a shake of the head and nothing more. Lida had regained some strength but was still unable to do so much as sit up by herself. Emmy didn't mind tending to her grandmother; it was the settling of the house, the dark rooms with their dusty furniture, the small noises of animals in the eaves, the large noise of the wind howling across the fields outside, and the cows lowing out in the barn, preparing to give birth, that set Emmy's teeth together. Her parents had put their faith in her ability to handle this situation. She hadn't dared mention that she was scared to death to stay out on the farm practically alone.

Her father had checked both of the expecting animals before heading back to town with her exhausted mother and sister, and the Branns' cattle hand, Pedro, was to drive by and check the cows in the middle of the night. The heifer was likely to calve early, and there had been talk about how restless she'd been during the day. Even though she'd known Pedro and Maria Gonzales since she was small, the thought that anyone might drive into the yard while Emmy was asleep made her uneasy. She went to the window at the sound of a scraping branch, but met only the reflection of her face, startled and pale. The warp of the old glass distorted Emmy's features, turning her normally small and pert nose into something flat and slightly askew. Bending her knees just a bit, she watched as the warp moved to her wide-set eyes and accentuated the space in between, giving them a pitched alien look that wasn't entirely unpleasant. The longer she gazed, the more the hinge that held her fear in check creaked open toward mild panic.

The radio was on and playing a violin concerto, and Emmy picked up the Bible and tried to soothe herself with the Book of Psalms until she could grow sleepy enough to go up to the cold bed that had been her father's before he had married Karin. Too distracted to fully take in the words, Emmy thought instead of the rapid passing of the previous week and tried to absorb just how much had happened in the small slice of time.

Sunday they had packed the car with clothes for her mother and Birdie and driven directly from church to Grandmother Nelson's, where Maria Gonzales had stayed by her bedside. Emmy hadn't had a moment to do right by Ambrose after the service, and the brief time she did meet his eyes, she still felt a hint of shame. She couldn't continue to look at him, though, as she felt the magnetic scorch of Mr. Davidson's stare affixed to her own. Christian had steered them all past the Brann pew without stopping to engage the three men. An hour later Ambrose had surprised Emmy by driving Pastor Erickson out to the farm to attend to Lida's prayers. She'd never missed a day of church under his watch, not for childbirth, not for harvest, not for blinding snow. Her face glowed at the approach of the pastor and the door swung shut behind the old man. What a gift that must be, Emmy had thought, and had hurried to bring them tea in order to witness Lida's powerful faith. But Ambrose had intercepted the tray and carried it up himself, asking her to stay and wait for him in the kitchen. When he had returned, he preempted her desire to confess the details of her night out by getting down on one knee in front of her.

"I'm no good for you, Emmy," he'd said, looking at her hand. "But if you'll consider me, I'd like to make our engagement formal as soon as possible, and put all others aside."

The heat on Emmy's face had risen hotter, and she had stayed perfectly still, finding herself incapable of returning the sentiment. This moment had been expected for so long, and yet it had none of the thrill she had once imagined it would have. She wanted to be swept with the notion that Ambrose would always take care of her, but all she could see was the small spot of scalp that was slowly being revealed on the very top of his head, a spot that foretold nothing but sheer, rapid decline. There were a few gray hairs mixed into the sandy brown she'd taken for granted, and from this angle, she could see the first deep lines etched into his brow. The handsome lanky boy had somehow vanished while he'd been away at school, leaving behind only sinew and the grit of being a Brann. He was already old. She hadn't even started being young.

"Oh." Her voice had caught, as she knew she must say something and fast. She could sense her mother lingering just outside the kitchen door, quietly folding napkins on the kitchen table, her hushed whispers to Emmy's father an indication that she was anxious for a response. Emmy had no choice. "Well, yes, I suppose that's right."

Ambrose had leaped to his feet and drawn her into his arms, bending over to bury his face in her hair. Suddenly and inexplicably unable to return his tenderness, she had tensed up with the urge to push him away. The shame of such an ungrateful feeling consumed her, so she had held his embrace as long as she could stand. When they at last parted, she gripped his arm with her right hand, counting to ten before she let the touch fall away. Now that their union was suddenly real, the affection she had for Ambrose was like a window shade drawn against the weak light of a slivered moon, cutting off the warmth she had expected to feel, even as she realized there was so little there.

The effect that Ambrose and Emmy's official engagement had on Karin was like boiling water poured over a block of ice. Emmy had never felt so genuinely respected by her mother before, nor treated as though her opinion held weight. Every night after school, Karin had telephoned from the farm to make suggestions to Emmy of things she should be doing over the next year, in preparation for both the wedding and for married life. Karin had also told her of Ambrose's frequent visits to the farmhouse, his kind gestures to Birdie, and his constant help. When he had offered for Pedro to check the gravid cows every night, Karin insisted on paying for the help, even though it was understood that Ambrose would merely roll the cost up into the accounts of his eventual ownership of both farms. Emmy had only begun to grasp the method by which the Nelson farm acreage had slowly seeped over the years since Grandfather Nelson's death into the Branns' sugar beet expanse, but she was all too aware that the grim necessity of her central role in this usurpation was to be accepted with fortitude and grace.

Sitting in the cold parlor with the Bible open in her lap, Emmy felt the constricted mobility of her situation hem tighter and tighter around her heart, until hot, silent tears slipped down her cheeks as she listened to the low undertones of Lida snoring away upstairs, a fine companion sound to the doleful strains of the violin on the radio. The car ride with Bobby Doyle felt as if it had never happened. Ambrose was certain to appear at the farmhouse bright and early; it was best that Emmy try to sleep. She exhaled and was surprised to see her breath plume out into the room. The temperature had dropped considerably and the wind was howling yet more frigid gales out in the yard. Emmy checked the thermostat on the wall. The needle hovered around fifty degrees. She tapped it, frowning. Rubbing her hands briskly together, she first went to the kitchen to put a kettle on for filling hot water bottles. Dreading the trip belowstairs into the cobwebby undertow of the cellar, she recalled her father's detailed instructions on how to relight the pilot on the furnace should it snuff out, which it most likely had.

There was no way she could let it slide until the morning or pretend the heat had failed while she was asleep. She would have to face down her fear of the dark spaces buried under the house and do her best to fix the thing without help.

Once the water was hot enough, she filled the red rubber bags, screwed on their tops, and slipped them into the cozies her grandmother had crocheted. Emmy then took a deep breath and walked the ten paces across the kitchen to the door that led to the cellar. She touched its smooth wood and slid her hand down to the glass knob. Straightening her shoulders, she rolled her eyes at her own stupidity and jerked open the door—it had always stuck a bit at the top—and holding the rail banister, she leaned over the flight of planked stairs to grope for the fine metal chain that attached to a bare bulb. The sulfurous smell of the leaked gas caused her to sneeze.

She couldn't remember the last time she'd ventured down these stairs, with their open backs and rough-hewn unfinished wood, worn smooth in the center of each plank by the boots and shoes of three generations. This was her grandfather's sacred place. When she was really small, she would have to sit down on the top step and carefully move her bottom down each board, afraid of slipping as she bumped her way into his lair. The basement hadn't been touched since his death, and as the bulb swung from the motion of being pulled on, she caught sight of his carefully arranged animal traps hanging from their looped chains along the wall at the bottom of the stairs, furred now only with dust. At one end were the small gopher traps with their toothless arching jaws snapped still; in the middle the slightly larger, smoother traps that Grandfather Nelson had used to trap the money pelts—fox, raccoon, badger. Emmy grimaced as she approached the biggest one, reserved for coyotes and the occasional wolf. The jaws here were immense, slotted, and cruel. She could see him even now, slipping a live mouse into the tiny cage at the spring of the trap before prying apart the jaws and setting the pin, having already secured the loop of the chain with a long spike driven into the ground. Grandfather Nelson had taken her along to check the traps until the time they had found only the gnawed ankle of a bobcat, the sight of which caused Emmy to imagine such suffering that she never went near the gun-metal traps again.

Out of instinct, Emmy reached up into the middle air of the cluttered cellar and drew on the chain of the next light, relieved that it still worked. She could make out where her father had walked across the hard-packed dirt floor toward the squat white enamel machine sitting in the corner where once a coal burner had sat. Grandfather Nelson had replaced the back-breaking beast long ago, proud of his switch to all-gas appliances years ahead of most farmers. Without further hesitation, Emmy marched to the corner of the room, ignoring the scurrying sounds of wintering rodents, and it wasn't until she had twisted shut the gas valve and was kneeling in front of the furnace that she realized she had made this journey without matches or a flashlight to see the small pipe that needed reigniting.

Emmy sat back on her heels and looked around for matches. An odd feeling of association rose in her as she remembered a long-ago hot summer day playing down here even though she knew she wasn't allowed, poking around in an olive green metal box that held linens and leather-bound books and old newspapers. She'd dug past these dull objects to the bottom, finding a delicately carved wooden trinket box. Inside was a ring so large she could fit two of her fingers inside of it. A delicate scene of an armor-clad knight high on a horse was carved on the flattened oval surface. Emmy had loved it instantly, imagining within the small circle a vaster place of castles and kings, princes and princesses, maybe even dragons. She had slipped the object into the treasure pocket that her grandmother always sewed into her summer dresses with a small drawstring ribbon to lace up the top. Emmy had re-ordered the large box before crawling into her favorite hide-and-go-seek space near the cool darkness of the coal bin to wait out the scorching sun high outside.

Time had passed while she daydreamed about fairy tales, maybe as little as an hour, maybe as much as three—Emmy's grown-up grasp on the order of childhood events collapsing into the singular moment when she had realized that Grandfather Nelson had descended into the cellar. She could see now through her child's eye the old man slumping on the short stool, opening the metal box and drawing out a rectangular white sheet. He had held the fabric in his hands for quite a long time before unfolding it and draping it around his shoulders like a cape, smoothing his hands over it as though stroking the fur of a newborn pup. She had held her breath from the dark retreat as he had then taken a smaller length of fabric—a pillowcase?—and placed it high up on his head. The tall point of it dipped limply, reminding Emmy of a storybook drawing she'd once seen of a white-faced clown wearing baggy pajamas with large black buttons down the front. She had giggled, slapping a cold hand over her mouth as Grandfather Nelson had dashed the hat from his head, taking three large strides in Emmy's direction. Her mirth had pitched into a squeal as she tried to scurry away from his outreached hand, her bare feet scraping across the dirt floor as she was lifted swiftly up by her dress and tossed toward the stairs, where she had gained her feet and scrambled up, away from his bellowing voice, past her grandmother and mother in the kitchen, and out through the yard until she had reached the creek's bank, where she had climbed the familiar limbs of a gnarled old beech tree and sat there silently weeping, terrified that her grandfather would hate her now, that he would replace her companionship with Birdie's.

Emmy's grandmother had brought her a sandwich at suppertime and had handed it up to her, and Christian had come out at dusk with a ladder to carefully pluck her sleepy body out of the tree. Grandfather Nelson had died not many months after, and somehow Emmy still felt the two events conjoined, regardless of the stroke that had claimed his life. On the day of his funeral, Emmy had slipped the stolen ring into the hole they had dug for him, but the guilt of her theft still burned on her fingers eight years later.

Emmy looked around at the makeshift shelving that had been fashioned from boards wedged between the wooden supports of the house, sifting through the many canning jars filled with assorted sizes of screws and nails, the small paper boxes containing broken watches and pennies from emptied pocket change. There were milk-colored glass insulators from when the electricity was first strung to the farm from town and the linemen working on the project had given them away as souvenirs. Dust seeped into Emmy's fingertips as she turned over objects she hadn't been allowed to touch as a child. In fact, she had only ever come back down to the cellar when she had to fetch something for her mother. Her fingers began to ache with the cold when upon a high shelf she found a box of safety matches, which she took to the boiler, lit one for illumination and another for the gas, and, rubbing her eyes of the creeping memories, restarted the furnace and made her way up the stairs in time to hear the clank of the heat beginning to pump through the arteries of the house.

After shutting down the lower floors, Emmy carried the hot water bottles up the polished stairs and stopped at Lida's door, listening before slowly turning the doorknob and easing herself into the room. A small lamp glowed beside the oversized four-poster, Lida's frame tiny in the middle of her bridal bed. Emmy stroked the dear old woman's forehead lightly and pulled her hand back as Lida's eyes opened. She looked at Emmy and reached out the arm that hadn't moved since the stroke, guiding her granddaughter to her side. Emmy climbed into the bed, slipping the covered rubber bottle between the sheets and blankets at Lida's feet.

"Are you in any pain?" Emmy whispered.

"No, dear," Lida replied, her voice weak but clearer than Emmy had expected. "I'm at peace."

"Is there anything you need?"

"Just you."

Emmy curled herself on the bed next to her grandmother and listened intently to her rasping breath, counting each one in order to placate the fear of the sound stopping.

"Tell me," Lida said. "Do you love the Brann boy?"

"I don't think so," she said, surprised by how quickly the answer flew from her lips, and by how what she really meant was *No.*

"Good. Love never works," Lida said in a small voice, almost like that of a child. "I loved Stephen, but he loved Josie, and she loved Ray. I didn't love Ben, but it was a good marriage."

Emmy sat up at the strange squeak in Lida's tone. "You mean Grandfather?" she asked. She had so infrequently heard his given name that it sounded as foreign as the others in her grandmother's grasping list.

"Read to me, Emmaline," Lida replied, sounding more like her usual self, as though a different part of her had come for a visit and then left on the same train. "From the Good Book."

Emmy tucked the old woman tightly into her sheets, and then read aloud a few verses from the New Testament until Lida dozed back into a deep sleep. Wide awake, the confusing advice complicated further by the jumble of unfamiliar names, Emmy turned to her studies. She crossed the length of the room and rolled up the front of her grandfather's old desk in order to spread out her geometry homework. She turned on the green-shaded lamp that sat on the shelf where the rolltop rested and opened her textbook to page 159 before realizing that she didn't have a ruler, which she needed in order to even start the homework. She stared at the small compartments lining the interior of the desk and knew they were too small to hold even a six-inch length of wood. With an uneasiness ingrained during a childhood of being told not to open other people's drawers, Emmy wrapped her fingers around the handle of the large file cabinet down and to the right. It stuck a little, and then slid open in response to added force, revealing nothing more than a stack of old cigar boxes, topped by one which had a colorful drawing of an Indian in full, feathered dress. Emmy slid her index finger across the gilded image, flipping open the lid and finding it stuffed with bundled squares of paper. No ruler. Her mind drifted back to the unfamiliar names—Josie, Stephen, Ray—and her grandmother's sleepy confession. Had the stroke affected Lida's brain in a way that could result in shifting memory? Emmy quickly searched the other drawers and came up empty-handed. She decided to move to the rocking chair next to the warming radiator with her history book instead. She read about the Civil War for a long time, and well past the moment when Pedro Gonzales's headlights moved shadows against the wall as he passed through the yard, stopped, and then they swept back again, she finally slept, dreaming of the one thing she had successfully placed out of her mind all night: the car ride with Bobby Doyle.

Five

To Hold a Thing Unknown

Emmy woke with a start in the pitch black as the sound of slamming pickup truck doors jolted her out of sleep. She chased the tail end of her dream, searching for meaning, but it was little more than guilt-flecked vapor in the cold room. Emmy rubbed her face and rolled her head around on her stiffened neck before moving to the window. Ambrose's truck was in the drive. Pausing to watch him unfold from the vehicle, Emmy held to the curtain, trying not to wish that it were Bobby out in the yard. She slapped her cheek lightly and turned away from the window. Still dressed from chores the night before in overalls and flannel shirt, she added an old beige cardigan that her grandmother favored with her dark dresses—a dead man's remnant. Emmy rushed downstairs and into her work boots, pulling her father's barn coat around her as she swung open the door to find Ambrose standing there, blowing into his cupped palms.

"That heifer's having trouble," he said, skipping pleasantries. "Dan Wallace is on the way. Put up a pot of coffee and call your father." They turned away from each other as Emmy closed the door, hurrying to the kitchen to do as she was told. A surge of feeling useful coursed through her as she set to her tasks. Maybe she could do this after all, be this wife, till the fields and relight the home fires. If love never worked, then perhaps the way to a deeper meaning could be through the work itself. After all, her grandparents had trained her for this life, and her mother's tireless efforts had set her an example that Emmy had already more than lived up to; she shouldn't have been surprised that going through the middle-of-the-night movements of a typical farmwife felt familiar. Emmy measured out the coffee and set the pot on the stove, and then picked up the phone.

"Hello," Birdie answered, a bit out of air on the fourth ring.

"Get Dad. The heifer's in trouble," Emmy rushed. She wrapped the phone cord tightly around her finger as she waited for Christian to come to the phone. Only then did Emmy look at the clock and see that it was four in the morning.

"Emmy, we'll be there as soon as we can." Karin's voice came over the receiver as though a thousand miles lay between them instead of fifteen. "Go to the barn and wait."

"Ambrose is here," Emmy said. "Dan Wallace is coming."

"Good. Then stay put and make some coffee." Karin hung up.

The back door opened as Emmy was cutting slices of bread for sandwiches, and Ambrose brought a gust of biting air into the room. He took three steps across the large kitchen, welcoming the steaming mug she poured for him. He drank it black, not hesitating against the heat of it.

"Sorry," he said, and removed his cap and sat down at the table. His closely cropped hair stood up in places, revealing more spots where it had started to thin. "I think she'll make it, but Dan's going to have to pull the calf. Is your father up?"

"Yes," she said. "They'll be here soon."

"Okay, then. Come to the barn."

Emmy filled a green metal thermos with the remaining coffee, grabbed a handful of tin cups, and placed the sandwiches into a picnic basket. This is what a farmwife would do, what I will do the rest of my life, she thought as she quickly raced up the stairs to check on Lida before heading out to the barn.

❧

As Emmy crossed the frozen yard—lit to a garish yellow by the one pole light in the center of the farm—another truck pulled into the drive and

Emmy's pace relaxed with the sight of Dan Wallace, the only veterinarian her family trusted. What a life he must have, she thought, with constant middle-of-the-night calls that started in the dead of winter and kept coming well into the thaw of spring. Midwife to a cow. Emmy had seen many things over the years, but never this particular event. Being the substitute man of the house for now, she would wear that sweater and coat as best she could. She was a Nelson, after all, and they were strong people of the land. This last thought struck her as ridiculous the minute she had it, and it was with a laugh in her throat that she greeted Dan as he stepped out of his truck.

"Hello yourself, Emmaline," he said as he went to the back of the truck and pulled out a large canvas bag that looked heavy and sounded ominous with the tools inside it clanking together. "I'm not sure this is a mirthful occasion, though." Even as he admonished her, there was a twinkle in his eye. He had been a boy when her grandfather ran the farm, following behind his own father at visits such as these, learning the job from the hay up. By the time Emmy was a teenager, the practice was Dan's. He was tall like Ambrose, but as thin and strong as a white birch, swaying slightly in the frigid night air. The hair on his head was completely white, even though he couldn't have been much more than thirty. He was the kindest person Emmy knew.

"You're right, of course," she said. "I've got coffee, if you're interested." He ruffled her hair, a feeling she had once hated but welcomed now for its sheer infrequency.

"You should have a hat," he said as they crunched their way over the crusted snow to the barn, where the sound of an animal laid low suddenly pierced the air. Emmy stopped. Dan put a hand on her shoulder and nodded her forward.

It was below freezing, and all the cows were inside for the night. Most were lying on their sides, a few were starting to rise and stamp, the breath streaming out of their noses in the slightly warmer room. Emmy could remember a time when this barn was end to end with animals, but now there were maybe a dozen left. It was getting toward milking time, and the cows who were accustomed to being drained first were beginning their restless shuffle, the heaviness of their udders pulling them up out of sleep.

Here and there a tail lifted and a hot river of urine hit the floor. It was rank and earthy and sweet-straw-scented in here, and Emmy loved it. This was comfort to her, a place she could hide away when she was small and stroke the wet noses of the large, gentle animals. Equally as pleasant in memory were the afternoons spent playing in the hayloft of the Brann barn—the prickly straw felt through layers of outerwear as she hid from Ambrose, who always pretended he couldn't find her though it mustn't have been very hard. If she held her own in this fraternity she would be treated as a peer, and eventually a matriarch. A calm aura descended over Emmy as she strode forward with a new purpose: She would make her grandmother proud, at least for today. The golden-haired boy of her dreams was no more than a fantasy. This was real. This was her life.

In a corner pen at the far end of the barn—between Ambrose and Pedro—lay the moaning cow. The three men moved around the stall as Emmy glanced at the lowing animal long enough to see two small hooves protruding from her back end. Emmy turned hastily to the basket and set up the coffee and food on a stack of hay bales outside of the pen.

"She's anterior. Third one tonight," Dan said upon observing the heifer. "I can't reckon why so many are coming early this year. Can't be a good sign. We need to pull her." Ambrose and Pedro nodded in silent agreement as they drank from the cups Emmy offered. Then, as if directed by some whispering conductor, the men set quickly to work: Dan slipped his arms into long black rubber gloves, scooped ointment from a large bucket, and massaged it into the cow's birth canal; Pedro drew two chains and folded cloths out of Dan's bag, along with an instrument with a flat metal plank attached to a long rod; and Ambrose stood off toward the face of the cow as he tipped some liquid out of a bottle and into a thick sponge before fitting it neatly into the end of a metal cone.

"Ready?" Dan asked, and Ambrose nodded, looking to Pedro for the second nod. Then, in concert, they moved into swift action, with Ambrose slipping the cone over the cow's muzzle and tapping a few more drops from the bottle through a tiny hole in the end of the cone. Emmy could see that the mask was open on the end and assumed that was how the cow would keep from suffocating entirely.

"Emmy, put this on," Dan said, handing Emmy one of the cloths as he unfolded the other and slid his arms through two holes. As Emmy fumbled with the material, he gave her a blanket and then broke some fresh straw under the back of the cow. The animal had grown eerily still, as if she knew the moment had arrived.

"Now, Emmy," Dan said, bending over and looking her square in the eyes. "This isn't easy, and you can tell me if you're not up for it, but I need you to catch the calf. It'll be heavy."

She nodded and unfolded the blanket where he told her to, cradling it in her arms in a way that anticipated an eighty-pound animal. Dan quickly looped the chains around the calf's hooves, positioned what turned out to be a brace against the cow's lower hip and handed one of the chains to Pedro, who expertly looped it around his forearm. Dan and Pedro sat, placed their feet against the brace and in turn pulled on the partially born calf's legs with a gentle back-and-forth motion until the cow's eyes went wild and her head bucked with the force of a fresh contraction. Ambrose gave the bottle a small tap, and just like that the calf's head was out. Dan put his hand up and everyone stopped what they were doing as he moved up to the cow, grasped the calf in a headlock, and rotated it within the birth canal. This caused the animal to take in air, and Dan exhaled loudly at the sound and wiped his brow on his shoulder. The next contraction started to shake the cow and Dan picked up the chain and said, "Now!"

The calf slid out and into the blanket, along with a rush of blood and fluids that splattered them all, but nearly soaked Emmy, who had been squatting but now lay on her back in the straw, holding the bucking calf to her chest as Pedro removed the chains. Dan clamped and cut the thick, pulsing, umbilical cord. The way he moved his hands through the motions of tying and sewing and then once more gently yanking—this time on the thick cord—caused Emmy to fall into a small trance until more tissue issued from the heifer. The entire mess of it hit Emmy square against the legs, and if Pedro hadn't at that moment taken the squirming calf from her, she would have dropped it. Yes, she'd dressed a deer, but that was death; this was life, throbbing and ugly and bloody and wonderful.

"Bueno," Pedro said to Emmy as he set the calf on its feet. Ambrose removed the cone, and the cow turned her sloping head in the calf's direction and licked at the matted fur, clumsily urging the calf toward her udder. That's

right, Emmy thought, this is good, and she went out the back door of the barn to gain some air, surprised to see the sky lighter than when they'd gone in.

Ambrose emerged and lit a cigarette, which she took out of his hand, drawing the harsh smoke into her lungs with the cold morning air. She coughed a little, but then inhaled again.

"You're good, Emmy," he said, proud. "Strong."

"Thanks," she said, feeling as though everything that she had just witnessed hadn't happened, as though she had stood behind the barn for a very long time looking out at the ashen sky. "It smells like snow."

Ambrose took the cigarette and dropped it under his heel. He cupped her chin in his hand and placed his mouth on hers, his lips parting slightly, waiting for her to respond. She didn't know how to kiss a man, and was grateful when she heard the family car in the distance. She wasn't as resistant to his touch this time, though. Curiosity spread through her limbs and she felt tingly from the sensations of the morning. They stood apart as Christian's car moved up the drive. Emmy pushed the loosened hair out of her face and felt the stickiness left behind by the already standing and nursing calf. Emmy looked down at her afterbirth-slicked clothes and ran off to the side of the barn, where she vomited onto the hard-crusted snow.

❧

The sun had not only risen, but was about to set when Emmy awoke hours later. She'd slept upright in a large wing chair next to her grandmother's bed, an American history textbook splayed out across her lap. Rubbing her neck, Emmy remembered that after she had bathed and washed her hair and left the rest of the daily farm chores to her family, she'd come in to try to catch up with her languishing homework, reading perhaps two pages about the battle of Gettysburg before she dropped off into a blissfully dream-free sleep. Emmy yawned and stretched her arms over her head. It couldn't have been much later than four in the afternoon, but she smelled onions frying and heard the subtle noises of a table being set. Lida was sitting up with a half-eaten bowl of milk toast on a tray by her side. The old woman was staring at Emmy, and it gave her an odd start, like falling within a dream.

"Good sleep?" Lida asked.

"Well, yes, more or less," Emmy said, feeling a dull ache at the base of her back, where it had strained against her unnatural position. "How are you feeling?"

"Better. God is good to me."

"Are you hungry? Do you need me to help you finish your meal?"

"I've eaten. How was the calf?"

"Wild," Emmy said, moving the tray over to a table and settling lightly on the edge of the bed. She took Lida's hand in hers, and was pleasantly surprised to find it warm but not too warm. It had been cold since the stroke. On impulse Emmy felt her grandmother's forehead, but it was papery and cool. The old woman smiled sleepily.

"You are so much like Josie was at your age," Lida said, stroking Emmy's cheek. "You have her hair, and her eyes."

"Tell me, who's Josie?" Emmy said, putting her own hand over the one on her cheek. It was still warm, but she felt a strange chill.

"Shame," Lida said. "We were once so close." And with that small teasing statement, she fell into a shallow sleep. Emmy was amazed anew at her grandmother's ability to do this neat trick: start a fire and then throw sand on it in the same breath, even though Emmy understood well that there were certain things in life that adults knew, and others that were shared with children. It wasn't unusual to discover a piece of information that had seemed not to exist in the moment before it was issued. A decade before, she'd gone with her mother on a long train journey to a grassy graveyard outside of a small town north of Minneapolis. She had stood next to Karin beside a freshly mounded grave, the rich black soil showing slick pink worms that had made Emmy's feet twitch inside her tightly laced shoes. She was desperate to be back at the creek fishing with Grandfather Nelson. There had been no marker on the grave to offer Emmy a clue, and she hadn't asked Karin where they were going or why they were there, because by that age Emmy knew that the answer would likely be "You'll know when I tell you." She had heard these words enough times to think them already etched on her own tombstone. Emmy had watched her mother's tightly closed eyes and folded hands, her lips moving in a wordless prayer, at the end of which Emmy had heard Karin whisper, "Good-bye, Father," as she turned and walked away with her head still bowed. They'd gone back to the train station, waited quietly for the return train to come, unwrapping cold roast beef sandwiches from their damp papers and chewing in silence. In Emmy's experience, this was how information was shared—sparely, and without the luxury of further commentary.

Lida's bedroom door opened a bit and Karin poked her head through the gap and motioned for Emmy to come with her. Once in the hallway, Karin looked up at Emmy, holding her by the arms and smiling.

"You've grown so much," she said. "I'm pleased with you, Emmy, I really am. You don't know what it means to us that you are marrying Ambrose. He'll take good care of us."

Emmy shrugged her mother's hands from her. "Who's Josie?" she asked, testing her right to ask questions now that she was considered an adult. Karin's face closed like a screen door in a high wind on a hot day—snapping to, yet still revealing the cool interior unchanged by the weather.

"What did she say?" Karin asked with a nod at the door.

"Not much, just something about love, and that I looked like Josie, whoever she is."

"Your grandmother once had a sister," Karin said plainly. "Don't trouble yourself or her about it. Come."

Emmy hesitated, wanting to ask more questions, yet knowing that the answers wouldn't unlock her mother's firm hold on their family's history. Karin didn't believe in the past, only the future. It had served her well through more than one tragedy, and Emmy had no choice but to respect her mother's desire to find distance from what she called painful, pointless nostalgia. Besides, dead siblings were not uncommon—Emmy had one herself, after all—and it was easy for her to imagine one day saying something about Daniel to her own granddaughter, folding the information into a tossed-off story of *There once was a boy I never knew.*

Karin led Emmy down the hall to Lida's sewing room and opened the door. The lights were blazing in the narrow room where the old foot-pedal Singer sat in front of a bay window that looked out on a wide field during the day. Next to the cutting table stood a dress form, and on that form were the makings of a formal white gown. Emmy raised a hand to cover her mouth. Karin gave her a small push forward and Emmy saw her mother's reflection in the darkened window: tight-lipped smile slightly turned up in a way that made small pockets of flesh push downward at her jawline, hair grayer than Emmy had taken time to note. Karin was willowing away at a rate that made her seem much older than her forty-some years. Emmy walked to the dress. It was a ghost of the garment it would become, with an under slip of silk covered in a veil of homespun lace across the high-necked sweetheart bodice. The skirt was pinned to the mannequin, the yards of supple rayon peau de soie gathered and hemmed at tea length. It would accommodate a very large crinoline, or perhaps even a hoop. Her mother must not have slept much of the previous week, by the looks of the amount of work already finished. Emmy had never imagined Karin had this much lightness in her.

"It's stunning, Mother, really," Emmy said, but couldn't bring herself either to touch the garment or turn away from it. The white of the fabric was like the snow outside—cold, harsh, and beckoning with its icy perfection.

"I'm glad you like it." Karin bowed her head. "I'm not much of a seamstress, but I want it to be as perfect as God will let me. Tell me if there's anything about it you don't like so far, and I'll change it." Emmy knew that her mother hadn't worn a wedding dress. Women during the Depression were lucky if they had a new suit, and Karin hadn't been particularly lucky, not for many years.

"Oh, no." Emmy turned to her mother. "Don't change anything. Do exactly what you think will look best. It's already perfect." She went to Karin and held her by the arms, as the older woman had done to her moments before. "Thank you."

"Don't thank me, thank God," Karin said, evading the embrace and going over to the dress as she slipped a small threaded needle from the front of her house apron and clicked a thimble-covered thumb against her front teeth thoughtfully. "You're going to make a beautiful bride."

Emmy looked around the room and noticed a wooden chest that had been painted a soft blue with swirls of delicate flowers, stems, and leaves interwoven in harmonizing dark blue, red, and cream colors. The top leaned open on its hinges, revealing a good deal of folded linens stacked inside. Embroidered with red thread onto the dusky blue cotton fabric lining the lid were the letters EBN.

"Mother," she said, approaching the trousseau as though it were a casket. "Why is this already so full?"

"Isn't it lovely?"

Karin turned her attention to the box, lifting a lace-edged sheet and smoothing an undetectable wrinkle with the edge of her hand. "The Branns had it made in Norway years ago. We were thinking that since your grandmother is ill, it would be best to have the ceremony as soon as school ends."

"Were you planning to tell me?" Emmy asked, a snap in her voice. It stung not to be consulted.

Karen stood straight. "I just did. Now go downstairs and help Birdie with supper. That girl burns everything she touches." Emmy backed out of the room slowly, trying to undo the time that had just run past her and tied down her future more neatly than the stack of lace doilies she tipped over as she bumped into a small table. She turned and left them scattered for her mother to collect, no longer able to deny that this path forward promised only more of the same disregard for what she wanted.

❧

At supper, Ambrose was clean-shaven and had slicked back his hair from a side part. He smelled somewhat soapy and was wearing one of his good Sunday shirts. Emmy found his pale features to be more delicately arranged than she had taken the time to notice in the many years they had changed and grown beside each other. His nose was narrow and sharp at the end, dividing the planes of his cheekbones and the misaligned eyebrows with the slightly askew placement of a hastily set table. The betrothal had caused Emmy to see him through a new glass, one that had always been at her disposal but never needed when viewing someone who was merely a friend. She fought away a sense of urgency, a slowly rising desire to measure the banks of his character. Contemplating the scant five months between turning eighteen and the finality of her upcoming marital vows compressed her lungs to the point of dizziness. Flashes of Bev's tart laughter, Howie's jet hair, the Kratz sisters jockeying, the Halsey boy's flashing eyes . . . Bobby's toothy grin . . . only made her vertigo worsen. All of them had so much unexplored life ahead of them, while Emmy knew hers would soon be tempered by the expectations of the handful of grimly determined people at the table in front of her.

Dressed in a similar fashion to his son, Delmar Brann raised a glass of milk in celebration of Lida's improved health and his son's betrothal. Next to these immensely self-assured men, Emmy's father seemed shrunken and a bit grizzled. Christian hadn't shaved and he was still wearing his weekend attire of bib overalls over a red cotton long john, topped with a flannel check shirt. It was a typical country outfit—more colorful than his usual gray work pants and shirts—but somehow the calamitous ensemble only made him seem pale and insubstantial. At the same time he carried an air of detachment as he sat quietly spooning sautéed liver and onions onto his plate.

Karin was in full bloom, having donned a dress that must have been Lida's in a distant decade—a sapphire blue serge that draped over the rise of Karin's bosom before pleating in at the waist and swirling below the knee. Mr. Brann was seated at the head of the table, Birdie to his left, and Emmy on the right—the chair closest to the kitchen, her grandmother's usual place—and Ambrose next to her. Karin had scooted them in these seats without comment, placing herself at the foot, and Christian completing the circle next to Birdie. The quiet of the table was marked by the beginnings of serving—utensils against china, bowls of roasted turnips and boiled potatoes passed and settling on the linen-clothed wood with gentle thumps and spoon scrapes. No words were spoken until the last plate was filled. They had set out quite a meal for the guests, and Emmy's hunger peaked as she held her hands tightly in her lap.

"Delmar, would you be so kind?" Karin asked, bowing her head.

Mr. Brann closed his eyes and tilted his face toward the ceiling. "Our Dear Lord, Your blessing be upon us as we gather Your bounty before us, and give our sister Adelaide the strength to return to Your table so that we may once again enjoy her company as we bathe in the spirit You have given us through the sacrifice of Your only Son, Jesus Christ our Savior. In His name we pray. Amen."

Emmy looked up to see her mother's glowing approval alight on Mr. Brann. Something about the exchange sparked, and Mr. Brann held the gaze as he began his usual dominance over the topics of conversation—a habit of his to which Emmy was so accustomed that she typically found other things to think about while his voice hummed on in her ear. Tonight, however, she was seated between the Brann men and knew that her mother was watching her closely. As Emmy lifted her fork, she turned her head attentively in Mr. Brann's direction.

"When we put our faith in Eisenhower, he promised that the immigrant stream would be stanched," he said with grave disappointment. A white string of spit danced between his lips as he talked, and Emmy had to look away as he continued. "But it shows no signs of it. Our community cannot afford one more impoverished foreigner washing up from Italy or Ireland or Spain. Before you know it, they will let all the Mexicans in, and our community will be overrun with this threat to our God-given sovereignty. At least our *betabeleros* know their place in our society, unlike those people out in California."

"They're decent folks," Christian said, barely loud enough for Emmy to hear over the sounds of eating. "Trying to feed their children, no more or less than you or me."

"Yes, brother Christian, the ones that have grown up amongst us are decent," Mr. Brann rejoined. "In fact, I couldn't run my farm without Maria and Pedro. But look at all those criminals they rounded up in Operation Wetback. Some say as many as ten thousand had fled to California from Mexican prisons!"

"Some say," Christian said in a way that could have been mistaken as agreement. "I just know that there's never been a problem with the contract workers."

"What about that one up in Hillsboro, who robbed and—excuse me ladies—accosted a teacher in Moorhead? Or the murder in the Andersens' cornfield last year?" Mr. Brann shook his head in outrage. "Don't tell me there's never been a problem."

"None of those men were sugar beet workers." Christian wiped his mouth with his napkin and fell silent.

"Exactly my point," Mr. Brann said, thrusting his knife in the air. "They were all foreign nationals, all working without documents in the onion fields. Where there's no regulation on these immigrants, there will be crime. These people don't even bother to learn English."

"I'm a bit confused," Emmy said, delicately interrupting. "Weren't our ancestors immigrants?" She looked around, attempting to find a sympathetic connection to how Mr. Brann's vitriol had made her feel. "And didn't they speak Norwegian?" Mr. Brann dropped his knife on his plate, and all heads but Christian's turned to Emmy. Her father was smiling at something in the middle of his plate. A hot blush itched her cheeks as she tried to think of how to better explain what she meant. But as she opened her mouth, Karin kicked her under the table.

"Emmy," her mother said, cutting a slice of meat and holding it in midair. "This roast is perfectly cooked. Isn't it, Ambrose?"

"Yes, ma'am," he said, before turning to Christian. "Looks like we're in for some real snow this evening, Mr. Nelson. I don't think the dam will calve tonight, though I'm happy to come by and check on her."

Emmy's cheeks burned harder with the pointed change of subject, but she was even more concerned by the simmering silence she felt from Mr. Brann's stillness and closed eyes.

"That's okay, son, we're as likely to stay tonight." Christian seemed amused by Emmy's discomfort and she stared at his plate as he continued to meticulously mix the beef, potatoes, and turnips into a kind of stew. He then reached for a slice of bread from the stack on the table and after smearing it thickly with homemade butter and currant jelly, he used it to push his dinner bite by bite onto his fork. Emmy wiped at her lips with her napkin, and everyone but Mr. Brann fell back to their meals until he opened his eyes, at which point all eating stopped.

"My dear child," he said to Emmy, laying a heavy hand on her shoulder. "When my grandparents left Troborg and traveled first by boat and then train, and lastly a horse-drawn cart up the side of the Mississippi, they broke the soil of this territory and with it their bond to a foreign land. They became Americans. They changed their last name from Brannveld to Brann, and they spent hours studying the language of their chosen country by reading aloud from the Constitution and the King James Bible. In Norway they had been little more than slaves. In America, they were their own lords, the landowners, and they did their own work instead of stealing life and blood from others."

He paused, waiting for something, and Emmy nodded her head to show that she was listening. No one else moved.

"The United States government gave our people what they needed to make their own way, and to in turn create a place where our children could be safe from unwanted worldly influence. It's with God-grateful humility that we chose to become Americans, and so when any immigrant refuses to learn our language, or carries his former heritage with pride, or, in the case of the Catholics, chooses to serve a master in Rome above our president, it tears at the fabric that our founders knit with their very blood, so that we could come here and practice the good Christian faith of this country. It's unpatriotic and flies in the face of all that America just did to save the blasphemers from Hitler's evil."

He lifted his hand from Emmy's shoulder and picked up his fork. "The roast is indeed good."

"Thank you," Emmy said, her voice barely a whisper. "I should start the coffee." She left the table and walked to the kitchen with her head down, a pain in her chest pressing darkly at the edges of her vision. For the second time that day, she drew the tin marked COFFEE from her grandmother's shelf, spooned the right amount of grounds into the top of the already water-filled percolator, and secured the lid with a practiced twist. Tightly bridled exasperation churned through her movements, her breath coming in shallow gasps as she felt emotion pinch her shoulders until a calm settled thinly enough for her to raise her chin level and return to the table with the brewed coffee, her eyes dry and clear.

The room was as she had left it, with one exception: Birdie had moved to Emmy's chair and was relating a story that held everyone's attention.

"And then I showed Mr. Haarsager that neat little trick with the chisel that you taught me, Ambrose," Birdie said, lightly touching his arm. "He'd never made a joint in that fashion, and had me show the rest of the class." Birdie wore a tight-fitting pearl pink sweater dotted with tiny white beads across the shoulders. Her manner was likewise confectionary, and Ambrose smiled down at her.

"You must be quite a sight in that woodshop," he said with an admiring laugh. "Not many girls interested in the craft."

"I'm very interested," Birdie said. "And there are a few other girls like me who would rather know how to make things than stick around a hot kitchen cooking."

"How's the calf?" Emmy asked Ambrose, and Birdie jumped to her feet.

"Oh, tell Emmy what we named her," Birdie said as she returned to her place.

"We named her Emmaline," Ambrose said. "After you."

"How sweet," Emmy said, pouring a cup of coffee for Mr. Brann before setting down the pot and moving the sugar bowl within his reach. She started clearing the dishes, but Karin stilled her with an upturned hand.

"Birdie, please help me clear." Karin's voice was not exactly pleasant, and it gave Emmy a small rush to feel like the favored child. Emmy sat stiffly next to Mr. Brann, watching him swirl excessive amounts of sugar into his coffee before moving his spoon back and forth, clinking in rhythm with the clock on the wall behind them. This would, over time, likely drive her mad.

With a shriek of wood on wood, her father pushed his chair back.

"Delmar," he said. "I'd like to go look at that calf if you care to." Emmy gave her father a nod of thanks as the older men went to the door without their coats, Mr. Brann starting in again on Eisenhower. She and Ambrose were suddenly alone, and his nearness caused in Emmy a feeling of hundreds of small birds trying to take flight within her. Ambrose took her hand and she closed her eyes, seeing Bobby's face lit in the sweet-smelling pickup cab, his soft, full lips slightly open in a partial smile. It had been a week since her big night out, a week since she'd felt possibility instead of place. She drew a long breath, testing the netting she felt holding back her better sparrows, and found her lungs slowly gaining capacity. She squeezed Ambrose's hand; gathered her will.

"It's not that I disagree with your father," she said. "But if we are Christians, then we need to help those who have come here to make a better life. Not treat them as criminals."

Ambrose stroked her palm. "As you get older and have more experience with the world, it will make more sense," he said.

Emmy sat straighter, opened her eyes wider. "I can only hope you're right," she said, her back teeth clicking together. "Because right now, I find no sense to it at all." Her head shook from the effort it took not to speak her mind more fully.

"You have four months, Emmaline," Ambrose said, his face as impassive as his voice. He stood and let his napkin fall to the floor, where she stared at it as though it were a thing given and refused. "If you are to live in his house, you will manage to do so with respect."

Six

A Reflection of Human Frailty

The Nelson family slept in the farmhouse on Saturday, and then Emmy and her father drove to Moorhead on Sunday night. She was relieved to be returning to the less complicated demands of high school and homework. In the wake of her maddening conversation with Ambrose, Emmy had applied her logic to the disappointing realization that her hopes of finding ownership in her soon-to-be household were no more than the idle dreams of a sheltered girl.

By the time she opened her locker at the end of school on Monday, she began to think that maybe this was just how all marriages were entered into, and like a garment cut for sewing, each rule had to be laid out, pinned, and adjusted until everything came together to create something whole. If she could picture Ambrose's warning as merely a sleeve or a placket, then perhaps she could find a way to set down a stitch or two of her own. Emmy was staring into the metal hull as though she might find the diaphanous tissue patterns of matrimony somewhere deep inside of it when she felt a quick poke to the ribs.

"Hey!" Emmy said, turning her annoyance on the prankster. Her anger disappeared at the sight of Bev, the one person she'd been looking for all day. "Bev! Where have you been?"

Bev shook her head in wonder. "Never mind about me, you little minx. You want to explain how you managed to fall into the arms of the dreamiest boy who ever lived?"

Emmy shrugged into her coat as the crush of jabbering students jostled past them. "What boy?"

Bev whistled low. "You really know how to get lost, don't you? Bobby Doyle!"

"I wasn't lost," Emmy said, closing her locker and shouldering her bag for the walk home, a hopeful chord of muted possibility sounding in her chest. "How do you know Bobby?"

"This is a small town, you unborn." Bev rolled her eyes and latched firmly to Emmy's upper arm, marching her down the hall toward the exit while passing a small, neatly folded slip of paper into Emmy's hand. "He gave me this after church. I don't know how you did it, but that boy is snowed!"

Emmy tucked the white square into her glove, where it stayed until she got safely home and in her room with the door tightly closed behind her. With a hand pressed to her damp forehead, Emmy read Bobby's unfurled words from the distance she felt safe enough to take them in: an arm's length away in the other hand.

Dear Miss Nelson:

Please forgive the un-invited note, but ever since we met last week I have racked my brain to figure out how I could find you again without actually pulling up to your door and knocking, which I finally did, tonight, Saturday, but you weren't home. Then it occurred to me that you must go to school with my friend Bev, and so I am taking the chance on sending a note through her, if I'm lucky enough to see her at Mass tomorrow morning.

I am thunderstruck by you. That's all.

Please let Bev know whether I can call.

Yours sincerely,

Robert (Bobby) Doyle Jr.

Emmy sat down. The note fell to her lap and then to the floor. She stared out the window toward the east, toward Ambrose. The clock ticked. She calmly pulled off her school clothes and on a pair of dungarees and an old sweater. The weather had warmed considerably and most of the snow that had fallen two days before was reduced to black dirt-mottled puddles of ice. It was four o'clock, time to do her homework. But to what end? She was to finish school and then marry Ambrose. What could she possibly learn in the next four months about world history and Shakespeare, and, for heaven's sake, *geometry* that could make a bit of difference to her life going forward? She tried to pull her study books out of her bag, but dropped it all listlessly onto the bed, and, kicking the note out of her way, went downstairs to find something, anything, to clean.

Tuesday was home economics, and though she preferred the exotic stories of her comparative literature class, or the world of ideas that Mr. Freydahl's history lectures had packed into her head, she knew that learning how to balance a kitchen budget and sew a French seam would probably be the best use of her remaining high school time.

The day's assignment was to plan and cook a fancy dinner menu, keeping frugality in mind while preparing an appealing meal. Each pair of girls was responsible for one dish, and Mrs. Hagen had passed out a stack of colorful cookbooks to help them choose. Bev and Emmy were in charge of the salad course, and they were picking their way slowly through *The Essential Homemaker,* stopping to laugh at some of the more outlandish photos.

"Would you look at those wieners," Emmy said as casually as if the note from Bobby had never happened, which she had decided was the best way forward. She had given Ambrose her word and knew that no one had made her do so. It was time for her to stop acting as though she was disappointed at the prospect, and begin accepting it for what it was: a fortunate match. Emmy showed Bev the picture, which featured a pot full of baked beans with about a dozen sausages sticking as straight up as any tube of meat could out of the mess. Surrounding the dish were the torsos of swell-dressed people, holding cocktails in their hands and no doubt having a gay old time.

"Forget about the salad, for crying out loud," Bev whispered, leaning in close. "Do you have a note for Bobby or not?"

"Not," Emmy said, and turned the page. "I'm committed."

"To be circled?" Bev yelped. Mrs. Hagen gave her a sharp look and Bev calmed her voice. "Tell me, when did this happen, and how could you not call me?"

"If by 'circled' you mean married, then yes, it happened last week, and no, I could not call you. It didn't seem worth mentioning." Emmy flipped ahead to the salad section, which featured the headline: "Molds and Other Delights." "Holy Christmas, look at this one." It was a shimmering tower of aspic topped with gelatin, the bottom of which encased sliced cucumbers and chunks of salmon, the top of which was crowned with a lemony-looking pile of goop, studded with small marshmallows and maraschino cherries.

"Emmy, we must!" Bev's green eyes sparkled mischievously. "It's perfectly awfully dreadful, don't you think?"

"Perfectly awfully so. Let's do it." Emmy opened her notebook and started writing down the ingredients they would need to accomplish the two-course monstrosity. She could feel Bev's stare.

"Ambrose?" Bev asked.

Emmy laughed through her nose. "Of course."

"But that's good, right? Make your parents happy?"

"I suppose so," Emmy said, closing the cookbook. She knew as much as she needed to execute the salad tower. "How's your cousin Howie?" A look of mild despair colored Bev's features as she took Emmy's hand and led her to the pantry next to cooking unit one, using the large door to shield their conversation from the rest of the meal-planning girls.

"Howie is my second cousin, once removed, if you must know," Bev whispered. "The keepers said we can't see each other anymore. They figured out that we've been fooling around."

"Are you in love?" Emmy asked, a large round copper mold shaped like a fish eating its own tail in her hand. Bev took it from her.

"Desperately," she said. "You know, there's hardly any chance of genetic mutations; they've done studies." Bev took more molds out of the cupboard, stacking them one at a time on the fish. "Besides, it's the sort of thing that royalty relied on to keep lands in the family, with no worse results than the occasional hemophilia."

"I'm sorry," Emmy said, shaking her head at the crown mold Bev tried to balance on the top of the heap.

"Franklin and Eleanor Roosevelt were cousins." Bev put her hands on her hips. "King Richard the first and Eleanor of Aquitaine. Albert and Elsa Einstein. Josephine and Raymond Randall."

Emmy set the copper pans on the preparation counter. "Who?"

"Josephine Randall, the writer," Bev said, opening the pantry and handing Emmy the tin of sugar and a box marked KNOX. Something about the way Bev was looking at the floor as she spoke was odd. "It's kind of a famous story, she even wrote about it in her novel *The Family We Keep*."

"Good for her?" Emmy supposed. Bev bit her lower lip and wrung her hands together, as though wrestling with an internal thought that was about to win.

"Look," she said, blowing at her reef of bangs. "I'm not supposed to say anything, but Josephine's your great-aunt. She lives north of Moorhead and married her first cousin Raymond."

Emmy blinked down at the orange box in her hand; the cameo of a cow smiled up at her. Josie. She blinked back. "What do you mean?"

"Your grandmother's sister." Bev squinted. "I promised not to tell you, but really I don't get why it's such a *secret*. From what they say, it all happened so long ago I figured you probably knew all about it anyway."

Emmy thought about her grandmother's confession, her mother's confirmation. "I don't know much of anything."

"Oh, dear," Bev said, stroking Emmy's arm. "Mother insisted you wouldn't know, and now I've gone and done it. She said your parents should be the ones to tell you."

Emmy shook her head. "My mother never tells me anything."

Bev blinked twice, a thought maturing into decision. "Well, it was quite a falling-out, apparently." She set the dry ingredients on the counter one by one. "Adelaide—that's your grandmother, right?"

"Yes," Emmy said, setting the box of gelatin next to the sugar canister. "We call her Lida."

"Well, when she and Josephine were younger, they were courted by the same man—some sort of traveling preacher." Bev said the words as though they tasted sweet. "I don't know the details, but it was during the war, and I think he either moved on to the next town or went to Europe to fight. Lida married your grandfather and never spoke to Josephine again. It's all so silly because all along Josephine only ever loved Ray—she just couldn't tell anyone or do anything about it, because they were cousins, like me and Howie." Bev sighed and touched a small silver heart on a chain around her delicate neck. "Jo's a friend of the family. Wait until you meet her. She's the limit."

"That's what Grandmother said," Emmy echoed. "Stephen loved Josie, but Josie loved Ray."

"So romantic," Bev said, and began to order the selected ingredients into a neat row on the counter, writing down the things they would need Mrs. Hagen to purchase for Thursday's class. Bev stopped her busy movements and turned her full green eyes on Emmy. "Speaking of, I need a favor," she whispered.

"Of course." The bell rang. Emmy looked up at the clock; it was three forty-five.

"Can I come over to your house after school?" Bev said, tidying up their workstation so it would be ready when class resumed on Thursday.

"There's no one there, so I can't ask," Emmy said.

"Perfect," Bev said. "I really need someplace to meet Howie without my parents finding out."

Emmy smiled shyly at the feeling of being needed by Bev. She knew her father wouldn't be home until at least eight, and her mother and Birdie were out at the farm. "I don't see why not."

"Thanks, kid." Bev grinned. "You're a real peach."

❧

Bev drove north on Eighth Street and crossed over Main. As they passed the winter-shuttered windows of the Dairy Queen, Emmy saw Howie's sleek hot rod glide out of the empty parking lot and into the lane behind them. A train was crossing up ahead, and Bev coasted to a stop as they waited for a long line of freight cars to rattle by. They were loud and heavy, and

Bev had turned the radio up full the moment she'd started the car. Jerry Lee Lewis was blasting out of the speakers, his throbbing voice and the vibrations from the thundering rails putting Emmy on the edge of the aqua seat. Bev pushed the lighter into the dash and pointed at the glove compartment.

"Do me a favor, would you," she shouted. Emmy pulled out a fresh pack of Camels. Bev took them from her and tapped the small square box daintily against the palm of her hand before extracting two cigarettes and lighting both at the same time. She gave one to Emmy and turned down the radio.

"Want to hear more about Jo? I have to admit, I'm a little obsessed with her," Bev said, exhaling a thick cloud into the space between them. She then continued to talk without waiting for Emmy's response. Her heart jumped greedily as Bev began to pour out the details of Josephine Randall's life, including her days as a suffragist with Bev's grandmother, and how she started a newsletter just for women during the Second World War—information on rations, war effort meetings, help for new widows, and other ways to get assistance while the men were so far away. According to Bev, Josephine also took care of her elderly relatives, and for the longest time never married or showed any interest in men. "Which led to the kind of gossip you might expect about a woman who always wore pants," Bev said with a knowing smile.

Emmy wasn't sure what kind of gossip she was supposed to expect, so she kept quiet as her cigarette burned unsmoked in her hand, the paper slowly receding into rings of ash as Bev rambled on about Josephine's love for her older cousin Raymond, who was sent off to Minneapolis, with the parental expectation that he would find other interests. Bev tapped her fingers on the steering wheel in time with the passing train. "That's what my parents want." She glanced in the rearview mirror and smiled with her lips pursed. "Anyway, Josephine stayed on the family estate, living with Raymond's widowed mother while taking occasional trips east and beyond. I think she lived a sort of double life, wandering for a few weeks in Morocco or Prague, then coming home to spoon-feed Raymond's mother on her deathbed. Can you imagine?"

"No," Emmy said. She marveled at the details of Bev's storytelling, suspecting that just a smidge of it might be embossed with her friend's romantic gilding.

"I wouldn't be surprised if she secretly went on those trips with Raymond," Bev said wistfully. "At least I hope she did. Otherwise it would be just too, too desperate a life to live without him."

"But you said they married," Emmy said, dropping an inch of ash into the tray before extinguishing the stub.

"Right, they did, about ten years ago, after his mother finally died. There was a bit of gossip, but Josephine has never cared what people say about her."

Emmy leaned against the seat. "At least they're together."

"Not exactly," Bev said, rolling down the window and tossing her cigarette out into the street. "Raymond died two years ago, heart attack. He was quite a bit older, but the years they had together were good ones. And like I said, I'm pretty sure they didn't go all that time completely without contact, though it is tragic to think so." She looked again into the rearview and pressed her lips together, corrected a small curl that had flipped the other way on her forehead. "How do I look?"

"Perfect."

"'Chances Are'!" Bev said, cranking the radio dial. "Oh, God, Mathis is my absolute favorite!" The train ended and the gates went up. The cars in front of them crept and then moved forward more swiftly. Emmy listened to Bev's sweet harmonizing as they bounced up and over the rails, into the north side of Moorhead, where the houses quickly diminished in size and quaintness. These were modest two-story homes with atticlike second floors, mostly square boxes with small square yards, many built in the years after the war to provide cheap housing for veterans. Emmy thought about her great-aunt, whose life was so different from Lida's. At the last note they swung in front of the Nelson house, and Emmy suddenly realized how tiny and careworn her life looked from the outside. In the wake of Bev's colorful love story of Josephine Randall, here Emmy could see only the brackish end point of Adelaide Randall's choice. Having the family's history revealed changed nothing for Emmy.

Bev killed the engine and in the side mirror Emmy could see Howie already leaning against the front of his car, carefully combing his hair into place. Bev shook some tiny Sen-Sen squares into her hand and tossed the pack to Emmy before bolting from the car.

Emmy watched in the reflective oval as the scene unfolded. She considered what forbidden love must taste like, and how it could unravel even the most neatly woven lives. It looked a good deal more exciting than kissing Ambrose. The idea of his stiff frame bending enough to accommodate the kind of temperature that existed between Bev and Howie made Emmy feel something akin to despair. A spiraling sense of panic wormed inside of her, and her eyes filled with the frustrated tears of hewing too closely to her mother-manicured life.

Emmy dried her eyes on her beige sleeve and opened the door. Bev spun around and smiled, her hair messy, her coat undone. The couple's happy gaze fell upon Emmy and she let herself feel the pull of it and its heat, moving her forward, into life.

❧

At half past five Emmy meticulously refolded the note from Bobby Doyle and yelled upstairs to Bev that it was nearing six o'clock. For the previous hour Emmy had been alone in the kitchen, first finishing her homework, and then preparing her father's supper from a slab of veal that Ambrose had sent home with them on Sunday. Stroganoff, that's what she'd made, from a recipe in *The Fargo Forum*. She didn't have any broad noodles, though, so potatoes would have to do. As the sauce had simmered, she'd read Bobby's neatly penciled words for the millionth time, even though she knew them all by heart, and also knew that they were nothing more than a collection of symbols that over time would point to a tiny moment of her premarriage history.

For the third time she heard her own bed scraping in little bursts against the floor above, Bev's shrieks and giggles, Howie's low "atta girls'" growled as much as spoken. Intercourse had never been a great mystery to Emmy, who'd seen plenty of couplings on the farm, but this was different. Though she had been embarrassed by the noise at four o'clock, now she was sighing in boredom, having finished her homework and exhausted all the possible ways she could think of to ask her father about Josephine. He had never been much of a storyteller, and besides, they clearly considered it a closed subject.

Minutes later the couple came racing down the stairs, Bev pushing Howie in front of her and out the door before she circled back over to Emmy and drew a small but thick black book from her schoolbag.

"Thanks," Bev said, her lips fuller, her cheeks redder than they had looked earlier. "This is for you. I just finished it. It'll blow your mind!" On the cover of the book was a striking image of a train station with a woman standing on the platform under the large letters *Peyton Place.* Just the Sunday before, Pastor Erickson had decried the book as filth to the nodding congregation.

"Oh, I can't have this in the house," Emmy said, backing away from it with her hands up. "My mother would kill me if she found it."

"So don't let her find it," Bev said with a wink, and dropped the book onto the table. Her nonchalance was emboldening. "You are the best friend, *ever.*" She hugged Emmy quickly to her chest and went out to her car, giving a little wave as she disappeared into its plush interior. That car is bigger than this room, Emmy thought, swinging the door shut and lifting the book from the table. She had two empty hours to fill before anyone would be there to object.

During study hall the next morning, Emmy was asked by the monitor to report to Mr. Utke's office. Emmy had assumed that after her parents had shown no interest in the high scores she had routinely earned on the aptitude tests, she had fallen off of Mr. Utke's radar completely. It was with dread that Emmy approached the window-paned door stenciled with REINHOLD UTKE, and saw five other kids, four boys and a girl, waiting in the hard-backed chairs. Just as she leaned against the wall, Mr. Utke opened the door and Katie Howell, the Moorhead Spud most likely to succeed, walked out, laughing as though she'd just been visiting an old friend.

"I'll certainly try!" she exclaimed, and gave Emmy a warm smile as she passed. No wonder everyone likes her so much, thought Emmy. She doesn't need to give me the time of day, yet here she is, smiling at me as though we are friends. Emmy stood up straight and returned the smile as Katie sailed past her and yelled down the hall to one of her actual friends. Mr. Utke glanced over the seated group, a look of exhaustion on his face, and then brightened when he saw Emmy.

"Miss Nelson, come right in," he said. "The lot of you can wait." As he closed the door behind her he said, "What you have there is the Society for the Prevention of Doing Anything Constructive. They've been meeting in the chemistry lab at lunchtime and leaving cryptic formulas and obscure quotes on the chalkboard. Mr. Stenoin has asked me to put them someplace else."

"Oh," Emmy said, still standing as Mr. Utke wheeled his chair up under him to his desk with a harsh creak. He looked at the papers on his blotter for a moment, motioned for her to sit down and it was then that she saw it: a copy of *Peyton Place* on the left side of his desk. She suddenly felt sweat drip down her spine and she knew she must have been the color of a freshly cut beet. The bookmark that was sticking out of the pages was Bobby Doyle's well-folded note. She straightened her skirt over her knees and sat as still as she could.

"Miss Nelson," Mr. Utke said, still looking through the glasses on the tip of his nose at an open file. He had straggly gray eyebrows, and a small brown mustache lined his thin top lip. He was somewhere around her father's age, Emmy guessed, but stouter and with slightly more hair. "Is it possible that you are unaware that this book"—he laid his hand on it and paused, as though trying to remember which one he meant—"this book is not allowed on school grounds?"

"Yes," Emmy said, staring down at her damp hands. He quickly looked up at her, over the lenses.

"Yes, you are unaware, or yes, it's not allowed?"

"Sorry. Yes, I'm unaware."

"Well, it was banned by the PTA. Imagine my surprise when it turned up during locker check this morning, in your possession. You're one of the few kids who has never missed a day or given any teacher any trouble, Miss Nelson. Don't think that goes unnoticed." He folded his hands. "We're very disappointed in you."

"I'm so sorry." Emmy leaned forward to take the book off the desk, and he moved it out of her reach. She had been up most of the night reading and desperately needed to know what fate would hand Selena Cross.

"I'll take care of it," he said, and then pulled the note out of the book and handed it to her. "You may keep this." She got up to take the note from him, and then turned to leave without meeting his eyes.

"Not yet," he said. She sat back down. He propped his fingers together and rested his bottom lip on his thumbs. "I would tell your parents about this—it's the school policy—but I know that they're under some strain right now, with your grandmother's illness."

"Pardon me for interrupting, Mr. Utke, but how do you know about my family?" Emmy asked, embarrassed that her story was so pitiable.

"I grew up in Glyndon," he said, a tiny smile finally softening his stern expression. "I need an assistant. One of my girls has had to drop out of school." Emmy knew that the girl in question was Karla Bossert. It was common knowledge that she was pregnant and had been sent off to her grandmother in Duluth to wait out her time.

"Thank you," Emmy said. "But I'm afraid I'm not much of a typist and I don't know steno, so I can't imagine how I could be of use."

"Just show up after school and let me worry about the rest," he said, folding the newspaper that lay on his desk and handing it to her. "Read something useful, please. Your critical thinking scores are much too high to waste on prurient pulp."

The bell rang, but Emmy didn't shift, confused by whether she was being punished or rewarded, yet feeling that it was a little bit of both.

"Well, go on." Mr. Utke stood. "I'll see you later."

❧

Bev caught up with Emmy in the hall just after Emmy had closed her locker at the end of the day, determined to try her best to accomplish whatever task Mr. Utke had in mind.

"Hey, doll," Bev said affectionately, putting an arm around Emmy. "Why so glum, chum?"

"Mr. Utke's put me on his after-school staff," Emmy said, returning the hug. The girls walked down the hall. "Seems *Peyton Place* is not exactly recommended reading."

"Oh, gee." Bev stopped and smacked the middle of her forehead with her palm. "I'd heard they were doing a locker sweep, but I didn't know for what. Wow." Emmy was cheered by the warmth of her friend's voice. She turned and looked at Bev, at the pink cashmere coat slightly open, revealing the dress that she'd recently shown Emmy in *Vogue* magazine: a bright green no-waist sack-style dress that obscured Bev's curvy figure, in loud contrast to all the pinch-belted shirtwaist dresses and flaring poodle skirts populating the halls. Bev shrugged. "Well, it's better than detention, though, right? What do you say I come back and give you a ride home when you're done?"

"You'd do that?" Emmy asked.

"Of course, silly. Mother won't mind—she wants to meet you anyway—so you think we can swing by my house first?"

"I don't see why not," Emmy said as they continued down the thinned-out hall and stopped in front of Mr. Utke's office.

"See you soon." Bev released Emmy's waist.

"Don't be late." Emmy waited a moment before opening the door for the second time that day. A girl looked up from a filing cabinet where she sat with a stack of files on her lap, working her way through the alphabet.

"There you are, Emmaline," Mr. Utke said, strolling in behind her. "Thank you, Betty, you may leave the files on the shelf until tomorrow." The girl set the neat stack where she was told and silently left the office, eyes focused on her feet. Mr. Utke motioned to a chair set in front of a small table. "Sit down, please."

Emmy sat, looking at the blank sheet of paper, pencil, and a book titled *The Caine Mutiny* set out for her.

"I don't have any work for you today, so I want you to just read for the next hour. Feel free to take notes." Mr. Utke moved to his desk and worked there quietly.

She put her hand on the top of the thick book, opened it to the first chapter, and began to read.

After what seemed like ten minutes, Emmy felt Mr. Utke's tap on her shoulder. "Time to go," he said.

"May I take it home with me?" she asked, not wanting to stop reading.

Mr. Utke laughed. "Sure you don't want your other book instead?"

❧

When Emmy walked out of the school doors and into the dark, frigid early evening, Bev's car was not there. Emmy scanned the reaches of the parking lot before she realized who was standing right in front of her: Bobby Doyle, leaning against his cream-and-red pickup truck, grinning widely. She'd already started to descend the short flight of steps and caught herself, nearly tripping down the entire set. She stopped where she was, a jolt of hot energy surging through her, a warning in her head telling her to go back inside the school.

She forced one foot down in front of the other, hoping to make her descent without further gracelessness, keeping her eyes glued a few inches in front of her feet. She knew she looked a fright. It was the night she usually washed her hair, which meant it was slightly too limp under her brown cloche hat. Beneath her battered but trustworthy coat she had on a heathered sweater that her mother had knit. As the most comfortable thing she owned, it was the least flattering. Her mother had attached the wrong cuffs to the wrong sleeves and so it would occasionally twist under a coat, which was happening now as Emmy tried to pretend that the sight of Bobby meant nothing more to her than a worn-out piece of scribbled-on notepaper.

"Hello," she said, walking slowly up to Bobby and lifting her eyes to his face. He was even more handsome than she remembered, with a brimmed baseball-style cap that folded down to cover his ears and most of his hair. One small curl had snuck out and down his forehead, and Emmy wished she could spin the hair around her index finger. "Why are you here?" she asked, letting her hand drop to her side. Impossible, but his smile grew wider. His teeth were perfectly aligned and shone brightly in the glow of the parking lot lamps.

"Bev thought you might be mad," he said, his hands jammed deep inside the pockets of his red letterman's jacket. "But it was all my idea."

"Mad? No." Emmy walked to the passenger side and waited for Bobby to open the door. He laid a hand on her back and once again she felt that curious warmth. She stepped up into the truck and leaned against the seat while she waited for Bobby to get in his side. The engine was running and the cab was warm. This had always been her favorite part of winter: the immersion in a well-heated car right after absorbing the chill of an icy night wind.

"I'm not the type to take no answer for an answer," Bobby said, putting the truck in gear and driving slowly out of the parking lot. "And even though Bev tells me you have some sort of fella out there, I'm still not giving up hope. In fact, I'm just going to drive you home, because Bev couldn't make it, and she asked me to do her the favor. But don't expect me to do it without trying to convince you that I deserve a shot."

"You are some talker," Emmy said, laughing. "And don't tell me it's because there are eight kids in your house."

"Funny thing about that. My mom had me when she and Dad were eighteen, so they're kind of kids, too. Which makes ten of us. You can see my problem."

"Oh, I can see your problem just fine." Emmy reached to turn up the radio, and Bobby grabbed her hand without taking his eyes off the road. She pulled against his grasp slightly before letting her arm go weak, and he rotated it slowly, circling his thumb and index finger delicately around her wrist before letting her have it back. She closed her eyes briefly, as though to blink away her betrothal, if only for the instant.

"Do you need to go straight home?" he asked, turning the wrong way on Main. "Or can I steal you away and show you something?"

Emmy looked at her watch, feeling the burn of his fingers to the right of the band. "I have time."

He grinned. "You could come sit over here, where I can hear you better, you know."

"Or I could stay here, where it's safe from boys like you," she said, the state of her hair and clothing making her more nervous than she liked.

He widened his eyes. "You know a lot of boys like me?"

"Not one," she admitted, unable to resist moving toward him, a foot closer and yet still a foot away. It was either a mistake or a very smart decision, but in either case, the way he smelled like vanilla and peppermint drew her over another inch.

"See that parking lot?" he asked, after they had crossed the Main Avenue Bridge and reached Broadway.

"The one that looks like a parking lot?" she said.

"You're a laugh riot. Yeah, that one. Doyle and Sons concrete, all of it."

"That's very impressive." She laughed.

"There are more where that one came from," he said, starting to poke fun at himself. "But even more exciting is our new contract, to build the new interstate highway from here to Bismarck."

"The tavern or the city?" she said as they cruised past the neon sign of the former.

"I have half a mind to take you straight home," he said.

"What about the other half?" She was surprised by her ability to be so light in the presence of a boy.

He snagged her hand again and pulled her closer. "You really like this other guy?"

"What other guy?" she sighed, wishing Bobby would stop making her remember Ambrose. She took off her hat and ran a hand through her unwashed hair as Bobby pointed out a Doyle concrete building going up at the college, and a plan for Doyle affordable housing along a strip of tornado-flattened property in the Golden Ridge section of North Fargo. Emmy listened to the simmer of his deep voice, comparing it to the reedy tones of Ambrose's. Bobby turned the truck down a bumpy lane on the outskirts of town.

"Another Doyle and Sons road?" she asked, the headlamps illuminating a rutted dirt path lined with a few other cars, all pointed in the same direction. Bobby parked the car in a space along the row and turned off the lights.

"Hector Field," he said, just as a long vehicle dotted with lights sped in front of their view, lifted at an angle, and took flight. He looked at his watch. "That's the 6:10 to Minneapolis. We poured that runway."

"It's so pretty." Emmy laughed, nervous in the quiet car.

"You might find it funny," he said, all his mirth leveled. "But I know what I'll be doing in five years. And ten. Mom wants me to be a priest, but Dad sees my potential."

"I didn't mean to make fun," Emmy said, abashed. "I wish I had potential."

Emmy tipped her face up to Bobby's and looked into his eyes, the pupils so large in the dim light of the dashboard that the blue irises seemed gone. He stared back, and her mouth fell slightly open in a way that made her painfully aware of how much she wanted him to kiss her. A thrill started low in her spine and moved both down and up rapidly, simultaneously. He leaned toward her, and like magnets turned the wrong way, she pressed apart from the current she felt between them.

"Wow," he said, low and dry. "Did you—"

"I should get home," she said, afraid of how good this all felt, certain that there would be some kind of punishment awaiting her if she went too far.

He acquiesced and the raw relief inside of her sunk like an anchor without a boat to secure or a silt-thickened river bottom to settle into. It was agony. Uninvited longing held through their small talk, and when they got to the top of her street, she was startled out of her daze by a light on in the house.

"Quick," she said, pulling on her hat. "Leave me here. I have to pretend I've walked."

When Bobby brought the pickup to a stop, he took her by the shoulders and steadied his gaze once more. Her breath came in tiny whimpers until she broke free, out of the truck, her head pounding with the effort of not looking back.

"Wait," she heard him call from the cab, but she refused again to turn, even as his footsteps hit the pavement and rapidly approached.

"Emmy, stop," he said, directly behind her. She obeyed, wanting the weight of his hands on her, but instead he moved as close as he could to her without touching.

"I'll find you," he whispered next to her ear, a moment so perfect that Emmy tried hard to suspend herself within it.

"I hope you do," she replied with the half hope he wouldn't. There was no future to be had with Bobby, and so she folded the memory into her heart and gathered her courage to go. She walked briskly up the street, toward the cold reality of her foreseeable future.

Seven

A Delicate Web Unwoven

Days flowed into weeks as Emmy's life returned to a deceptively normal state. Grandmother Nelson regained enough strength for Birdie to go back to school, Karin resumed her Glyndon schedule, the Branns ate Sunday dinner at the farm with the family after church each week, and Emmy worked an hour after school every day in Mr. Utke's office with the blessing of her parents. Birdie had matured considerably the three weeks she had lived out on the farm, and seemed determined to take over Emmy's after-school chores. Birdie was an adequate cook, but Emmy found she often had to secretly make modifications to the dishes, as the younger girl frequently neglected important ingredients, usually salt.

The one thing that set Emmy adrift in her once comfortable habits was the scissor cut of Bobby's failure to reappear. No matter how many times she told herself that it didn't matter, that a chance with Bobby was never meant to be, an unreasonable part of her longed for a note or a hint, anything that would crack into the tedium of her slow march forward. The night in his truck had become an unwelcome shadow dream to Emmy, his "I'll find you" darkening her movements and haunting her skin where he had touched her. The few times the telephone had rung, she thought she would become ill waiting for the voice on the other end, which was invariably her mother's from out at the farm, since Karin was the only person who ever called.

Emmy was stunned by the betrayal of her aching fingertips, and how in her heart there was a constant, throbbing twist. At first the feeling had been excruciating, as she imagined him around every corner—each truck that passed her on the street, every blond-haired boy in the school hallways. Within the first week, her uncontrollable anticipation had turned into a desperate thing, howling inside of Emmy up in her cold room on windburned nights.

Further complicating matters, Emmy's helpful messenger had vanished. Emmy had eagerly sought Bev's advice the day after she went with Bobby, but instead found only empty seats and a vacant locker. Hallway whispers indicated the same fate suffered by the Bossert girl, and Emmy could not deny the probability after what she had overheard at her own house. She had written a note for Bev to pass along to Bobby, but now that slight piece of lined notebook paper grew increasingly dog-eared in whichever pocket Emmy held it. She mostly kept it clutched in her left hand, fearful of losing touch, losing the memory of that night, losing her small grasp on the last moment's fierceness and beauty.

After the first week, Emmy had asked Mr. Utke if he knew what had become of Bev. Perhaps she was sick? Lots of kids had gotten the flu. Emmy had heard of pneumonia taking a long time to cure, and that mononucleosis could knock you flat. He merely grunted at her passel of suggestions, his avoidance an indication that like most good rumors, this one was true. Now three more weeks had passed and she still had not heard from Bev.

❧

On an early spring Friday, Emmy waited for Ambrose to take her on their first official outing to the Spuds' basketball game. Christian and Karin had apparently decided that no harm could come from an athletic competition. Emmy paced around the carpet in her Jeanies, blouse, and new peach sweater, her hair in a high bouncing ponytail, waiting for the sweep of Ambrose's headlights to pull up the street. When they finally did, she sprang out the door and ran to the truck, not really minding the thawed-mud-splattered old gray vehicle. Its relative dullness reminded her of where she belonged, and for that, she was increasingly grateful. Ambrose reached across the seat and pushed open the door on her approach. She stopped short, surprised that he didn't get out of the truck to open her door. She was further dismayed when she saw that he was wearing a western-style brown striped cotton shirt with pearl snaps on the closure and pockets—the kind of thing a person wore to a rodeo, not on a date. A beige cardigan was folded on the seat between them, and the cab was hazy with tobacco smoke. Emmy stepped into the truck, pressing a glove under her nose.

"I thought we'd maybe grab a bite at the Black Hawk before the game," Ambrose said, taking his red plaid newsboy-style cap off and laying it on top of his sweater.

"Oh, I'm not hungry," Emmy said, even though she was. She was strangely reluctant to be seen with Ambrose at the Black Hawk, which was certainly going to be full of town kids going to the game. "Popcorn's fine by me."

"No, I insist." Ambrose put the car in gear. "Only the best for my girl."

"Got a smoke?" she asked, trying to subdue the disjointed feeling of being with Ambrose while wanting so keenly to be with Bobby.

"Here," he said, offering one with his Zippo lighter. She struck the wheel, touching the smooth surface of the cool metal as she inhaled a long drag that brought the sting of butane into her lungs. "Rough thaw this spring." Her thumb rubbed the small cross on the other side of the lighter as she handed it back to him, and an image of holding the same object in her much smaller hand floated up—her grandfather's pipe, the smell of cherry tobacco, the clear blue of his eyes as he held her hand steady. Grandfather Nelson's hair had still been mostly black before he died, the skin where he parted it on the side showing milky white.

"Not too bad out by us, but the low houses are getting swamped," Ambrose said, lighting his own cigarette. She watched his profile and tried to see what her grandfather had seen in Ambrose, and whether there was something beyond fealty, or inheritance, or the simple ease of moving the chess pieces across the board in the order they were laid out. The harder she tried, the more she kept coming back to feeling the pawn.

They arrived at the tidy popular restaurant on Center Avenue just as

Emmy saw a sleek, familiar black-and-white car start to inch away from the curb.

"Pull over," Emmy said, opening her door before they had come to a complete stop and running up to the Bel Air, knocking on the window. Her breath came in small bursts as she half hoped to see Bev snuggled under Howie's arm, throwing her head back in a laugh. The car stopped and the window opened as Emmy leaned down, putting her hands on the sill and looking past Howie. There was Donna Kratz, moved up in the world to the front seat.

"Hey, kid. What's the panic?" Howie said, chewing a large piece of bright pink gum and looking past Emmy and over at Ambrose. "Going to the game?"

"Yes, we are. Hi, Donna," Emmy said, fighting against the sting in her vision and trying to figure how to get to the truth with Ambrose close enough to hear. She had to know. "Have you seen Bev?" she asked. Donna shook her head and pulled down her visor, looking in the small oval mirror as she applied fresh lipstick to an already crimson mouth.

"Look, kid. She's gone to visit her aunt, okay?" Howie bit at his lower lip and revved the engine.

"When is she coming home?" Emmy asked, unsatisfied.

"In about nine months." Howie raised his eyebrows and hit his palm against the steering wheel. "Get me? Better go feed your hillbilly. He looks hungry." Howie threw the car into gear and tore off as Emmy stumbled back away from the curb, bumping into Ambrose and almost knocking him over. She could tell by his disapproving grimace that he'd heard everything.

"Let's go in," Ambrose said, wrapping his arm around Emmy's shoulder and guiding her down the sidewalk. During the awkward meal that followed, Emmy made it through a burger and fries without realizing she had eaten, and enjoined light conversation without having any recall of the content, so wholly absorbed was she by the confirmation that her best friend—her only friend—was expecting. How alone Bev must be, wherever it was she'd been sent. Even as she worried over her friend, Emmy's pride hurt that Bev hadn't at least reached out, and that Emmy was clearly one of the last to know.

After dinner, they walked the few blocks over to the gymnasium. The flow of excited students and parents swept Emmy along the sidewalk, the proliferation of red letterman jackets with the word DEACONS scrawled between the shoulders steadily raising the flesh on her arms. When she read the marquee outside of the building: TONIGHT AT 7! MOORHEAD SPUDS VS. SHANLEY DEACONS, Emmy stopped and stared at the sign, her eyes those of a wild animal caught in its own trap.

"It's the Catholic school over in Fargo," Ambrose said, mistaking the look on her face for confusion when it was simply sheer, horrible panic. They moved up the sidewalk, toward the door. "A school run by old nuns." He shook his head in disgust. "They teach them all sorts of communist papist ideas."

Emmy latched onto Ambrose's arm to cover her momentary shock at the cool revulsion of his words. "Let's not go," she said. "If you feel so strongly about it."

He shook his head and took some change out of his pocket, handing two dimes to a man sitting at a small wooden table, who in turn placed a mark on the backs of their hands with an inky fingerprint. Emmy looked around at the laughing couples, the clutches of families, the children playing tag in the hallway that led to the gymnasium, and shadowed herself in Ambrose's height, following him to the popcorn stand, where the salty air made her mouth water as she practiced feeling nothing if and when she should see Bobby.

Ambrose hung her coat on a hook, and when they entered the tensile energy of the junior varsity game in progress, they discovered that the only seats left in the gymnasium were right down front, across from the players' benches, on the opposing team's side. Emmy sat in a sea of Shanley fans: Any one of them could be a Doyle, and many looked related to Bobby. Emmy couldn't focus on the game other than trying to spot a Doyle brother on the floor—she was pretty sure the boy wearing number ten must be Bobby's brother; he had the exact same smile and curly hair.

Ambrose cheered loudly for the Spuds and was often the only person standing on their side of the gymnasium. More than once he was told to sit down, and Emmy slouched into her sweat-soaked blouse until finally, mercifully, the game ended and the JV Spuds won. A few people on the other side of the gym filed out and Ambrose crossed the floor in his hard-heeled boots, grabbing two of the vacated seats ahead of the fans waiting at the door. Emmy looked in the direction of the exit as she followed him and contemplated an escape. The noise in the gym escalated to a fever pitch, with cheers from both sides of the room thundering as the two teams entered. The Shanley team blurred past her in a hailstorm of pounding basketballs, their red satin uniforms catching the glow of the bright lights that hung from the ceiling. Emmy ducked her head and took her place next to Ambrose, the empty space on the bench accommodating the way she suddenly felt—small enough to disappear.

Bobby wasn't hard to spot, and at first Emmy did her best not to look his way, instead focusing on the Spuds and telling Ambrose the names of various players in an attempt to latch onto the more tangible aspects of their increasingly awkward date. He, in turn, remarked on which were younger brothers of people he had played ball with in high school, and pointed down the floor, singling out Bobby.

"That's their best player," Ambrose said. "I hear he's pretty good, for a Catholic."

"Oh," Emmy replied. "Yes."

The game began and people all around Emmy stood up and sat down, yelled and cheered, but she mostly did whatever Ambrose did, the tiny strings of assumed matrimony fastening her to him. The gym was hot and Emmy was thirsty, but she didn't dare move for fear of Bobby seeing her. He was a magnificent athlete, with speed and grace and fierce competitiveness. He handled the ball more than anyone else on his team, and nearly always passed it to a teammate. Emmy watched his beautiful, graceful body—sweaty and lanky in his red uniform—and began to understand that she had hoped for an unattainable thing. He certainly deserved a better mate in life than a girl whose only evident talent was catching a newborn calf in a barn. He'd find a Bev or a Katie or even a Donna—a girl who knew how to wear stylish clothes and throw fancy dinner parties. That wasn't at all what Emmy had been designed for, and the list of her deficits was almost too long to consider. The sum total would never be enough to fit in his world. She had glimpsed at it, and that would have to be enough.

As the game wore on, she slowly began to tune out the loud demands of city society, turning her ear closer to Ambrose and accepting his quiet words during halftime, when he talked about many things: how many children he wanted to have—five; how soon he wanted to have them—right away; where they would go to school—here in Moorhead, as he had; how he planned on becoming a hugely successful farmer like Paul Howell and move his family into town. It was this last part that turned Emmy's head as the two A squad teams dribbled back out onto the floor. His dreams were bigger than she'd known, and with the idea of a solid future once again in mind, she placed her hand in his. Calmed, she gazed out at the players and instantly found Bobby. This time he saw her, too, and a large, lovely grin spread across his face as a ball struck him in the chest, uncaught.

Emmy turned to Ambrose and saw him staring past her, at Bobby. "I think I've seen enough basketball for one night," she said, unable to bear another moment of the pining that wouldn't stop bubbling under her resolve to see things through with Ambrose. She desperately needed to put Bobby, and everything he stood for, out of her sight.

Ambrose squeezed her hand and led her out of the gym, to her coat, and down the sidewalk, wordlessly shepherding her to the truck. If he suspected anything, she couldn't tell, nor would she deny it if he asked. He didn't.

They drove east out of Moorhead on the road that had so often led her to the familiar surroundings of home and church. As they left the city limits he reached over and drew Emmy toward him. She went.

"Maybe we'll have enough boys to create our own team," he said, pressing her closer.

She didn't know where they were going and didn't care. Emmy needed to move forward, and if Ambrose wanted to drive east, then east it would be. He hummed along to Conway Twitty on the radio, some tune about a man being in love with a woman who isn't in love with him, the country strains of it sounding like any other drive out of Moorhead in her father's car. Twitty's aching voice repeated the plea for God to answer his prayers and one day the girl will care, but he knows, he knows it's only make-believe. Emmy stole a glance at Ambrose, who sang the last few words out loud.

Emmy cleared her throat, searching for something to say. "Well," she ventured. "Girls are nice, too."

"Then five girls!" he confirmed. "As long as they're as pretty as you."

Emmy smiled, unused to the directness of his compliment. "Do you really want to live in town?" she asked, crossing her fingers inside of a pocket.

"I want more than that." He turned the truck onto a gravel road that eventually winnowed down to a two-track prairie lane that would soon be sprouting grass through its center and wild pink roses along the sides. "I've become involved in the Citizens' Council," he said with an air of already improved status. "Curtis thinks that I have what it takes to become mayor of Moorhead someday, but we'll start with the local township elections next fall."

"Mayor?" Emmy said, surprised by the mention of Mr. Davidson's first name and the familiarity that Ambrose attached to its use. She'd somehow assumed that the odd man had moved on, out of their lives, and back to Indiana. "What a thought!"

The muddy road had frozen with nightfall, and the truck bounced hard on the cracking puddles and ruts. Emmy felt a little sick, but whether it was from the jolts or the idea of something physical about to happen between the two of them, she couldn't be sure. In the middle of this empty little road to nowhere Ambrose parked the truck and switched off the engine. The music stopped and Emmy's ears rang in the silence following the cacophony of the gym. Underneath it all she could just barely hear her own heart beating.

"It's become clear to me that things are going in the wrong direction in the world," he said, his voice lower than usual and oddly authoritative. "The council meetings have shed a lot of light on what's wrong with this country, and I aim to be part of what sets it straight again."

Emmy smoothed her coat on her lap, unsure of what to make of this newly voiced ambition, rooted as it seemed to be in the dinner table conversations she'd had so much misfortune trying to engage. She felt unsettled by her inclusion in his plans, seeing as how she hadn't had much time to consider being a farmwife, much less a town wife. That she might someday be required to stand next to Ambrose and agree with his views in a very public way was dumbfounding.

"I know you share my love of country," he continued excitedly, sounding less like himself—and more like his father—with every word he spoke.

"But things are changing and we need to prepare, or our way of life will be destroyed. Black Monday could happen here, if we allow the liberals to take away our Bibles and our right to choose the way we want to live." He reached past Emmy and opened the utility box, drawing from it a folded newspaper and turning on the dome light. Emmy squinted in the harsh glare, surprised to see the words *The Citizens' Council* instead of the customary *The Fargo Forum.*

"Look," he said, pointing to a headline that read "Forced Immigration Seen as Leftist Scheme." "It says right here, 'Forced immigration and forced integration are twins in the struggle to destroy American Sovereignty.'"

"Where did you get this?" she asked, quickly scanning a few other headlines, all of them seeming to align on the same spectrum of distrust and fear of communism, the NAACP, and in particular, President Eisenhower. She pushed away the paper.

"It's what everyone should be reading," he said, a glow in his eyes matching the fire of his words. "Instead of that filth written in the *Forum.* I tell you, all of our newspapers and radio and television just fill people's heads with ideas that are foreign, corrupt in morals. The compass needs to be reset before the commies take over every corner of government, forcing us to abandon our Bibles and our traditional patriotic way of life." Ambrose turned off the light and stuck the paper under his seat.

"I thought it was the liberals," Emmy said, unable to make sense out of the concepts he was rapidly declaiming with such fervor.

"They're one and the same, Emmaline." He rolled down the window a crack and flicked his cigarette through the small space.

"I don't see how segregation can possibly matter here," she said as he rolled it back up and in the next movement brought his right arm around Emmy's waist. "We're all the same."

"That's just it." He pulled her closer. "It says in the paper that an entire suburb of Chicago has been settled by southern Negroes, and parts of Saint Paul are rapidly filling. It's only a matter of time before we're seeing the same thing in Fargo Moorhead." The disquieting quality of his words had sent her to shivering, and he held her tighter. "Look, I'm not saying that there's anything wrong with Negroes, but we have enough problems with outsiders in general, not to mention most immigrants are Catholics. We don't need more."

"What's wrong with Catholics?" she asked. "There were plenty in that gym and they didn't seem so bad to me."

Ambrose clucked his tongue, a sound that raised the hair on the back of Emmy's neck in frustration. "It's simple," he said, squeezing her arm. "They listen to the pope, not the president. They're un-American."

"You can't be serious," she said, pulling away slightly. "I know plenty of Catholics and they are as American as the rest of us."

He drew her tighter. "On the face of it, maybe," he said. "But over time, through school boards and city councils, they have tried to change good Christian policies that undermine the will of the people, and they run that school over in Fargo for immigrant children, in *Spanish*." He laid a heavy hand on her upper thigh. "It's all connected, Emmy, with the eventual overthrow of the government. We won't sit by and watch what our ancestors built for us be taken away by a heathen population."

"I guess I haven't given it enough thought," Emmy said, frustrated by her own lack of knowledge.

"Well, I have, plenty," he said excitedly. "It's what the council is dedicated to—defending peace, good order, and domestic tranquility in our community, and the preservation of our state's rights. You'll see. Everything is going to be just fine, with men like Curtis and my father leading the way."

Emmy sat still in Ambrose's arms, sensing his face coming ever closer in a kiss, moving his mouth on hers, even as she felt like pulling away and telling him No, I won't see, because it doesn't make sense. She broke the embrace and shifted toward her side of the cab, all of her steadfast efforts to convince herself that she could do this thing—marry this man, be his wife, and follow his ways—skittering away like tailless mice, uncatchable in their flight.

"It's gotten cold," she said, hoping he would be satisfied with the one kiss and take her home for the night. Instead he turned the truck and the heat on, took off his cardigan, and drew it around her. He sat back for a moment before reaching under the seat, having made a decision of some kind. He brought up a small bottle and unscrewed the top, offering it to her first.

"Schnapps," he said. "Peppermint. You can't tell our parents." She looked at the bottle, stunned that he could so easily reconcile one moment's speech on morality with the next moment's abandonment of a piece of their own religion's code—and top it off with a vowed lie. With a shaking hand, she took the minty-smelling liquor from him and sipped a small amount, hoping for the kind of reckless high she'd had in Howie's car to chase away the creeping dread. She coughed against the sickly liquid and handed it back. He drank down half without stopping, handed it back to her. They passed it back and forth in silence, pretending that they weren't going to hell as the heat blew out at Emmy and warmed her on the outside as the booze warmed her on the inside. He switched the truck off, and the silence of the prairie night filled the cab.

"I didn't know you drank," she said, feeling the prickle of the alcohol hot on her face.

Ambrose looked at her. "There's a lot you don't know." He laid his thick hand on her neck and rubbed, his calloused touch scratching at her delicate skin. Too hot. She wasn't inclined toward more kissing, even as her body started to tell her it wasn't such a bad idea. She removed his hand and awkwardly scooted away, remembering how much sweeter Bobby's cab had smelled.

"Please," she said. "I'd like to go home." The attempt to deny her baser instincts felt sluggish in her tingling mouth.

"Shhh," he said. "Come here."

She slid toward him, and he was suddenly at her, kissing her hard on the mouth and wrapping his arms around her body. She fell across the seat as he pushed her down onto the length of it and stretched out on top of her, the points of his boots tapping against his door. She couldn't fully inhale with the pressure, yet her body automatically reacted and she arched up at his kiss, meeting him full on the lips, leading him back down when he pulled away in surprise. This could be her strength, she thought as they continued, the pull and push of necking developing a rhythm she controlled. There was none of the tender feeling of place she had felt with Bobby, the sweet seesaw of drawing together and pulling apart. This was a mismatch of throttled desire, and the more keenly he responded, the less she wanted to go further. She broke the clumsily mashing kiss, staring up at the starlit sky through the window as his mouth sucked away at her neck. Suddenly repulsed, she pressed him away with both hands.

"No more," she whispered, wanting to be clear about her change of course. He closed his eyes, and roughly pushed his right hand up her shirt as the left one became entangled in her hair. His hand was on top of her brassiere, then it was under it, next it was unbuttoning her pants at the side of her waist, and in a rush of panic, she began to fight every advance, pushing to make him stop, begging for it to end.

"I know your game," he said, gathering her wrists tightly into one hand in front of her and lying heavily on them as his other hand went to work. Her pants were down in seconds despite her attempt to raise her knees in defense, and it was only the moment that he moved his restraining fist to gain a better position that she was able to free her right hand and slap him hard across the face. He grabbed the offending hand and twisted it away from her, ignoring the rest of her pleas. The shock of inevitability silenced her and she began to sink back in time—past Howie's face leering at her on the curb, past the dulcet moment of staring into Bobby's eyes, past the sounds of her bed and her friend Bev getting this very thing done to her, but with the kind of joy and appetite that were painfully missing in this moment. From far away she felt his thighs pin her legs apart and she saw him long ago in the broken cornfield, bracing the doe for evisceration. The piercing pain that followed elicited a curdling growl from her throat, and she found her right arm free enough to pull back and land squarely on his slackened jaw. In return, a sharp sting of pain sliced at her cheek.

"How dare you," she hissed. She wasn't scared now; she was furious. Ambrose held still for a moment as the ugly fire slowly died out of his eyes, and then he sat up and slumped behind the wheel, silently adjusting his trousers.

Trembling, Emmy collected her torn clothing and dressed herself in the hot, stifling odor of the cab. A storm began to brew in her that threatened her reason. Leave this place, it said. Open the door and walk away. The buttons on her shirt were half missing, her pants were damp in spots, and her bra was impossible to refasten. Get out before he does it again.

"I want to go . . ." she started, but he muffled her shaky words by loudly turning over the engine and reversing the truck up the road the way they had come. The radio blared to life, and as she listened to Johnny Cash sing about a teenage beauty queen, Emmy gathered her unasked-for mementos: buttons, ribbon, glove. She smoothed her hair and refastened her ponytail with a shaking hand, pulling her sweater over her torn blouse and buttoning it up as best she could. All the while, she watched his face in the flickering lights of town as they drove into Moorhead and past the familiar landmarks. His jaw moved as though he were chewing on something inedible, his cheeks drained of color from the effort. Only when they pulled up in front of the small house did she break her stare.

"This won't happen again," she said, her voice hushed but hard.

He smoothed his left hand across the dashboard as he prepared to offer whatever defense his silence had conjured during the drive. "Emmy . . ."

She threw open the door, her body quick to leave the space before her mind was forced to consider more words. "Good night, Ambrose."

"Emmy, is that you?" her mother called from the darkened living room as Emmy slipped into the house. "Come in here and say good night."

The floor sloped down under Emmy's left foot as she tried to take a step in Karin's direction. Holding her sweater more tightly with one hand as she smoothed her hair with the other, Emmy peeked around the corner to see her mother knitting by a dim light. Karin looked up and smiled.

"How was it?" she asked, setting down the yarn.

Emmy moved her hand over her tender cheek and said, "He hit me," in a bewildered tone. She waited for her mother to rise and ask her more, to prod Emmy through the entire chain of events with outrage and shifting plans, until the ultimate solution of not marrying could be arrived at without Emmy's instigation.

"How did you provoke him?" Karin asked, holding still in her chair.

Emmy took a dizzy step forward. "I don't know," she answered. She misjudged the distance and nearly tripped. But *hadn't* she made him think she was willing, and hadn't she indeed struck first? How could she begin to explain the sequence of events when she didn't fully understand what pieces of it were due to her own desires? She had drunk the schnapps, returned the kiss—and yet also slapped his face and begged him to stop.

"Go lie down," Karin said, picking up her knitting. "I'm sure he'll forgive you."

Slowly turning her aching body, Emmy made her way up the stairs and into the bathroom. In the harsh light over the medicine cabinet, she took a disassociated inventory: pale green bruise high on her cheek, dark blue smudge on her neck—how had that happened?—light red mark on one wrist, a darker one on the other where they had been crossed and held. She gasped and, feeling a sharp pain in her stomach, sat uneasily on the edge of the tub, peeling off her jeans and standing naked before the sink, the white of her slim thighs cool against the porcelain as she tried to scrub the bloody evidence out of her clothing, the murky water swirling around the drain until it finally ran clear. Though they had been groped, her breasts sloped in their resolute fashion, full and round above her soft belly. Emmy put a hand on her navel, knowing that what had happened could lead to a more complex situation than she was prepared to handle. Had her mother moved up the wedding date with this sort of event in mind? A tap at the door startled her, and she grabbed her nightdress off its hook on the back of the door before responding.

"Are you better, Emmaline?" her mother asked through the thin wood. The knob began to turn and Emmy slipped the edge of her foot against the door. She closed her eyes and wished for the assurance that telling her mother everything would somehow bring forth any other outcome than more advice on how to make amends.

"Yes," Emmy said instead, clearing her throat of the stoppered emotion enough to sound almost normal.

"This is what happens," Karin said in a faraway voice. "It's how it is."

"What?" Emmy squeaked. Beyond all reason and nearing complete collapse, she collected her clothes from the floor and opened the door, where her mother stood, both hands wrapped around her own throat, as though saying the few words had left it aching.

"Dad?" Emmy asked, fearing what she might hear next.

"No, not him," Karin said slowly, her eyes slanting to her bedroom door, a hint of gratitude underneath the sadness. "Now go to bed."

Emmy bundled past her mother down the hall and to her room, shoving the dual disappointments to the back of her mind. Mercifully, Birdie was out at the farm, and in the moonlit hours that stretched before her, Emmy systematically sewed the buttons on her shirt, fixed the zipper on her pants where it had been torn from its seam, and mended her brassiere, working until all evidence of her shameful evening was meticulously erased by repair and her eyes smarted from the chore. When she finally rose and turned out the light, the sound of a revving engine drew her to the window, where she watched, horrified, as the old brown pickup truck crawled down the street until it disappeared from view.

Part II

Doubt Grows with Knowledge

Eight

Candles in the Wind

On Sunday morning Emmy lay in bed, sick. The thought of seeing the Branns at church had sent her straight to the bathroom to vomit, proving to Karin that the illness wasn't false and that Emmy needed to stay home. Though by the way Karin cast her eyes to the floor rather than witness the bruises on her daughter's body, Emmy knew that her mother was relieved to leave her behind.

Once the house was quiet, Emmy lay on her bed, staring up at the ceiling and considering her options. She tried to imagine ever kissing Ambrose again, letting him touch her, or even looking him directly in the eye without feeling the horrible hatred and fear that bubbled up with a fresh round of violent illness that sent her straight to the bathroom. It was as though her body were trying to purge the memory along with anything that had been inside of her when it had happened: the popcorn, the hamburger, the schnapps. She wiped her mouth of the acrid mint and moved back to her bedroom, undressing and gently touching the multitude of bruises polka-dotting her skin, as though the light pressure would produce a different tune. The trance she had been trapped in since the night before snapped, and Emmy hastily dressed in flannel and overalls, tying a small silk scarf around her neck to hide the marks there. She drew a notebook from her schoolbag and began to consider what she needed to do in order to release herself from the web: school, work, college. Enough self-pity. She had a choice.

Over the month that she had worked for Mr. Utke, he'd repeatedly encouraged her to consider studying for a teaching degree. She had thought his advice akin to a barber suggesting a haircut, but now that she was in need of any shred of hope, she grasped at his belief in her ability to succeed. She would also need to earn some money, and hoped that the clerical work she'd done for him was enough for him to recommend her elsewhere.

"If you promise not to tell my mother," Emmy said to him in his office after school the next day, "I'd like your help with college."

"What happened there?" Mr. Utke asked, pointing to her cheekbone. Emmy's hand fluttered against the greenish mark for a second.

"Kicked by a cow," she said, a feeble lie.

"Sit down, Emmaline," he said. "If you don't want to tell me the truth, then I won't ask you twice. But I'm not comfortable lying to a parent, under any circumstances."

Emmy felt her lip quiver. "Mother won't approve," she said. "And it wasn't a cow. My fiancé hit me, and I don't know what to do." A tear slipped down her cheek, and Emmy angrily batted it away.

Mr. Utke tapped the side of his nose with a pencil, his mouth a grimly set line beneath his mustache. "I see. Why don't we start with the admissions test, and see how things go from there?"

Emmy drew a shallow breath and said, "I read there's one in May."

"I have no doubt you'll pass it." He pulled a small stack of paperback booklets from a desk drawer and laid them on the blotter, sealing his part of their unspoken agreement. "It's little more than a formality for the top students."

"And I've been thinking about studying home economics," Emmy said, finding courage in having told Mr. Utke the truth. "I could eventually do what Mrs. Hagen does, teach girls how to cook and sew."

"Then we should aim for NDAC over in Fargo." He gingerly set the thickest book on the top of the pile. "But at some point, you will have to tell your mother."

"I'm eighteen," Emmy said, twisting a damp hankie around her index finger so tightly that the pain kept her from showing any more evident anger, in particular directed at Karin.

"So you are," he replied. "That is a valid point."

"I need a job, too," she said. "I won't be able to afford the tuition on what you pay me."

"You're a funny one." Mr. Utke smiled kindly, knowing that she wasn't being paid for her work. "I'm afraid I can't give you more than a ten-cent raise."

"Ten cents are better than the current rate." Emmy laughed, a bitter tone revealing how trapped she felt. "I'm a hard worker, if you know of anyone who needs one."

He sat quietly for a minute. "I can certainly ask around." His smile faded as he leaned forward and looked at Emmy's cheek more closely, a thundercloud of protection gathering in his expression. "We'll find you something. In the meantime, steer clear of that cow."

On Thursday afternoon, Mr. Utke announced that he'd found Emmy a job at the Moorhead Theatre, selling concessions. The pay was $.75 an hour, and she could start on Friday night. The girl who had been working the candy counter had quit, and Mr. Rakov needed an immediate replacement. After Emmy had struggled through the five-minute interview, barely able to understand through Mr. Rakov's thickly accented and broken English that she could have the job, she sat in Mr. Utke's car, pointing the directions to her home. This was happening faster than Emmy could quite grasp. It was nearing six; her mother would already be there, her father home soon.

"How do I tell her?" Emmy asked herself out loud, even as she hoped that Mr. Utke would have an answer.

"Part of becoming an adult is facing hard situations with truth," Mr. Utke advised.

Emmy filled her lungs with air. "I doubt she'll like this idea much."

"With doubt comes experience."

Emmy plucked at a loose string on her skirt. "You always know what to say," she said. "Thank you for helping me."

Mr. Utke parked at the curb in front of her house and turned slightly toward her. "You have great potential, Emmaline. Don't lose sight of that."

Emmy nodded, frozen to the seat. She heard the words but didn't entirely believe the sentiment.

"I've known your mother since I first taught school out in Glyndon and you were just a baby," he said, opening the door. "I have every reason to think she'll understand."

Emmy closed her eyes. "I'm not a baby anymore."

"The first step is the hardest, you'll see." Mr. Utke got out of the car and Emmy sat with her eyes closed until she felt the air rush in against her right side as he opened her door and offered a hand up and out of the temporary safety of the car.

She led the way up the walk, noting that the house was dark except for a light in the kitchen, which was not a good sign. When Karin had had a particularly long day she liked to keep the house stone quiet and underlit. She never complained, but it seemed to Emmy that her mother suffered some kind of deep pain on nights like these.

"Maybe tonight's not the best time," Emmy said, hesitating at the front door. Mr. Utke gave her a little punch on the shoulder and knocked. The door opened.

"Hello, Reinhold," Karin said, showing mild surprise. Emmy had not seen her mother since the night before and she did not look particularly well. There were dark moons below her eyes and one corner of her mouth drooped down a tiny bit, not really a noticeable flaw, but one that caused Emmy to bite the inside of her cheek.

"Emmy," Karin said. "It's later than usual. Please, come in." The formality of the statement unsettled Emmy even more, and she hesitated on the threshold as Mr. Utke waited for her to enter first. Karin turned on a lamp in the parlor as Emmy took Mr. Utke's coat and hung it with her own on the coat tree, hugging both for a moment and gathering her will.

Her mother and her guidance counselor chatted about people in Glyndon, catching up on the local news, and Emmy took the opportunity to find something to offer Mr. Utke. Birdie was not in the kitchen, nor could Emmy hear her upstairs. She found some bread and cut it into pieces, made toast out of it and smeared a bit of butter on the triangles, arranging them on a plate as she'd seen in a cookbook at school. She peeked in the oven and saw a roast surrounded by potatoes and onions—more of the endless Brann side of beef. She pressed a hand to her mouth, forcing the thought of anything related to Ambrose quickly and sharply away.

Emmy offered Mr. Utke a piece of toast with a small linen napkin and a glass of tap water. It was meager but clearly appreciated as he took a bite and set the appetizer on his knee, then lifted it again to his mouth and so finished the bread swiftly but elegantly by setting it down after each small bite. Emmy offered him another before taking one for herself. She was spinning inside, waiting for the right moment to announce her news, and when the topic predictably turned to the weather, she broke in.

"Yes, it's certainly gotten cold again," she said to Mr. Utke, and then turned to Karin. "Mother, I've taken a job at the Moorhead Theatre. It pays almost a dollar an hour, I'll be working three nights a week and Saturdays, and it starts tomorrow. I won't be watching the movies, just selling popcorn, candy, pop, and chocolate, and I'll come home straight after, so you don't need to worry."

Karin looked blankly at her daughter, then looked at Mr. Utke and narrowed her eyes. "You were supposed to keep her out of trouble, not to fill her head with ideas." Before she could say more, the door opened and Christian walked in, took note of their guest, and greeted Mr. Utke with the same degree of warmth that her mother had. Emmy could see a look pass between Christian and Karin, but another round of weather pleasantries, and how-is-the-beet-plant questions, and you'll-never-believe-who's-getting-married exclamations unfolded until Birdie walked in the door, followed closely by Ambrose, the two of them laughing over some shared joke. Emmy dropped the empty toast plate, and Mr. Utke stood suddenly at the sound.

"I should get on home," he said, breaking the awkward moment with his calm voice. Emmy knelt on the hard floor and gathered the pieces of porcelain, cutting the edge of her palm in the process.

"I wouldn't hear of it," Karin said. "Set one more place for dinner, Emmaline. Our future son-in-law has been quite generous to provide tonight's roast." Emmy looked up at her mother, a plea in her eyes, only to realize that Ambrose had already been invited without her knowledge.

"I'd be honored to join you," Mr. Utke said, his hand firm on Emmy's elbow as he helped her stand. "It's not very filling being a bachelor at my age."

"Let's take a look at that cut," Karin said as she led Emmy by the wrist into the kitchen, away from the three men and Birdie. Emmy's hands shook the pieces of plate together as she carried them to the sink, where she let them fall again as her mother turned on the cold tap and held Emmy's palms under the stream.

"You need to make amends," Karin whispered. "He'll do whatever you say now, but not if you take on airs."

"And if I don't want to?" Emmy said through her chattering teeth.

"Then you can find a new place to live," Karin said, as though she had already packed Emmy's bags and left them on the stoop of her disappointment. She let go of Emmy's hands and opened a cupboard, pulling a plate from a stack. Then, gathering utensils from a drawer, she set the extra place for Mr. Utke. Emmy looked at the damage on her palm through the rushing water and understood with stark clarity that this was how her life would be if she continued to follow her mother's advice: one small cut after another until her heart had bled out completely through her thickened skin.

❧

"It's a lucky thing our future son-in-law is so generous," Karin said again as Christian carved the roast. "It makes it so easy for us to add a guest to God's table." Emmy was surprised by how hard her mother was trying to impress their company—she'd even changed into one of her better dresses before supper, and mentioned Birdie's position in the school choir, and how Mr. Utke should consider a place for the girl in the one he directed at the Moorhead Lutheran church. For her own part, Emmy had deftly avoided being near Ambrose by seating herself between the other two men, forcing her mother to take the spot open beside her fiancé. Silenced by the situation, Emmy poked at her food and noticed how Ambrose dominated the conversation, a role he had clearly learned from his long-winded father. She barely listened as the meal wore on, the topics as unchanging as they ever were. Her hand throbbed when she tried to cut through the roast, and eventually she gave up trying to eat at all.

"Let me ask you, Mr. Utke," Ambrose said, shifting toward him.

"Please, call me Reinhold," Mr. Utke replied. "You're long out of school."

"As an instructor, do you find the desegregation of schools and what it's done in Little Rock to be a positive thing?" Ambrose asked, his voice level but his eyes narrow in a way that showed he expected a certain kind of answer.

"I don't find that it affects me," Mr. Utke replied. "But yes, I do think it will eventually be a positive change."

"Now, son," Christian said to Ambrose. "You know I don't like talking politics at my dinner table."

Ambrose coughed into his napkin, a sound of slight disrespect. "This isn't politics, sir. It's a matter of grave concern that all knowledgeable citizens should discuss openly."

"One man's concern is another man's politics," Christian replied. He moved his chair away from the table an inch and folded his arms across his chest. Karin stood and began to clear the table.

Ambrose laid his hands on either side of his plate. "Forgive me for saying so, but I disagree. The NAACP is moving more and more coloreds up north, and their branch in Minneapolis has been corrupting the unions and schools, suing regular citizens for not wanting to send their children to school with Negroes."

"I don't think I'd want to go to school with a Negro," Birdie said, her voice filled with its usual melody. "I mean, I wouldn't feel safe, really."

"Help your mother, Birdie," Christian said in a tone Emmy had heard only when one of them was in trouble with him. Birdie rose quickly and took her father's plate as Mr. Utke passed his along to her as well.

"Ambrose," Mr. Utke said, "the NAACP is safeguarding the rights of humans, regardless of their skin." He leaned forward on his elbows, a pose Emmy knew well, one that always preceded some morsel of salted wisdom. "You do know that most Negroes came to this country against their will, as slaves, yes?"

"Yes."

"And that the North won the Civil War, ending slavery?"

"Of course," Ambrose said, sparking at the words. "But see, that's just it. The war is long over. They can all go back home. There are many countries in Africa that would benefit from a population increase. There's plenty of farmland there, and Negroes have learned well how to cultivate fields."

Christian began to speak, but Mr. Utke put his hand on Christian's arm. "Is this something you learned in Wisconsin?" Mr. Utke asked calmly.

"No, sir," Ambrose replied, taking a folded newspaper from his back pocket and opening it up. Emmy saw the masthead *Citizens' Council* above the headline "Violence Grips Integrated Schools." "See, it's all in here. It even says that there's scientific proof that race mixing is wrong. There was no problem until people started desegregating. Everyone was happy."

"Emmy, go help your mother," Christian said without shifting his gaze from Ambrose.

"I can't," Emmy replied, showing him her damaged hand. She had no intention of leaving the table, even if she wasn't in pain.

Christian nodded. "Look, Ambrose," he said. "There was a time, many years ago, before you were born, when an organization much like your Citizens' Council came round here and stirred up a lot of trouble. Curtis was part of it then, and I suspect he's up to no good now. Stay away from this, son."

The light in Ambrose's face dimmed and he refolded the paper. "This is not the Klan," he replied. "Curtis knows that what they did down South was wrong, but this isn't about all that. This is about states' rights, the rights of Minnesotans to keep their state the way they want it without interference from Eisenhower and the communists."

Mr. Utke laughed sharply. "It's communists now, is it? Son, I think you need to go back to college and learn some things the right way around." He shook his head and stood, dropping his napkin on the table. "I've enjoyed this evening, Karin. Thank you for having me." Karin returned to the table, wiping her hands on her apron.

"You are welcome any time," she said, ushering him toward the living room. "Birdie, go get your things and Ambrose will drive you back to the farm."

"I'll walk you out," Christian said to Mr. Utke, and Birdie smiled as though the fraught conversation had never happened, cleared a few more of the dishes to the counter, and slipped into the living room behind her parents. Suddenly Emmy was alone at the table with Ambrose. A tense silence fell between them as Emmy stared at the bandage on her hand.

"I think you should go now," she said quietly.

"Emmy," he said, all of his hubris gone in one word.

"Please," she whispered. "I can't. Not now. Not yet."

"I will make it right," he said. "If you'll let me."

She closed her eyes and waited, listening to the old clock tick on the wall, waited for the scrape of his chair, the fall of his foot. She didn't flinch when he touched her shoulder, even though she could feel a bruise where his hand was. She pressed into the subtle pain, let him leave, the mild murmurings of her parents as he moved through the house, Birdie's hasty footfalls on the stairs, the second funnel of cool air as the door opened and closed one last time for the evening. Opening her eyes, Emmy stood and cleared the salt and pepper shakers, the napkins, and the butter server from the table and moved around the kitchen, letting the welcome calm of restoring order descend. Her parents' voices murmured from the other room, Karin's slightly louder and more vehement than Christian's.

The arguing stopped and Emmy heard the tired tread of her mother's small footsteps go up the stairs and creak along the floorboards above. Christian grunted a little as he came into the kitchen, and Emmy took up scrubbing the roaster with her unbandaged hand.

"You can't see any of the movies," Christian said wearily. "And you will come home immediately after work is finished."

Emmy looked up at her father. "Thanks, Dad," she said, relieved.

"You're eighteen," he said, his brow creasing. "You don't need our permission. Reinhold told me that Mr. Rakov is a fair and decent man. That's good enough for me."

She nodded, a lump forming in her throat. She wished she could ask him why he was so agitated by Ambrose's cold diatribe, or tell him why she needed the job—end the charade of being strong—but she realized that if she was going to change the course of things, she would have to keep her own confidence for a while.

"Okay, then." He turned from her and left the room. A minute later she heard the radio, and knew that by the time she finished wiping down the kitchen and putting everything away, she would find him sound asleep with his head tipped back against his armchair. She felt a pang of nostalgia for the way things had once seemed so simple, though to be honest, she knew that all of her current complications arose from exactly that simplicity: She'd been a simple girl, but she would not be a simple woman.

❧

Emmy's curiosity led her to the school librarian, who was more than happy to show her the long shelf of books that comprised the works of Josephine Randall. Her first book, *Candles in the Wind*, was one of Miss Lily's favorites, written when Josephine was twenty-four. It took Emmy no more than two days to tear through the book, a process that felt like falling off a cliff and into a vast ocean of prairie grass, populated with roaming herds of buffalo, scores of Indians, and a handful of rugged settlers who were likely modeled on her own ancestors. Though she knew it was a work of fiction, Emmy couldn't help wondering how much of it was true, and whether she fit the mold of sod-house builders, wide-hipped women undaunted by the locust-infested broiling summers or the endlessly dark and brutally cold winters. She traded that book for the one Bev had mentioned, finishing it just as quickly and with the feeling of having found in Josephine Randall a voice that rang truer than any of the ones she'd heard growing up. The delicately drawn romance between the cousins at the center of the book made Emmy miss Bev more keenly. Emmy decided to go past her house one more time, and with the Langers' help, meet this unknown aunt—and maybe she would be able to contact Bev, as well.

The Langer house had a high, pointed roof, with two quaint windows protruding like the eyes on a bullfrog from the dark shingles where the attic floor would be. Unlike any other house in Moorhead, theirs was painted a robin's-egg shade of blue, which cheerfully nested in the snow-dusted evergreen shrubs that surrounded the porch and lined the walk all the way up to the street. This is where Emmy stood, bracing for the conversation she would have with Mrs. Langer, a woman she hadn't yet met and knew very little about. Emmy could only hope that Bev's mother was less formidable than her own. The shades inside were closed, which for a moment made Emmy think that no one was at home. The sudden barking of a small dog suggested otherwise, drawing Emmy up the walk. She reached for the door knocker as she heard the latch slip its bolt on the other side.

There stood Bev. Emmy gasped. Her friend was not only rounder, but her condition lent her an ethereal air, as though the child growing within her had whispered some secret only Bev could hear. A jolt of elation overtook Emmy as her hand stayed suspended in mid-knock.

"Hallelujah," Bev said, joy lighting her full face. A tiny white dog barked at her ankles. "Don't just stand there looking goofy." She pulled Emmy in by the sleeve, closing the door neatly behind them, wrapping her arms around Emmy, and rocking her back and forth. "It's been too long, dear friend," she said, her belly hard against Emmy's. "Let's go to the kitchen, I'm starved. I'm starved all the time!"

Bev led Emmy by the hand through the living room, which was decorated with emerald green wall-to-wall carpet and two gaily flowered davenports on either side of a brass-accented stone fireplace. They passed a large dining table stacked with an assortment of Bev's schoolbooks and papers, looking as though she'd just left them in the middle of an assignment.

"That's my desk," she said, pushing open a swinging white door to the kitchen, the dog racing ahead and looping in a circle around a smaller table upon which sat a bowl of fruit. Bev bent the stem of a banana, stripped the peel, and took small bites while she talked. "Mr. Utke brings over my schoolwork twice a week. I won't be at graduation, but I'll get my diploma, all right." Bev dropped onto a cushioned chair, and the tiny dog leaped into her lap. "This is Kitty. I know, stupid name for a dog, but that's what happens when you let your ten-year-old brother pick the name." Her hair had grown in a bit and softened her once-sharp features with new unfussed curls. "At first I wanted to go spend my time in New York with my mother's sister, but then I realized I'd be miserable there, without my family and Howie. Now that I'm nesting, all the parents have come around. Once we both finish our studies, we'll make it official. I'll have the baby in July, and then we'll move to Paris, where my uncle has a job for Howie all lined up at the embassy. No one there will even know that we're cousins, if they were to care. I would have kept going to school, but my mother felt it would send the wrong kind of message, you know, about *s-e-x*." Bev rolled her eyes, and Kitty jumped from her lap. "As if half the school weren't already well aware of the outcome. It's astonishing how stupid grown-ups are, thinking we don't have urges until we graduate and marry."

Emmy felt the blood drain from her face and her hands go icy, even though she hadn't yet removed her hat or coat and was standing too close to the warm stove.

"What's wrong?" Bev stood suddenly, alarmed. The sound of her friend's pinpoint concern pricked at the bubble that Emmy had settled over the image of the truck parked on the deserted road.

"It happened so fast," Emmy whispered, closing her eyes. "I'm not even sure what it was."

Emmy felt Bev touch her cheek—the same one that had been bruised that night—and all of the strangled helplessness she had dammed up in the absence of maternal comfort pushed forth in a sodden rush.

Bev braced Emmy's arms and eased her into a chair before carefully kneeling on the floor. "Tell me, please?"

The crying wouldn't abate now that it had started, so Emmy did her best to work the words into sentences, to get the details out from where she had them hidden. "I tried to do it, to kiss him that way. . . . I even wanted to at first, but then I didn't. . . . He pinned me down and tore my clothes, so I hit him . . . and then he hit me, and didn't stop and . . . and . . . and," she sobbed in a deep breath, stretching her hands toward Bev, who grasped them tightly. Emmy dropped her head onto their joined fists, fighting out the last horrible fact. "I couldn't make him stop."

"There now. You're safe here," Bev whispered in her ear, stroking Emmy's hair and exhaling small shushes until the sobbing slowed. "Have you had your monthly visit since?"

Had she? Emmy sat up. "Yes." She remembered. "Yes, of course I have."

"Good. Then you're going to be fine." Bev crossed her arms, her tear-stained face full of anger. "What did your mother say?"

Emmy shook her head slowly. "I tried to tell her. She wouldn't hear it."

"What about your dad?"

"I could *never*," Emmy said, humiliation filling her veins at the thought of it. She swiped at her cheek, done with crying. "Besides, I've decided to find my own way out. Mr. Utke's helped me get a job, and when I have enough money, I'll call off the marriage and find a place to live."

Bev laced her fingers across her stomach. "Maybe you could live with Josephine. She's got that big estate all to herself and has a reputation for taking in wayward souls."

Emmy's embarrassment intensified. "I'm ashamed to say that I came here to ask your mother to introduce me."

"You're a silly goose," Bev said, swatting Emmy's knee and moving from the floor to a chair. "Who cares *why* you're here? You were absolutely right. Mother will know what to do."

"Honestly, I don't know how I've managed without you." Emmy stood and buttoned her coat.

"You've managed just fine," Bev said. "I'll pass you a note through Mr. Utke."

The mention of his name calmed Emmy enough for her to let go of one more fear, and she realized that no matter how much she might have felt alone, there were now at least two people she could count as friends.

❧

A week later Emmy took account of her plodding resources while she waited at the theater for the main feature to finish. She had made some progress toward figuring out how much money she would need to strike out on her own, and at less than a dollar an hour, six hours a day, four days a week, it would take up to a year to make the move. On a good day she imagined living like a boarder in her parents' home, coming and going with the hands of the clock. Other days she knew that breaking off the engagement would bring a swift end to this dream.

The days had nonetheless slid by in a blur of chores, school, work, home, study, sleep, and chores. Work was easy. She showed up Monday, Wednesday, Friday, and Sunday nights, went through the theater and down the aisle to a door that led to the basement, where she changed into her mustard yellow uniform, went back up to the concession counter, and surveyed the chaos left from the night before. The girl who worked the other nights wasn't as meticulous as Emmy, and she only truly enjoyed setting up on Monday, when she found things perfectly ordered from her own closing the night before. Cindy was a college girl who sometimes worked the ticket booth on her off nights, and she had once worn Emmy's uniform by mistake, spilling something on it that Emmy had to scrub out in the cold water of the sink in the basement, hoping it would dry in time for opening.

Next she turned on the popcorn machine, checked the fluid level in the pump, and loaded more of the thick coconut oil paste into the hopper if there wasn't enough to get her through the night. Once it had melted, she pumped a small amount into the kettle and added a scoop of presalted kernels, waiting for the fluffy bits of corn to spill over and fill the glass box. She loved the smell of it all and even liked the way the oil slicked her hands and the salt stung her lips. Before long, the audience would start to trickle in, and she and the ushers would buzz around one another in a subtle ballet, darting to the popcorn, the candy counter, the cash register, the seats. Pointing out the ladies' room and asking patrons to please put out their cigarettes before entering the theater, even though they knew some of them would light new smokes once inside.

While the movie played, Emmy cleaned up the machine and started it fresh, filling bags for the occasional bored or hungry moviegoer who would slip out for a break and chat with her about the weather. Then she'd prepare for the onslaught of the next audience, and at the same time begin to shut down and set up for the following day. If there was popcorn left after the late show, she would bag it for mixing into the first batch the next night. Then she would spray down the glass of the machine and put the gears into a bucket to take back downstairs and wash before she changed to go home.

Sometimes during the movie she would peek through the round theater door window and listen to the murmuring tones of movie stars, but usually she used the time during the movie to study or to read more of Josephine Randall's books. The novels had run the gamut from the original sod-breaking heroines to banner-waving suffragettes, each narrated by a woman whom Emmy imagined to be a thinly veiled version of the author. With every page she read, Emmy's scope grew in an increasing circumference of time and space, rippling over the Red River Valley, past the Upper Midwest, into the soft deltas of the South and the frozen tundras of the North—back to pockets of Renaissance Europe and even a stop in ancient Greece. Emmy's appetite for the books had grown to the point where she was walking to school with one in hand, falling asleep with another on her chest. At some point it occurred to Emmy that neither her house nor the farm nor even the Brann house contained any books. Yes, there were Bibles aplenty, and her grandmother kept a shelf of *Reader's Digests* that they weren't allowed to touch, but beyond that, Emmy could not think of a time when any member of her family had ever read anything other than a newspaper.

Emmy folded the cleaning rag and put it under the counter with the glass spray. She was pleased with her work and felt ready for the night to be over. She set a stool behind the popcorn machine in order to read. One hour to go before the movie ended, then a brisk walk home in the cool spring air. Emmy couldn't figure out why Mr. Rakov was against shutting down the stand early, as she had never once sold a concession during this last long stretch of time. It must have had something to do with the way he'd done things in Russia, though she certainly could keep her uniform at home and wash it herself rather than have the theater spend the money on dry cleaning. Lost in a fog of minutiae, Emmy didn't notice the door to the theater swing open and close until through the glass of the candy case she noticed a pair of dungarees folded once at the ankles over a pair of red high-topped athletic shoes.

Emmy glanced up from her book to see Bobby Doyle examining the selection of Sno-Caps, Jujubes, and a variety of licorices. She nearly dropped the novel as she leaned back on her stool, hoping he would decide he wasn't hungry enough to buy anything. Emmy attempted to rely on the charade she had practiced so well: She wasn't interested in him anymore, nor any boy who passed her way. There was a dull pulsing in Emmy's wrists and temples, and she suddenly needed the bathroom very badly. The ushers had all gone with the ticket girl to grab a burger at Wolf's and wouldn't be back until closing, so she did the only thing she could: She stood. Bobby put his fingers on the countertop and peered around the popper. Emmy's heart stopped, then started again, faster than before. They looked at each other for a long moment, during which it occurred to Emmy that *he* might be mad at *her*. She looked away, irate, and slapped her book onto the stool, moving behind the counter in a spell. When she stood in front of him, his face opened into a bottomless grin, and he practically leaped over the narrow counter to take her shoulders in his hands.

"It really is you, isn't it?" he asked, his eyes locking onto hers. "Bev said you were here, but when I came in, I didn't see you." She wouldn't let his charm win this time, nor would the mention of Bev's name sway her determination.

"I beg your pardon," she replied, removing his hands from her uniform. He let her, but his smile didn't fade. "It's not like you can just blow in and out of my life, unannounced."

"You didn't get my note?" He stood with his hands retreated to his pockets, casual, so sure of himself. She fell back against the wall, her well-manicured position on Bobby suddenly overgrown and unruly in an irrational wish. She wanted him to touch her again.

"Note?"

"Darn that Pete," he said, somewhat to himself. "He was supposed to give it to Bev to give to you."

"What did this note say?"

"How about I write you another one and give it to you myself?" He leaned forward again on the case, reaching as if to hold her hand. She let him, and the cloud of melancholy that had clung to her since she had seen him last shifted an inch to the right.

"I'm here again Wednesday night," she whispered, lowering her forehead so it almost met his. "Looks like you'll need to see the movie again anyway."

"I like the picture out here better," he said, propping his chin in his other hand and turning his full blue-eyed attention on her. They stayed that way until the movie ended while they chatted about the mundane activities of high school life. She told him about Mr. Utke's kindness; Bobby told her about learning how to arc-weld in shop class. She didn't tell him that she'd known how to weld since she was twelve, but instead listened to his explanation without interrupting his smiling monologue. As the crowd filtered out of the theater, Bobby wove his way out the door through the dispersing crowd, turning and touching his index finger to his brow in a last salute as he disappeared.

Emmy hastened through her basement clean-up routine, changing out of her uniform and hanging it neatly on the rack, washing and rinsing the slick coconut oil from the gears of the popper and wiping them dry. The last of the ushers, having finished his sweep of the theater, held the front door open for her as she flew down the sidewalk, her head full of bees from the excitement of seeing Bobby.

It wasn't until she turned onto the darkened residential stretch of Eleventh Street that she noticed headlights casting her shadow long before her on the pavement. The pace seemed to match her own—not nearing, just remaining the same eerie distance away. Emmy glanced over her shoulder, lengthening her stride at the sight of Ambrose's truck slinking along, then speeding up until it passed her and stopped a short distance ahead. The door swung open, and he appeared, wearing dark slacks and a long-sleeved white shirt, a slim black tie around the collar.

"I want to tell you something," he said, closing in. She stopped, her high spirits draining into the gutter at their feet.

"I don't want to hear it," she said. The shaking started in her arms and rapidly moved to her torso, up to her mouth and teeth. She made an effort to relax her muscles, but when she looked up at him, a fresh chill bloomed at the sight of his face, shadowed by the moonless night.

"I want you to stop working at the theater," he said. "It's run by communists."

She shook her head, bewildered by Ambrose's insistent tone. "Mr. Rakov is not a communist."

Ambrose counted on his fingers, "He's Russian, an immigrant, and a Jew. He plays foreign movies. There's no possible way he isn't a communist."

"You're nuts," Emmy said without mirth. "Even if he is a communist, it's no business of mine."

"Well, it is mine! I can't let you take that chance." He moved one step closer and hung his head. "I want to make things right with you," he said toward his shoes. "Whatever it takes."

Startled by the change of subject, she detoured around him, not wanting to hear any compassion in his voice. He caught her by the upper arm. She looked at his hand. "Please just let go of me."

"I can't," he said, as though he was the one wounded. "We have a wedding to plan."

Emmy bit her lower lip at the thought. "Yes," she said, trying to remain calm even though his touch made her want to run. "I suppose we need to do something about that, but not tonight."

"Let me know when," he said, and released her from his grip.

"Thanks. I will." She continued on her way, slowly, but with her shoulders squared and her head high.

"Let me drive you home," he shouted after her. "It's not safe."

"I'm fine," she said over her shoulder, stubbornly walking on as she talked. "I do this every day." Once she had turned the corner and was certain he wouldn't follow, her nerves shattered, and the cold night air drew the tears from her eyes as she ran the remaining five blocks home. The well-oiled machine of her childhood was obsolete to her now, and as she slowed her pace upon reaching the walkway to her house and dried her cheeks on her sleeve, she knew that she would have to dismantle it all on her own. *I can say no*, she thought. Oddly, this notion didn't raise more tears, but Emmy instead felt as though a dozen small hot air balloons had taken flight inside her chest, lifting her spirits and leaving her elated at the new possibilities that could come from simply letting go.

Nine

The Fragility of Stars

The days passed, and Emmy's resolve to become independent grew stronger. Turning the wheel of habit away from the curb was slow work, though, and Emmy knew that until she had enough money tucked away and her high school education finished, she couldn't do anything that revealed her intentions.

A note from Bev arrived via Mr. Utke the next week, suggesting that Emmy come over on Easter Sunday to meet Josephine Randall, who had just returned from Europe. Emmy scribbled out a reluctant refusal, knowing that regardless of the way she felt about Ambrose, she was duty bound to spend the day at her grandmother's table. *But please,* Emmy closed the note, *do let me know when I can meet her any other time.*

The Friday before Holy Week, Emmy went home after school, prepared dinner, made certain that Birdie was studying, and then as the clock struck five put on her hat and coat and said, "See you later." She wasn't going to work at the theater as expected, but merely walking there in order to meet Bobby before heading over the river to Fargo for the Crystal Ballroom's Friday Night Dance Canteen. The opulence of the words made Emmy swallow hard. Dancing. And with a Catholic boy, no less. She laughed out loud in the spring night air, giddy with the thrill of the forbidden.

All she could think about lately was Bobby, Bobby, Bobby. He had shown up at the movie theater on Wednesday night as promised, and she was ready, her hair washed and freshly curled late the night before, her uniform spot-cleaned and pressed stiff, her cute little saddle shoes, the black parts shined, the white parts chalked. She'd never forget the moment when he'd walked in, ordered a box of popcorn, paid her his dime, and then turned away—the whole time with a small, shy smile on his face. Only after he had passed through the inner doors did she realize they hadn't said another word, but when he gave her the coin his fingers raked her palm in such a subtle way that she didn't immediately notice the small folded piece of paper dropped there along with the money until he had walked away and the next guest repeated "Miss" for what must have been the tenth or twelfth time. She had put the dime in the till and slipped the note into her pocket, where it stayed until the movie started and the ushers had gone outside for a smoke.

You will be mine.

Her heart had thundered as she quickly refolded the note, unfolded it again, read it again, folded it, ran to the ladies' lounge and sat on a vanity stool, attempting to catch her breath. It was no use. She'd gone to a sink and splashed cold water on her face, and then she'd held tightly to the porcelain edge, gazing at the girl in the mirror. Her eyes had never been so clear, her lips so soft, and her brow so smooth. And yet a ripple of insecurity played there, barely detectable. How could Bobby be so sure of everything? She was only just learning to trust her instincts and here was this boy—man—who was so confident and divine. After the movie had finished, he'd asked her with due formality for a date, to this dance. They were starting from the beginning, with all the proper etiquette lending the courtship a languid kind of old-fashioned romance she desired in the wake of her recent disillusionment.

Emmy briskly walked up to the theater a few minutes early. She couldn't see the Fargo Sweptside on either curb, so she ducked inside to primp in front of the mirror. On Wednesday after school she had taken the bus over the river to the Herbst Department Store and carefully selected a few items of makeup. When the woman behind the counter asked her what she needed, Emmy had turned so red that the woman laughed and said, "Well, I guess it's not blusher!" This made Emmy laugh, too, and the clerk showed her how to apply the powder from a compact and blusher with a small, soft sponge.

When she got to work that night the makeup was still on and she noticed how the male customers looked more carefully at her as they paid. Before she had gone home she had assiduously removed all signs of the paint. She didn't need Karin to give her an ironic lecture on what happens to painted girls. As Emmy delicately reapplied the foundation and powders, she tried a little fox-trot move in front of the mirror, steps she had surreptitiously learned from a library book during study hall. Asking Miss Lily for the book had filled her with a wicked shame, but so many nice boys and girls went to the canteen and to the dances and proms. Certainly they couldn't all be bound for hell?

Emmy threw everything into her purse and ran out of the theater. There he was, standing in front of the gleaming Sweptside in the last light of the day. He opened her door, and a streetlight flickered on, creating in Emmy a dazzling surge of energy that started somewhere in the middle of her chest and spun outward to where Bobby's fingers touched hers as she climbed into the cab. She settled within the heady cocoon, letting it be real, no longer just the memory of a cold night spent in his company.

"Gosh, Emmy," he said, entering from the street side and starting the engine. "It feels like a lifetime since Wednesday. I thought I would die before tonight arrived."

"I sort of feel like I have," she replied, laying her hand open on the seat between them and closing her eyes at his melting touch. "I don't see how heaven could be any sweeter."

Cruising Broadway this time was much different than the night she had gone with Bev and Howie. Then she'd been trapped in the middle in the backseat of the car; here she was riding high up on the thick red upholstery, deliriously happy to be out with Bobby and far away from any single person who knew her as Emmaline Nelson. You couldn't help looking twice at the

Sweptside, its cherry red and vanilla paint swanning from the headlights to the taillights, where the truck bed widened instead of narrowed.

"She's the only truck made with fins," Bobby said. "Bought her with my own money, just this year. All that work for my dad finally added up to something."

Emmy gazed at the other, older cars that most teens drove. "It's something, all right. Like an ocean liner, almost."

Bobby slapped his thigh. "That wasn't what I was going for, but now that you mention it, yeah, I guess it kind of is."

The Fargo Armory loomed up ahead at the corner of Broadway and First Avenue South, its somber façade adorned with a few fanciful crenellations that did nothing to subdue the forbidding nature of the architecture.

They parked across from the entrance, a small white colonnade that was attached to the side of the building, and over which was a brightly lit sign. As Emmy watched smartly dressed young people hurry through the glass doors, she suddenly didn't feel as bold about her ability to fit in. Her spring coat seemed shamefully old and threadbare in the light of the cab as Bobby opened her door.

"Ready to have some fun?" he asked. Emmy nodded, letting his evident glee overcome her doubts, and walked up the path on his arm.

Inside, the band was in full swing, playing "Satin Doll." People were everywhere, on the dance floor, by the concession stand, sitting along the side tables. There were a few kids her age, but mostly it seemed to be a slightly older crowd, with some patrons older than Emmy's parents populating a nondancing section near the band. From a distance she noticed a gray-haired couple who looked as though they were dressed for church, sitting with a man in a dark suit, and it dawned on her that people could be here for the music as much as for the dance. Bobby took her things to the coat check as she watched the explosion of colorful dresses spinning and crinolines flashing out on the floor. There were many full-circle skirts, propped by acres of tulle, but there was also the occasional sack-shaped dress, and even a few fashions that were considerably out-of-date. Emmy looked down at her own gray wool pleated skirt and Birdie's fitted short-sleeved pink sweater. Pretty enough, but decidedly humble—the skirt had been advertised as reversible, which had seemed clever at the time of ordering it from the

Sears, but felt a good deal less so in this grand room. Apart from the skirt, it was her slope-heeled Sunday shoes that she knew would expose her for what she was—a girl from the wrong side of the river, north of the tracks. Her eyes stung as she gazed up at the sparkling ball hanging from the middle of the room, but before she could give in to the rising fear of not belonging, Bobby came up beside her, put his arm around her waist, and escorted her out onto the floor. She had no idea how to dance to this music, so she looked deep into Bobby's eyes and let him lead her into an effortless swirl of movement.

"Emmy," he whispered into her ear. "I've been dreaming of this moment my whole life. Feeling like this, with someone like you." His smooth cheek brushed against hers as he swung her in a circle and held her eyes with his own.

"You know, don't you?" she replied in wonder. "You just know." The slight smile slipped from his face, revealing all the vulnerability that lay open, ready for her to claim, beneath his effortless charm. He tightened his grip on her and she managed to avoid stepping on his feet too much, closing her eyes against joyful tears. He smelled of Ivory soap—clean and perfect and male. She let go of all her thoughts and wrapped her senses in the moment, the throb of the standing bass, the salty taste in her mouth, the scent of Bobby, the softness of his hand in hers. She opened her eyes and knew that she could live here, right here, under the light-splitting scales of the rotating crystal ball, even if it meant never again knowing anything or anyone familiar or safe.

"Hey, Doyle!" Pete Chaklis appeared out of nowhere with a petite woman nestled under his arm. Bobby let go of Emmy, turning back into his easygoing self. Pete looked at Emmy, smirked, and drew Bobby slightly away.

"Hey, Pete!" Bobby shook his friend's hand. "When'd you get home?" Bobby grabbed the woman to him in a huge hug. "Sally, I'm so sorry about your mom. You okay?" Emmy stood aside, unnerved by Pete's disregard, as though she were nothing more than a floor lamp waiting to be turned on. She retreated a couple of steps, contemplating a run to the bathroom or perhaps right out the door. This was not the place for her at all. Sally's dress was beautifully cut, covered in black lace and trimmed at the collar with just a bit of fur. It wasn't a spring look exactly, but it was stunning and the shoes were tiny, perfect patent pumps that even though they must have been four inches high didn't lift Sally up to Emmy's chin. The band finished its tune and announced a ten-minute break. When the silence momentarily fell before the rush of conversation, Emmy stepped forward and tugged on Bobby's sleeve.

"Oh, gosh, baby. I'm so sorry." Bobby put his hand at the small of her back. "Sally, this is Emmy Nelson. My best girl."

"Well, Bob," Sally said, poking him in the ribs, "you found a beauty, didn't you? Pete didn't mention any Emmy." They all turned to Pete and he shrugged. Emmy saw a look of some sort pass between Bobby and Pete, a moment broken by Sally wanting a drink.

"There's no alcohol here," Pete said. "Where do you wanna go?"

"I haven't been to the Bismarck since we got back from the funeral," she said. "I could easily murder a sloe gin fizz. Leave the coats, boys. We'll be back in fifteen."

As she followed the three friends to the door, Emmy thought she heard her name. At first she ignored the trill of a woman's voice, certain she'd been mistaken, but then Emmy felt a hand on her arm and turned to see Svenja's bright face.

"Emmy! I didn't think it could possibly be you, but it *is*," the girl exclaimed, hugging Emmy awkwardly. Emmy couldn't help seeing Svenja take in her waiting companions in one swift glance. "Is Ambrose here, too?"

"No," Emmy said, considering what being out on the town in strange company might do to her reputation, and seizing on the opportunity to fray the leash. "I'm here with friends."

"So I see," Svenja replied, tilting her head to get a better view of Emmy's company. "You know Mr. Davidson, of course."

The older man turned from the coat check behind Svenja and put his hand on the middle of her back. Emmy recognized him in an instant—the well-tailored suit, the large ring, the curdled color of his skin—and felt the hair on her arms stand in alarm.

"Hello," she said, taking a step backward. He closed the space as effortlessly as if they were dancing a waltz.

His small eyes drew slightly wider as they shifted from surprise to amusement to hooded judgment. "Hello, Emmaline. Having a night out?"

"Yes," she said, trying to gauge the level of his scrutiny. "I'm here with friends."

Mr. Davidson took Emmy by the elbow, pinching lightly at her skin. "As are we. We're meeting the Hansens to hear some music and celebrate Svenja's betrothal to their son."

"Yes," Svenja said without enthusiasm.

"Congratulations," Emmy said, suddenly placing the trio she'd seen near the bandstand. "Aren't you pleased?"

"He's a good man, one of the council's hardest workers," Mr. Davidson admonished Svenja.

"I'll be a June bride after all," Svenja said lightly. "See you on Sunday." She kissed Emmy's cheek and headed into the ballroom.

"Watch yourself," Mr. Davidson said to Emmy in a much harsher tone. "Coming here to listen to music is one thing; dancing with a Catholic boy when you're spoken for, quite another. But, of course, Ambrose knows of your whereabouts."

Emmy shook her head slightly, as much a yes as a no. Viewed from the outside, her actions were decadent, unconscionable, no matter how justified she had felt entering the hall. The smirk on Mr. Davidson's face clawed at her. "He will soon," she said, her voice stronger than she felt.

Mr. Davidson watched Svenja cross the room. "Pity he chose you," he said, licking at his moist lower lip. "She's much better suited for breeding."

"How can you say such a thing?" Emmy said slowly, her temper barely controlled. "She's not a farm animal."

"Of course not." Mr. Davidson laughed, the sound deep in the barrel of his chest. "I was just going after your goat, which was far easier to get than I imagined." He touched his fingertips to his brow in salute. "Until next time," he said, and turned to find the Hansens.

Emmy watched as he made his way across the floor as though he had cut the wood planks and laid them himself. She rubbed her arms and jumped at Bobby's hand landing on her shoulder.

"You ready?" he asked, turning her around.

"I need to go home," she said, bringing to a sudden end her experiment in dangerous living. "I shouldn't be here."

Bobby motioned to Pete and Sally to wait another minute by the door. "What's the matter, baby?"

"I'm engaged to Ambrose," she said quietly, pinching her eyelids shut. "Until I break it off, this can't be." Emmy bowed her head, relief winning out over her confusion. He lifted her chin and she met his understanding gaze.

"When you break it off," he said, glancing at Pete and whispering, "I'll be right here."

❧

Emmy waited for the news of her debauchery to swing through the community and turn up in her own house. But the closer Easter Sunday crept without so much as a whisper, the more likely it seemed that her secret had gone unshared. She could only surmise that Mr. Davidson preferred her marrying Ambrose to not, and that Svenja wanted Emmy's track to remain twinned to her own. Palm Sunday came and went in an uneventful blur as she slipped out of church untested, driving the family car directly back to Moorhead without stopping for dinner at the Branns', using the excuse of science exam studying as her shield. No mention was made by either of her parents of her night out dancing. The burden of ending the betrothal remained squarely on Emmy like a chafing yoke.

By the time the two families were once again gathered at Grandmother Nelson's meticulously set Easter dinner table—the company china, the polished silver, the slick ham, and the buttered mashed potatoes—Emmy was determined she'd get the refusal out immediately after, when she planned to ask Ambrose to drive her into Moorhead for her Sunday shift at the theater. But as she sat in the yellow full-skirted cotton jumper she'd made in home economics, and watched Mr. Brann cut the honey-glazed ham into thick slices, and endured her sister's incessant twittering, and abided the endless political diatribe of her erstwhile childhood companion, each sweep of the second hand moved her closer to having to sit in that truck cab and suppress the anger of what he had done to her that night; stomaching how able he had proven himself to lunge past it all in his boorish way. She knew that without a witness, any proclamation she might make to him would rest unheard, providing him with ample opportunity to restake his claim.

"Emmaline," her mother barked, snapping Emmy's ponderous stupor. "You haven't plated or passed."

Emmy looked at the empty white circle in front of her and suddenly stood. All sound stopped, and she could finally hear in her head what she then said aloud. "Ambrose, I am sorry, but I can't marry you." She sat, resettled her napkin, and waited for the storm.

Everyone turned to Ambrose, except for Christian, who cleared his throat with a grunt, a noise that bolstered Emmy's resolve.

"You can and you will," Ambrose said. For once it was his face that purpled with embarrassed constriction.

"I can't and I won't," Emmy said as slowly and gently as she would to an infant. "You understand."

Mr. Brann stood over his son. "Do not just sit there," he said, taking Ambrose by the collar and yanking him up by the neck like a limp puppy. "I've heard enough." They moved in a huddled mess toward the door, followed swiftly by Birdie, who was just as immediately restrained by Karin, and turned to the staircase, where the girl broke free and ran upstairs in a clatter of tears. Karin stopped.

"You will make this right," she said, addressing the floor before following after Birdie.

Perhaps, Emmy thought as she looked at the uneaten food around her—the usual assortment of vegetables that had hibernated in the basement all winter in either jars or burlap bags, the giant muscle of a once beloved animal, slicked with honey and spice. Perhaps not. The uplift of an unplanned action lent itself to a banquet of new possibility, and she picked up a fork, speared a pale green bean as though it were as important as what had just happened, folded it into her mouth, and chewed. Her left hand lay calmly in her lap as her father eased up out of his chair and helped Lida away from the table and into the parlor, her grandmother murmuring a dismissive "She'll come around; they always do." The rest of their conversation was lost to Emmy, and she felt strangely cleansed by the sound of frantic pacing and door slamming that was coming from the women upstairs. It made what had happened real in a way that eased her conscience for the first time in weeks, maybe even months. She glanced at the ceiling, wondering how long it would take Karin to regroup and come downstairs to level whatever judgment she was contemplating.

Emmy watched as Christian tuned the radio to Easter-appropriate music to soothe his mother, and then walked past Emmy before going to consult with his wife. He patted Emmy on the head, but she was unable to tell if it was out of pity or pride.

"That's one way to do it," he said, a small hint of approval in his voice. He sighed as he climbed the stairs.

Emmy took a bite of the ham, chewed it until the honey taste drifted away and only pulpy salt remained. Swallowed. Listened to the music swell in the other room, and above that the guttural sound of her grandmother snoring. Took a sip of water. Then they came, the footsteps that would either fall behind her or turn away. Christian walked into the room and handed Emmy her spring coat and small, straw hat.

"Saddle up, little sister," he said, using a term of endearment she'd not heard in years—the one he'd given her when Birdie was born and Emmy was just a tiny little thing hanging off his flexed arm. He went out the front door, pulling his own coat solemnly over his shoulders. She took one long look around the room, touched the tablecloth, stood and walked over to her grandmother. As she leaned over to kiss Lida on the forehead, Emmy's eyes remained as dry as the dirt on a drought-parched summer's day. She put on her coat and slipped a hand-crocheted antimacassar from under Lida's arm and into her pocket before walking out the door and into the welcome unknown.

Ten

A Wet Seed Wild

Small green shoots of fresh crops dotted the recently churned and planted black fields that sped past outside of Emmy's window on the endless drive from the ruined Easter dinner back to Moorhead.

"She hasn't decided yet what to do," Christian said, his voice little different from how it ever was, which gave Emmy a deeper worry than if he'd been yelling. "But I suspect she will want you to quit the movie theater and your work with Reinhold. She seems to think you've become corrupted by one or both."

"What do *you* think?" Emmy asked, a simmering disquiet gathering steam from his relay of Karin's predictable thoughts.

"I think there's always more to the story. Are you going to tell me?" he asked, his voice unchanging.

"No," she said. "Would it matter if I did?"

"Most likely not," he admitted. "Unless there's a chance you might change your mind."

"I'm not quitting my jobs," Emmy said, ignoring his suggestion. He hadn't turned on the heat during the drive and Emmy was numb above the cold ice of her blood, her body racked with shivering that showed no signs of stopping. When they finally pulled up in front of the small house, Christian rested one hand on the top of the steering wheel, letting the car idle.

"Go inside and take your time before you make any decisions. I might be able to bring her around, but it's doubtful. She's got a mouthful of hornets like I've never seen."

"If bringing her around entails me changing my mind, then you certainly haven't seen them," Emmy said, the quaking hurting her jaw as she spoke.

Christian looked at Emmy, his eyes clouded by frustration, yet each time he blinked they were cleared for a moment by freshly unspent tears. "I'm afraid that unless you stop all of . . . this"—he gestured above the dashboard, an action Emmy took to mean breathing—"and fix things with Ambrose, then I don't think she'll bend and let you stay."

"What does that even mean?" Emmy's face burned as she bundled her fists deeper into her coat pockets. She felt a small rip beginning in the lining of the right one and eased up. "*She* won't bend," Emmy said, a strangled note. "It seems as though *I'm* the one who is expected to do all of the bending. Well, you can tell her if I'm made to choose between *this*, as you call it, and turning myself into a Brann, then I will gladly choose this."

"I can't argue," Christian said, taking his wallet from his pocket and drawing out some bills. "You might need this before too long, and I don't want her to know that I gave it to you. It's my emergency money."

Emmy counted. Fifty dollars. It was more than she could make in a month. "If there were any other way," she said, looking at him and letting the tears slip over her lower lids. "But there isn't. Please believe me." The pain in her heart felt angular, unruly.

His own tears welled. "Okay, little sister," he said. "I believe you." Christian put a hand on Emmy's shoulder and squeezed it like a board in a vise. "Still, I doubt that I can sway her. I wish I could."

Emmy dried her cheeks and met her father's gaze. "I wish you could, too," she said. "But I honestly don't care if you do." She opened the car door and strode up the walk to the small house as she heard the car start behind her and drive off back to the farm.

Emmy unlocked the front door with her key and then slipped it onto its hook on a little wooden plaque her father had crafted out of oak that hung on the wall by the coat closet. She touched the key to stop it from swinging and slowly turned her head to the right in order to make sense of the slice of time that she had stepped into—on one side her childhood, on the other, everything else. The house slept on, tidy in its frayed collection of cast-off furnishings, its scant bits of homey touches or decorations. Jesus on the wall, standing in front of a door and raising His hand to knock. A calendar from the sugar beet plant hanging on a nail over the cold black telephone. Reaching for it, Emmy dropped her hand, raised it to the calendar, and put her left index finger on the date: April 6. She licked her finger and flipped up the page, counting and scanning the boxed increments of time before coming to the conclusion that graduation was six long weeks away. She flipped another page and saw the June wedding date noted in Karin's compressed scrawl.

A sudden calm rushed over Emmy. I am free. The words drifted over and over through her head as she paced slowly toward the kitchen, throwing her coat on the davenport as she passed through the living room and not stopping until she reached the sink. Turning on the cold tap, Emmy leaned over at the waist and drank directly from the icy stream of it, deep and long until her teeth hurt and she forgot that she was drinking water but instead felt as though air were entering her mouth in a new, refreshing way. She gripped the counter with both hands and righted her body before turning off the tap and pushing away from the kitchen, and went back through the living room and quickly up the stairs into her bedroom. She didn't bother to change out of the dress that had given her so much pleasure to sew, and instead set about packing.

It didn't take Emmy long to stack her possessions on her bed. Plenty of worn coverlet showed in a neat rectangle around the clothes and books like a picture frame around how small and uncomplicated her life had been up until this moment. Snapping her fingers, she remembered the small pearl-white suitcase her mother had bought for her with nine books of carefully saved Green Stamps. It was meant to be a wedding present. Emmy rushed into her parents' bedroom and located the case inside of their closet, resting on the floor between Karin's few pairs of shoes and Christian's only other pair. Is it mine? Emmy wondered, puzzled by the rules of this game. She remembered the trip she'd taken with Karin to the Green Stamps store, walking down the aisles and letting her fingers dust the lovely objects that the coupons earned from many months of buying groceries and gasoline. In particular she had settled on a jewelry box that looked like a miniature dressing table, with red velvet compartments for rings, slatted shelves for clip-on earrings, and tiny hooks from which to drape necklaces. Emmy didn't own any of these objects, but the whimsy of the tiny piece of furniture made her smile until Karin had said her name and told her to hurry along to the suitcase section. This was the one Karin had picked out as "dainty, good enough for a three-day trip," as though that was the limit of time anyone needed to be anywhere else. Emmy hovered over the suitcase for a protracted moment, her head throbbing with the desire to be gone by the time her mother returned.

Emmy lightly slapped her own cheek, stood up, and grabbed the handle of the suitcase, walking briskly and evenly down the hall, where she set the thing on Birdie's bed, unclasped the brass hardware, and flung open the top half, which landed against her sister's coverlet with a dull thud. Quickly placing all of her possessions into its void, she realized that she had only acquired enough in her life so far to be away for three days anyway.

She scrawled a note that simply read *I've gone to stay with my friend Bev Langer*, and left it on her neatly tucked bed. After looking around her bedroom one last time, Emmy checked her watch and hurried down the stairs to the phone, calling Cindy at home and asking if she could cover at the theater until Emmy arrived, just in case she was waylaid. A manic energy began to bubble as she sped up the pace of departure, closing lights and doors behind her as though a vacuum were pulling her out the front door and off down the street, ten blocks south, five blocks west, two more blocks south until she stood quite still at the top of Bev's walk, swaying a bit from the effort it had taken not to abide by Karin's rules for one more second. A chill spring gust blew up her skirt and swept her hat into a budding apple tree. Emmy pinched the bridge of her nose. There would be no crying, she told herself. The sound of Bev's door opening caused a brief moment of panic—what if they didn't take her in? Foolishness. She snatched her hat off the branch, gripped it firmly to her brow, and walked toward the house.

"May I help you?" the woman at the door asked, a look of suspended merriment on her face. Her snowy white hair peaked at each temple and was pulled into a high bun, which matched the color of her simple silk blouse. It took Emmy by surprise to see that the woman was wearing wide-leg burgundy slacks on a Sunday. Even though her skin showed far fewer of the lines and spots of age than Lida's, the woman was easily old enough to be Bev's grandmother. Sounds of laughter and curiosity flowed from the dining area, where Emmy could just make out the end of a long table covered with food. The warmth of the room pulled her a step forward. It was then she remembered that it was still Easter Sunday, and that she had been invited to this very dinner. Her chest tightened as she took a closer look at the woman holding the door open.

"Are you Josephine Randall?" Emmy asked.

"I am." The woman nodded. "And who might you be?"

"Emmaline Nelson," Emmy said, holding out her hand.

"Well, I never." Josephine gripped Emmy's arms with hands that were as strong as they were gnarled, steadying Emmy for a closer look. "Is it really you?" Mirrored in Josephine's face were Emmy's own fine, high cheekbones, deep blue eyes, and full, curved lips.

"We look alike," Emmy said, unaccustomed to finding familiarity in another's face.

"Perhaps once," Josephine said, gently pulling Emmy into the room and closing the front door behind her. "Are you hungry?"

"Oh, Emmy, you did come!" Bev emerged from the dining room and rushed to Emmy in a newly clumsy way, her joyful greeting subdued by the sight of Emmy's suitcase. "What's wrong?"

"I left," Emmy said. "I broke the engagement off and left." Once she had said it aloud, the cumulative import of her actions shocked through Emmy, draining her of the energy with which she had done it all.

"Bev?" A woman wearing a blue satin chemise that matched the color of the house came into the room, still holding a cream linen napkin. "Everything all right here?"

"Yes, Mother," Bev said with a proud grin. The roundness of her stomach had taken on an oblong, pointed shape under her empire waist dress. "Better than all right." She took Emmy's empty hand and squeezed it. "Everything is just fine. This is Emmy."

Mrs. Langer extended her arm and beckoned. "My dear, come join us at the table." Emmy detected in the handsome woman's expression a hint of pity, enough to indicate that Bev had told her mother the grimmest details of Emmy's life.

"Thank you very much for the offer." Emmy glanced at her watch, surprised to see that it was already time for her to be at the theater. "But I'm late for work, and I really just came to . . ." She looked at Bev, then Mrs. Langer, and finally Josephine. The shine on their expectant faces urged Emmy to let go of her doubt, and accept that they were all prepared to throw feathers under her head should she slip and fall. "I . . . I came to ask if I could stay for a little while."

"Oh, Mother," Bev said. "We must."

Mrs. Langer hesitated. "It's that serious?"

Emmy nodded. Her knees began to wobble, and she gripped the edge of a nearby armchair. Why had she thought this would be the easier way? The Langers had enough problems of their own, and Emmy knew she'd made a terrible blunder. "I'm sorry, I should have thought this through."

"I'm sorry, dear, but my parents are in the guest room, and, well, you can see that Beverly's nearly due." Mrs. Langer looked at Josephine and raised her shoulders. Josephine snapped her lips like closing a purse, a look of contemplation building in her eyes.

"Listen," she said to Emmy. "I'll drive you home, and you can talk this over with your parents."

"Thank you very much," Emmy said, taking an unsteady step backward. She fought the burning sting of tears that threatened to cloud more of her judgment even as her brain started hurtling toward other possibilities. Perhaps she could ask Cindy at work for a night on her couch, or maybe Emmy could just wait until the movie theater cleared out and sleep there for the night. "But I'm late for work at the movie theater, and I can walk the six blocks just as easily." Her armpits went damp, and there was nothing she wanted more than to undo the past fifteen minutes, maybe even the past fifteen hours.

"I'll drive you," Josephine said as she retrieved a camel hair cape from the coat closet. "We can talk on the way."

"I'm truly sorry, dear," Mrs. Langer said, opening the door. "The Langer house is already up to the rafters with its own nonsense. I doubt you'd find it comfortable here."

Bev hugged Emmy. "It will be okay, I promise. Trust me when I say it could be worse."

"Perhaps," Emmy said, wishing she could afford her friend's easy optimism.

Josephine linked her arm in Emmy's and led her up the walk. "My car's right over here. Let's get out of this wind. I hate wind."

"So do I," Emmy said as they approached a well-kept emerald green–colored station wagon with wood-paneled sides. It was exactly the kind of car Emmy had imagined Josephine Randall owning.

"Wait." Josephine turned her head just as the town siren began to wail. "Smoke. Let me take that." Josephine pointed at the suitcase. It had been clutched so hard in Emmy's right hand that it had begun to feel as though her fingers had grown into the leather handle. She released it, the burning smell intensifying as the siren rose into its fourth signal.

"It's close," Josephine said as the air seemed to fill with the smaller, jarring shrieks of fire trucks.

They hurried into the car and Josephine swung the tail out into the street, smoothly completing the turn and pulling onto Eighth Street behind a careening ambulance. Emmy looked at her watch. She was late enough that Cindy would have started the popcorn and set up the counter for the early show. As they neared the onlooker-choked intersection at Main Avenue, Emmy's dread spiraled into panic as she saw the black plume of smoke rising down the street. Josephine stopped the car and Emmy leaped out, pushing through the crowd, her feet swiftly rising with the throttle of her heart. She came to a sudden stop as she saw the flames licking at the high point of the Moorhead Theatre sign.

"Good Lord," Josephine said as she came up beside Emmy.

"I was supposed to be there," Emmy said, moving forward more slowly, her pace slackened by the surreal spectacle of the neon lights still aglow inside of the flames. They made their way up the street, to where two police cars were parked at a slant, and a handful of men were directing traffic and people away. Three fire trucks arced in front of the theater, streams of water shooting uselessly into the rapidly disintegrating façade.

"Come on." Josephine strode forward and Emmy followed her toward a barrier in front of the candy store where a crowd stood—some with

Easter-bright clothing visible under their hastily donned overcoats, others holding the hands of wide-eyed children. Josephine nodded at one officer and then walked up to a second, who was holding a bullhorn.

"Hello, Eli," she said, shaking his hand. "How'd it start?"

"No idea," the officer said. "Won't know until they put it out, but the smoke came from the back, possibly the basement, and spread fast." He glanced at Emmy. "We pulled a girl out of the basement, but everyone else walked out."

"Is she all right?" Emmy asked, sickened by how close she'd come to being that girl, then doubly worried when she realized that Cindy could be hurt.

"Don't know," Eli said, taking off his cap and wiping sweat from his bald head with a large white handkerchief. "They took her over to Saint Ansgar's."

Emmy spotted Mr. Rakov near the farthest fire truck, sitting on the curb, with a blanket wrapped around his shoulders, his face streaked with tears as he watched the building burn. He lived alone in a small apartment over the front of the theater. Emmy looked at Josephine. "I should go see if Mr. Rakov needs anything."

"Would that be all right, Eli?" Josephine asked. "Emmy's my niece. She works here. Or, at least she did."

"Tough break, kid." Eli took a step back. "Just be careful, and stay out of the way."

Emmy nodded and moved through the loud and chaotic space as carefully as she could manage, the heat and the smoke blowing into her face with the gusts of wind. Mr. Rakov was staring straight past her as she approached, the flickering light of the fire dancing in his watery gray eyes. His thin body curled like a cooked shrimp, rocking slowly and causing the wisps of loose white hair on the top of his scalp to float like a gossamer halo.

"Mr. Rakov," Emmy said gently. "Are you all right?" She carefully sat next to him on the curb and touched his shoulder. He started and the blanket fell around his waist. His shirt was torn on the left sleeve, revealing the pink underside of his forearm, where a series of blue numbers was inked in a line, underscored at one end by a tiny triangle. He looked up at her and followed her gaze, quickly pulling the blanket around his arm.

"I am not bad guy," he said in his dolefully accented English. "I don't want trouble."

"Of course not," Emmy said, her own struggle dwarfed by his anguish. "I'm sorry."

"Why this?" he cried, pushing her away. "Go." His head sank to his knees and his body shook. Emmy patted his back for a minute, then stood, awkward in her inability to know what she should do.

"Just leave me be!" he shouted, and Emmy jumped backward.

"I'll pray for you," she said, shaken, turning away. Emmy rubbed her brow with a soot-smeared sleeve and, momentarily blinded, nearly tripped over a snaking hose.

"Get out of the way," a fireman yelled, grabbing her arm. She looked up to see Pete Chaklis. "You?" His annoyance flared with recognition. "What the hell are you doing here?"

Emmy shook her head. "I was supposed to be at work."

"You're in the way," Pete said. He walked her away from Mr. Rakov.

"That's my boss," she said. "He needs help."

"We've got it," Pete said. "Run on home now."

She nodded, turning away and walking back to the barricade, where Josephine was talking to a man with a fedora slanted in such a way that Emmy could not see his face.

"Emmy, this is Jim Klein," Josephine said as Emmy approached. "My grandniece sells tickets at the theater."

"Popcorn," Emmy corrected, as though it mattered anymore. Jim tipped his head enough to see her sideways from under the brim of his hat, and then raised his square chin toward the marquee.

"Shame. I wanted to see that one," he said.

Emmy stared at the title she knew so well, *The Brothers Karamazov*. She'd watched parts of it through the round window two nights before, drawn by the sultry cadence of Yul Brynner's voice. "It's Russian," she said, shaking her head. She looked at Jim.

"So I've heard," he said. He took a long notepad from his pocket and a stubby pencil from where it was perched over his left ear. "What's at the back of the theater?" he asked as he jotted something down.

Emmy hesitated. "Why?"

"Jim works for the *Forum*," Josephine said. "I got him his first job there, in fact."

"She never lets me forget it, either." Jim smiled gratefully.

"The alley door, where employees enter," Emmy responded. "Sometimes boys sneak in that way to skip the admission, but Mr. Rakov mostly keeps an eye on it."

"Where's it lead?" Jim asked.

"There's a door into the theater, and to the left a flight of stairs to the basement, where there's a storage area and slop sink," Emmy replied. "Not much else. Does it matter?"

"Probably not," Jim said. "Can just anyone gain access?"

"I guess so," she said, worried about Cindy. Past Jim and far down the street, beyond the barricades and onlookers, she thought she could see the rectangular brown nose of Ambrose's truck parked two blocks away. Her rejection of him seemed decades removed, not a handful of hours earlier.

"Excuse me," Emmy said, her voice husky from the scorched air.

Exhausted and dismayed, she walked away from Jim and Josephine, dodging rescue workers. Ambrose walked toward her at the same measured pace, and a flood of sympathy overwhelmed Emmy's grip on the day. Had she acted in haste? Was it possible that her decisions had set bad things in motion? She couldn't weigh the responsibility of it all, nor could she comprehend why he would be here now. They stopped with three feet between them.

"Thank God you're okay," Ambrose said, his hands shaking in the void, without a welcome place to alight. "I came straight here as soon as we heard."

Emmy touched his fingers, surprised to find them cold. "I wasn't here."

"That's good," he said, jerking his hands away and shoving them into the pockets of his jacket. "You need to come home."

She shook her head, an automatic response. "I can't."

"Your parents are worried," he said. "They found your note, but you weren't at your friend's house when I got there."

Emmy took a step backward at the notion of being tracked around town. "I thought you said you came straight here?" Over Ambrose's shoulder her gaze was drawn to a match flaring in the passenger seat of the truck.

Ambrose turned to look at what she saw: the jowled face of Curtis Davidson lighting a cigarette and casually tossing the stick out of the window.

Ambrose turned to her and lifted her hand. "Yes, after we went there."

"Why is he here?" Emmy asked, a knot of anger rising inside her. "Did he come to watch the Communist Party burn?"

"We can still get married," Ambrose said, ignoring her comment. "If you'll apologize."

"Apologize?" Emmy asked, withdrawing her hand sharply. "For what?"

He looked surprised at her refusal. "You've done me and your family wrong." He glanced away, at the fire, his jawline white with the effort of holding it firm. "We're meant to be. Don't you see?"

Emmy studied his face and comprehended for the first time the wreckage her actions had blown apart in him. "No, I don't see," she said, grounding her words in compassion. "I didn't plan this."

"The plan isn't ours, Emmy," Ambrose said, and straightened his posture until he loomed over her. His expression resumed its angular formality as he gazed heavenward. "Curtis says—"

"Is there one thing," Emmy interrupted, then paused. She thought back, way back to when she was small and recalled how often Ambrose would say things like *your grandfather says* and *my father thinks*. He was a funnel for every thought poured into him by the nearest influence. "Is there one thing you say or do because it's your idea?"

His face crumpled. "Is that how you see me?" He squeezed his angular nose, wincing with the pain. "It's God's plan, Emmy," he suddenly shouted. "Not mine, not anyone's. You must see that."

Nodding slowly, Emmy moved away from Ambrose. "You may be right," she said, backing up the sidewalk in the direction of Josephine's car, away from him. "But I don't forgive you."

"*You* don't forgive *me*?" he spat, pointing his finger at her. "And He said, 'though your sins be as scarlet, they shall be as white as snow; though they be red like crimson, they shall be as wool. If ye be willing and obedient, ye shall eat the good of the land.'"

Emmy shook her head slowly. "I have to go," she said, and turned away, stung by the hypocrisy of his words. She shouldn't have said the things she'd said, shouldn't have tried to hurt him. It wasn't in her nature to be mean, and the way it made her head throb caused her to hug her arms around her waist in an attempt to navigate the sidewalk without tripping again.

By the time she reached Josephine's car, Emmy was so overcome with emotion that gripping the door handle and squeezing the button with her thumb was more than she could do. She checked to make certain that Ambrose hadn't followed her, and was relieved to see Josephine approach. Emmy gathered up the might to open the door and eased onto the rough fabric of the seat.

"I'm sorry about this," Josephine said as she started the engine. "Rotten way to strike out on your own."

"I'm just so tired," Emmy said, resting her head against the cool window, not wanting to talk about how she really felt: desperate, sad, and alone. "I know you think I should go home, but I really can't do it. If you know of a cheap hotel, I have enough to cover tonight."

"Nonsense," Josephine said. "You'll stay with me."

"I'd be very grateful." A rush of relief came over Emmy, but then she remembered Cindy's predicament, and all self-pity fled. "Do you think she's okay? The ticket girl?"

"Probably not," Josephine said, patting Emmy's leg once. "But you will be."

They drove up Eleventh Street, past the sugar plant and around a bend in the road that curved past a cemetery. The sky had clouded and large drops of rain splashed the windshield. Josephine turned on the headlights and the wipers.

"This rain could have happened sooner," she said, leaning forward to look out at the sky. "I'll have to show you around the place after school tomorrow. You can take the car, I'll use the truck if need be. When you get back, we can go to your parents." The wagon slowed as they neared a stretch of enormous elm trees, and Josephine turned the steering wheel to the left. They drove down a lane that opened into a yard encircled by a series of low-slung white buildings that dotted the perimeter of the drive where Josephine parked. A porch light glowed from the one that looked most like a house.

Emmy followed Josephine to the door and into a well-lit room that was half kitchen and half dining room, dominated by a round oak table with claw feet and cozy-looking chairs set next to the coal-fired heater, in front of which a cat lay curled, asleep.

"That's Flossie," Josephine said as she slung her cape over a chair. "Don't even bother trying to get to know her. She only has eyes for me and will break your heart if you dare to think otherwise." On mention of her name, Flossie looked up at Emmy, yawned, and set her chin back on her crossed paws, leaving her eyelids slightly open as she returned to her doze.

"I've never had a house cat," Emmy said, resisting the urge to stroke Flossie. "Mother always said she didn't need another mouth to feed."

"Well, maybe when you graduate, she can get one." Josephine cocked an eyebrow and moved through an arched doorway into the parlor. A small stone fireplace framed the wall on one side, and the rest of the room was filled with a collection of old and new pieces of furniture whose unifying theme seemed to be comfort over beauty. The room was a bit disheveled, with a used teacup delicately perched on a side table, magazines strewn across the umber velour fainting couch, and an overflowing ashtray sloped on the arm of a chair. It occurred to Emmy that Josephine didn't need to bother with tidiness if she didn't feel like it, as there wasn't another person to notice the mess. In the far corner of the room was a narrow staircase. Josephine disappeared up it with the suitcase, causing Emmy to leave her inspection of the lower floor for later.

"My bedroom is below this one, but I mostly sleep out in the Jeep house, as I tend to work best when the world is asleep, and then I can't be bothered to come back inside," Josephine said as Emmy reached the top of the stairs and found a small landing, to the left of which was a fairly large open room wallpapered in dusky red roses. The ceiling slanted mere inches above her head at its highest point, necessitating Emmy to duck down a little as she moved around the welcoming space. Josephine went to the bed and swiftly gathered sheets of newspaper that had been laid on top of the coverlet. "Keeps the mice off," she said. "Without the stink of mothballs."

"It's charming," Emmy said, noticing a gabled nook where a foot-pedaled sewing machine exactly like her grandmother's sat next to a stack of neatly folded cloth of varying hues. "Do you sew?"

"Not as often as I would like." Josephine lifted the topmost cloth from the pile, letting the blue seersucker material drape to the floor in front of her. "I thought this might make a nice skirt for summer, though I don't know why I would think that since I prefer to wear pants. I just can't seem to resist buying beautiful fabric."

"I could make one for you," Emmy said, taking the cloth and carefully refolding it. "I made this dress. It was really hard right here, where it gathers at the waist, but I only had to rip out the seam once."

"It's truly beautiful," Josephine replied, looking at her watch and going back down the stairs. "There's a bathroom off of the kitchen," she called in place of good night. "And fend for yourself for breakfast. There's eggs."

"Thanks, I will," Emmy called back, suddenly feeling very alone. She sat on the edge of the blue chenille bedspread, not wanting to mess up the tightly tucked corners, and listened to the rain pellet down on the roof. It was a sound reminiscent of the years her family had lived in the migrant shack. Before she could think any more about the day, Emmy laid her head on the pillow, curled her feet up under the crinoline underskirt of her dress, and drifted into a restless sleep.

Eleven

A Goodly Heritage

The high-pitched sound of an animal shrieking jolted Emmy awake, and she rushed to the window, where the first light of day was breaking behind a tiny white house in the backyard. Another louder cry echoed on the other side of the main house, and Emmy hurried into her shoes and down the stairs, careful not to hit her forehead on the low overhang at the bottom of the flight. The screams were now coming from either side of the house. She opened the front door, and there stood a large bird with a dark blue body and a tail that stretched out far behind, dragging in the grass. At the sight of Emmy, the tail flipped up and fanned out until the feathers reached a height of nearly three feet, resplendent in their multicolored shades of blue and green. She'd never seen anything like it. The bird elongated its neck and let forth with yet another shocking scream, answered almost immediately by a softer yelp from the other side of the house.

"Oh, stop already," Emmy cajoled, shooing the beautiful creature around after its mate. The two birds ran off into the trees, reunited. She looked down to see her Easter dress completely rumpled, and she caught a whiff of the smoke that clung all over her. The miniature abode behind the main house was dark, and the dampness of the grass caused a tremor to shoot up Emmy's calves, making her run back to the house and into the bathroom, where she filled the tub with water as hot as she could stand. Looking in the mirror, she was dismayed to see the dark blue shadows under her eyes and a smudge of soot on her forehead. Her hair was matted all over, even though she had washed it two days before.

She peeled off her clothing and stepped into the rising water, sinking into the heat of it and closing the taps with the balls of her feet. The length of her body distorted under the rippled surface of the bath, her breasts two small white islands breaking the surface. From this vantage, her flesh became less important, more ordinary than it felt when covered with the conventions of clothing. Eve had left the garden like this, and Emmy had now bit into her own apple of knowledge. Somehow her transgressions didn't feel like sin. She wanted to honor her parents, but she could neither make herself love Ambrose nor allow him to subjugate her body again.

It couldn't be much past seven, she figured, as the room grew slowly lighter with the sun. Emmy closed her eyes and rested her neck against the porcelain edge, and tried to think of the words she could use to best explain to her parents the pain in her heart. No matter what she conjured, she knew that Karin would not listen, and fresh hot tears leaked down her cheeks and into her ears. A draft blew across her shoulders, a feeling as though someone had entered the room. She opened her eyes and sat bolt upright in the tub at the sight of Flossie crouched on the back of the toilet, staring right at Emmy.

"Oh, you gave me a fright," Emmy said, covering her nudity out of instinct. "I thought you didn't like people."

Flossie licked a paw and then stepped down from her perch, passing Emmy with a flick of her tail. Emmy looked around the room for a towel, realizing too late that she hadn't had the foresight to fetch one from the washstand in her room. A swell of loneliness rose in her heart as she realized she couldn't simply yell out to Birdie to bring her one. "One small moment at a time," she said to the air. "That's how I'll do it." She hoisted her bright pink body out of the water and stood on the bath mat, wet and weary, waiting for her skin to dry.

The lunch bell rang, and Emmy rose from her desk in the study hall, passing by Mr. Utke's darkened office once more before heading to the cafeteria. She had sought him out before school, and at least twice since, hoping he would have some suggestions on where she might find a new job. The pungent smell of boiled meat permeated the short stairway leading down to the lunchroom, and Emmy's stomach lurched against the idea of the hot lunch that she had requested and paid for in first period homeroom. Josephine's larder contained only coffee and eggs—no bread or milk, nor even a pat of butter—and Emmy had been unable to pack any sort of lunch for herself. She took her place in line, picking up a metal tray and utensils and moving along the service counter, where scoops of pinkish beef, orange macaroni, and slippery halves of peaches were loaded onto plates and bowls. Following the lead of the girl in front of her, Emmy selected her meal, moved down the line, and chose a small glass that she filled with milk from a large stainless steel dispenser. Turning, she momentarily froze at the sight of so many rowdy students swirling effortlessly among the tables and benches, free of the kinds of challenges she had brought to rest upon her own shoulders. She saw a half-empty table near the back of the room where she and Bev used to sit together, so she wound her way there in search of a quiet place to think. Though she'd eaten her bag lunch in this room all year, the weight of the tray balanced in her hands somehow made the atmosphere feel as though the gathering were a thing of the far-distant past, or a place where she might one day come for a reunion, her hair gray and teeth long. Her outsider status within the school walls was amplified in her head by the self-eviction, and yet somehow she no longer felt it set her apart. One class after another would pass, and one day after the next as well, until all was finished and she'd turn her books in with the scant memories of being a Moorhead Spud. If it weren't for Mr. Utke's support of her studies, Emmy would simply drop it all and find a job. She had no intention of returning home, even though she hadn't quite figured out an alternative solution.

Once seated, Emmy drew from her book bag a copy of the morning's *Fargo Forum*, which she had bought at the grocery across the street from the school. She had already mined every line of the article about the fire, and there wasn't any sense of how the fire had started, though it was still assumed to have been a wiring malfunction. There was a passing mention of one girl injured, but beyond that, Emmy hadn't been able to find out how Cindy was faring. Instead of reading the articles again, Emmy opened the paper and turned to the back page, scanning through the four items she had circled in the want ads. In Help Wanted, she decided the only option was a position open at *The Fargo Forum* itself, for a part-time switchboard operator. It probably didn't pay much better than popcorn girl, but it was the only job where experience wasn't required, and after-school hours were available. She had also found a small room for rent in Fargo, though the notion of calling the number and taking the bus across the river to look at the desolate space sat less satisfyingly than the small bites of vile-tasting beef she put past her lips while she contemplated her future.

Emmy glanced again through the other ads, and was about to give up on the meal and prepare for her afternoon English exam when she looked up to see Birdie standing next to the table, a brown paper bag in her hand. Her eyes were puffy, as though she'd spent a good deal of time crying. A ripple of regret swelled in Emmy, and she stood, hugging her sister tightly.

"I'm so sorry I left without saying good-bye," Emmy said, releasing the girl. They sat opposite each other.

"I'm just happy to see you're okay." Birdie opened the sack and withdrew a large wax-paper-wrapped sandwich, the sight of which made Emmy's mouth water. Birdie held it in midair, a peace offering. "Looks like it's going to be ham all week. Halvsies?"

Emmy took the offered triangle and sunk her teeth into the familiar yeasty white bread. Her throat constricted with emotion and she had to drink milk to help ease the food down.

"They're waiting," Birdie said in her delicate way. "They think you're coming back. Are you?"

"I don't think so," Emmy said. "No."

"Well, Mother says this is all your fault," Birdie said. "We haven't heard from the Branns at all, not even Ambrose, and she's frantic for things to go back to normal."

Emmy dropped her sandwich, her appetite drained. How had Ambrose known about the note? "I've seen him."

"You have?" Birdie's face tensed, a slow half smile pushing across it like a wary snake. "Will you give him another chance?"

"I'm sorry, but I just don't love him. No." Emmy watched as the snake of her sister's smile retreated, leaving behind a small, inverted crescent of relief mixed with what looked like wounded consternation.

"That's all right," Birdie said, her voice like the warble of a small yellow bird in springtime. "I don't want you to."

"You don't?" Emmy could see it now: the limpid gaze; the high, fevered cheeks—the way she herself had looked in the mirror after reading Bobby's second note. "Oh, Birdie, you're too young," she scolded, knowing full well it wouldn't matter what she said if Birdie felt as strongly about Ambrose as it suddenly appeared.

"I wish I could help the way I feel." Birdie bit the corner of her lower lip with a pointed tooth, looking as though she might start to cry. "But he's really wonderful, Emmy, no matter what you may think."

"What I think," Emmy said slowly, "is that you should wait for your own beau." Her memory pivoted through the drunken roughness, the indecency, and her face evidently showed this. She wanted to tell Birdie everything, but shame stopped the words.

Birdie folded the paper around her uneaten sandwich, her eyes cast down and brimming with tears. "I knew you wouldn't approve," she said, distraught. "I really haven't told him anything, I swear. He doesn't know how I feel. If you'd married, I would have taken my feelings to the grave."

Emmy envied the easy drama of Birdie's emotions, the childlike fluttering of her eyelashes and wringing of her dainty hands, as though the girl had stepped out of the kind of dime-store novel Bev always liked to read out loud, a hand thrown back against her forehead. Of course, this was the way Emmy felt every time she pictured Bobby in the movie theater lobby, slipping her that tiny folded square of paper. "Just don't rush," Emmy said with as much generosity as she could muster. "There's no hurry for you."

"Oh, thank you, thank you," Birdie said, a fresh glow replacing the ashen fear of a moment before. She shifted her eyes to a point over Emmy's head as a hand lightly settled on Emmy's shoulder. She tipped her head to see Mr. Utke.

"Ah, good," he said. "I've been looking for both of you." The bell rang, ending the lunch period. Birdie hastily repacked her lunch bag and sprang to her feet.

"Hello, Mr. Utke," Birdie said, staring at her shoes. "I don't want to be late for class."

He cleared his throat. "Girls, your mother is parked outside, waiting to take you back to Glyndon High School. I did what I could to make her see otherwise, but it seems she doesn't feel the atmosphere here is conducive to proper behavior."

"But that's not fair," Birdie said. "My concert . . ." Her face crumpled and she started to cry.

"You'll have to go without me." Emmy stood and squeezed her arm, worried that her sister had set a course for the misery Emmy had avoided. "Maybe I can . . ."

Birdie wrenched herself away, sniffing back the tears. "You can't, Emmy. Not anymore."

"She's waiting," Mr. Utke repeated. "Go get your things."

Emmy turned to her adviser as Birdie ran away down the hall. "I'm not going."

"I surmised you wouldn't," he replied, watching the door to the cafeteria as though he expected Karin to burst through. "But frankly, I'd rather not know the whys, if it's all the same to you. Your mother is remarkably capable of speaking her mind, and at great length. It seems that I've corrupted you by supporting your wild dreams and opening your mind to literature."

"You have," Emmy said, looking around the quiet room. She extended her hand to Mr. Utke. "Thank you."

"You're welcome." He shook, bowing his head slightly.

"I wonder if there's anything in your books about operating a switchboard." She unfolded the newspaper and nervously showed him the advertisement.

Mr. Utke looked down through the bottom part of his glasses. "No, but your cousin works there—ask for Dorothy Randall. She should be able to get you in the door."

❧

At three o'clock, Emmy left the school grounds in her aunt's wagon, and ten minutes later she reached the parking lot across from a grand five-story brick building, topped on one corner by a tall spire with the letters *F-O-R-U-M* stacked on all four sides. Emmy studied the colored lights that illuminated the sign and tried to decipher their meaning while she listened to the engine quietly ping and tick as it cooled. Her nerves were jumping, but in a way that propelled her from the car, across the street, through the front doors of the building, and rapidly up a flight of stairs that led to another set of doors with FARGO written on the glass rectangle of one, and FORUM on the right. Nodding to herself for courage, she pushed against the brass handle and found the large oak door to be lighter than she'd expected. The massiveness of the open room caught her by surprise. It encompassed most of the second floor and soared up at least two floors, with windows along two sides and offices on the third. Filling the space in between were rows of desks populated by a number of smartly dressed people, including two women in fitted suits.

Emmy approached the long oaken counter that separated her from the news floor, and waited patiently as a young woman sitting in front of a large switchboard on the other side of the counter held up a finger and then pulled a cord from her desktop, expertly plugging it into a hole at the top of the board. The operator had white-blond hair just like Emmy's, a reassuring sign that she was in the right place.

"May I help you?" the woman asked Emmy.

"I hope so," Emmy replied, managing to quell her excitement at the prospect of working in such a fascinating place. She held out the well-worn newspaper. "I'm here about the switchboard job?"

"Hallelujah and hello." A red light blinked on the desk, and the woman pressed the switch under it.

"Good afternoon, *The Fargo Forum*, how may I direct your call?" she said into a mouthpiece that connected to her headset. "Oh, hiya, Carlene, it's Dot. Hang on, I'll get him for ya." She strung another cord, and a phone rang at a nearby desk. Emmy watched the man at that desk pick up the receiver, at which point Dot flipped another switch. She then turned to a girl passing with a stack of papers. "Louise, take the board for a minute, would you?" She handed the headset to the girl in exchange for the papers and stood in front of Emmy, extending her right hand over the counter. "I'm Dot Randall. These are edits. Follow me."

Emmy quickly passed through the swinging half door at the end of the counter and fell into step. "I'm Emmy Nelson," she said, expecting her name to elicit some sort of response. It didn't. "We're cousins, I think."

Dot stopped midstride and gave Emmy the once-over. "Well, I'll be damned," she said with a distinct air of bemusement. "Did someone die?"

Emmy laughed, caught off guard by the question. "No, why?"

"My mother said we'd meet over your mother's dead body." Dot shrugged.

"I'm staying with Josephine for now." Emmy lifted her shoulders. "I don't even know how you and I are related."

"Let's see." Dot scratched her head at the point where her blond ponytail was secured with a red piece of ribbon that matched the gingham blouse under her gray split-front jumper. "My father's father was Aunt Jo's older brother—right, and Adelaide's, too—which makes you and me second cousins. Technically, she's my *great*-aunt, since she was my grandfather's sister. He died in the First World War, long before I was born. So did his older brother, Hans. Tragic story—they died within two days and ten miles of each other in the battle of Meuse-Argonne, probably killed by distant relatives on the German side. Jo and Adelaide had some sort of falling-out after that, and Adelaide left, never to be heard from again. Though I guess you know that part. Anyway, Aunt Jo find you on the side of the road?" Dot tilted her head in a way that made her ponytail brush her right shoulder.

"You call her Aunt Jo?" Emmy asked, holding back the flood of questions that Dot's easy information sharing prompted.

"Yeah, but boy, does she hate it." Dot laughed. "Says it's too *Little Women* for her taste, though if you ask me, that's a pretty great book, and she's a *lot* like that Jo."

"I haven't read it," Emmy said, increasingly won over by Dot's patter.

"Well, you should." Dot put her hands on her slim hips. "You ever run a switchboard?"

"No," Emmy replied, surveying the rack of pegs and holes. "I've never even seen one."

"It's not trigonometry or anything. My mom used to run it, and Aunt Jo before her. It's sort of in our blood, I guess." Dot waved Emmy around the counter and led her past the desks, only half of which seemed to be occupied. "The job's a few nights a week, while I study for my exams. Though we could also use a copygirl, if you're interested in more hours. Louise is leaving at the end of the month to get married. We have a lot of turnover in that job, for that reason."

"I'd be happy to take whatever you have," Emmy said, following Dot through the room. "Though don't I need to formally apply? Mr. Utke at Moorhead High said you could call him on my behalf."

"To be honest, we've only had a few applicants," Dot said, winking. "The job's pretty much yours if you can do it. How is old Reinhold, anyway? Have you read *The Caine Mutiny*?" She said the title with a deep, dour accent. Emmy laughed, making Dot smile at her own cleverness. "Do yourself a favor and skip right to *Marjorie Morningstar*. To, die, for. Just don't tell him I said so." They stopped at a larger desk, set apart from the others in the front of the room, where a heavyset man wearing a sweat-stained white shirt rapidly drew lines and circles on a typewritten sheet with a thick red pencil.

"This is the boss," Dot said, and the man looked up from his work. "He looks big and mean, but he's as harmless as a baby wasp."

"Stan Gordon," he said, sticking the pencil behind his ear and extending a hand. Emmy shook it.

"Emmaline Nelson."

"She's our best shot," Dot added. "If you want, I can get her trained and see how she goes."

"Carry on, then," Stan said, reclaiming his pencil as though he'd been temporarily missing one of his fingers.

"He likes skirts, if you know what I mean," Dot whispered, leading Emmy to a door marked ARCHIVES. "This is the morgue. Don't let the name scare you; it just means where all the dead files are kept. There's a nice big table in there for doing research, should you need it. Some people take naps in there, don't ask me why. Those are the ladies and gents, and this is the most important place of all." She stopped at the final open door. "The break room, where we do our best work."

"Where you do your only work." A man's voice echoed from inside of the room. Emmy followed Dot in and realized the fellow was the reporter she'd met the night before. Hatless, and with his sleeves rolled just above the elbows, he looked much younger than she'd thought at the time. She watched him fill a cup with coffee from an aluminum urn that took up a good portion of the short counter. An odd sense of familiarity hit Emmy, almost as though she'd been waiting to see him again after a long time apart.

"Oh, Jim, you're so droll," Dot said, handing him the stack of papers. "Here's your slug copy." She hooked a thumb over her shoulder. "That's my cousin Emmy Nelson, aspiring switchboard operator and probable copygirl. Be nice."

Jim crossed the homey room, having to weave his way around two leather armchairs and a low-lit lamp that had a topaz-colored glass ashtray encircling its brass post. "Aren't you the girl from the fire?" He squinted and sniffed, as though trying to smell the evidence of smoke on her.

Emmy nodded.

"Your friend's going to live," he said, sliding his hands into his pants pockets and shrugging. "But it's going to be a hard few months."

Emmy nodded again, sick to the heart that she'd ever asked Cindy to take her place. She attempted to change the subject. "I read your article three times today. It was really good."

"Only three times?" he cajoled. "It couldn't have been very good if you didn't read it four times." Emmy smiled at him, thankful for the lightening of her mood.

"I said *be nice*," Dot said. "At least until she says yes to this crazy place, though I wouldn't wish it on my worst enemy."

"Too late." Jim lightly punched Dot's shoulder as he went through the door. "You are your worst enemy," he said with a laugh.

"Droll, droll, droll," she said to his back, and then turned happily to Emmy. "He's a little more puffed up than usual. We just heard this morning that the paper got a Pulitzer for our tornado coverage last summer."

"Is that a good thing?" Emmy asked.

"Yeah," Dot said with a bemused shake of her head. "Real good. So when can you start?"

Emmy peeled off her lightweight jacket and hung it on an empty hook on the wall, readjusting her A-line worsted beige skirt and tucking her blue nylon blouse firmly down the front. "I wouldn't mind starting now, if it's all right with you?"

Dot's smile was as big as it was instant. "Okay, cuz, I like your attitude. Monday's always quiet, so it's a good time to train. If you can't hack it, we'll know right away."

Emmy's gaze hung in the space of the empty door where Jim had just passed. "I can hack it," she murmured, and cleared her throat. "With your help."

❧

By the time her training was over at eight and she was on her way back to Josephine's, Emmy understood that the evident upside to having a cousin who talked a lot was the amount of readily transferred knowledge Emmy now possessed. She had become as intimately acquainted with the inner workings of *The Fargo Forum* as if she had been born in the break room. First, she'd committed to memory the numbers on the board that correlated with the various reporters and their names, what areas they covered, and where they all sat in the newsroom. She knew which outboxes to empty and when, how to tell if the newswire machines were jammed, and to frequently check for photographs coming over the wire on a special machine that she watched, mesmerized, as it transmitted a picture of a lady in a monstrous Easter hat from a parade in New York City, one line at a time. Her initial anxiety over whether she could handle the job ebbed as she learned each piece of it. The switchboard was the most formidable, and oddly, therefore, the easiest thing to learn. Dot was impressed by how quickly Emmy learned, and had asked her to come back the next day for a test drive on the machine by herself. If she did well, she'd have her own shift by the end of the week, at improved pay of twenty-five cents more an hour than her theater salary. The notion of having a real job, with interesting work and energetic, friendly people, settled the worry that the theater fire had begun, though she still felt distraught about Mr. Rakov's catastrophic loss and was worried sick about Cindy.

Emmy steered the wagon onto the soft dirt drive of the estate, happy to see the warm lights of the cottage. If only Emmy could find a way to explain to her aunt why she couldn't go back to her parents' house, even for one more night, she could then ask Dot if she knew of a place where she could stay longer.

The temperature had dropped considerably, with frost predicted overnight—or at least that was the weather report Dot had shared as Emmy left the building. Music could be heard as Emmy neared the front door, a song that she remembered from her childhood, something low and sweet in its yearning vocals. The words *smile the while you kiss me sweet ado* popped into Emmy's head as she heard them float through the slightly open door.

"Hello?" Emmy entered the kitchen, and her stomach growled. She realized she hadn't eaten a bite since her half of the ham sandwich at lunch. "Josephine?"

"Bring yourself a glass," Josephine said from the parlor, her voice loud over the strains of the song as it wound down, only to scratch and start again, Josephine's sweet soprano slightly higher than the tenor's rich notes. "There's a song in the land of the lily . . ."

Emmy took a glass from the cupboard and a piece of fried chicken from a discarded plate on the counter. She went into the cozy room, her eyes slowly adjusting to the dim light enough to see her aunt standing next to the wide horn of a Victrola with a delicately formed goblet in her hand that swayed to the tune as she sang it through to the end. Her hair had been released from its bun and floated in a white cloud around her shoulders, which were draped with a flowing silk gown printed with long-legged white birds. The glow of the fireplace lit Josephine's face, contorted with the sentiment of the song. At the words *till we meet again*, she held the glass in the air toward Emmy, the exquisite fabric swinging loosely from the sleeve and almost touching the floor. A messy stack of black records, some in brown paper sleeves, others without, gleamed next to the player on a side table.

"Not that glass." Josephine folded onto the fainting couch; her legs tucked one at a time under the robe. The magazines from the night before toppled onto the floor, but Josephine didn't seem to notice or care. She removed the stopper from a crystal bottle that was surrounded by more of the tiny stemware on a table next to her. The thick log in the fireplace popped and hissed in concert with the needle of the Victrola clicking around the finite circle at the center of the record. Emmy flipped the heavy round head of the player in her palm and swung it aside before selecting a goblet and holding it under the unsteady trickle of dark liquid that Josephine poured. "Claret. I only drink French wine."

"I thought you worked at night," Emmy said, perching on a rocker next to the fireplace. She took a cautious sip of the wine, expecting it to taste sweet like the grape juice used for communion at church, but found it bitter instead. The chicken, however, was delicious.

"You pay attention. I like that," Josephine said, draining her glass and refilling it. "Today's a holiday."

"Yesterday was a holiday," Emmy corrected softly. "Today's just Monday."

"See, that's where you're wrong. Some holidays are celebrations of the self, of having lived long enough to have not died." Josephine burst into a cackle, covering her mouth with a hand that had taken on spidery dimensions in the low light. "In other words, it's my birthday." She raised the glass, found it empty, and refilled it, making Emmy wonder why she didn't simply use a larger one.

"Happy birthday," Emmy said, tilting her own wine a bit less tentatively. "If I'd known I would have planned something nice."

"You *are* something nice, dear girl," Josephine said, stretching out along the couch and resting her head on her propped-up right hand. "Besides, when you reach sixty-six alone, there's hardly any reason to celebrate. Instead, I mourn." She laughed again, the sound of it like breaking glass.

"You have an odd way of mourning, I must say," Emmy replied.

Josephine leaned forward just enough to look as though she might tip onto the rug between them, and focused her gaze on Emmy. "Scarlet fever took Mother when I was ten. My father drank himself into the grave next to hers when I was fourteen. My brother Hans joined the army and enjoyed it so much that my other brother, Otto, went right along after, leaving his pregnant wife and four children behind. If you want to meet my brothers, you'll have to make your way to Romagne-sous-Montfaucon, in France. The cemetery is quite beautiful." She looked at the glass. "French wine for American blood. A paltry payment, but it will have to do."

"What about my grandmother?" Emmy asked, eager to shift to the living.

"Oh, Adelaide," Josephine murmured, and closed her eyes as though picturing the end of a tragic play. "That was the hardest blow. You recover from the dead."

She told Emmy of how Lida brought her up after their mother died until 1915, when Lida ran off to marry Ben Nelson. It was clearly hard for Josephine, the way Lida erased her family in order to stitch up her own scars, blaming herself for not being able to save their father. "Though God knows he was hell bent," Josephine said through a gargle of wine. She gestured around the room. "All of this was eventually left to Raymond, and it wasn't much at the time. I've built most of it with my own money."

"I see," Emmy said, knowing her understanding was insufficient solace.

"Ghosts," Josephine barked in reply. "All of them now. They haunt me, Emmy. When I close my eyes at night they are there, waiting to ask me for a way home. It's why I built the Jeep house after the second war, so I could find a place to sleep and work without their voices beseeching me to call them up." She drank down the contents of her glass. "It makes for great novels, but not a very good life."

Emmy trembled at the thought of whispering ancestors. "It doesn't seem so terrible." She had been trying to mollify her aunt out of her wretched mood. Instead Josephine's brow drew tighter and her lids dropped low enough that she tipped her nose to look down along it.

"It wouldn't look bad to you, all this *cushion*, but it hasn't broken my fall." Josephine tapped a thick nail against the crystal. "Eighteen is such an *important* age. Everything is felt so *deeply* and *poignantly*. I know you think what happened to you with that boy is unique, but it's not."

Emmy's cheeks heated up. She hadn't realized that Bev would tell Josephine about Ambrose. "It wasn't what it should have been." She tipped the contents of the glass through her lips. "He attacked me, forced me . . ."

"You honestly think there isn't some girl out there in a car tonight losing her virtue to the wrong man in the wrong way?" Josephine turned her eyes to the ceiling and then brought them back to Emmy with all the power of a door slamming. "It's not original."

"Well, it was to me," Emmy said, this new aunt's harsh words stinging. "It happened to *me*." Her spirits, lifted so high by the excitement of her new job, sank under the same old weights. "And now I don't know how to step over it, but I am trying, I really, truly am."

"Then you're where you should be," Josephine said. "Choosing not to be a victim is brave. I may not like my sister's choice of leaving her family, but I have to admire her courage for sticking with it, no matter how stupid it seemed from the outside. I'm the one who has to live amongst my mistakes."

Emmy licked the bitter residue of wine from her teeth, wishing to end the fraught conversation before she learned too much all at once. "It must have been quite a loss."

"You've only begun to learn about loss," Josephine said, the hardness of her expression honing to an edge that was just as quickly softened by a passing cloud of melancholy. "Wait until you have something really worth losing."

Emmy stood, wary of what confession Josephine might make next. "I have homework," Emmy said. "I hope it will be all right to stay one more night. I will find a place tomorrow, I promise."

"You can stay here," Josephine said without indicating if she meant for one night or many. Her leveled gaze pinned Emmy with its intensity. "You're strong enough to make your own way, if the world stops being so damn soft on you."

It was Emmy's turn to laugh. "I suppose you're right about that," she said, feeling strangely lighter than she had since the conversation had begun.

"Help me to bed," Josephine asked. "I think I'm just drunk enough to brave that room now. I normally wouldn't risk it, but I'm in need of new material." A sly smile worked at the corners of her mouth. "You will forgive me anything I've said poorly."

Emmy helped her aunt to her feet and slung a supporting arm around her tiny waist. "I will," Emmy soothed. "I will."

Twelve

The Beauty of Patience

Emmy heard the screen door groan open and then snap shut, followed by the sound of her aunt rustling around in the kitchen. It was finally lunchtime, and Emmy hoped that Josephine would be pleased to see the table properly set, with bread baked that morning and wild-flower honey collected from the beehive behind the old machine shed. Emmy had also picked some fresh green peas from the garden, blanched them, mixed in some sour cream and dill, and then placed them in the icebox to chill.

As the morning summer sunlight pooled in a patch on the day porch's floor, Emmy looked around the funny little house and marveled at how quickly she had taken to the place. Something about the ancestral objects—portraits of immigrant grandparents, a small handmade chair with a thatched seat, a ceramic washbasin and pitcher full of water on her dresser, which she filled every night and used every morning while imagining having to break the ice on a cold winter's past—felt right to Emmy. She had slipped easily into this place and began to understand more about herself and her desires as she learned more about her family—the family that existed beyond the place she had grown up in, which had simply become the "small house" in her new lexicon. That seemed like another existence entirely, being a small person in the small house. Now she felt somehow taller, more fleshed out, as though someone had been drawing her and finally decided to set down the pencil and pick up the paint. Even her clothes had color now, the old gray skirts and coats given away. She looked down at her lap and admired the pretty red gingham peasant skirt she'd made for herself. It felt wonderful to have the layers of silk and crinoline fluffing the ruffled layers as the fabric circled her where she sat. Emmy had always liked sewing, but after a few weeks of playing with all the wonderful fabrics that Josephine had collected, Emmy had developed a passion for the skill and tirelessly put together an entirely new and grown-up wardrobe. She'd made Josephine some items by way of thanks: slacks and skirts, a sash for her hair, even a new gardening coat festooned with bright blue roses against a white background. Mostly though, Josephine would ramble around the farm in a pair of jodhpurs and a long-sleeved white shirt, and whether she had just gotten off a tractor or emerged from an outbuilding, she looked as though she'd been riding her horse, Kid, nonstop her entire life.

Emmy set down the copy of "The Yellow Wallpaper" that Josephine had suggested she read, pressed herself up from the wicker rocker, and went to help her aunt. Moving through the ancient house, Emmy took in the portraits of immigrant grandparents and tried to imagine what it must have been like for Lida to be a girl in this space, until one day the dolls of childhood lay forgotten, slumped in the corner where they still lay.

"I'll get those cooked," Emmy said, taking the egg basket from her aunt. After the night of the Victrola, they'd never talked again of Emmy staying or not, but fallen instead into a companionable pattern welcome to them both. At times, when Emmy came home after work to find Josephine at the kitchen table, there was a sense that her aunt was happy to see her in a way that felt like relief that Emmy had, in fact, returned.

"Put these in that vase," Josephine instructed, handing Emmy an armful of gladioli and pointing to a ceramic urn. "I need to wash up."

Pouring the freshly beaten eggs into the hot pan, Emmy waited for the bottom to set before pushing them around with a wooden spoon. She gazed out the window over the adjacent sink, trying to imagine how she would feel when Bobby drove into the yard in half an hour. She wondered whether he had changed much since she last saw him the night of the canteen. She certainly had changed. The separation had been good for her, though, as she had begun to reconcile the cocoon in which she'd been wrapped with the enormous width of her new, damp wings. A too-familiar spell of uncertainty overcame her, a cold wariness that had filled in the space between her disappointment with Ambrose and her hopes for Bobby. She'd known Ambrose so well for so long, and had been so wrong. How could she possibly be right about Bobby, and if she were, how could she ever know for sure?

"Emmy?" Josephine said, emerging from the washroom and startling Emmy, the spoon in midair over the scrambling eggs.

"Oh." Emmy smiled, shaking her head. "They're done." She divided the eggs between two plates and spooned the cool sauced peas over the top of each, adding a sprig of parsley before placing the food in front of her aunt and sitting down. The steam of the hot eggs drove the earthy scent of the herbs into the air, where it mingled with the fragrance from a twine of pale honeysuckle that Josephine had wound into the long stems of scarlet gladioli.

"I don't think I can eat," Emmy suddenly said as her stomach drew into a knot. She looked down at her lap and tried to picture Bobby's face. The memory was hazy at best, causing her doubts to escalate.

"Exhale, Emmy," Josephine said, an uncommon look of concern on her face. "He's just a boy. Not the first, and possibly not your last." Josephine got up from the table and collected her cigarettes and lighter from the counter, a green glass ashtray from the windowsill. She sat back down, lit two smokes, and handed one to Emmy. Josephine drew deeply on her cigarette, exhaled a long ribbon of smoke from her mouth, and then stubbed out the remaining tobacco. "Now eat your food," she said, unfolding her napkin.

Emmy put the cigarette in the ashtray and let her hand fall back to her lap.

"Perhaps it was too soon for Charlotte's book," Josephine said, her eyes carefully trained on Emmy's face. "I see you've sought some solace in domestication."

Emmy looked around the immaculate kitchen. "I thought you'd be pleased," she said, confused.

"I'm always happy to have a meal cooked for me," Josephine said. "I just don't want you to feel compelled."

"I don't," Emmy said, still sensing she'd done something wrong. "I only meant it as a gesture."

"Gesture accepted." Josephine picked up her fork. "I love peas."

"So do I." Emmy took a bite, chewed carefully, and swallowed, only slightly less overwhelmed by the flavors. She looked at her empty fork, considering how rare it was to enjoy the simple pleasure of eating. Emmy slowly let the air out of her lungs, put out the cigarette untouched, and took another bite. She had never tasted a fresher egg or sweeter cream or a saltier piece of . . . salt. It was all too much to consume, especially in light of the countless tasteless and unadorned tables she had sat through in her life. Why couldn't her first eighteen years have been likewise filled with the casual beauty of God's world? "We never ate like this at home."

Josephine narrowed her eyes. "With forks?"

Emmy laughed, her cautious mood tempered by the joke. "No, of course we used forks. It's just that Mother always seemed so suspicious of ripe vegetables, always pickling and canning everything only to hide it all away until it turned gray enough to eat in the middle of the winter."

"We always had such wonderful meals when my mother was alive," Josephine replied, resting her chin on her hand, her long fingers rubbing a temple. "Her father was a baker, and she could make such delicate pastries, even out here in the middle of nowhere, in a wood-burning stove. I think she would have started her own bakery if she'd lived long enough to be finished with rearing the four of us. Five if you count little Charlie, but then he died right alongside of her."

"You've never mentioned him," Emmy said, fascinated by the incessant revelation of unknown relatives. Her great-grandparents had homesteaded the land, building the house out of trees they'd cut down, milled, and eventually covered with clapboard, adding rooms as the family grew to twelve children and countless descendants.

"He was practically born with the fever," Josephine said. "She had him, and neither of them got up from that bed."

"In the back room?" This was a place Emmy still hadn't ventured, especially after her aunt's ghost stories.

Josephine nodded. "That summer Adelaide found her true religion. There was a Chautauqua a month later out in Detroit Lakes, and Father took Lida and me, thinking it might cheer us up. His brother Johan had a little fishing cabin out on Big Twin Lake, so we stayed with them for the week, going to town to hear the talks."

Emmy held back her questions, waiting for the story to add its own dots.

"Oh, it was marvelous." Josephine's voice raised in pitch to that of a girl's. "Tent after tent of lectures, sermons, and little theatricals, set up in large brown pavilions down at the end of Summit Avenue on the edge of Detroit Lake. It was like a slow-moving parade, with women in long summer-white dresses and lacy parasols strolling arm in arm on the lawns along the shore. At first we stayed in our little group, but by the afternoon, Father had met up with some drinking companions and let us wander on our own. Raymond was there. I hadn't seen him in a few years and he'd become so handsome! Truly, Emmy, there never was anyone else for me, no matter what I tried."

With a jolt, Emmy remembered her plans for the afternoon. She glanced at the kitchen clock—fifteen minutes. "I wish I'd met him."

"He would have liked you," Josephine said with a sorrowful smile. "I left Lida, and Raymond snuck me into a tent through a flap along the side—and there sat a woman on a high stool, a book in her hand. She did nothing extravagant, had no props or a costume other than the fashionable dress of the time, and yet the tent was filled to the poles with captivated men, women, and children. Her name was Margaret Stahl, and she read something called 'The Dawn of a Tomorrow.'" Josephine cleared her throat and held a steady hand out toward Emmy. "'There . . . is . . . no . . . death.' Remarkable. I saw her do the same reading five more times in my life, and even when she was sick with cancer and barely able to hold the book, at least one girl in the audience fainted, every time. I'm pretty certain that was when I fell in love with the written word."

"What about Grandmother?" Emmy finished her food and wiped her mouth.

"Well, my dear sister Lida, who was as devout as Mother, went in a different direction, winding up in a temperance revival tent . . ." Josephine's lower lip moved, as though she were missing the words she wanted. "She went in a Catholic and came out a prohibition-crazed Lutheran. Maybe it was Mother's death or Father's drinking. Who knows? Lida was already prone to holiness. Not gullible exactly, but the religious equivalent. She became fired by the cause and picketed with other ladies outside of Uncle Johan's tavern just up the road here. She'd walk right behind Father the whole quarter mile, a Bible in one hand and a hand-lettered sign in the other. They'd take up their positions and eventually come back home, where I'd have some sort of supper waiting for them. Usually eggs. Clearly, Father won that battle—they were both so damn stubborn—by going to the grave a good year before the Volstead Act." Josephine laughed as though it were a fonder memory than it appeared. "After the war took our brothers, her faith ossified. She always had a flair for the dramatic."

"Is that what caused your rift?" Emmy asked, and just as quickly wished she hadn't when she saw the fury clouding Josephine's brow.

"Not today," she barked. Her words hit Emmy with a sting akin to a fast slap. Josephine speared a glistening pea and held it in the air between them. "Religion is an accident of birth, no more, no less. This small green orb makes as much sense to me as any religion I've encountered. It's at least as nourishing and far less judgmental." Josephine pushed back her chair and began to clear the lunch dishes.

"Please let me do that," Emmy said, recovering from the shock of her aunt's changing moods. "I promise not to let it domesticate me." Emmy winked and then clumsily caught the older woman up in her arms. They stood there together for an awkward moment as Emmy waited for Josephine to give an indication that she'd had enough. Finally her aunt gave her a small squeeze and they dropped the embrace in unison. When Josephine stepped away, Emmy saw a slight ripple of surprise pass over her aunt's face, and she suddenly realized that Josephine had not been held affectionately in a very long time, a feeling no more familiar to Emmy. A car horn blared outside of the house and Emmy jumped.

"There he is," Josephine said. Emmy looked quickly out of the window and then at the collected dishes. Josephine picked up a linen dish towel that was dotted in embroidered strawberries and snapped her with it. "Go on, now get lost in *love*."

"Do I look all right?" Emmy asked, ruffling her fingers through her hair, which she had cut short the week before. It wasn't quite as severe as Bev's once was, but fluffy and sweet in a softening way. The look had gained her second glances from grown men, and she hoped that Bobby would like it, too. She wasn't sure about love, but the feathers inside of her were already flying.

"I'm sure you do." Josephine turned Emmy by the shoulders and pushed her toward the door. Emmy quickly straightened her clothing and stepped outside, instantly visoring her eyes with an upheld hand at her brow. Bobby slung his thumbs into the loops of his dungarees and squinted before shaking his head and breaking into a radiantly white smile. Emmy laughed and crossed the freshly cut lawn to stand in front of him.

"Isn't it heaven?" she asked, looking around at the place.

He took her hand. "It sure is."

She accidentally bit down on the side of her tongue and winced. "You want the tour?"

"Oh, you bet," he replied.

"Well, this is the main cottage, which my ancestors homesteaded," Emmy said, feeling her hand heat up in Bobby's grasp as she led him along a blue-and-white-tiled pathway around the house and through a vine-laden trellis that opened on a wide field lined with rows of heavy stems in full multicolored bloom. "This is the gladiola garden, my aunt's passion."

"I've never seen so many flowers," Bobby said, touching a pale pink blossom. "It's magnificent."

"She also grows tomatoes, cabbages, cucumbers, onions, you name it, and a man named Mr. Green sells whatever she grows at that little stand across the road," Emmy said, her voice wobbly because Bobby was near. "I kid you not, that's his real name." She continued walking and talking, scared to turn her head and find him gone. "And in the fall the pumpkin patch next to it opens for people to come out and pick their own."

They fell into an easy pace as they continued past the old milking barn.

"That's where Kid lives," Emmy said. "There used to be cows here, but I'm relieved not to have to milk anything anymore, and besides, he's a fine old horse."

Bobby stopped walking and looked at her hand in his. "I'm sorry about your engagement." He tapped her palm. "Actually, I'm *not* sorry."

"I'm not, either," Emmy said, trying to sound casual. "I don't know whether

I'm fit for marriage in any case. I might just choose to be an independent woman."

"I'll get married. It's part of the plan." Bobby glanced at her and started walking again. "What's that down by the river?"

"Oh, it's a chicken coop," she said, happy to change the subject. "Apparently, when Uncle Ray was still alive he had at least a hundred chickens. Now there's maybe a dozen roaming the place and laying eggs down there. That and a pair of peacocks."

"I saw them," Bobby said. "They're pretty."

"Pretty loud, more like." Emmy laughed. "The male sits on one side of the house and calls to the female over on the other. It's sure annoying when it happens in the middle of the night. Sometimes Aunt Josephine is still out in the Jeep house working and will shoo them back together to restore peace." As if to prove her point, the two birds mewled shrill notes between them. "See what I mean? I swear they sound like tomcats in heat."

"I guess so, a bit," Bobby said, laughing. He took off his cap and scratched the top of his head. "I've been wondering about you, Emmy. Worried, more like. This is good to see you here, with all this beauty. It suits you." His staggered speech wasn't that of the Bobby she'd remembered and dreamed about. Emmy leaned into the thought that he too was nervous. "I've been pouring cement since graduation," he continued. "Dad says I'm the hardest worker on the site."

"Mr. Utke gave me a satchel," Emmy replied. "And Aunt Josephine gave me Ray's car." She gestured to the maroon-and-black Crestliner sedan parked next to Josephine's wagon in the yard. It was more than six years old but drove like new. "She said it makes her happy to see it out again."

They walked over to a small wooden bench next to the water pump and sat, staring at their own feet. Emmy gazed off toward the tree line, seeing movement, dismissing it as the peacocks. She cleared her throat as she tried to find something to say that wouldn't break the fragility of the moment. "I help out the best I can, though Aunt Josephine has a field hand who does most of the heavy work, in addition to Mr. Green. It's much easier here than back on the farm, that's for sure."

"What was that like?" Bobby said, lifting her hand and placing it once again in his own. She felt every bit of his skin where their palms connected.

"When my grandfather was alive the place seemed happy, but after he died it sort of lost its features." Emmy glanced at Bobby, realizing how little they really knew about each other. "Grandfather Nelson was very quiet and strong. We'd go fishing or trapping or looking for arrowheads. I wasn't good at the heavier chores, but I could collect eggs." Emmy laughed and Bobby smiled. She leaned a little against him. "I miss the smell of freshly baled alfalfa, though, and all the dogs, especially Sky. She was this pitch-black lab who never left my side when I was a kid. After we moved to town, Mother didn't allow any pets." Emmy's nervousness grew with Bobby's silence, and she pressed on, trying not to think about what it would be like to kiss him. "I hope to have a puppy someday. Wouldn't that be nice? I mean, you do like dogs, don't you, because I love them and if you didn't . . ."

Bobby pressed Emmy's hand. "Stop talking," he whispered, and drew the top line of her lip with the tip of his index finger. She opened her mouth to ask about his life, but he gently pressed the finger against both lips and then slid his knuckle under her chin, tipping her head back slightly. His lips pressed against hers, and the soft warmth of his kiss began the flow of yearning that she had nearly convinced herself she could live a lifetime without. When the tingling reached her toes, Emmy drew back and sighed.

"I'm sorry it took me so long to invite you out here," she whispered. "I wasn't sure you'd want to see me."

A wrinkle crossed his nose. "Don't ever think that," he said, and drew her into an embrace that brought a rush of longing up her spine. Their lips welded together in a feverish crush. They kissed like this, sitting in the middle of the yard, hands roaming and eyes slightly open, until Emmy's senses prickled with something else: beyond the tree-filled lawn that separated them from the drive was the unmistakable brown slouch of Ambrose's truck.

"Stay here," she said to Bobby. She stood and wove her way back through the pergola and into the front yard in time enough to see Ambrose emerge from the cab with a stack of newspapers in his hand. Emmy caught sight of Josephine paused at the door to the old barn, arms folded, standing sentinel there.

"Hello," Emmy said to Ambrose, echoing her aunt's posture with the hope of finding some common strength.

"Good day, Emmy," Ambrose said, removing a lightweight fedora-style hat that seemed to be woven from fine straw and was wrapped with a black band that sharpened the look of his black trousers and short-sleeved white shirt. Around his neck was knotted a thin tie that seemed out of place, and over the left pocket of his shirt Emmy noticed a small, embroidered cc. "I've come to personally invite you to a ladies' gathering for the Citizens' Council. And to give you these to read and distribute." He extended the newspapers between them, where Emmy let them fold over his hand in midair.

"No thank you," she said. "I'm working at *The Fargo Forum* now."

Ambrose took a step forward and pressed the stack a foot closer. "That's why it's important you read these, Emmy, before it's too late." He looked over her shoulder and withdrew his arm. Emmy turned and, seeing Bobby, felt suspended on a tightrope between the tangible future and the dissipated past.

"Hello," Bobby said, crossing the short distance with his hand extended. "I'm Robert Doyle." Emmy had never heard him use his proper name, and given the circumstances, its invocation had all the gravity of a tricycle.

Ambrose shrugged away the handshake by elevating the papers and hat slightly, and Emmy was speechless, stunned by Bobby's slightness next to Ambrose. "You're that Shanley kid, right?" Ambrose asked.

"Yes, sir," Bobby replied, sharpening the disparity of age and Emmy's chagrin at the same time. It occurred to her that she had kissed both of these men, with far different results. Embarrassment pounded in her ears as she tried to figure a way out of the unhappy scene.

"Bobby, this is Ambrose," she said, propping her fists on her hips. "My oldest friend." She suspected that explanations weren't necessary, and yet, having placed a true name on the nut of her relationship with Ambrose, Emmy knew she'd moved beyond everything they had attempted to be other than what they were. Friends.

"I see I've come at a bad time," Ambrose said, and settled his hat in a way that Emmy read as disagreement with her assessment. He nodded slightly at her. "I'll try you again another day." He began to turn toward his truck, stopped, and swung back, holding out the newspapers one last time. "Just take a look. It's all I ask."

Emmy pushed the damp hair from her forehead with the back of her hand before reaching out and taking the papers in a roll, the rough print feeling as though it would scratch fine lines into her palm. "Thank you, I will." It seemed easier than trying once more to say no. This time when he turned to go, he completed the effort without further words, not even a goodbye. Emmy held a flat hand above her eyes and watched his dusty departure down the road.

"That went well," Bobby said, and she smiled with relief at his small joke, tossing the bundle of papers through the open window of her car as they walked together, hands entwined, to his truck.

"I haven't even asked you what else is new," she said, trying to look into his eyes and wincing with the effort of diminishing the brightness of the sunshine bearing down all around them.

"Let's see," he said, lifting one of her fingers at a time as he talked. "I graduated high school, I'm working for my father on the road crew, Pete and Sally's going to have a baby, and this fall I'll go to college at NDAC." He stopped at her thumb, folding her hand inside of his slightly larger one. "Just regular stuff, I guess."

"I guess so," she whispered, closing her eyes and leaning into the relative shade of his chest. Her head tipped neatly onto his shoulder and she stayed there, still, until the heat of the day pressed them apart.

"So where do you want to go from here?" he asked, an uncommon shyness in his voice.

"I suppose we could see a movie," she said. "That would be nice."

Thirteen

All Progress Is Precarious

June bloomed and greened its way into the hottest July on record, and as the days snapped back from the long stretch of the solstice, Emmy eased into the trappings of her new life, distrusting the comfort even as she welcomed the routines. In particular, she looked forward to the long, looping afternoon drive from the estate to the *Fargo Forum* building, and the freedom she felt behind the wheel of her own car, going to earn her own paycheck. Even more than her growing relationship with Bobby, the work gave her a sense of security and place she hadn't before known. A bird would only have to fly about a mile or two from point to point, but Emmy had to make her way over the Red River, a meandering coiled creature with its closest two bridges in opposite directions from Oakport Township. She could turn left out of the driveway and head up old Highway 3, ford the river just north of Hector Field, and then take Thirteenth Street along the edge of the college campus and down to First Avenue. Or she would go down Eleventh Avenue to the Second Avenue crossing and up Broadway. Either way it took about fifteen minutes, and she greatly preferred the country route with its wind-slanted fields of mellowing grain, the occasional sight of an airplane landing, and cruising her car along the edge of the place where she hoped to eventually study. Taking this route also meant avoiding the Crystal Sugar factory and thoughts of her father. She missed his silences more than their talks—his ability to calm her with his steady presence—but she wasn't quite ready to seek him out and explain why she had left his house. In fact, the more she learned about the family rift, the less she understood her father's ability to let it happen again in his own.

Meanwhile, the slow waltz into courtship with Bobby had guided Emmy through a thicket of new people and experiences. She hadn't been able to imagine what it would be like to have seven siblings, all younger, and not until she had set foot in the Doyle house had she considered the amount of noise that many children were capable of making. She was used to the quiet of the small house, and the stillness of the people it held—it was almost as though the Nelsons had needed to maintain quiet and a safe distance from each other in order to stay upright. Not so at the Doyles', where the television was always on in the living room, the radio always chirping and chatting away in the kitchen, and a constant flow of inquisitive curly heads would pass by Emmy, asking her questions as the children touched her—on the arm to get her attention, on her skirt to admire a new pattern, on her cheek to feel if it got as hot as the blushing made it look. All this touching would only increase Emmy's flush, making the assembled clan attempt new approaches and excuses for embarrassing her. Emmy liked Mrs. Doyle in particular. She was young and beautiful and as full of the ability to enjoy life as Karin was devoid of it. Mrs. Doyle had long, thick, wavy auburn hair that was often swept up under a kerchief but occasionally was left wild. At the start of the summer Emmy had cropped her own hair into a pixie-style shag, short and simple. She'd been so giddy walking out of the salon—her first time in one—watching the men on the street turn their heads as she passed. The new look made her feel mature and independent, but around Mrs. Doyle, with her bounty of hair and stable of children, Emmy still felt small and awestruck.

As the car crossed over Thirteenth Street Emmy checked her watch. She had forty-five minutes to spare before her shift started, so she impulsively decided to detour toward the river and stop by the Doyles'. They lived on a charming street called North Terrace, which curved along a bend in the river on the way to Oak Grove Park. The house had been built by Bobby's grandfather, who had learned his trade of stonemasonry in Ireland before coming to America between the wars. Bobby's father had made many of his own remarkable improvements, including an attached garage with an apartment above it, wood-burning fireplaces in the living room and basement, and a concrete swimming pool in the backyard. This last detail had really knocked Emmy over when she first saw it; she'd never even thought such a thing was possible. Bobby's grandfather had switched from the stone business to pouring cement at the right time, and in the past years, Doyle and Sons had grown to be the largest construction company in the area. Work was already under way for the new four-lane express highway that would connect Fargo to Michigan in one direction and stretch all the way to the Pacific Ocean in the other. Over the spring, the crew Bobby worked on had poured countless loads of cement between Jamestown and Valley City, and the groundbreaking for Fargo to Casselton would happen at the end of the week.

Emmy turned onto North Terrace and saw a few of the Doyle children playing in the front yard with a garden hose. She couldn't tell at this distance which of the kids they were, and wasn't so swift to tell them apart even when she got closer. They were most likely the middle three, born within two and a half years of one another—a feat that Mr. Doyle liked to call "Irish triplets." Emmy knew that their names were Michael, John, and Thomas, and that they were twelve, eleven, and ten, but she really couldn't see much difference among them, other than one having red hair, and that should have made it easier, but it just didn't. She parked the car in front of the house and the boy holding the hose wheeled around and sprayed her as she walked up the driveway. She shrieked and held her hands up in front of her face, but behind them she was smiling. The cold water felt good on a ninety-degree day.

"Stick 'em up," the redhead said, pointing the makeshift gun at Emmy. She instantly put her arms in the air while the other two boys wound a section of hose around her waist, dragging her across the lawn and to the front door.

"Don't hurt me, please, I come in peace," she said, feeling the heat of the rubber tubing through the thin cotton dress she had slipped on in the face of an increasingly muggy afternoon. One of the boys had a band of feathers strapped to his head and war-paint markings. The other was wearing a black mask and cowboy hat. None of them had shirts or socks or shoes on, just dungarees that had been cut into shorts, the white fringes hanging down in places from a makeshift hem.

"You're going to tell us where you hid the dynamite, or we'll tie you to the rail," the redhead yelled, and the other boys let out whoops and whistles. The cowboy drew a silver toy gun out of his waistband and shot off a couple of caps. Mrs. Doyle emerged from the open front door and leaned against the frame, holding two-year-old Mary—whom everyone called Ruby—on her hip. Ruby was the baby, the first girl after seven boys, and was rarely seen more than a foot away from her mother outside of the house. Emmy took a quick measurement of the girl with her eyes, determined to make a sunsuit for her.

"Michael, put down that hose and let Em go." Mrs. Doyle sighed. "And wash your brothers off once she's in, then pick up this mess. Lord knows why you can't play in the backyard, out of sight of the neighbors. You look like the ragpicker's children." She shifted Ruby to the other hip. "Ah, Em, you look fresh and lovely in this heat," she said, tucking an errant strand of hair into a blue scarf, which clashed in a cheerful way with the orange housecoat she had on over denim pedal pushers. "If I'd known you were stopping by I'd have put on something decent. You'll have a cup of tea with us, won't you?"

Mrs. Doyle managed her household with ease and iron, switching from coddling a bloody nose to shaming the child behind the bloodletting without hesitation. Her children both feared and loved her, with the fear being of the practical sort, the kind that gets you to the table for supper on time with your hands washed and folded in prayer. Emmy followed Mrs. Doyle into the house, through the foyer, and past the large living room cluttered with tidy chaos and an older boy stretched out in front of the television, watching teenagers dance to "At the Hop" on *American Bandstand.* Along the hall there were shoes of all sizes, lined up neatly but not in any particular order. Above these were a series of hooks holding lightweight outerwear, with the names of each child painted above. The only empty hook was Bobby's, as he had moved into an apartment over the garage upon graduation and employment in the family business.

"You must think us savages; this house is such a pigsty," Mrs. Doyle said, setting down Ruby and taking off her housecoat to reveal a surprisingly tight pink buttoned shirt that gapped open between the strained buttons. "I pick up after them as fast as I can, but by this time of day I've about had it."

Emmy looked around while Mrs. Doyle took cups out of the sink and gave them a quick rinse. The kitchen was narrow but bright, with the appliances grouped down the front end, and a long table, with a booth-style seat on one side and a freestanding bench on the other, filling the oddly rectangular shape. It was a lovely room, lined by windows on all sides. It had once been a sun porch, but as the Doyle family expanded, so had the kitchen. Off to the left and wrapping around to the living room was a formal dining room with a massive mahogany table at which Emmy had eaten a number of Sunday dinners after attending Mass with Bobby. The Catholic service had seemed so foreign at first, but after a few weeks, Emmy had begun to prefer the solemnity of the Latin rituals to the simplicity of Pastor Erickson, and found the congregants to be not only welcoming but also genuinely pleased to have a new parishioner in their midst. She'd dutifully learned the Pater Noster, letting the melody of the odd language float from her mouth. It was the same prayer as the Our Father, after all, a fact that Emmy found the hardest to reconcile when contemplating the stark line drawn by her family between Catholic and Protestant. Viewed from this other side of the supposed abyss, the prejudice simply didn't exist. The only things the Catholics wanted to know were whether and when she might convert, and if she had a strong enough voice to join the choir. The simple acceptance was at times too foreign for Emmy to trust. It would take her time to get to know her place in the church, but first, she needed to figure out the Doyles.

"This'll just be a second, I've already got water boiling," Mrs. Doyle said as she slid Ruby into her high chair at the head of the kitchen table. Emmy noticed Patrick, the quiet, pale, and freckled six-year-old Doyle, tucked into the corner of the booth, his head bent over a piece of paper on which he was drawing what looked to be an epic battle scene. This boy's name she knew—he was her favorite due to his dulcet outside and simmering inside. His demeanor reminded her of how she'd been as a child, yearning for attention but mutely accepting that it wasn't in the cards. He'd been the baby until Ruby picked up his universe with her stubby fingers and put the whole thing in her pocket.

"Hello, Pat," Emmy said, and ruffled his hair. He looked up at her from far away. "What's that you're drawing?"

"Gettysburg," he said above a whisper, with the hint of a lisp in the middle of the word. He gave her a slight smile and returned to his art. Ruby grabbed a fat crayon off the table and Patrick handed her a piece of blue construction paper without breaking his own concentration.

"Let's go outside, then, shall we?" Mrs. Doyle elbowed the door to the patio open and stepped down the drop, easily balancing a tea tray set with two cups, a cozy-covered pot, sugar, milk, lemon, and some assorted pastries. "Pat, mind your sister."

"Oh, you didn't need to bother," Emmy said, springing to the door and holding it open, grateful for the opportunity to leave the cluttered interior and be outside. "I've only got a few minutes anyway."

"I need to fatten you up," Mrs. Doyle said. "You might blow away come the winds of fall." They sat down at a small iron table topped by a tiled mosaic of a three-leaf clover. The backyard was as chaotic as the front, with toys and bikes and swimming rafts littering the concrete deck of the pool. There was a high wooden fence enclosing the madness, covered with thick overgrown ivy and climbing red roses. Off in the corner leaned a small swing set, and Emmy jumped a little in her skin when she realized Jesse Acevedo—or tornado boy, as she'd come to think of him—was sitting at the top of the metal slide, unmoving, watching them with his shallow gaze. Emmy had tried to get used to his quiet lurking, and understood that the care he was given was both communal and foster until his father could become well enough to come back to claim him.

"We took him to see his father last week," Mrs. Doyle whispered as she poured Emmy's tea. "The two of them just sat there, looking at each other for fifteen minutes, a couple of ghosts. God bless their souls."

"Where exactly is his father?" Emmy asked, keeping her voice similarly hushed.

"Down in Fergus Falls, at the state hospital. Poor fellow's really done in by it all." Mrs. Doyle leaned closer; lowered her voice even more. "They don't know if he'll get better at all."

"Doesn't his mother have family that can take him?"

Mrs. Doyle frowned. "They don't want him," she answered. "Cut her off from the family when she married a Mexican. They blame Mr. Acevedo for what happened."

"That's terrible," Emmy said, her heart stinging for the boy. "What will you do?"

"Mr. Acevedo has a sister in Grand Forks." Mrs. Doyle blew on her tea, talking across the steaming surface without sipping. "He's asked us to take Jesse to her next week. They live ten to a shack on a beet farm up north and drive to their home in Texas every winter." Mrs. Doyle shook her head. "We have plenty of room here, but it's time he goes to his own people." She looked around the backyard, clucked her tongue, and resumed her cheerful tone. "It's quite a show, isn't it?"

"A bit." Emmy forced a smile that felt hampered by the sad tale. "In a good way."

"I married for love, but thank God that came with enough money to provide for this reckless army." Mrs. Doyle laughed lightly at her own good luck—almost as though she were touching a piece of wood to ward off the kind of misfortune the Acevedos had been served—as she poured milk into her tea. Emmy sometimes felt intimidated by Mrs. Doyle's easy strength, but her embrace of life was so penetrating it made Emmy forget that they weren't peers of any sort.

"How's your aunt? Her health strong?" Mrs. Doyle asked as she handed Emmy a plate of baked goods to go with her tea. As hot as it was outside, the steaming smell of mint felt surprisingly refreshing.

"Yes, thanks," Emmy replied, taking a small slice of bread from the plate and sinking her teeth into the cloudlike substance. It was crumbly and soft, melting on her tongue and revealing its little golden treasures, which she chewed into her teeth. A little burst of caraway set the raisin in contrast, and Emmy smiled at the simple pleasure of the treat. She stole a glance at her watch as she sipped from her teacup. Twenty minutes. It would take only five to drive to work and even if she were a minute or two late, the woman who worked the earlier shift was always happy to take a quarter to cover the time difference. A cloud passed over the sun and the atmosphere stilled. "It looks like it might storm."

"It has every day this week," Mrs. Doyle said as she crossed herself. "Please God we won't have any more tornadoes. They're still working on the high school, and my sister Clare's moved in with the orphans while the convent's roof is repaired. Imagine, a whole year later."

"Your sister is a nun?" Emmy asked. Bobby hadn't mentioned this aunt. "What's she like?"

"Oh, a bit like you and me," Mrs. Doyle said, winking. "Without the fun." Emmy blushed but smiled.

Emmy looked past the pool as a strong wind scattered green leaves across its surface and a rumble of thunder boomed off in the distance. Jesse sat with his body rounded into a tight, quivering ball at the sound. She wondered what it must be like for him to be so permanently lost, stripped by fate of the elementary pieces of having a place, or a people, to call home. Her own minor devastation, though akin, seemed trite to her in a way she'd never had to think about. Leaving her family was a struggle utterly falsified by knowing where to find them if she so chose. Jesse had no such luxury to ease his heavy heart each night when he folded his hands in empty prayer.

Before Emmy could voice her thoughts to Mrs. Doyle, three Doyle boys ran full speed around the corner of the house, followed by fourteen-year-old Billy, who was chasing them with a garter snake, its yellow and green markings bright in the increasingly overcast backyard.

"William Reilly Doyle!" Mrs. Doyle yelled and stepped between the teenager and his brothers as the younger three went screaming into the pool, the redhead diving, the others grabbing their knees in tucked orbs that threw water up and onto Emmy's dress, soaking her through.

"Oh!" she exclaimed, standing as the water dripped down her front. There was always a danger of being soaked around this many children, but Emmy was now going to be both late and wet for work. Mrs. Doyle put an arm around her and grabbed the snake out of Billy's hand.

"I don't see how this is my fault," he said, pushing his fists into his pockets and sulking back around the house.

"Well, maybe your father will show it to you in a way you'll understand," she yelled after him and dropped the snake into the peony bushes that surrounded the patio. "Let's go get you a dry shift, Em. I'm sorry for my boys."

"Oh, I'm not," Emmy said, having regained her sense of humor. "At least I didn't fall into the pool this time!"

"Ah, there's your silver lining," Mrs. Doyle said, and laughed with a brightness that belied the rumbling sky. "Get your sorry selves out of the pool and into the house before you're electrocuted!" she yelled at the boys. "And bring poor Jesse down off the slide, would you?" As the boys scrambled around Emmy and Mrs. Doyle, the redhead—whom Emmy suddenly remembered was Michael, like the archangel—picked up the tea tray without being asked and scooted it through the door as the first fat raindrops splashed indigo circles onto the parched blue tiles.

❧

By ten o'clock the switchboard had fallen silent for the evening. This was the magic moment: when people in the city were either asleep or watching the local news on television, and Emmy had only an hour to go until her shift was over. She leaned back in her chair and stretched her arms over her head before taking off the operator's headset and fluffing her hair. She could safely predict only a couple of calls would come in the next hour, and she liked to use this time to read newspapers from other cities or sift through the edits and rewrites that had landed in the scrap pile at the end of the day. There seemed to be a rhythm to reporting that Emmy read like musical notes, and she kept a spiral-bound pad on her desk to jot down frequently used words or particularly pleasing turns of phrase. On the nights when she was off the switchboard and on the floor, the swirl of copy routing mesmerized her brain in a way that made her eager to learn and do more. Her desire to take the college entrance exams lessened with each shift; there didn't seem to be a better school than the one she had lucked herself into. The idea of teaching home economics now made her laugh, especially in light of Josephine's disdain for the domestic. The only skill she used from that goal was sewing the increasingly more mature clothes, the pencil skirts, shirtwaist dresses, and trim blouses she normally wore for work. Still, Emmy quite often found herself daydreaming about Bobby, and what it might be like to someday cook his meals, have his children, and sleep all night in his arms.

The office grew quiet, with no major stories reported or circulating, and the morning edition's presses beginning to rumble in the floors below. Most calls had come from men who followed local baseball sensation Roger

Maris's career with first the Indians at the beginning of the summer, and now the Athletics, wondering what the score was and how he was hitting in the game. The sports editor had arranged with a friend at *The Kansas City Star* to call Emmy at the end of each inning with updates. The Athletics had won in the last inning, 4–3, against the Red Sox. In the half hour since the end of the game, all the calls had died off, and Emmy tapped a pencil on the counter and looked around the room. Of the thirty-some scattered desks, only six were occupied. Mr. Gordon, the city editor, was at his post at the front of the room, his feet up, head tipped back into an uncomfortable position. He was sound asleep. Emmy laughed a little to herself, which caused Jim Klein to look up from his work and raise an eyebrow. She met his look and glanced over at the main desk. Jim picked up his phone and called the switchboard. Emmy replaced her headset and plugged the extension into the board.

"Hey, kid, put me through to sleeping beauty," he said, winking at her. She pulled a red cord and did as she was asked, trying not to giggle. When the ringing filled the otherwise quiet room, Mr. Gordon shot upright and nearly fell out of his chair in an attempt to answer. By the time he did, Jim had quietly replaced his receiver in its cradle and had his eyes fixed on the copy in front of him. The editor looked over at Emmy once his barked hellos met no response. She shrugged to cover the prank and pulled the plugs. He resumed his slumped position and promptly began snoring again. Jim pretended to applaud her actions, but Emmy waved him off as if it was nothing, then pointed to the board and mouthed, "Would you?" He nodded and she got up from her desk and went down the hallway, stretching her arms overhead on her way to the archives, that place casually referred to as the morgue.

Part of Emmy's duty as copygirl was to sort through the clippings of articles and photographs that various reporters felt were worth filing, and then attempt to find the best category for the clip, and store it in the appropriate envelope or file, depending on how long a subject had been morgued. She checked the inbox on the side table and saw a grouping of tagged photos bundled there. On the very top was one of the Moorhead Theatre, ablaze. As she lifted it, a small ache of guilt passed through her. Cindy's family had moved down to Minneapolis to be near a special hospital that worked with burn victims. Mr. Rakov had left the Midwest for a job at a distant cousin's factory in a place called Poughkeepsie. Turning the photo over, Emmy saw the elegant writing of Cal Olson, staff photographer: *Movie Theater Fire.* Emmy went to the drawer marked MOA-MOZ, pulled on the metal handle, and walked her fingers through the tabs until she found the matching envelope. Pulling the folded clips and pictures from the file with care, she flipped through them, expecting the routine backlog of history to unfold—which it did, until one headline in particular caught her eye. "Strand Theater Engulfed in Easter Day Fire." She glanced at the date, April 2, 1923, and took the clipping down the hall to Jim.

"Don't thank me," he said as she approached. "No one called."

"Hey, keep the flirting down." Fred Simmons, the sports writer, looked over at them. He was a very small man with a very big voice. His teasing was just in fun, though, as everyone treated Emmy the same exact way: like a daughter. "Good night, lovebirds," Fred said as he dropped his final in front of the sleeping Mr. Gordon.

"Look at this," Emmy said, handing Jim the article and crossing her arms around her waist as she watched him scan through it. "Don't you think it's strange?"

"Which part?" he asked, squinting up at her.

"It's the same sort of fire, isn't it?" she said, pulling a chair from a nearby desk and sitting. "And also on Easter Sunday. I was filing this photo in the morgue." She set it next to the article, her confidence flagging. "It just seems odd, is all."

Jim pushed the copy he'd been revising aside and laid one hand on the Strand article, the other on the Moorhead picture. Emmy quietly watched him, imagining small cogs and wheels turning inside of his head. The night had cooled since the storm had passed, but it was still quite stuffy in the office, even with the ceiling fans on full above.

"I see what you mean," Jim said, leaning back. "I'll do some digging around."

Emmy put a hand on her cheek, hoping it wouldn't betray her as she gathered her will. "If you wouldn't mind, I'd like to help you. I mean, I'd like to learn how to dig around." The words felt stupid in her mouth, but she kept talking. "I promise not to overstep."

Jim laughed. "It's your nose, kid, not mine."

"My nose?" Emmy said, confusion warming her hands. Her left one flew up to her face, alighting on her cheek.

"It's an expression," Jim said, glancing down. "You smell a story here, and you may be right."

"Oh," Emmy said, inching Mrs. Doyle's skirt along her leg where it had crept to reveal more knee than was necessary. A buzzing sound came from the switchboard and Emmy jumped up.

Jim narrowed his eyes and smiled kindly. "Your phone's ringing."

She looked over her shoulder, knocking the chair down as she hurried back to the switchboard, where all three incoming lights were blinking. Mr. Gordon looked up from his snooze just as she eased back in front of the board, her hands shaking as she pulled the cords and went through the routine of patching calls with a new exhilaration until all had been dispatched and she sat back against the green leather padding of her wheeled chair, rubbing her nose to keep from smiling at the tiny step forward. The spring dreams of a college enrollment in the fall had faded with each passing day she spent in the newsroom, fixated on Jim's work. Each article he wrote was tight and finished, no matter how much or how little time he spent writing it. More than that, though, he was so passionate about every story, every minute of his workday. Now that she'd gotten his attention—*You smell a story here*—she knew that no matter how deep or cold the water felt in this instance, all she wanted to do was swim harder or drown trying. The light went on again, and Emmy plugged in and answered.

"Hi, Emmy," the friendly woman on the other end said. "It's Elise Klein. Is Jimmy still there?"

"Sure," Emmy said, used to this nightly reminder call, and put Elise through to Jim. A few minutes later, he donned his hat and left without another word.

❧

"I can see the fireworks reflected in your eyes," Bobby said, hovering just a few inches above Emmy the next Friday. "They look like the beginning of the universe—like God's first thought." She loved it when he talked like this, when he made her feel as though she were the most important person he'd ever met. Emmy sighed and pushed her hands deeply into his soft hair.

"Sweet talker," she whispered, and pulled his lips to hers as even more fireworks exploded over the tree line in front of them. They had climbed up onto the machine shed roof at Josephine's insistence, rightly claiming it to be the perfect place to view the display announcing the closing of the county fair across the river in Fargo. She had joined them for a picnic supper of chicken Emmy had fried earlier in the day, and a German-style potato salad studded with bits of sweet pickle and hard-boiled egg. Once the fireworks started, though, Josephine had excused herself. She said she'd seen them so many times before, but Emmy knew that her aunt was slowly winding down into one of her darker moods, and could hear the Victrola wheezing its ghostly melodies from the house. Emmy wondered what significance the fireworks actually played in Josephine's memory. Was it a happy time when she was young and still had parents and a houseful of siblings, or did they sound like bombs falling in a French forest with no place for her brothers to hide?

"Hey," Bobby said, pulling away slowly. "Where'd you go?"

Emmy gave her head a small shake. "Nowhere important," she said. "France."

"You're the limit." He laughed and went back to his steady necking.

Bobby was sometimes an eager kisser, pushing against Emmy's lips in a manner that could make her think more of eating, except that the delicate searching with which he moved his tongue over and between her teeth would erase the thought as soon as it surfaced, and she'd be pulled down under into his embrace, senselessly kissing back as best as she could. Other times, like now, he would be exceedingly tender but somewhat methodical. She didn't mind, as it gave her time to think about what she was doing with her mouth, and she'd attempt to find small ways to please him and draw him into a more heated round of kissing. For the most part, he kept his hands at or around her waist, though if they were kissing standing up he would occasionally let one hand drift down to her bottom and let it linger for a moment or two before once again grasping her waist. He showed a great deal of self-control and whenever she would let her hands move toward his more private places, he would wordlessly redirect her, then come up for air and strike up a hushed conversation. It was like living inside of a dream, where unbridled passion was kept in a box, wrapped up tight and waiting for the appropriate event to celebrate. When that would be she couldn't guess, but she found herself hoping it would be with fireworks lighting up a dark summer's sky. The slow pace of Bobby's seduction had helped Emmy heal the wounds inflicted months before. She was aching to consummate the way she felt about Bobby in a way that would erase the remaining scars. She put the index finger of her right hand into the waistband of his denims. His kissing intensified. This was good, she thought as she pushed against his lips.

Bobby moved on to her neck and kissed along the collarbone as she pulled him closer at the waist, wrapping her right leg around his left. She could feel him strain against her, and just as she prayed he might move his lips down to her carefully displayed cleavage, he rolled onto his back and looked up at the sky, taking her right hand and pressing it to his slightly open mouth. Emmy sat up and leaned over him, but he wrapped his arm around her shoulders and eased her beside him. She sighed. Tapped her fingers on his chest. Sat up again. He was definitely distracted by something; he kept looking away from the fireworks and out at the road. She followed his gaze.

"Don't you like this?" she asked without first thinking the words. He propped up an elbow and put a finger on her chin.

"You're nuts, you know that?" He ran his fingers up through her short hair. "I love this."

"Love what?" she asked, leaning into his hand.

"Your hair. Your eyes, this night. You." He put his arm around her and this time she relaxed into his embrace. "You know, Emmy, I never thought I could be this happy. I mean really, truly happy. Ever since I met you, well, it's just been great, you know? And that's just the beginning. Oh, the world is just right out there at our fingertips, Emmy, exploding with possibility like those rockets." She looked to see him grinning with all of his perfectly square teeth. For a moment she wasn't sure what she was looking at or whom. For a briefer instant she felt as though she'd never seen this man before, but then his smile eased and his features came back into focus. "What's wrong, kitten? Are you okay?" She looked at him harder and she smiled, brushing some hair from her forehead with the back of her hand.

"Yeah, sorry," she said. "Guess everything is just a little overwhelming at once, and all."

"You're telling *me*?" he replied, his voice full of excitement. "All I think about when I'm out at the site is you, and getting to see you at the end of the week."

"Me, too," she said, straining to match his emotion, even though she knew her week had flown by without much thought to Bobby at all. It was puzzling how little she could miss him when he wasn't around, and then here he was, the same adorable Bobby. "I had a wonderful break at the paper this week." She sat straighter and folded her hands on the broad swath of her layered peasant skirt. "Jim said I could help him with a story, one that I think I found myself, if it turns into something, that is."

"That's swell," Bobby said, rubbing her back.

"It's more than that, don't you see?" she asked, annoyed by the way his calloused palm snagged the back of her silk blouse.

"Do you have any idea how much you fill my heart?" Bobby took one of her hands and slipped it under his shirt, where he held it tightly against his chest. "Feel that. It's going awful fast. Now wait a second. I can slow it down just by looking into your eyes." As she matched his gaze she felt his heart slow considerably.

"That's me?" She sighed, cajoled by his intensity. He nodded and then placed his free hand on the back of her head and pulled her mouth toward his own. She moved her hand across his bare chest and around to his smooth shoulders. His kiss was hungry now, the kind of kiss she remembered from the first days of necking in his truck. He urged her down onto the blanket, and she welcomed the confidence with which he did it, putting up the opposite of a fight, melting into the night air, which felt increasingly cooler on her skin. He slung his leg over her and lay down with one knee braced between hers against the roof. Her hands were now tangled in his hair, grown lanky and honey blond from long days working out in the prairie sunshine. She closed her eyes and realized that she was barely breathing, silently urging him on with subtle motions to keep going, keep going, keep going—wherever it may lead. She didn't worry about the potential consequences of these actions. She just wanted him to take charge, be done with this yearning that she felt whenever they necked like this. His hand found her breast and stayed there, hesitating, then moved down to the hem of her skirt and slipped around her thigh. He gasped, stopped kissing her, stopped moving his hand, and bit his bottom lip. She arched up to him, completely lost now, wrapping her arms tightly around him, her knees falling open, welcoming the thrusting motion he was making there. She could feel him through his dungarees and her skirt and her petticoats and right through her underpants, which were damp from the friction and heat.

"Please," she whispered in his ear. "Please don't st—"

He froze above her and looked out at the road. His face was suddenly lit by a sweep of headlights passing into the drive.

"Pete's here," he said, out of breath, pulling away, up, and tucking his shirttail into his pants.

"Oh, Bobby, you didn't." Emmy's hands flitted around; adjusting, smoothing, buttoning.

"C'mon, baby. we're going over to Fred Johnson's barn, remember?" he said, helping her up and wiping his mouth on the back of his hand. He stopped moving for a moment and looked at her, the wild light deep in his expression still there but muted at the approach of his friend.

"You didn't tell me he was coming," she whispered.

"We're up here." Bobby waved to Pete as Emmy folded the blanket into sharp creases.

"I really thought it was just us, here, tonight," she said, hearing the pout in her voice. "Besides, Pete never seems that keen on me."

Bobby helped her over to the ladder. "Be sweet. You know he's bored stupid with Sally laid up in bed until the baby comes." He circled his hands around her waist. "We'll have fun." He looked past her, toward Pete, and at that moment the last of the fireworks—the big, booming display that marked the end of the fair—made Bobby's face glow with what could only be described by Emmy as certain, uncharted bliss.

❧

Fred Johnson's barn hulked alongside Highway 10 just a few miles outside Arthur, North Dakota, to the northwest of Fargo. They drove the twenty minutes from Oakport in Pete's Ford Fairlane, the top down and Emmy's short hair wild in the night air. She couldn't hear a word the two men were saying in the front seat and she didn't really care. It was probably about baseball or the youth group at church, or perhaps Pete's job at the Fargo

Fire Department, none of which particularly interested Emmy. Not only did she feel that Pete didn't really like her, she also didn't like the way Bobby acted when Pete was around. It seemed as though the only time Bobby ever drank alcohol was with Pete, and then he'd drink until he was slurring his words. She'd never known for sure what they were drinking or when, as Pete kept a flask in the dashboard and hadn't offered her even a passing sip after she turned him down the first few times. Tonight would be different, she thought. Tonight I am no longer a temperance-raised prig. She reached over the front seat as they raced north alongside a freight train, and grabbed the booze out of Bobby's hand, tipping the flask high as she stood up straight in the backseat, letting out a yell as the alcohol burned her throat.

"Well, all right!" Pete shouted as she sat down, dropping the empty flask onto the seat between the men. He slowed the car as they entered the tiny town of Arthur, cruising to a stop in front of a small storefront with the odd sign DICK'S BRA swinging on a pole over a wooden door. "I'll be right back. It seems the lady requires refreshment." After Pete disappeared into the bar, Bobby grabbed Emmy by the collar and kissed her hard on the lips.

"I love you," he said as Pete emerged much more quickly than expected from the bar, tossing a brown sack to Bobby. He let go of Emmy and her skin tingled all over. He loved her. It was finally, truly, said out loud. She exhaled and tilted her head against the seat, searching her heart for the echo of his words, unprepared for the flat surface they slid across instead. She shook her head and took a drink from the offered bottle, assuming the prairie of doubt inside of her was nothing more than a field planted by her own limited experiences. If tilled and seeded properly, love would grow there.

By the time they got to the barn they'd all had a few swigs from the new bottle and Emmy was ready to dance. The makeshift parking lot was packed with cars, so Pete parked the Fairlane in the ditch across the road. Even before the car had rolled to a stop, they could hear the rock and roll music pumping out into the warm night air. It would be sweaty inside the barn, but Emmy was well past feeling temperate about life and wanted to burn it up. She stumbled arm in arm with the two men up to the building, which was long and wide with a curved roof and gray shingles. Emmy figured it had to be almost as tall as the *Fargo Forum* building and nearly as wide. Through the downstairs barn doors they could see a man pitching hay into countless pig stalls; he stopped long enough to nod at the young people on their way.

Once they were inside the cavernous wood-lined space, Pete swept Emmy onto the highly polished and buffed planks of the dance floor. She saw many familiar faces from school, including the Kratz sisters and the Halsey boy, who were all laughing at some shared joke at a side table with a group of likewise well-heeled friends. Seeing them made her miss Bev's lively company, and even Howie's surly drawl, but with the baby arrived, they'd been swept off as a little family to live in France with Bev's uncle. The magic that money sprinkled on Bev's situation impressed Emmy, but not in a way that she envied. As smooth as her friend's road looked from the outside, it wasn't the path Emmy would ever choose for herself. In fact, it was too similar to the one she had blown up everything to avoid.

The bandleader's voice filled the air, introducing a song called "Boom Diddy Wawa Baby," and the orchestra drove into a fast boogie beat. Pete started swinging Emmy in every direction, gripping her hands and twirling her away, and then back again in repeated frenzy. As they neared the front of the room, she caught sight of the band and was surprised to see that they all had dark skin. "Who are they?" she asked, stopping in midswirl.

"Preston Love's Orchestra," Pete replied, tugging on her hand and folding her into a rapid embrace.

"I've never seen a Negro," Emmy said, trying to get a better look at the one woman in the band over Pete's shoulder. She was tall and deeply brown, swaddled in a sheath of bright copper silk. Her hair was swept into a high crown of large curls, with a short straight bang sharply cut one inch above perfectly arched eyebrows. Her lips were painted a hot shade of red that matched the color on her nails, and a pair of ruby gems hung from her ears. The song slowed, and the woman began to sing low and soft, putting Emmy into an instant trance. "She's so otherworldly."

Pete laughed, saying, "She's not the first colored person to step foot in North Dakota, you know. Though compared to the Cities, Fargo's a little backward."

"So what does that make Moorhead?" Emmy asked, snapping with defensive pride that masked her deeper embarrassment of being exactly what Pete meant. "Or Glyndon, for that matter." She stopped dancing. "And who are you to say?"

Pete lightly grasped her arm as couples swirled around her and the lead singer moved her voice through a throaty ballad. "Look, girl," he said, pointing toward the stage. "Not one member of that band is allowed to stay in the Cooper Hotel downtown because of the color of their skin. They travel in an old school bus with seats that fold into beds when they encounter hicks out here that don't want their pretty white sheets sullied. For as far north as we may be, there are those around here who would fit in just fine down in Dixie."

Emmy held his stare as long as she could, knowing exactly the kind of people Pete meant. Her family's association with the Branns burned a guilty hole in her racing memory. She shrugged his hand off to stop the flow of unwanted images. "I'm not them," she said plainly. "It's why I left."

Pete tipped his chin over her shoulder and she turned just as Bobby handed them a couple of Cokes.

"Your friend here thinks we're backward," she said in an attempt at levity, and poured the sweet liquid into her mouth. It was shockingly cold and deliciously spiked.

Bobby shook his head. "We are," he said, punching Pete in the arm. "We like it that way."

"We do, don't we?" she echoed, focusing on Pete's face, which fired with its own high color. "I get it, you're jealous!" She pointed her finger, gunlike, at him. Pete put his hands up in surrender.

"You got me," he said, moving his right hand to his heart, pretending to be shot. "I envy your freedom. Wait until you're married with a kid on the way. It's all downhill from here!"

The ballad ended and the band went right into a hard-edged version of something called "Country Boogie," and the crowd erupted with shouts of approval as farm kids and town kids alike packed the floor. It felt to Emmy that everyone there was dancing with everyone else; that there was complete abandon erupting all around her. Bobby set the Cokes on a table and grabbed her right hand as Pete pulled her on the left.

"So this is why it's bad to dance," she said, letting out a delirious laugh. Her mind floated away as she let her body do whatever it wanted, sweating and laughing some more and feeling Pete's arm around her waist, then it wasn't there, then Bobby was spinning her and the three of them were flowing together, the friction she'd earlier felt all but forgotten.

❧

There were many trips to the car that night, and around midnight Emmy leaned against the Fairlane next to Pete, smoking and passing the bottle between them. She wasn't sure where Bobby was, but they had run into boys from Shanley High, so it was likely he was off reliving their glory days.

"That's quite a moon, huh?" she said, finally feeling some sort of ease in Pete's company.

"Sure is," Pete said, handing her the bottle. "Look, Emmy, I need to talk to you about something."

She took a drink. "If it's about that backwards comment, I forgive you," she said, looking at him. It required effort due to the tilt of the road and the spin of the stars. She smiled.

"Never mind that." Pete drew a circle in the dirt with the heel of his shoe. "Well, it's about Bobby, see."

She nodded. Stilled her head, considering the sudden movement a bad idea.

"He's about the best guy in the world, and I don't think you should hold him back, is all." Pete put a fresh cigarette into his mouth and flipped open his lighter, roughly engaging the potent-smelling flame. "He's too young to be tied down."

Emmy stopped smiling.

"You don't know him like I do," Pete continued. "He's just not ready for anything serious. He needs to get out there and see things, *become* someone, before getting married and having kids."

She stood up and ground her cigarette under her heel. "What are you trying to say?" she asked, fear blaring in her head. "I'm not good enough. Is that it?"

Pete shook his head. "I'm trying to tell you that he'll never love you the way you think he will, so it'd be best for you to let him go now."

"Pete," she said, laying a hand on his forearm and forcing a laugh. "Don't tease me. You can't be at all serious."

"That's just it, Emmy. I'm as serious as a heart attack."

Emmy forced a composure that wove itself against the grain of her doubt. The effort resulted in an acridly benevolent smile brewed in hard liquor and insecurity. "It's very kind of you to intervene on my behalf," she slurred. "But we'll be just fine."

"He's got big dreams, bigger than marriage." Pete took a swig and offered her the bottle of gin. She refused. He finished it and threw it into the ditch. "Look, you're a nice kid. I don't mean any offense. I just think you should have your eyes open if you won't look at what I'm trying to show you. He doesn't really love you, Emmy. He never will."

"For someone who never means offense, you sure are offensive," she said, her laugh now bitter and too high for her own taste. She knew that he'd won whatever game he was playing at, and it took all of her restraint not to slap him. Instead, she pushed away from the car, hoping the weakness in her legs was due to fatigue and not defeat. "I'm quite certain I didn't ask for your advice."

Pete grabbed her arm and moved close to her face. She realized he was far more drunk than she thought.

"You know what you are? You're the kind of girl who breaks hearts." He let her go and she tripped backward into the road just as a car went flying past, laying on the horn and causing her to stumble forward into Pete, who caught her. In a rage, she threw off his arm and ran blindly across the road, tears of acute humiliation clouding her sight. As she reached the front doors, a pair of large men carried out a much smaller man who was throwing his elbows in an attempt at release and yelling words that Emmy didn't understand. All she knew was that they sounded ugly. It was Frank Halsey, but none of the other kids were with him now.

"My grandfather used to preach against this," he shouted. "Thirty years ago he warned that the wolf would be at our door!"

"Go on home, son," the man on the left said. "You're drunk."

Emmy backed quickly into the shadow of the barn before Frank could see her and draw her into his drama. Up a back staircase she slipped, clumsily pushing through the crowd only to see Pete already at the pop stand, laughing and gesturing to Bobby. Humiliated, she hurried out of the barn and found a quiet spot out back. She sat down on a bale of hay, pushing away the spectacle and replaying Pete's words over and over again in her head. *He doesn't love you. He never will.* The music and laughter from inside the barn rose and fell and overlapped as Emmy's thoughts hurtled down a tunnel, plunging her into the starry darkness that had earlier held such promise. Her frustration broke open the nut of mistrust she had tried so hard to squirrel away. The image of the fireworks over Bobby's strong shoulders retreated, only to be replaced with the one of him standing inside the barn, drinking a pop and laughing with Pete at her stupidity. Poison can seep in two directions, she thought. Emmy wanted to vomit, to purge the entire evening along with the alcohol that was blurring her senses. When that didn't happen, she instead began to breathe more deeply, and counted to sixty over and over again while she waited for the full moon above her head to cast a stiller shadow on the ground at her feet.

It took about thirty counts to collect enough sense and stand up without feeling the need to sit back down. She'd tried once at fifteen, and then again at twenty. The worst of her imaginings had come and gone along with a number of couples looking for a spare bale on which to neck.

"There you are," Bobby said, in front of Emmy before she'd seen him coming. Her eyes must have been closed. She looked up at him and wrapped her arms around her waist.

"Here I am," she said softly, unable to see the expression on his face or calm her paralyzing fear of imminent rejection.

"What did you say to Pete?" Bobby asked.

Emmy stood, a stamp in her feet against the soft earth. "What did *I* say to Pete? What did *Pete* say to you?"

"Slow down," Bobby said, placing his hands on her shoulders. "He just said that you'd had a fight. Wouldn't tell me about what."

"If you must know, it was about you." She pushed his arms away. "Your good friend Pete doesn't seem to think that you love me." The music was quietly hammering on, and she could hear some people hanging about in the parking lot around the side of the barn.

Bobby took a step back, a cloud of compromise shading his face. "I think maybe you've had too much to drink."

Emmy scoffed. "I've had too much to drink? That's your answer?"

"Of course not," Bobby said, his voice sounding a higher note than she was accustomed to hearing from him. She waited through his silence, determined to find her answer in his words, and not by picking through the million furies of doubt that were flying through her head.

"I should get home," she said, gathering her emotions in order to hold it together long enough to be clear of this place. Then she remembered how they'd gotten there.

"Now you're being ridiculous, like Pete said." Bobby kicked at the dirt and straw. "I don't know how to get it into your head how I feel."

Emmy caught on the first part of Bobby's words: *like Pete said*. She pressed her lips into a hard line and walked past Bobby, her eyes blurring again but not failing. He caught her by the wrist. She stopped. Didn't turn.

"I've been thinking," he said, moving behind her and speaking over her shoulder. "I wonder if I might call on your father, and if he would see me."

Emmy felt a sharp pain in her heart, in the very place where her love for her father bumped up against the way she felt about Bobby. She didn't reply.

"I want all of this to be done right, in a moment of well-planned surprise. Not in a pile of hay behind someone else's barn." He drew his other arm around her waist and she let her head fall against his shoulder. "You're the only reason I get up in the morning, the last thing I think about when I fall asleep at night. I know we've only known each other a short while, but I felt it from the first time I saw you at the back door of the church, that you could be my salvation." He kissed her softly below the ear. "So tell me, Emmaline Nelson, will you grant me a bit of patience?"

Bobby's jeans felt rough against Emmy's calves where they were bare, and it was all she could think of as she let the question drift. If she didn't move, didn't respond, didn't breathe, then this moment would never go away, and Pete's words would disappear. If she died in this embrace, then this is where she would live forever—in the before time. For even as he asked her to be patient, what she couldn't help hearing was that his request was balanced on a fulcrum of doubt, with her on one side and Pete's influence on the other. Try as she may, it was impossible to peel away the residue of Pete's words that now shook her confidence in Bobby. She closed her eyes and inhaled the sweet smell of climbing roses, and hay and pigs and

Bobby and her own stale breath all around her, palpable, real. But then there was another smell, darker, growing stronger. Bobby moved his hands suddenly to her waist, turned her around. He was looking off at a distant light, commotion seeming to erupt all over the farm.

"Something's burning," he said, and grabbed her hand, running with her to the edge of the barn. The music had stopped, sirens could be heard in the distance, and patrons were pouring out of the building. Emmy couldn't see any smoke yet, at least not from the windows or doors. As they turned the front corner, down past the high silo obscuring the moon, she stopped and gasped, her hand covering her mouth. There, in the middle of the adjacent wheat field, a wooden cross at least six feet high was aflame against the dark sky. By the time they reached the semicircle of onlookers, only the arriving fire trucks made any sound as the clumps of huddled crowd tried to make sense of an object they had only read about in history books or seen in the newspapers related to things happening far away down south. Pete ran past them, tossing his car keys in a large arc to Bobby.

"Get her out of here," Pete yelled as he loped off toward a wailing fire truck. Bobby barred an arm across Emmy's chest and pushed her away from the scene. As she turned in the direction he led, she saw the reflections of the evil deed splintered among the trumpets, trombones and saxophones resting, silenced, in the hands of the musicians who had all gathered in a tight knot near the edge of the field. Emmy gazed upon the sheath of copper silk in the middle of the band, momentarily meeting the singer's dark brown eyes, weary-struck against the warm prairie night.

Fourteen

Unseen Feet

As Bobby drove the convertible down the straight rural roads with their high-grass shoulders, Emmy tilted her head back in the warmth of the night air and stayed silent, grateful for the noisy wind that baffled her thoughts. The police had questioned them at length, but Emmy hadn't seen or heard anything useful, and Bobby's answers had been even less informative than hers. As they'd moved to the car she'd seen Jim arrive with Cal Olson, but Bobby had steered her away from any more conversations.

Emmy looked out into the dark night speeding past and closed her eyes. She'd read about burning crosses in Little Rock and the firebombing of churches in Alabama. Her brain curved around its illusive logic and wound past the theater fire, and just as quickly took a sharp turn back in time, to the long-ago conversation in Ambrose's truck and the newspapers she'd thrown away without curiosity. How he'd carried on about segregation and the Negro "problem" heading north. It wasn't hard to know what kind of person could strike such a match of hatred. Could it be Ambrose? she asked herself, falling more steadily into her memories of childhood, searching for any indication that Ambrose had such a thing in him. She came up empty. She pressed on, feeling keenly that something else was at work here, something connected to the other fire. Jim hadn't brought it up again, and suddenly she wondered if he'd been humoring her when he said she had a nose.

Pete's car quieted as they glided into the yard, and Bobby slid the gear into neutral, letting the engine purr under the soles of Emmy's shoes. She felt his palm warm her cheek.

"You're home," he said, clearing his throat. Emmy turned her head but left her eyes closed.

"Thanks," she murmured, somewhat lost in her maddening chase. "It just doesn't make sense."

He coughed. "I want you to stop thinking about it," he said.

"I can't." Her eyelids strained against the weight of the scene. "I won't," she whispered.

"You can't do anything," Bobby said. "Leave it to Pete and the police. They'll know what to do."

Emmy frowned at the mention of Pete's name. Where had he been when they were talking behind the barn? "How can you be so unmoved?"

"I'm not," Bobby said, looking out the window. "It's just not our place to get involved."

"I disagree," Emmy said. She opened her door. "I should go in."

He clutched at her hand. "You didn't answer my question about your father."

Emmy looked at Bobby's night-darkened eyes and felt the first shiver of dew. "I'd like to not talk about anything happy tonight. It's not right." She thought about the musicians, standing around the lead singer in the tall grass, weathered disappointment sloping their shoulders. Bobby's haste to move past the worst of it unsettled her. "Can you imagine growing up with that kind of hatred?"

"Of course I can't imagine," Bobby said. "Nor should you want to." He sighed and opened his door, walking through the shaft of insect-stippled light cast by the headlamps and around to Emmy's side of the car. He swung the door and held out a hand, lifting her up and out. "Will I see you tomorrow?"

"I'm going to the lake with Dot, remember?" She put her arms around his neck and softly kissed his lips. He smelled smoky. "Call me Monday?"

"I'll call you Sunday," he said, and released her. She was relieved to hear the telephone begin to jangle from inside of the house.

"I should get that," she said, running up the tiled walk, surprised to find the door ajar and the kitchen lights on. As she picked up the receiver, she peered into the parlor, where Josephine lay on the couch, snoring softly with a small glass of wine wrapped in a hand that rested daintily upon her chest. "Hello?" Emmy said into the phone, out of sorts with the sobering challenges of the evening.

"Hi, it's Jim. I saw you out in Arthur." The phone line crackled around his voice. "What happened?"

"Oh, Jim, wasn't it horrible?" Emmy asked, taking a quick inventory of the dishes her aunt had left: a plate with uneaten fried chicken, a second glass of wine, an ashtray full enough to indicate two people smoking. Emmy held it in midair, noting a small red circle around the words *Lucky Strike* on some of the stubs. Josephine smoked Camels.

"Looks like another act of juvenile delinquency, like that *M* on the Fargo South lawn last winter," Jim said. "The mayor wants a citywide curfew. Thinks kids have too much time on their hands."

Emmy flinched, having been one of those kids. "I don't think that's it," she said, then hesitated, intent on launching her own theory. "Look, I can't stop thinking that this is related to the theater fires." She swallowed hard at the ensuing silence, placing the ashtray back on the table and winding the phone cord around her finger.

"Sorry, kid," Jim finally said through a sigh. "The first fire was electrical, and the Moorhead Theatre happened because someone dropped a cigarette in a bin of oil rags by accident. I didn't want to tell you. The rest was just coincidence. Sometimes that's what smells funny. It's a rookie mistake."

Emmy sat down and winced. "Still," she said, concealing her embarrassment, "I think this one's more than a bunch of kids, don't you?"

"Look, they've got one kid in particular in custody." Jim paused. "A bad egg."

"Frank Halsey?" Emmy drank the last of the wine. "I saw him escorted out."

"Yeah," Jim replied. "Not his first offense, but his father's powerful enough to get him out of anything, and to keep his name out of the papers."

"How is that right?" Emmy asked. "Just because he has money?"

"Yes and no." Jim sighed. "Sometimes you have to keep something quiet to make it right. If we write an article that a cross was burned outside of a Negro dance hall in North Dakota, it validates the sentiment and invites more of the same. There are too many people holding matches in this town, waiting for a reason."

"But that should be reason enough to show that it's wrong," Emmy said, her skull tight and throbbing. "You can't convince me otherwise."

"Get some sleep, kid," Jim said, his voice hoarse. "I'll see you on Monday."

❧

At noon the next day, Emmy sat in her car out front of Dot's house on Fifth Street South, waiting for her cousin to emerge from the sweet pea-colored structure. Unlike the other houses on the block, the Randalls' roof had a slight curve down from its second-story peak, and looked like a little flipped-up hairdo on an old woman. She tapped the horn and Dot came flying out the door, a small suitcase in one hand and a collection of garments arrayed haphazardly over her other arm. Seeing her cousin's huge smile helped dissipate some of Emmy's remaining fatigue and confusion from the night before, but not nearly enough.

"I'll be right back," Dot said, slinging all her things into the backseat through the open window and returning to the house, where she disappeared for a few moments longer. Emmy kept the car quiet, tired of searching for even one report of the fire on the radio. Jim was right: Frank's father was powerful enough to keep the whole thing quiet. She'd had a late night, managing to get Josephine tucked into bed and then cleaning the house before packing for the trip to the lake. Not wanting to disturb her aunt, Emmy had slipped out early and eaten breakfast at Wolf's, reading the bland news of less disturbing events. The paper spent most of its local coverage on the end of the state fair, with a brief mention of Mayor Lashkowitz pressing once again for a solution to the teen delinquency problem—the closest wink Emmy could find to anything unpleasant. This time the city council planned to enact a cruising curfew that would clear Broadway of its weekend show of beautiful cars. By the time she'd finished her coffee, Emmy felt that the burning cross might actually have been a dream, which only made her feel worse: If it had been reported, she wouldn't have to carry the burden of witnessing alone.

Dot emerged from the house, struggling under the weight of a large metal cooler with a red-padded top. On the side was a red-stenciled logo for Hamm's beer. Emmy got out of the car and helped carry the heavy thing by one of its red handles.

"Let's put that in the trunk," she said as they swung it between them. "Gee, what've you got in here, your little sister?"

"I wish!" Dot laughed. "No, Mom asked me to bring the beer and the steaks so Dad wouldn't have to bother tomorrow. We just need to stop out at the tavern and get some ice before we hit the road." She slammed the trunk and a good deal of dust rose into the hot afternoon air. "Ready to get out of Dodge?" Dot asked, brushing the dirt from her hands.

Emmy looked down at the ground. "Yeah."

"I heard on the radio that it's suppose to hit one hundred here in the valley today," Dot said as the girls got into the car. "This heat wipes me out."

"You know, this is my first time to a lake," Emmy said, trying to find a way to tell Dot about the fire, yet at the same time wishing away the last of the images. Sleep had never really come for her the night before, and now that she was in the hot car headed to the coolness of a summer lake, her eyelids felt like burned toast scraping against her smoke-tired eyes.

"No kidding!" Dot said, hitting her on the arm. "How is that humanly possible? Even the poorest kids down by the river go somewhere in the summer."

Emmy ignored the implication. "There was always too much to do on the farm."

"It's rustic, but it's heaven, away from all this heat and noise." Dot stuck her arm out of the window to gain some air.

"This is noise?" Emmy smiled. "I can't imagine it being much quieter." She headed the car back up Eleventh Street, toward the estate, and within minutes pulled into the parking lot of the Trail Tavern. It was a long, low cabin built out of logs and reminiscent of pioneer times. Emmy wasn't old enough to have stopped before, though she knew from Josephine that the building was once run by the family as a green market, until Uncle Raymond built the new one across from the estate and turned this place into a bar. Just north of the tavern loomed the sugar beet refinery, the sight of which caused Emmy a pang. She'd driven by the old house a number of times, but the lights were never on, nor was the car ever in the drive. A part of her needed to be just a little more settled, a tiny bit more successful in her new life before she spoke to her father again. The image of handing him a copy of *The Fargo Forum* with her name as a byline to an important article compelled her onward; she needed the evidence that she was doing everything she could to make her own way. This ground felt less than solid after her setback of the night before.

"Hey, come on in with me, I'll need help with the ice," Dot said as Emmy turned off the car.

"I'm not twenty-one," Emmy replied.

"It's okay. I'm not either," Dot said as Emmy followed her through the parking lot, waves of heat shimmering a foot above the pavement. "Besides, we're just running in and out. I do it all the time."

As Emmy entered the cool, dark interior, it took her eyes a moment to adjust to the low light, but she could make out a row of booths to the right, small tables and chairs anchoring the middle of the room, and a bar to her left. Straight ahead a jukebox was playing a song she hadn't heard since she was a young girl, and though she couldn't recall the name of it, the words flowed in her head along with the music. Something about a girl named Mona Lisa, sung by a richly sweet and longing male voice that reminded Emmy of the band at the barn—this same tune had been playing when she and Bobby were out in the hay, arguing about stupid and solvable things.

Dot took Emmy by the hand and led her over to the bar, where Irv Randall polished a glass with a white linen cloth. His dark hair was slicked in combed rows away from thick eyebrows, his darkly tanned skin contrasting against his neatly pressed white shirt.

"Hey, Pops, we're here for the ice," Dot said, her voice filling the room.

"Hello, Cousin Emmy," Irv said, putting down the cloth and taking her hand. His typically jovial disposition seemed held in check.

"Hello, Cousin Irv," Emmy said, returning the formality.

"How much ice does your mom need?" Irv asked Dot.

"More than I can carry."

"The ice is in the cellar," Irv said to Emmy as he opened a small bottle of 7UP and set it on the bar with the clean glass. "We'll be right back."

"Thank you, I could use that," she said, taking a long sip.

Irv hesitated. "There's someone here who'd like to see you," he said, nodding past her toward the open room beyond. "We'll be right back."

Emmy turned from the bar as Dot and Irv went down a flight of stairs. She took a long sip of her pop and looked more carefully around the room now that her eyesight had adjusted. The entire bar was very tidy, and smelled of stale beer and cigarettes, over which was a cleaner smell, of wood polish and floor wax. She walked over to the one occupied booth, which stood in the corner next to the jukebox.

"Hello," she said politely as she approached a man seated in front of a glass of beer and a copy of *The Farmer's Forum*. He looked up from the printed green paper slowly and Emmy took a quick step back. She barely recognized her own father in the delicate features and thinning hair of this slight man. He pulled a handkerchief out of his front pants pocket with a pale hand, and used it to first wipe his eyes and then his mouth. Emmy felt her legs weaken as she slipped into the hard bench across from him.

"Irv told me you'd be here this morning," he said. Emmy's eyes stung, but she resisted the urge to rub them.

"I'm glad he did," she quietly replied, wanting to say all the right words. "Every time I pass the factory I think of you. Sometimes I even drive past the old house." Her voice trailed off and silence settled over them until Emmy broke it. "I have to say I'm surprised to see you in a bar, drinking."

He turned his glass. "Ginger ale." She looked at his gray work shirt, the mechanic's mix of dirt and oil under his fingernails, the ashen quality of everything about him. Had he ever been young? she thought, and then realized that he didn't really look all that much older than he had when she'd left; she was just seeing him clearly for the first time.

"How's Mother?" she asked.

He sat straighter, groaning with the effort and rubbing at the small of his back. "She's moved out to the farm," he said as Irv and Dot came out of the storeroom and looked over at them.

"Need anything, Christian?" Irv asked. Dot looked at Emmy and shrugged a small apology.

"We're good," Christian responded. Irv and Dot went out to the car with the ice, and Christian turned his eyes to Emmy. "Your mother left Moorhead when I wouldn't go after you. I don't expect her to come back."

Emmy sat straighter, a trickle of sweat slinking down her spine. "I'm sorry," she said, painfully aware of the ripples her actions were making around her.

"It's not your fault," he said. "Sometimes people need space."

Emmy's neck burned. She rubbed at her collarbone. "But if I hadn't left," she said, barely above a whisper.

"What's done is done." He folded the newspaper and laid it on the bench. "I think she mainly didn't want to be there every night, waiting for you to come home. You're both so darn stubborn."

"Why don't you move out to the farm?" Emmy asked, the pain of having caused her parents to live apart sharpening.

"I've always hated it," he said, finally shifting his gaze to the round paper coaster under his glass. "Even when I was small. And the more I hate it, the more your mother hates living in town. You know how she loves to embrace futility." He laughed, a small noise laced with a hint of anger. "Her and your grandma sure do see eye to eye on that." He took a square white package of cigarettes from his shirt pocket and slid one from the tear at the top, tapped it three times against a thumbnail, and lit a match. Emmy looked at the red circle, the words *Lucky Strike.*

"This is new," Emmy said, lighting one of her own and examining the logo on the end.

Christian exhaled and coughed. "One of the habits of living alone, I guess."

"You're not lonely?"

He put one finger on the side of his nose and shook his head. "Maybe a little."

"Enough to visit Josephine?" she asked. Christian's face softened.

"I needed to know you were okay," he said, his eyes tearing slightly.

"Oh, you could have called," she said, trying not to cry from the happiness his concern gave her. "I would have liked that."

He flicked the ashy end of the cigarette into a small gold foil tray between them.

"How about I come over on Friday night and cook you supper?" she asked. The glacial feeling inside of Emmy started to recede, leaving behind the rich scraped dirt of fresh possibility. "Would that be all right?"

He nodded, a slight smile of relief creasing the sides of his cheeks and making him appear suddenly younger, boyish.

"Good, then," Emmy said, her sense of purpose restored. "How's Grandmother Nelson?"

"Not well," he replied. "She rarely leaves her bedroom, except to go to church on Sundays. Your mother lets Ambrose run the farm, or whatever's not already Brann property." The resignation in Christian's tone surprised Emmy.

"Ambrose?" she echoed.

The door opened with a shot of blinding sunlight, and Irv came back into the tavern with a pair of customers who sat at the bar. Emmy waited for Christian's response. He pursed his lips and pulled them back into a grimace, sucking air through the space between his front teeth as though trying to reverse a disgruntled spit.

"He's marrying Birdie tomorrow." Christian stubbed the butt of his cigarette into the tray. "I thought you should know."

"Oh, I see," Emmy said, but she didn't see at all. Her sister was so young, and far more naïve than Emmy, or at least she had thought so.

"There's more to it." Christian tore the coaster in half, an internal struggle made manifest. "She's in the family way."

Emmy furrowed her brow over her sister's graceless lack of restraint. "This seems a bit sudden," she said, her dismay increased by an unexpected jolt of envy. Everything that was once laid out for Emmy as something special was now being boxed and embroidered for Birdie. "At least Mother will have only one initial to change on the monograms," Emmy quipped, the words uncomfortable in her mouth. "E to B should be easy enough."

"That's not you," Christian admonished, shaking his head. "But I get how you feel. He's filled her head with nonsense—Karin's, too. He's running for a seat on the township board, seems to have developed political aspirations." Christian said the last words as though they were coated in poison. "From the outside I suppose it looks a good match. They're at the church now, setting up for the wedding."

Emmy had never heard such deep opposition in her father's voice. "And from the inside?" she asked.

"It's been a long time since I knew anything." Christian leaned forward. "I'm sure it smarts, but you'll have your own wedding, by and by."

Emmy searched her heart for a charitable upside. "At least she loves him."

"Oh, she loves him," Christian said. "The way a toddler loves a kitten. I'll walk her down the aisle, but I won't be happy about it."

Emmy touched his hand. "And what if I need you to walk me down an aisle?"

"You have a boy?" Christian's face softened. She eased her mind away from Birdie and Ambrose and focused on something new, something that she just as readily understood could cause her a fresh round of familial grief.

"He's a Catholic," she said.

Christian smiled and scratched his ear at the crease. "She won't like that much, will she?"

"Add it to the list," Emmy attempted to joke. " 'Things About Emmaline That Disappoint Her Mother.' "

The door opened again, and Dot poked her head and shoulders halfway into the room. "Hey, Em, I'm dying out here and the ice is melting."

"Go on now," Christian said, taking her hand as though to shake it. "Tell your boy to come and see me. I want to get a good look at this one."

❧

Emmy left the tavern and met a wall of heat that made her think of Hansel and Gretel being tossed into the witch's oven. She got into the car with Dot and drove off east, toward the cooler promise of water.

"You could have warned me," Emmy said, squinting from the glare all around them.

"I didn't know until we got there," Dot replied. "How'd it go?"

"Good," Emmy said. She tilted her chin up slightly, considering whether to tell her cousin about Birdie. All the restraint that Emmy had shown in front of her father sparked on the simmering coal of betrayal. "My sister's marrying Ambrose." The plainness of the statement helped release some of the steam.

"Sheesh! The same Ambrose you were supposed to marry?" Dot exclaimed, rolling her eyes. "Did you have any clue?"

"I suppose so," Emmy admitted, realizing if anyone were to blame, it was probably her. The car thrummed over the hot paved road as they left the city limits, and over each small rise, Emmy saw what looked like a puddle of water across the road ahead—a glistening mirage, she realized each time they reached the dust-dry spot where the wet patch should have been. "She's expecting."

"At fifteen?" Dot asked, clucking her tongue.

"Sixteen next month," Emmy said, defensiveness conquering scorn. Still, she thought, How dare Karin judge her, when all along Birdie had been handing out the kind of favors that trap a man completely. Perhaps it had been the smell of the animals in the barn on those cool spring nights when Ambrose showed Birdie the way through her mathematics. Though once Emmy stopped to think more carefully about how far Birdie might be from conception, she went cold. The ruined night, the torn clothes, her sister's empty bed. He'd already moved on, well before the Easter upheaval. Without so much as a second thought, Emmy slowed the car as they approached the familiar turn, and drove down the rough gravel road leading to the small church on the high prairie. "I think I need to see her," Emmy said.

"It's your funeral," Dot replied, fishing a copy of *The Fargo Forum* from her bag. "I'm in no rush."

As the church came within sight, Emmy lost her nerve and pulled the car onto the soft shoulder a good length down the road that ran perpendicular to that of the church, and spied her grandmother's car, along with a few others, parked in front of the brick building. From this distance, Emmy could just make out the swift, tidy form of her sister, long hair flying in the hot, dusty wind, whipping across her face and making her white cotton shift paste against her middle. There was no denying it: That bulge was a small Brann on the way. When Emmy saw Karin emerge from the church to help Birdie lift a box out of the trunk of the old car, Emmy put the Crestliner in gear and spun out down the road, hoping they would look up from their task and see her driving away from them, from everything they were, everything she had narrowly escaped becoming.

"Whoa, cuz," Dot said, dropping her paper and clutching at the dash. "Take it easy."

"I've changed my mind," Emmy said around the lump stuck in her throat. She was seeing what could have been a moment from her past. Long-denied tears crimped her vision, even as she knew that she had never been freer than either of those women would be in their entire lifetimes. The wind stirred dust through the open windows as Emmy drove faster down the gravel road. The wheels lifted over a small rise in the road and only at its peak did she see a vehicle headed her way, the cloud of tousled dust rising into the blue sky above it. She swerved a little to the right to make room for the oncoming vehicle, but her back tires hit a patch of loose gravel and she momentarily lost control of the car. The ditch was steep on her side, with high prairie grass that bumped and jarred the car to a sudden, jolting stop. She looked over at Dot, whose eyes were wide with anticipated disaster. Emmy put her head down on the steering wheel for a moment of composure, and then looked up to see Ambrose emerge from the passenger side of the other car. Throwing her car into reverse, Emmy turned the wheels sharply, and the back end of the car fishtailed deeper into the ditch.

"We're going to flip!" Dot yelled, and Emmy tried to move the car forward more carefully, but the angle of the slope was not releasing them; instead, it seemed to be pulling them into a precarious angle.

"Let me help," Ambrose said as he approached with both hands out in front of him, as though Emmy were a cornered, rabid raccoon. Sweating now, Emmy tried to reverse one last time and could hear the back tires spinning in the slick grass until the engine harshly revved against the exertion of turning the axle to no avail. She struck the dashboard in defeat and Ambrose opened her door, holding it wide against the pull of gravity. Dot scrambled over the bench seat, through the back door, and up the ten feet of destroyed grass to the road, where she lit a cigarette with shaking hands. Emmy looked up at Ambrose. His thin black necktie fluttered in the hot breeze against the starched white of his short-sleeved dress shirt. Some sort of change had come over him; he looked quite handsome clean-shaven, and with a sharp beige woven fedora resting lightly on his closely cropped hair. Whatever transformation had started in the spring was now fully complete: He looked like any number of pictures she'd seen at *The Fargo Forum* of politicians campaigning on a hot summer day.

"Fine," she said in outraged defeat, pushing past his offered hand and stamping through the ruts the car had carved into the soil and up to the road, her newly purchased strappy sandals surely ruined before even nearing a patch of water. "That's Ambrose," she said to Dot as he slid behind the wheel and began to rock the car in fits and starts, back and forth, slowly undoing the damage Emmy's attempts had caused.

"Well, at least he's good with cars." Dot shrugged, making Emmy laugh at the sudden absurdity. Had she really expected everything to stop in her absence, that they would all sit around, cherishing the void that her leaving had created? The embarrassing answer was yes, she had thought the period of mourning would last at least until she'd had a better reason to return, triumphantly settled in her new life. Pride, she thought, that's what this is. The realization hardly made the situation better.

"He is," she replied, batting at a grass stain on the hem of her eyelet-edged skirt. Emmy rubbed her wrist where it had apparently slammed into the steering wheel, and turned to look at the other car. In the backseat were two young men she didn't recognize, dressed in a fashion similar to Ambrose, and behind the wheel was Mr. Davidson, his gaze trained steadily on her. He nodded and emerged from the car. All nascent mirth drained from Emmy as he approached in his light blue serge suit, a white straw boater slanted back on his head.

"Good afternoon, Emmaline," he said as he crossed the road. "Is this a prodigal return, or merely an accidental one?"

Dot whirled toward him, stepping protectively in his path. "I don't believe we've met," she said over the straining of the Crestliner, and extended a sharp hand. "Dorothy Randall." Though Dot was barely a year older, Emmy envied her cousin's calm maturity and tried to mimic it by standing taller and pushing away the uneasiness that always overcame her around the strange man.

Mr. Davidson narrowed his eyes and stopped just short of Dot's hand, the sound of loose gravel crunching beneath his heel as he ground out a dropped cigarette. "Irv's girl?" he asked, causing Emmy and Dot to look at each other, and then back at him.

"I am," Dot replied proudly, drawing her arm across her waist. "And you are?"

"Curtis Davidson," he replied, doffing his hat. "An old friend of the family."

"I'll tell you later," Emmy whispered to Dot as the Crestliner was released from the ditch and Ambrose emerged from the driver's seat.

"Thank you," Emmy said to him, wanting to be finished with the awkward gathering and on her way east.

"You're welcome," he said, glancing in the direction of the church. "May I speak with you for a moment?"

Emmy turned slowly in an arc from Ambrose to Mr. Davidson and then to Dot. "Why don't you wait in the car where it's cooler," she said to her cousin, even though they all knew there was no escaping the heat of the blazing noonday sun. Mr. Davidson smiled as though he had won an unexpected prize at the state fair, took a cigarette from its perch atop one ear, and struck a match on the tip of his thumbnail, all the while keeping his eyes trained on Emmy. She remained still as he drew the flame into the end of a cigarette, and then held the match between them, shaking it out and letting the small burned stick fall to the ground before turning and moving to his car, where he leaned and watched her from the distance. Dot made a noise that sounded like a rabid dog's growl before rounding the Crestliner and sitting in the car with the door wide open.

"We need to be getting on," Emmy said to Ambrose, who lifted her left wrist with one finger and held it in the air between them.

"You're hurt," he said, meeting her eyes for a brief moment before looking painfully away.

She let her fingers dangle, her palm moist with apprehension. "I know about tomorrow," she said.

He sunk the pointed end of a front tooth into his lower lip. Released it. "If you want," he said, barely opening his mouth, "I'll call it off."

Emmy yanked away her snakebit arm. "No," she whispered sharply. "Have you lost your mind?"

The knob of his Adam's apple pushed above the tight collar and then back down again as he swallowed, his eyes red-rimmed and moist. "I have always loved you," he said, his voice cracking. "And only you."

She slapped him, and the doors of the other car rattled open, the young men emerging. Mr. Davidson held his hand in the air and they froze in mid-motion. Emmy shook her head. "*Never* say that again. Do not even *think* it." She placed her stinging hand in the middle of his chest. The young men moved slightly, then sunk back into their places in the car as Mr. Davidson lowered his hand and tossed his cigarette into the road, where it smoldered. Emmy gripped her fingers around Ambrose's necktie. "If you ever hurt my sister I will come after you. Understand?"

Ambrose nodded and swiped at his face with a handkerchief, backing away from her and drawing the tie through her fingers as he went. "I'll try. For you." He walked to Mr. Davidson's car, and they drove off toward the church as Emmy watched, unable to move until the vehicle had gone over a small rise in the road and disappeared, no more a ghost from the past than it was a herald of the future.

"Come on," Dot said, slamming her door shut and opening Emmy's from the inside of the car, bumping Emmy's backside enough to put her into motion. Emmy got behind the wheel and wrung her hands for a moment before starting the engine.

"Your creepy ex-boyfriend left you a present," Dot said, tossing a sheaf of paper into Emmy's lap. "And what's with the geezer? 'I'm an old friend of the family.'" Dot perfectly imitated Mr. Davidson's growling baritone.

"I'm not really sure," Emmy said. She unfolded the latest copy of *The Citizens' Council* and then strangled it into a tight cone before sticking it under the seat and driving carefully down the road. "But I don't want to have anything to do with any of them, ever again."

❧

By the time Emmy and Dot pulled into the grass drive of the lake cottage, Emmy's temper had calmed and the mood was improved by Dot's increasingly funny imitations of Mr. Davidson and Ambrose. More than anything, she had helped Emmy understand that whatever had happened between Ambrose and Birdie was not Emmy's fault, nor was it something she could fix—if it even needed fixing, for that matter. They got out of the car just as the sun slanted behind the high treetops and the late afternoon smelled green and cool after the humid dust bowl of the valley. On the outside, the cabin looked fairly similar to the other buildings the various Randall men had built, constructed as it was from rough-hewn logs, with low roofs and square windows. But this house was painted a very cheerful red and trimmed with whitewashed window boxes, frames, and gutters. Along the small path up to the door was a smattering of wild flowers bending to the demands of heavy, buzzing bumblebees. Emmy spied a bird feeder hanging from an eave and saw tiny little birds sprinting to it, suspending themselves for a second, then flying off just as quickly. She ducked out of the way of one that seemed determined to dive right into her hair.

"What was that?" she asked.

"Hummingbird, farm girl," Dot said, nudging her forward with an elbow. "Wait until the bats come out." The white screen door opened in front of them and Dot's mom, Helen, came out to greet them, with Dot's eleven-year-old sister, Virginia, close behind. They'd arrived at the cottage a few days before, and both had a sunburn glow from long, lazy days spent beside the lake.

"Dottie, you'll never believe how many sunfish I caught. We're having them for supper," Virginia exclaimed. "And a big fat crappie!"

"How was the drive?" Helen asked Emmy, taking her bag from her and slinging an arm around her waist.

"The drive was the easy part," Emmy said, not knowing where to start summing up the past twenty-four hours.

"At least it's cooler here," Helen said, leading Emmy up the path.

"Get this," Dot said, holding the screen door open. "Emmy's old boyfriend is marrying her *sister*."

Helen's nose wrinkled across its aquiline bridge. "You poor dear."

"It wouldn't be so bad if he loved her, and not me." Emmy walked through the open door and into the house, which began with the kitchen and the smell of hot oil.

"How do you know that?" Helen asked. A number of small fish fillets lay on a towel, waiting to be battered and fried, next to a wood-burning stove supporting a frying pan.

"He *told* her!" Dot said, dropping her bag on the floor next to a round table in the middle of the room, already set with a handful of wild flowers stuck into a small white vase, and gaily checked napkins that matched the red tablecloth. The cabinets were all painted bright white and a small red hand pump sat next to the sink. Dot picked up Emmy's wrist and held it between them. *"I've only ever loved you,"* she mocked, standing stiffly.

Helen tilted her head. "Don't be cruel, Dorothy. The boy might have a point."

Dot rolled her eyes. "Sure, on the top of his head."

"Come with me, dear," Helen said to Emmy. She followed Helen into the living room, where there was a brown bearskin rug, complete with head and teeth, sprawled before a stone fireplace. The room was cozy but cool in the spackling daylight, and Emmy was happy to see a bundle of logs and twigs ready to be lit against the evening's chill.

"You're on this side with the girls." Helen pointed to a room behind the chimney with three twin beds. She turned and took Emmy by the shoulders. "We're so glad you're finally here."

"Don't get all sappy on her," Dot called from the kitchen. She was already frying the fish, slipping bits of firewood into the stove to make the flame hotter. "Em, get your heartbreaking skirt out here and toss the salad, would ya?"

"Sure thing," she said. "Just as soon as I wash up."

After the last tiny sunfish had been eaten and the peach crumble dishes cleared, Helen broke out a deck of cards.

"Do you play pinochle?" she asked, opening the deck, splitting it in two, and then effortlessly forcing the cards back together in a small arc.

"Mom," Dot said, shaking her head a little.

"Oh, right. Of course you don't," she said, putting the cards quickly back into their package. "Why don't we have some coffee by the fire instead?"

"Please let me light the fire?" Virginia asked. In the diminished light and with her ebony hair tightly braided, she looked a good deal younger than her eleven years. "You promised."

"Go ahead, firebug, it's not like we could stop you," Dot said, and Virginia stuck out her tongue as she ran into the other room.

"I would like to learn to play cards, though," Emmy said, wanting the cozy evening to stretch on forever. The good company and conversation had gone a far way toward keeping her mind from circling around the approaching hour of the wedding. Still, the tangle of emotions roped its way into her thoughts and fairly strangled any lightheartedness she might otherwise have felt in the happy collection of Randall women.

"Okay, then," Helen said, stretching the length of her tall frame away from the table and setting a coffeepot on the stove. "Maybe after Virginia goes to sleep."

"Oh, Mom!" Virginia complained from the other room. "I can hear you in here, you know."

"Then you can hear that you've got ten minutes to brush your teeth and get to bed," Helen said. She set an old tray with mismatched coffee cups, a bowl of sugar, and a small jug of milk, and handed it off to Emmy, who then carried it all into the living room.

"I'll take that," Dot said, emerging from the bedroom dressed in pink pinstriped pajamas. "Why don't you go change while the urchin is cleaning itself?"

The bedroom windows were open to the night and Emmy could hear syncopated crickets with their slowing chirps echoing around the cabin. She clicked open her small pearl-colored Samsonite case and took her nightgown and robe from the left side. She changed quickly, drawn to the murmuring voices on the other side of the door, thinking about how by this time tomorrow her sister would be married to Ambrose. When she tried to imagine the two of them in the front of the church it was like viewing the scene through a stereopticon—a great distance in front of her nose, split in two, slightly different and yet exactly the same. As she sat on the bed to pull on a pair of granny socks, it struck her that she should do something to stop the wedding, to save her sister from an unknown future. Imagining the scene that would ensue convinced Emmy otherwise. No, unless she was willing to turn back the pages of the calendar to Easter, ruining countless lives in the process, nothing about the situation could be set straight by her actions.

Besides, who was she to say what the future would be? Just as Emmy finished dressing, Virginia burst through the door.

"Hey, that's my bed," she said, and yanked down the white chenille cover. Emmy swept her suitcase closed and onto the floor.

"Sorry, Virginia," she said.

"Call me Gini, please?" she whispered, lying down and settling the covers under her chin. "I hate my name."

"You know, my full name is Emmaline, and I hate it, too." She kissed her cousin on the nose and went out to the living room, where the lanterns were all lit and the fire was ablaze. Helen and Dot sat next to each other on the couch, sifting through a box of photographs, the women's heads bowed together until they almost touched. Emmy's throat felt dry and hoarse, and she coughed a little to cover her swell of regret that she didn't have a mother who would ever sit so closely. They looked up at the same time and smiled—Helen with her crooked grin and Dot with her sweet, pressed-lip smirk. They looked nothing alike, but no one would ever doubt they were mother and daughter. Emmy observed them with the fragile desire of a child on the outside of a candy store window, pockets empty.

"Come sit." Helen motioned to the other side of the couch, and Emmy sat next to her. "Closer, so you can see. Dot thought it might be nice for you to see some old pictures."

"I love these," Dot said, lifting a small stack of black-and-white squares edged in white and carefully flipped through them, looking at the backsides, where names and dates were scrawled in a meticulous script. "Hey, here's a baby picture of Pops in a dress. Look at his hair!" She showed Emmy a picture of a small boy in a white shirt that went to the floor. Irv had short, straight bangs that framed his tiny face.

Helen laughed and pushed a pair of glasses up her nose. "That one always reminds me of one of the Stooges, what's his name?"

"Moe," Dot said, and filed the image. They sat quietly as Dot continued to sort through the moments of captured rural time, ranging from men gathered in front of a threshing machine, to ladies in flowing dresses crossing a croquet lawn, to formally posed stiff portraits of high-buttoned men and women. When she neared the bottom of the box, Dot stopped, holding up a very worn and yellowed photo. "Look at this one," she said. There were four young people dressed in brilliant white summer clothing complete with parasols and walking sticks, as though they were headed to church or even a wedding. The women were quite young, and one in particular had Emmy's high fair looks. "That one could be you, Em," Dot said.

Helen clucked her tongue. "That's Jo," she said, tapping the photo with her index finger. "So that must be your grandmother, and there's Uncle Raymond." The finger rested on her lower lip for a moment, scratching at memory. "I don't recall this fellow, but then, it's well before I was born. It's not Irv's father." She flipped the photo over and read the inscription: "Detroit Lakes Chautauqua, 1919."

Emmy took the paper from Helen, careful to keep her fingertips on the white scalloped edge. She held it closer, astonished to see her grandmother looking like a girl, when she'd always seemed to Emmy as though she'd been born old—even more surprising was her own resemblance to Josephine: the high sculpture of her cheeks, the clear eyes, the pale hair braided down to her collarbones. The face of the slight man with his hand upon Lida's small shoulder was half shaded by the brim of his straw boater, which was practically glowing from the reflection of the sun. "It's not Grandfather; he was much taller. I could ask Aunt Josephine if you'd like."

Helen shrugged. "It's probably hers anyway." She grazed through the remaining photos at the bottom of the box. "Well, would you look at that? It's Daniel."

"My brother?" Emmy asked, looking at the image of a boy in a sailor suit pushing a tiny wheelbarrow. There were no photos of any sort in the Nelson home, not of children, parents, grandparents—of no one. It only struck Emmy as odd now, sitting here holding the ghostly image of her dead older brother, along with the pancaked images of her family's tree.

"I remember when your father gave this to Irv," Helen said, resting her hand on Emmy's knee. "Said Karin was throwing everything away, but he couldn't bear to let her burn this one."

"My father?" Emmy said, her voice breaking a little.

"He's always been in touch with us. I think it's been his way of defying his family. He's a good man to stick it out. You have to admire that, even if it seems crazy from the outside."

Dot got up and went into the kitchen. Emmy could hear her cleaning the final dishes and presetting the table for breakfast.

"Tell me," Emmy said, searching Helen's eyes. "Do you think I've done the right thing? Leaving home, I mean. It feels right most of the time, but I'm worried about my father."

"I think it's the best thing that's happened to Christian in a very long time," Helen said, turning to the box and re-ordering its contents. "You've done him quite a favor."

"I have?" Emmy asked.

"Your mother's not an easy woman, from all accounts."

Emmy looked again at Daniel. "Maybe if he hadn't died . . ." Emmy let the photo fall back into the box, among the still living and the long dead. "Maybe then she could have loved us all a little better."

Helen put the top on snugly and rose to place it on the shelf beside the fireplace. "Your mother loves you," Helen said with her back to Emmy. She turned and smiled. "In her way. Get some sleep."

Around the time the crickets finally stopped their lazy chirps and the frogs found something better to do than plague Emmy's ears with their croaking, she awoke from her fitful tossing to the sound of her name being whispered from someplace outside of the cabin. Pulling on her robe, she slipped onto the screen porch and attempted to still the pounding in her ears enough to listen more closely for the voice. A blue calm had infused the backyard, which was laden with long squat shadows and the occasional speck of light caused by some tiny insect. Taking a gray-hued throw from the glider, Emmy wrapped her shoulders and pushed the screen door silently open with her bare night-whitened foot.

"Hello?" she whispered, emboldened by the vibrant cast of full moonlight showing the emptiness of the yard around her. It must have been a dream, she thought as she wandered through the mulchy grass toward the shore, drawn by the melody of the ripples lapping up against the tiny makeshift boat dock. There, at the end of a length of floating slatted wood, the slight figure of a much younger Ambrose sat throwing pebbles into the distance, puncturing the still surface of the inky water, his shoulders sloped forward as though a great sadness was anchored around his neck. She knew him instantly as the lanky boy who had taught her how to shoot and dress a deer, a boy who had loved her more deeply and for such a long time that Emmy's heart sickened at her own callousness.

"Ambrose?" she whispered, her voice hollowed out by the salty thirst of midnight. The boy didn't respond, nor did he stop the perfect rhythm of the arcing rocks as he plucked each from his palm and sent them sailing against the dappled slash of moonlight stretching toward his feet. His blood-dark coat pooled behind him as Emmy set one foot on the dock and nearly fell into the water when it shifted and moved in front of her.

She started awake to find the cabin room around her, her cousins asleep in their beds, her aunt's quiet snore echoing up into the open rafters overhead. Very slowly, Emmy pushed into a sitting position and looked out of the lakeside's picture window. Though she could see that the dock remained bare, above the sleepy din of nocturnal solemnity, she could hear a noise that sounded like the quiet plinking of stones.

❦

After breakfast the girls changed into swimsuits and went down to the dock, where Emmy was pleased to find a tiny patch of rough beach. Her dream slowly dissipated with the warming of the day, and she did her best to slip into the enjoyment of a Sunday spent at the lake. Bobby would be at church by now, her usual space next to his crowded by another Doyle. The wedding in Glyndon would be easier to forget if only he were with her, Emmy thought as she slipped off her sandals and looped the ankle straps over a finger. The silty dirt at the water's edge felt cool under her tender feet as she dug her toes into its moistness. Looking around tentatively, she was somewhat relieved to see that the dock she had dreamed of in the night was farther away than she had imagined it. Exhaling into the damp air, she threw her towel down on a low-slung metal-framed chair with turquoise straps of woven material interlaced on the seat and backrest. She removed her slight linen cover-up to reveal an emerald green one-piece costume, cut low on the legs and high around the back, a halter tie around her neck. Into the warm, murky water she inched self-consciously, hesitating slightly at the pull of the sluggy lake bottom spiked with ankle-scratching reeds. The deeper she moved, the more real the world once again became and the tension she'd felt over the past days of calamity eased out of her joints and into the soupy foam swirling at her knees. Dot ran past her in a red two-piece suit with small Swiss dots and cute bows at each thigh and where the top met in the center of her ample bosom. She strapped a white cap with a large white flower onto her head and winked over her shoulder as she splashed into the lake. Gini hurried behind in a darling yellow maillot with tiny appliqued daisies along the trim. The sisters swam toward a raft that was anchored some yards away from shore. Emmy looked over her shoulder to see Helen in her pink chenille bathrobe already settled into a chair, a large-brimmed straw hat perched on her head and a magazine spread out on her lap. The day was a stunner—no clouds, no humidity, just dazzling sunshine and a slight breeze. Emmy shivered and waded deeper. She couldn't swim. In fact, the green one-piece was the first bathing suit she had ever owned or worn, and it was no small thing to have put it on and walked brazenly out here to the edge of her modesty. The girls reached the raft and Dot hoisted herself out of the water, in turn helping Gini before yelling back to Emmy.

"C'mon in!" Dot called from the raft, hands on either side of her mouth.

"I can't swim," Emmy said.

Dot laughed, lifted a hand to shade her eyes, and pointed with the other to the dock. "Use the canoe, and don't fall in!"

They passed the day sunning on the shore, paddling around on the lake, fishing from the dock, and wading to cool off. Late in the afternoon, Emmy picked up one of Helen's magazines and turned a few pages before settling into a kind of day-trance, letting the cares slide away from her tightly held grasp. She drifted around a bit through her thoughts, tried to focus in on Bobby, smiled with her eyes closed and her head tilted to one side. She wondered where he was right now this minute, and figured he was finished with Sunday dinner and back out on the road. The crew was working at full tilt, including Sunday afternoons, and Bobby's current role was to sweat it out alongside the guys who mixed and poured the cement. She pictured Bobby with his tanned back bared to the sun, using a long-handled hoe to move the wet mixture of rocks and cement evenly around the boxed form lined with thin iron reinforcement bars. He'd described the process in great detail, explaining to her how important the four-lane road would be, how it would open up the state of North Dakota to the rest of the world. His enthusiasm was intoxicating when she was with him, but here, far away on another shore, she turned her mind away from his ambition and pressed upon the thin ice of her own. She could see beneath her own mundane responsibilities a growing desire to take up a pen, to explore subjects, and perhaps unravel details that could be spun up into the kind of stories people would want to read. Surely Jim meant it when he said her instincts being wrong was just a rookie mistake, even though Emmy still felt stupid. There had been kindness in his voice, after all, and a kindred spirit in the way he shared the Halsey boy's situation. It didn't seem likely Jim would trust her unless he saw *some* potential in her. If she just kept trying, working hard and paying attention, she'd learn how not to make those kinds of mistakes and before long she'd have the assignment she craved.

And yet, here was where the hitch always happened—something in her gut told her that once she and Bobby were engaged, her work would fade away, and he would eventually insist that she give it up. All the more reason to work harder, prove herself so good at it that he could never question the way being in that newsroom made her brain buzz like no place else.

Deeper into a sun-snooze Emmy went, applying her logic first to the Arthur fire and then the one before it, which led her to see Pete's face shimmering in the heat of both—there to put them out even as he had started a fire of a different kind in her. A fly landed on her nose; she brushed it off lazily, annoyed at the disturbance it caused her train of thought. Where was she? Pete. At the car, telling her that Bobby didn't love her, couldn't. Why? Deeper still into the lull of the waves, the tinkling of ice in a brightly colored aluminum glass that felt cooler to the touch on her lip than the liquid felt on her tongue. A car door slamming, the sound reminiscent of Mr. Davidson's car on the high prairie road, Ambrose's profession of love, making her heart heavy in her chest. A hand on her shoulder, squeezing, gently shaking.

"Emmy, wake up," Helen's warm voice spoke from far off. Emmy sat up in her chair, wincing against the way the rays of the sun at this hour scattered across the top of the water. It hit her sleep-weakened vision with a million shards of dazzling light. She couldn't remember a thing she had been thinking, only that she was incredibly thirsty.

"Emmy?" It was Helen again, but more firm this time. "Irv just got here. Your grandmother is back in the hospital. You need to go."

Fifteen

My Peace Is Lost

The sun had set directly in Emmy's vision as she drove through Dilworth, her skin feeling hot, tight, and increasingly painful to the touch. At one point she had pressed a finger to her forearm and was shocked to see how white the impression was compared to the surrounding bright pink skin. As she pushed the gas pedal nearly to the floor, glancing in the rearview every few seconds to check for flashing lights, all she could hope for was to arrive in time to say good-bye to Lida. No matter how Emmy felt about her family situation, she still deeply loved the grandmother who had stepped in and nurtured her when Karin couldn't. In this way Lida and Josephine were clearly of the same blood—women who welcomed strays and reared foundlings as though they were their own children. Emmy felt lucky to have been cared for by both of them. The city limits finally closed in on the Crestliner, and Emmy made the turns toward the hospital as though pulled there instead of driven.

She walked into Saint Ansgar's just as visiting hours were ending. Even so, when she asked the sister seated at the front desk about Lida Nelson, she was directed immediately to the third floor. Emmy's pulse rose with the slow elevator, which rattled convulsively in a way that made her close her eyes. She'd never been in this hospital before, and suddenly wondered why her parents would bring Lida to a place run by Catholics. The large steel box shuddered to a stop and the doors made a scraping sound as they opened, over which Emmy could hear her mother's loud voice from around the corner of the antiseptic-smelling hall.

"How dare you come here like this!" Karin was yelling at someone, and the words cut through Emmy as though they had been said to her own face. Emmy got out of the elevator, and though she could not hear the murmured reply, the tone was Josephine's. "It's not *decent*," Karin continued with some restraint in her loud voice. "It's bad enough she wanted to be brought here, without you showing up *drunk*."

Emmy dug her fingernails into the flesh of her palms, focusing only on the sharp crescents of pain. She would have to take sides, as if it weren't already clear to this scattering of blood ties exactly where she stood. As she turned the corner, a grim tableau appeared, framed by the overlit white of wall, ceiling, and floor: Christian seated on a hard wooden bench, hat dangling from one hand, face propped in the other; off to his right Birdie stood, wearing what could only be described as a traveling costume—a loose-fitting powder blue serge suit with matching navy hat and shoes, no doubt part of her trousseau—leaning against a somber Ambrose; two nuns dressed in white from toe to wimple, hovering and shushing outside Lida's door.

"I showed up to make sure you did what she asked." Josephine's voice rose in volume to match that of Karin's. "This has gone on for long enough. Let her die in peace."

"I will not have it . . ." Karin yelled as she emerged from the room. She stopped short when her eyes met Emmy's and the fire that was smoldering there burst into squinted blue flame. "And now *you*." Karin looked up to the ceiling. "Please, Lord, give me the strength for all of this day." She turned away from Emmy and walked off toward the elevator, followed by one of the nuns. The other approached Emmy and took her hand.

"We haven't yet met, but I've heard a lot about you," she said, her voice as cool as her skin. "I'm Bobby's Aunt Clare." Emmy startled, taking in the sweet eyes, the smattering of freckles, all framed by the white wimple that fit tightly around Sister Clare's face, and so smoothly across the top of her head that it made Emmy wonder whether she had any hair underneath it at all.

"Oh, hello," Emmy said, managing a weak smile. "I'm glad you're here."

"I called him when I realized Mrs. Nelson is your grandmother, and he called your aunt," Sister Clare said, stroking Emmy's palm in a way that made her sleepy.

"How bad is it?" Emmy asked, letting her eyelids drop as she waited for the worst.

"Father Munsch is on his way for the last rites," Sister Clare said as softly as a drop of dew sliding down a blade of morning grass. "Are you ready to go in, dear? She's been asking for you."

"All right, then," Emmy said, and followed the sister into the room, which was even whiter than the hallway had been, apart from the cold steel bars of the bed itself, and the curtain rod from which hung a white cotton drape. Behind this lay Emmy's severely shrunken grandmother, whose skin seemed stretched tautly across her skeleton, as though it might take only a week for her to decompose. Sister Clare left the room with the door still open onto the murmuring hallway.

Josephine stood, wet-eyed, on the far side of the bed, gripping Lida's tiny hand in her own much stronger one; both were rippled with wormy veins. It seemed to Emmy that far more than five years separated the sisters, Josephine's loosely braided hair drawing back from her face in the same youthful way it had in the photo. I must remember to show it to Josephine, Emmy thought, but what did it really matter now, who the stranger was? Whatever had happened that long time ago was no weightier than the vapor of memory about to rise out of the room on the back of Lida's soul. History was nothing more substantial at this mortal threshold than something either long forgotten or not worth remembering in the first place. In any case, they would all be dust soon enough.

Lida lay motionless, her eyes closed except for a slight part where Emmy could see her grandmother's rheumy gaze, her chest barely rising and falling beneath a small black Bible. Are we already at the visitation? Emmy thought, unable to look away, unable to focus on what lay before her. Death in all of its acuity. The end of Lida. When her grandfather had died, the body was swept away, returned in a closed casket without so much as a final look, and lowered into the ground later the same day.

Emmy looked at her aunt, and Josephine met her gaze. There was a sweet smell in the air right over the bed. Funny Emmy hadn't noticed it before, but as she leaned in close to kiss her grandmother, the smell intensified, like a lilac or an Easter lily—cloying, inescapable, nauseating, pure. As her dry lips brushed Lida's cheek, Emmy felt the old woman turn her head toward the kiss. Emmy turned her head at the same time, aligning ear to mouth.

"Bitter," Lida rasped. Emmy waited, a dull pain in her lower back from falling asleep in the beach chair, sitting two hours in the car, hovering over the specter of death. Lida inhaled sharply, using the scant bit of air to say, "My rue is him." It was barely a whisper and Emmy turned her head quickly to use her better listening ear. She waited as her grandmother's chest rose, and on the thin exhale Emmy heard "My hurts unfair." No more words came, and after a few moments of wheezy silence, Josephine walked around the bed, steadying her wobbly shuffle by dragging one arm across the thin cotton blanket, and eased Emmy up to standing. The inflammation of her skin where her aunt's hand pinched as she led her toward the door shot sparks of light into Emmy's vision. A different sort of spoiled fruit smell emanated from Josephine, as though she'd been working hard at pickling a patch of overripe watermelon.

"Your mother can be such a witch," Josephine said, easing her grip and leading Emmy to the door. "Acting as though she owns my sister." The participants in the hallway had shuffled about in their dour assemblage. Ambrose took a step toward Emmy but just as quickly retreated. She looked at her small, rounded sister, whose hand was attached to the crook of Ambrose's elbow.

"Congratulations," Emmy said without inflection, accepting that there were many things beyond the reach of her concern. Christian rose from a bench set slightly down the hall and embraced Josephine.

"I'm sorry," he said, helping her to the bench and seating her there. Emmy followed as Sister Clare bustled past in her starched long skirts with a cup of water and a small blue book into Lida's room.

Emmy sat next to Josephine, wanting both to run from this painful place and to stay as long as it took. She looked up at Christian. "Why are we in a Catholic hospital?" Emmy could hear the mumble of Sister Clare quietly saying a prayer to the rhythm of small clicks. "I don't understand."

"Your grandmother asked to be taken here," he replied. "I'm not sure why."

Sister Clare leaned into the hallway and beckoned at Christian. He went.

Josephine put a hand on Emmy's leg. She flinched. "Sunburn?" her aunt asked, a slight slur on the *s*.

"I guess so." Emmy lifted her skirt just high enough to reveal the deep red skin and touched it, amazed by how it ached. She suddenly felt feverishly cold.

"We should get you home and take care of that," Josephine said without moving, gazing at the wall with her head tilted at an odd angle. She sighed. "You know, dear, they say that when you are ready to face God, you tend to revert to the simplest prayers. Maybe we become children in that moment. I guess that makes sense, though I can't imagine ever saying a Hail Mary again." She drew her mouth into a terse smile and tipped her head against Emmy's.

"No, I can't imagine that, either," Emmy said, a slinking helplessness clouding her spirit. She had tried to follow along with the Latin Mass in the Doyles' pew, and had finally become accustomed to the constant up and down, kneel and stand of the intricate Catholic ceremony. Still, it felt as though it would always be too foreign to embrace fully. Emmy held the hot palm of her hand to her even hotter forehead. She'd seen a few people in coffins, but she'd never seen anyone this close to the other side of one. What if those had been her grandmother's final words? It was Emmy's burden now to understand them and comport their meaning into the world, to learn from her grandmother's life before utterly ruining her own. Emmy looked at Josephine.

"Did you hear her?" Emmy whispered, bereft.

"Yes," Josephine said.

"What did she say?"

"She said *'Beten, meine Ruh ist hin, mein Herz ist schwer,'*" Josephine said in flawless, dramatic German. "It's from *Faust*: 'My peace is lost, my heart is heavy.' Father used to read it to us. As if growing up on the prairie weren't grim enough."

"Oh," Emmy said, feeling the heaviness of lost peace in her own heart as well. "But why is she beaten?"

"*Beten*, Emmy," Josephine replied as she fanned away a fly from her nose. "It's German for pray. Though if you ask me, it's too late for all of that—not that it ever seemed to do her any good in the first place."

Emmy snapped open her purse, hesitated, and then withdrew the small sepia square nestled into a side pocket, thinking it might give her aunt some relief. She held it out in front of Josephine. "You were both so beautiful."

Josephine slowly turned her head from the photo to Emmy, her sad expression curdling into something more deeply primal. "Where did you get this?" she hissed, snatching the paper so quickly out of Emmy's hand that it left a small cut on her forefinger, which she instantly held to her tongue.

"At the cabin," Emmy said around the wound. "Helen gave it to me."

Josephine ripped the photo in half before shredding it into tiny pieces that lay in an ashy pile in her lap. Once it was destroyed, she stood, letting the miniature blizzard dust the floor as she walked down the hall to a watercooler and stayed there, not drinking or moving.

Emmy quickly collected what she could and threw the pieces into her purse, abashed for not having thought through her actions. She stood and moved back to Lida's room and saw Christian standing next to Lida's bed. The doorway framed her father in his stooped sadness, a vision of a young boy buried inside of an old man. It was clear to Emmy that not only did he love his mother very deeply, but also that he had been loved by her in return. The empty spot inside Emmy widened, and she returned to the bench, feeling insufficiently prepared for the rapid approach of death. The elevator groaned open and Emmy's stomach lurched toward the sound, all of her muscles tensing against a fresh encounter with Karin. Instead, there stood Bobby, smiling at her with his soft lips.

"Go on, Emmy," Josephine said as she turned toward the sound, an acrid hiccup in her drawl. "Leave death to the dying. You've said your good-bye."

Emmy parked the Crestliner in the yard and Bobby drove in right behind it, stopping his truck at a neat angle. Hunger began to fill the void made by Josephine's dismissal, and Emmy began to regret not stopping for a bite as Bobby had suggested. The ache all over her skin settled into a deeper, rougher pain even as the murmurs of the lake licked at her ears in the upholstered silence of the car, caressing Emmy's weary body with the promise of its cooling undercurrents. She closed her eyes and leaned into the heat all around her, inhaling deeply the smell of fish on the dock and wild mint in her iced tea. There was a tap at the window and Emmy turned her head toward the sound. She expected to see Bobby, but instead there was a dark brown muzzle and deep chocolate eyes peering out of an even darker, velvety coat. Emmy reached for the door handle, wincing at the tingle of scathed skin.

"Oh, Bobby, he's perfect!" Emmy took the pup from his outstretched hands and buried her nose in the silky fur. It smelled like new shoes. "Is he mine?"

"He's a she," Bobby said, clearly delighted that he'd done the right thing. "One of the guys on the crew had a bunch of these little guys, and when he asked me if I knew of anyone who could use one, I figured you could." He scratched the pup behind an ear.

Emmy cradled her closer and walked to the house. "Coffee?"

"Sort of a funny name for a dog, but I guess she's the right color." Bobby put his arm around Emmy's shoulder. She winced and pulled away.

"I think I burned my skin a little," she said, holding the pup to the porch light. "She is the right color. Hello, Coffee. Welcome to the Randall Estate, home for wayward girls."

"You'd better put her down before she pees on you," Bobby said. "She has a habit of doing that sort of thing."

Emmy looked at the dark house, and for the first time felt that she had perhaps overstayed her welcome. She settled Coffee on her large feet. "I'd better ask Josephine if it's okay," she said, the paper cut from the photograph stinging as though it had happened to her heart.

"It's okay," Bobby said. "You didn't think I'd clear it with her first?"

"She doesn't mind?" Emmy asked, squinting the water from her eyes.

Bobby shook his head. "She said she likes dogs." He brushed her nose with his lips.

"Ouch," she said. "Even that hurts."

"Sister Clare said you looked a little lobstery." Bobby took a small blue jar out of his pocket. "First-aid cream. She said it might help."

"You think of everything, don't you?" Emmy tenderly kissed his lips and opened the front door. Bobby whistled and Coffee wound around his ankle, sniffing the air at the threshold and making a softly nervous sound that was too meek to be a growl. She looked up at Emmy and tipped her head so quickly that one of her floppy ears landed across her brow. She shook it off with a full-body shudder, as though unaccustomed to the feel of the world.

Emmy knelt and scratched the offending ear, smoothing it into place. "It's okay, girl, that's just Flossie. She's too old and self-satisfied to care about a dog." Emmy picked up Coffee and whispered, "I was afraid of her at first, too. You'll be fine."

Once they were inside, Bobby set up the coffeepot, produced a steak bone for Coffee to gnaw, and Emmy went in the direction of her room in search of a lightweight robe—anything to get the scratch of her crinoline away from her bristling skin. She had one made of silk that Josephine had given her, saying that all ladies should have at least one pretty thing to sleep in, but it seemed too risqué for the application of burn cream. Instead she painfully peeled off her top layer of clothing, and slipped into her bathing suit, as it was the only option that made sense—she certainly couldn't wear her bra and underpants in front of Bobby—besides, it clearly displayed exactly the parts of her that were in need of help. Carefully draping her slightly ratty beige nylon robe over her shoulders, Emmy steadied herself against the dressing table, nauseated by the fresh prickling of blistering pain caused by the sticky material. She suspended her arms in midair as she delicately made her way back into the kitchen, where she was surprised to see a candlelit dinner of sandwiches and cold milk laid out as though it were a much more special occasion. The perfection with which Bobby had made the table almost *too* romantic put Emmy back on the edge that she had tried to leave in the hospital, the precipice where her grandmother lay suspended in time, waiting for death. Emmy tried to smile in appreciation but knew the corners of her mouth rose far less than Bobby deserved for his efforts.

"It hurts to smile now," she said, sitting down gingerly and taking a large bite of sandwich. Bobby watched her eat and she became self-conscious of how ravenous she must look, instantly feeling her nausea rise back up and take hold for good. She put down the sandwich and pushed away the plate, drinking steadily from the cold glass of milk until the final drops collected at the corners of her mouth and she licked at them like a sated cat.

"I'm sorry, it's all so lovely," she said. "But I just can't eat."

"I can't, either," he said. "I feel so terrible for you." Bobby cleared the plates into the sink and returned to the table with the jar of cream. He moved behind her chair and silently slipped the robe from her, lifting her left arm tenderly by the fingers away from her body and slicking a long white line of cream from shoulder to wrist. The sharp smell of menthol permeated the room, untying the twisted knot in the middle of Emmy's brow.

"You don't have to do that," she said. "I can manage."

"Shhh." Bobby worked the soothing coolness in tiny feather strokes across her skin, limiting his touch to the barest tickle. By the time he had finished this rhythm down her other arm, she was breathing heavily with her eyes closed, the pain relief bringing on a deeper, richer heat. Bobby placed his fingers under both of her palms and indicated she should stand by slightly tipping her hands in his direction. With her eyes still closed, she lifted easily from the chair and followed him into the other room, where he laid her down on the davenport and knelt on the floor before her. First her left leg was lifted into the air, the long line of cream now making her shiver in the anticipation of its ability to soothe even as the right leg ached for the same treatment. Emmy began to feel as though her body were turning into points of light, each tiny pinprick saturated with desire. Bobby must have sensed this change—perhaps because Emmy knew her breathing had become labored, intense, and punctuated by soft moans—for now every other finger circle was countered with the slightest brush of what had to be his lips. She wanted to look but was afraid of disrupting the free fall of physical sensation. As he worked his way up her thighs, her body arched and next she knew he was hovering a bare inch above her, and his tongue slid into her open, panting lips. Only their mouths touched for long delicious minutes, and Emmy knew that she could go until they stopped, yearning for the exquisite pain of his rough skin shredding hers. A flash of light swept through the dark room and Emmy gingerly slipped out from under Bobby, going to the window in expectation of her aunt's return, which could mean only one thing. There in the yard sat Ambrose's truck. It idled only for a second before the gears shrieked and the flash of light passed once again through the house as he spun the wheels into reverse down the long drive. Emmy wrapped her arms around her waist, willing herself not to cry.

"Who was it?" Bobby said, at her shoulder.

Emmy shook her head. "No one," she said. "No one at all."

Sixteen

When the Soul Is Touched

There's a story breaking over in Fargo." A voice burrowed through the phone line and into Emmy's ear. It had taken a number of rings and more than enough barking to cause her to go downstairs to the phone in the chilly pitch-dark of middle night. It felt as though she'd maybe slept an hour or two, and her groggy mind didn't start easily, despite the welcome sound of Jim's voice. "You ready?"

"Okay," she replied, looking out the side window to see the Jeep house warmly lit from within. Josephine had finally resumed her regular night owl schedule of writing, after far too many days holed up in the back bedroom following Lida's funeral. There hadn't been enough time for a full reunion between the sisters, but Josephine had told Emmy it had been as though the time had never passed, the separation never happened. The past was not what mattered to Josephine—there had been too much of it—and so she'd thrown herself back into her work. Emmy had done likewise, taking every opportunity to prove to Jim that she was worthy of his increasing confidence in her. Emmy was relieved to have things moving forward, and thrilled to be getting this particular call. "What time is it?"

"Half past five. Get dressed. I'm picking you up in ten minutes." The phone went dead in Emmy's hand. Suddenly she was wide-awake, running upstairs to throw on whatever clothes she could get to first, Coffee close at her heels. Jim had promised her a ride along to his next big story, and this was her chance to learn something more interesting than pulling cords and routing copy. The more she observed the writers up close and felt the jolts of adrenaline that came with the ring of a phone or the pushing of a deadline, the more alluring the job of reporter became. When Emmy wasn't at work, she would devour the newspaper from headline to obituary, circling details and turns of phrase that she liked in particular, recognizing bits of copy that she'd read on foot the night before.

In the weeks that had passed since her grandmother had died, the hours of the day leading up to Emmy's work shift had become empty and monotonous by comparison to the rush of the newsroom, rarely disturbed by anything more than routine chores or a poignant feeling of absence in the shape of Lida. Even Bobby had become never-present with the advent of September and freshman classes at NDAC in addition to work on the weekends out on the strip of interstate that kept its steady pace, snailing toward Jamestown. When Emmy closed her eyes she could still feel his soothing caresses on her fiery skin, even though there had been no further intimacy in the weeks since. Sometimes she wondered if his busy schedule had some sort of intent behind it, a distancing of a different sort, but then she would see him in church on Sunday morning and hear him talk about his class load and work schedule, reassuring her that all he did, he did for their future together.

She stepped quietly into slim black trousers and a pair of ballet flats, choosing a maroon buttoned blouse, and then quickly dragged a brush through her tousled hair. It had grown in nicely from the severity of the cut she'd gotten in June, and she could finally tuck it behind her ears. As she stuffed a spiral notebook and three pencils into the small satchel that Mr. Utke had given her, Emmy welcomed the flurry in her stomach, the nervous feeling that told her she'd made the right choice to put off college for a year. Dot had packed up and driven down to nursing school in Saint Paul, and Bev's summer in Paris had turned into fall in London. The glue of shared childhood seemed to weaken on the brink of maturity, and as Emmy's smattering of friends ventured off into the world, she became more at home amid the thrum and energy of the wire machines and printing presses.

After a brief glance in the mirror, Emmy ran back down the stairs and cleared the front door just as Jim's car swung into the yard. Feeling the first deathly chill of fall in the mid-September air, she darted back into the house and grabbed Josephine's red-checked barn coat. She jumped in the car and shut the door quickly.

"Hello," Jim said, reversing down the drive.

"Stop here," she instructed as they approached the Jeep house. "I'll be only a minute."

Emmy ran up the tile-bordered walkway and knocked. After a moment, Josephine opened the door.

"I'm sorry to interrupt," Emmy said, surprised to see that Josephine exuded an alert calm after being up all night.

"What's wrong?" Josephine asked, looking past Emmy at Jim's idling car.

"I'm not sure, but Jim's asked me to go on a story with him," Emmy replied, holding her coat closed at the collar, a small smile pulling at her lip. "Will you take Coffee out for me?"

"I'll bring her out here." Josephine nodded. "She's better company than my current heroine."

"Thanks." Emmy raced back to the car, where Jim fiddled with the dials on the radio. "What's happened?" she asked him as they drove off.

"There's a body over in Golden Ridge." He glanced at Emmy, as though trying to gauge her reaction before going on with more details. "In the root cellar of a condemned house. A construction crew found it and called the police." Jim lit a cigarette and passed it to her without lighting another for himself. She took a long draw and let the smoke flow out of her nose.

Emmy shivered and buttoned up the coat against the unnerving thought of living in the basement of an abandoned house. "Why the middle of the night?"

"The coroner was in Chicago." Jim pushed his hat up from his forehead and whistled as they crossed over the bridge to Fargo and down to Nineteenth Avenue North.

"Do you always do that?" she asked.

"What?"

"Whistle when you cross a bridge?"

"I have no idea," he said. "Maybe."

"I know a boy who lived over there, before the storm," she said, warding off the gloom that had begun to settle around the word *body*. "Around ten, named Jesse. Such a terrible story, lost his family. Had to go live with relatives in Grand Forks."

"Acevedo?" Jim asked. "They got the worst of it, all right."

"You know him?"

Jim coughed. "I was the first reporter on the scene." He gestured toward the south. "Just live that way a few blocks."

"Was your house hit?"

"No. Elise and I went down to the basement at the first siren and waited out the fifteen minutes of wind. When we came up, the air was green and silent—sweet smelling, from all of the broken trees. Then the wailing started. I went out to get in the car, but a giant elm had destroyed it, so I started running toward the screams. I suppose that doesn't sound very smart."

"It sounds brave," Emmy said.

"Not brave at all," he said. "Look, I've learned that there are two kinds of people: those who run toward a problem and those who run away. One is no braver than the other. It's all instinct."

"What about those who just stand and watch?" Emmy asked.

Jim laughed through his nose. "You have a sharp way of seeing things, for a kid. Sure, I guess there are those who do that, too."

His mirth flattered her, even as the word *kid* made her feel too young. As they passed through the corridor along Twelfth Avenue that ran along the southern edge of the college and past Hector Field, Emmy noticed how a grid of lonely yellow lights stood out on the left, against a flat dark line of night. As they neared the neighborhood, she realized this odd pattern was caused by the sudden dearth of trees, and as they entered the dismembered neighborhood she was even more taken by the gaping holes between tiny houses where the tornado had randomly selected the more vulnerable structures. This area was much poorer than North Moorhead, and the Nelsons' small house looked palatial when compared to these tiny ramshackle abodes. There was scant evidence of rebuilding, and Emmy was stunned to see heaping piles of debris still mounded in the far corners of some of the lots, illuminated by the dingy yellow light of the streetlamps. It was hard to tell which houses were occupied, as even the ones still standing had cheap patching that could indicate either habitability or desertion.

"Take notes," Jim said, and Emmy fished a pencil and notebook out of her satchel. She pressed the lead against the open page, wrote "ramshackle" and "denuded." He turned one corner and then the next, the quiet car practically gliding over the empty re-paved streets until at last, turning the corner on Twenty-ninth Street, Jim slowed and pulled to the curb at the sight of a fire truck, ambulance, and assorted cars blocking off the end of the street. Killing the engine, Jim righted his hat and sighed.

"I've got a bad feeling about this," he said, shrugging more deeply into his camel hair coat.

"More than usual?" Emmy asked, disquietude scaling up her arms and neck. She shook herself to get warm as Jim threw open his door and approached a man in a police uniform.

"Morning, Jim," the man said as Emmy quickly caught up.

"Hey, Harry, this is Emmy Nelson. She's with me," Jim said, shaking the man's hand. "Okay?"

"Yeah, okay," Harry said, looking her over. He was quite young, she thought, possibly even her age.

"What you got?" Jim asked him, and Emmy turned her notebook to a fresh page.

"Some kid," Harry said. "Only dead a day or so, from what I hear tell."

Jim rubbed his chin. "Cause?"

"I'm just crowd control." Harry tapped a cigarette out of a pack of Viceroys. "Got a light?"

Jim struck a match and offered the flame. "How old?" he asked.

Harry blew smoke mixed with cold breath high into the still-dark sky. "Nine, maybe ten? Ask the boss."

"Okay, then." Jim looked at Emmy. She wrote down "9–10," and glanced at Jim, the hair on her arms goosed. They walked past Harry and down the street, Emmy falling a step behind and soaking in as many details as she could scratch down. Along the edge of the sidewalk was an empty lot, and she began to see the forms of familiar things in the tall dried grass—a few tree stumps, a child's wagon missing a wheel, a paper bag quavering in the breeze against an object that was pinning it in place.

"There's still so much debris," she said, and Jim nodded without turning until they reached the phalanx of emergency vehicles. "Why the fire truck, do you suppose?" she asked him.

"Search and recovery." He grimaced. "They have the axes and ladders."

The light grew dimmer between the truck and the ambulance and Emmy braced against them as she stepped more carefully toward a brighter light that drew her forward until she emerged to see a floodlit, half-demolished house with people milling about like termites in the process of stealthily removing every shred of human invention. Details began to come into focus as the sky lightened in advance of the dawn. One outer wall had been ripped clean away from the structure, leaving the half-lit rooms exposed, the cheap wallpaper of the living room and battered cabinetry of the kitchen looking like a haunted dollhouse. Most of the men were milling about an area in the yard, and from there a man wearing a long trench coat approached them. In one hand he held a boxy camera, the spent flashbulb of which he unscrewed and stuffed in a pocket as he walked.

"Hello, Ted," Jim said, extending a hand. "What you got here?"

Ted raised a hoary eyebrow at Emmy, drew a new bulb out of the other pocket, and talked around a wad of chewing tobacco as he pressed the tiny light into the camera's socket. "Runaway, I suspect. We haven't ID'd the body yet. Just finished up with the photos. Don says an inquest is unlikely."

"Who's Don?" Emmy asked. She wanted to ask what an inquest was, too, but held back, hoping to look less at sea than she felt.

"Dr. Lawrence, the coroner," Jim said, studying the house. "When'll they bring the boy up?" he asked Ted.

Ted stopped his fiddling and spit a long line of dark liquid from one side of his mouth. "Didn't say it was a boy."

Jim put a hand on Ted's shoulder and began to walk past as he said, "You didn't need to."

Emmy quickly caught up to Jim's side and gauged his expression. "Who is it?" she asked just as two men carrying a slight, sheet-covered body on a stretcher emerged from the slanted cellar door on the side of the house that still stood mostly unscathed.

Jim folded his arms and shook his head slowly. "I can't say for certain. But that's the Acevedo house."

Emmy's heart crimped. "Jesse?"

"I was here that night, saw them bring out his siblings. One by one." Jim's face was ashen in the first rays of daylight. "His mother."

"Well, I know what he looks like," Emmy said, and started toward the stretcher. Jim caught her arm and pulled her back as the two men carrying it made their way past Emmy and to the open doors of the ambulance. A pungency not entirely unlike the smell of a two-day dead and bloated cow hit her and she stopped, a quick hand over her nose and mouth.

Jim handed her his handkerchief. "You ever seen a dead body?"

She brushed off his hand, thought of her nearly dead grandmother, and then the last time she'd seen Jesse alive. "No." As she watched the ambulance drive off, Emmy wondered about the ages of the other children and where Jesse fit in, whether he was a help to his mother with all those kids, where he had gone during the storm in order to escape one fate but be so cruelly delivered to another.

"You ready to ask some questions?" Jim asked her in his full voice, and Emmy jumped.

"Oh, I don't know," she said, flipping her mind away from the personal and toward the morning's assumed goal. "What if it isn't Jesse? And if it is, why did he come back here, and how did he die?" Emmy searched the faces in the crowd, determining which of the men still milling about she should approach first. Harry didn't seem to know much; Ted didn't know a whole lot more. "I need to find the coroner, right?"

"That's a good start, but he's already gone," Jim said. "That was him with the stretcher."

Emmy turned in a slow circle in the crisp morning light, the investigators, police, and firemen moving around the yard, in and out of the house, or to their vehicles. She stopped when she saw Pete emerge from the cellar in his fireman's uniform, his face as ashen as the still-warming sky above them.

"It's Jesse, after all," she murmured to Jim. "That's Bobby's friend, Pete

Chaklis." Pete crossed the short distance between them, glanced at Emmy, and then continued to the fire truck, his eyes trained on the blank expanse in front of him.

"Looks like he's seen a ghost," Jim said, close to Emmy's ear.

"I suppose he has," she replied, the desolation of Jesse's certain demise settling upon her like a fine mist.

Ted ambled back over to them, his camera replaced by a notepad much like Emmy's.

"Look," he said to Jim. "We should have the investigation wrapped up in a couple of hours. I'll give you a call when I can get you down into the hole."

"Much appreciated," Jim said, and shook Ted's hand before directing Emmy to the car. "Let's go see what we can dig up?"

❧

Around noon, Emmy looked at the clock in the archive room and sighed. She stretched her arms as high above her head as she could get them and pushed her chair away from the table. She'd been scribbling down her impressions of the morning, crafting small sentences loaded with import as best she could. Very little in school had prepared her for this, but the rhythm of copy felt oddly natural to her, even though her writing contained more crossed-out words than not. There was something captivating in watching the nib of the pen soak the thin paper of the spiral-bound pad when she held a thought for too long, and the thin scratch of the ink when she wrote too quickly. She chewed on the corner of her left thumbnail all the while, releasing long enough only to turn a page forward to press on or backward to find where she might already have used an uncommon word, crossing it out, inserting something fresh.

On the table in front of her were the carefully spread-out pages of *The Fargo Forum* from June 21, 1957, the day after the storm. She pulled the front page to her for perhaps the twentieth time, mesmerized by the photo beneath the top-fold breadth of the tornado cloud in deathly midswirl. This other image was half the size but carried twice the blow: a young man with a shock of blond bangs hanging to the middle of his face, looking down at the limp body of a tiny child in his arms. She read the caption again, still unable to fully absorb the meaning of the words: "Off-duty Fargo firefighter

Peter Chaklis carries the body of Marcela Acevedo, 5. Three other Acevedo children and their mother died in the storm."

Emmy held the newspaper, transfixed by the limpness of tiny Marcela. She couldn't have weighed much more than a wet feather, and it was entirely clear that her form was already lifeless, every muscle having abandoned the urge to contract. Mrs. Acevedo and her four youngest children had taken shelter in the bathtub, of all places, possibly forgoing the basement due to her fear of the dark, or so went the story as reported to Jim at the time. Emmy thought back to her morning out in Golden Ridge, the broken dollhouse, and tried to restore the missing walls enough to envision those last moments as the windows blew out and the children were spun away from their mother. Emmy read on, fascinated to learn that Mrs. Acevedo was not from Mexico like her husband, but was a local woman whose family had come over from Europe after the war. That explained Mrs. Doyle's assertion that Jesse's maternal grandparents hadn't wanted him. It must have been the hardest part for the boy—knowing that the person he loved most in the world had parents who hated him merely because of his father. Emmy read on, but when she came to the detail that Jesse's given name was Jesus, she stopped reading, heartbroken that a child named after a man who gave so much to the world would have everything good ripped away. The sound of the windowpane rattling in the door behind Emmy startled her, and she turned to see Jim, silently reading from his notepad.

"I can't seem to come up with anything out of the ordinary," he said, flipping a page. "It's just a damn shame his aunt didn't call someone to follow up." Jesse had been sent to his aunt's family, Emmy knew, but hadn't heard that he'd left them.

"Maybe she didn't have a telephone," Emmy said. "Or money enough to make the call."

Jim shrugged. "Or maybe she didn't have any reason to be concerned." He looked over her shoulder and put his index finger on her copy, reading, "'Acevedo must have been frightened to death alone in that dark space.' Hmm." He picked up her pen and drew a line through "frightened to death." "This is what's known as a cliché, or a turn of phrase that's used too much. You need to beat them out of your writing, kid. You know, things like 'baby with the bathwater' and 'green with envy.'"

Emmy swallowed and looked down at the offending sentence, wondering how many more were in her piece. "Thanks," she said as a knock at the door broke into their conversation. Emmy stood, dusting her slacks of the tiny shards of newspaper that had collected from her research. A woman tentatively entered the room; a cloche was pulled down over her ears. It took Emmy a beat to recognize within the tightly huddled figure her old friend Svenja; her body had gained considerable girth, her ill-fitted skirt was frayed at the edges, and the thin cotton coat was slightly muddy and in need of a button in the middle of the row, where Svenja clutched at it, her glove gray.

"Emmaline," Svenja said quietly, turning her eyes away from Jim as he passed through the doorway and went back down the hall. Svenja bit her lower lip. "I didn't know where else to go. I'm sorry. I'd heard you worked here and told the girl out front that I was your sister."

"It's okay," Emmy said as she led Svenja to a chair, noticing a light green, crescent-shaped bruise just above her collar. Svenja's hand went there and pulled a scarf up out of the coat and around her neck. She sat carefully down on the hard wooden chair.

"I need money," Svenja said, placing her shaking hands on the newspapers and pushing them slightly away. "To buy a bus ticket."

"What's happened?" Emmy sat next to Svenja, steadying her arm. The girl flinched. "Does John know where you are?"

Svenja darted her eyes to Emmy's, then just as quickly refocused on the clock over the filing cabinets. "I can't tell you. I just need the ticket. There's a place in Saint Paul . . . I have an aunt. If anyone can understand, it's you!" Her voice caught on the edge of broken hope.

"You can tell me," Emmy said. "Has John done something?" It seemed an impossible idea. The John Hansen that Emmy knew would never do anything to incite such fear—he'd only ever been quiet and kind—but then she'd thought the same of Ambrose. If there was one thing Emmy had learned, it was not to base an opinion on a person's public behavior.

Svenja jolted her head, a nod that looked like a dismissal. "I can't go back, not now. Not while he's . . ." She burst into quiet sobs, her mouth contorting into a downward smile that neither confirmed nor denied her husband's role in her distress. Emmy wrapped an arm around her, rocking steadily as Svenja gave in to her tears, the flow of which eventually ebbed enough for Emmy to release the girl.

"The ticket's only three dollars and fifty cents." Svenja sniffed. "But whatever you can spare will be most appreciated."

"Do you think a good night's rest would help things? Why not stay with me and get a fresh look at it all tomorrow?" Emmy offered, only to see a wild hysteria wash over Svenja's face, the kind of look she'd seen in the rolling eyes of the birthing cow in the barn.

"He's—" Svenja said, slapped a hand over her mouth, pushed back the chair, and let it topple behind her in a noise so alarming that it brought Jim rushing into the room.

"We're all right, Jim," Emmy said calmly, and motioned for him to leave them alone. She reached into her satchel and unsnapped the interior pocket where she kept loose change and folding money.

"Here," she said, pressing a ten-dollar bill into Svenja's shaking hand and closing the fingers into a fist. "Get that bus. I won't tell John where you've gone. I promise."

"Promise me you won't tell *anyone* where I've gone?" Svenja begged, shaking her head and backing toward the door. "There are people everywhere who would tell, if they knew."

Emmy studied the paranoid fear contorting her friend's still beautiful face and detected something else, a roundness that belied a deeper and more protective vigilance blossoming within her, something Emmy hadn't seen since that cold day in Bev's kitchen. She turned to the table quickly and tore a strip of paper off the bottom of her notepad, scrawled her address and the office's phone number and handed it to her friend.

"Okay," Emmy said, hesitating, and yet recognizing in Svenja the kind of rickety decisiveness Emmy had once clung to herself. "On the condition that you write me the minute you get where you're going, and call this number if you ever need anything. I'm on the switchboard most nights, so make the call collect." Emmy pulled on her coat. "Let me go with you to the bus station."

A ghost of a smile drifted across Svenja's face and she hugged Emmy tightly, the protrusion of Svenja's stomach jarring in its hard fullness. "It's only a few blocks," she said, looking at her watch and working out a silent timetable. "I'll be fine now. They won't be back for an hour, at least."

Jim returned. "We're in," he said excitedly to Emmy as Svenja slipped past him through the door. "We can go into the Acevedo house." He watched Svenja go, perplexed.

Emmy grabbed her satchel and started to follow Svenja as Jim's words sunk in and she stopped short. She'll be all right, Emmy told herself, and went back for her notebook before hastening with Jim to his car. She saw Svenja already a block away. The bus station was only three blocks farther south. There would be an aunt at the other end. Svenja would be fine.

"You want me to tail her?" Jim asked as he started the car.

"If you don't mind," Emmy replied, unable to quell her doubt. They crawled along a fair distance behind Svenja, and when she slipped into the heavy wooden door of the station, Emmy relaxed and turned her thoughts to Golden Ridge.

Seventeen

By a Soft Whisper

It hasn't changed much in a year," Jim said as they drove back into the heart of Golden Ridge. "After the cleanup, that is. You should have seen it, Em, trees everywhere, cars upturned, houses flattened, bodies . . ." He blew smoke against the fogging windshield. "I was in the war, you know, and it looked like that. Devastation. Eerie quiet." He pointed at an empty yard to the left, where a small group of people was gathered. "That's where Minnie Campbell's house was blown off its foundation and turned on its side before collapsing entirely." Emmy could hear some sort of chanting rising from the crowd as the car drew closer, and she rolled down her window.

"What's going on?" she asked. Jim slowed the car to the curb and leaned across to see out of her window. She caught a mix of menthol, Brylcreem, and something else—boiled chicken?—whose blend seemed oddly comforting.

"Looks like some sort of protest." He shifted the car into park and pulled the brake. "Let's go have a look."

The closer they walked to the circle of onlookers, the clearer the chant became:

"Solstad for mayor!"

Emmy rubbed her arms of a sudden chill as she began to recognize various boys she'd known in Glyndon, all dressed in Ambrose's recent uniform of black pants, white short-sleeved shirts, and thin black neckties. The chant stopped and a loud, instantly recognizable voice boomed through the cool September air.

"My good people," Curtis Davidson said from his perch atop what was once Minnie Campbell's front stoop but was now just a stack of concrete steps to nowhere. "Thank you for coming out here today. As concerned citizens, we must stand together against the infiltration of lower-income housing development designed for the ceaseless flow of immigrants into our fair city, such as the one proposed for this very spot by, lessee here . . ." He looked down at a piece of paper. "Some outfit by the name of Robertson. This sort of pandering to outsiders seems un-American to me." Mr. Davidson paused as a murmur of agreement rose from the crowd. "My friends, where once stood an elderly woman's tidy home, there will be a concrete ghetto of shabby apartments designed specifically for luring cheap labor to the valley—labor that was once done with our own hands, alongside our sons, while our wives and daughters kept the hearth fires burning. That work is no longer valuable to the young men of our community. And the young women?" Mr. Davidson looked straight at Emmy. "They want *careers.* The old ways, where God and family came first, aren't good enough for our youth. Instead they drive around without purpose in cars every night, getting up to no good—from the rampage of two teenagers in Wyoming to the defacement of school property last winter, our children have lost their way, and we need to bring them on home."

A number of spectators began to chant again, and Mr. Davidson let them until he raised a hand and they went silent. His skin looked waxed and polished in the bright daylight; his eyes squinted to dots.

"Listen, my friends. This path of delinquency can be altered, but we need to take a hard look at where we place our own values, and say no to the influence of foreign ideas. Where once there stood the dream of a hardworking, native-born American son, there will soon be an immigrant family stealing our homes along with our jobs. The more this happens, the more dangerous our neighborhoods become. Why, right down the road here apiece a Mexican boy was found dead in the basement of his former home—*this* is their idea of taking care of their own. Mayor Lashkowitz's regime can talk all they want about rebuilding and how this project will create new jobs for Americans, but let's call it what it is: Herschel's betrayal."

"He doesn't even say how Jesse died," Emmy said to Jim.

"These types don't care about the truth," he replied. "Just what gets votes."

An older lady in front of them made a shushing sound, and Emmy quieted, turning her attention onto the crowd, where she noted a scattering of young men dressed in black slacks and white shirts, their skinny black ties and dark armbands easily setting them apart from the rapt, primarily elderly audience. She caught sight of John Hansen, who clearly had no idea that Svenja had just boarded a bus to Saint Paul. His expression was as open and simple as it ever had been, too lit from Mr. Davidson's words for Emmy's taste. She tried to imagine what he must have done to cause Svenja's agitation and her flight.

"Some say that being mayor isn't enough," Mr. Davidson continued. He wiped his dry brow with a handkerchief. "That Lashkowitz fellow has his eyes on governor, maybe even—" He stopped to laugh. "President." A unified gasp rose from parts of the audience. "Now, now, I say, that's all well and good, but when he's sitting all sheeny up in the White House, we'll be mopping up after his itinerant houses, and the inevitable destruction they'll bring to the peaceable homogeneity of Fargo and Moorhead."

Emmy glanced at Jim and was struck by how pale and angry his expression had become, almost as though he'd been slapped in the face and was preparing to throw his own punch.

"We should go," she said to Jim, covering her anxiety. "Before we lose the daylight." He didn't move.

"My friends," Mr. Davidson continued, his voice louder. "Right now, all over this Red River Valley, our good friends from Texas are hard at work in the beet fields. Why should they have to travel so far from home and do the work that our own sons are more than capable of doing? We've gotten soft, brothers and sisters, and our children softer, turning delinquent because they've forgotten how to work, because they haven't gone to war."

Someone in the crowd shouted, "Amen," and Mr. Davidson took a moment to smile and nod. Emmy looked in the direction of the voice and was startled to see Frank Halsey dressed the same as the other young men. She stared at his weaselly features as Davidson thundered on. "Of course, we welcome our friends from the border every season, but they are far happier living in Texas during our inhospitable winters. Why tempt them with some phony sense of capturing the American Dream through year-round affordable housing? Shouldn't we give those opportunities to bona fide, U.S.A.-born men and women? If we don't stand against these developments now, it's only a matter of time before the *pachucos* are in our midst, bringing their gang terror from Los Angeles, Chicago, even as close as Saint Paul. Organizing." He paused. Adjusted his tie slightly. "Dating our *daughters*."

Another voice yelled out, "What can we do?" Emmy snapped her head in its direction and saw Ambrose, a complicit smile of concern on his face. She took a step backward, desiring more than ever to be out of the sphere of Davidson's ugly influence and yet drawn to understand its heady power to attract so many acolytes.

"I'm glad you asked, brother," Mr. Davidson said. "Because I'd like to introduce you all to my friend Harvey Solstad. He's boldly thrown his hat into the ring for mayor, and I'd like you to get to know him. See, he's like you and me, a patriotic fellow who, through his hard work and God-fearing decency, has gone from being a lowly plumber to running his own pipe company. That's what the American Dream looks like. Let's give him a warm welcome."

Over the scattered applause, Jim said to Emmy, "I've heard enough. Solstad's a bigoted hack. Runs every year for something. Never wins."

Emmy turned for the car, staying out of Ambrose's view. "I know that other man," she said. "I don't much care for what he was saying."

"Imagined danger. It's classic fear-mongering," Jim said, opening Emmy's door. "The bread and butter of politics. If they can scare you enough, you'll vote for them to keep you safe. You get numb to it after a while, even though we shouldn't."

Emmy sat in the quiet car and looked out at the clutch of people, unable to shake a feeling of apprehension. Jim slipped into the car and started the engine. "Well, I hope I never get numb to it," she said. "It seems dangerous to me."

"It can be." He gave Emmy a thoughtful glance. "What's this fellow's name?"

"Curtis Davidson," she said. "He was my grandfather's friend."

"You know what they say, with friends like that . . ." Jim replied.

Emmy shook her head. "Did you see Frank Halsey?"

"Doesn't surprise me a bit. Water seeks its own level."

"Isn't that a cliché?" Emmy asked.

"When you write." Jim smiled as he pulled up in front of the Acevedo house. "Let's get back to work."

❧

Daylight was softening through the four-foot-wide opening above Emmy's head as she reached the bottom of the steep cellar steps and waited for her eyes to adjust to the dim glow of the lantern Jim handed down to her.

"Take your time," he said. "I want you to get your own impressions." She nodded up at him and shivered against the chill emanating from the unfinished earthen walls as she slowly turned toward the layout of the small space and stopped. The basement had mostly kept its seal, preserving the contents in the state they had been when the tornado hit. Why Mrs. Acevedo had chosen the bathroom over the basement, Emmy couldn't guess, but the tragedy of that choice knocked Emmy's breath into short bursts.

There was a rack of untouched dusty canned beans to the left, a pile of clothes dented by the shape of a sleeping boy to the right. Emmy put aside her feelings and opened her notepad, documenting the assortment of rags Jesse had chosen—almost as though he'd selected one garment from each family member in an attempt to reconstruct their life in the broken house above.

Emmy carefully lifted the lace-trimmed baby gown and felt the weight of each subsequent piece of Jesse's morbid inheritance—a flannel shirt, a floral housedress edged in bright orange now faded to brown except at the floured seams, where its cheery print hinted at happier days. A young girl's violet-bedecked sundress and a smaller version fit for a doll, both homemade. From slightly deeper in the pile, Emmy unearthed the doll, its broken head carefully glued and yet missing one blue eye. On the wall Emmy saw a colored drawing of a small blond child wearing white-and-red robes, his hands held out to the sides and a glowing halo crowning his golden hair.

She blanched at the idea of what must have happened that horrible June day—the images came to her of their own accord: a woman half pinned and paralyzed by the majestic oak that also destroyed her house; a man running toward the exploding homes, crying the names of his wife and children; a silent boy stumbling in the street, a shard of picket fence sticking through the front of his striped T-shirt. It had been an unbearably hot afternoon that turned ugly in less than an hour, the massive black clouds closing in on the western prairie and congregating like a ghostly herd of buffalo enraged and wild with fear.

Here in the cramped space inhabited by an unhappy boy, it was clear that Jesse had returned to the place where he last felt safe. He had constructed a utopia where his mother was about to serve them chicken she had fried in the early morning hours, before the heat of the day had seeped into the stuffy little kitchen. There would have been pickles and potato salad and other standard Midwestern fare—and perhaps a side of rice, or a pot of garlicky beans. Maybe someone from church would stop by to gossip about the latest inhabitants of the old Jenkins house on the corner—*Did you hear they're having another baby?*

The images came alive for Emmy, and she began to write the newspaper story in her mind; sitting at the oilcloth-covered table, watching as the smallest Acevedo slipped into the room to sneak a small chicken leg from the cooling basket only to get a sharp rap on the knuckles and a scolding yelp from the mama, who would perhaps have just enough time to get to the bathtub with her wailing children before being knocked in the head by a flying kitchen chair from three blocks away. Did she have a moment to think that perhaps she should have mellowed her voice, let the poor child eat, chosen a different place to hide from the storm? Or did she simply say the prayers of childhood, the Ave Maria, the Pater Noster, again and again? Emmy's image of the dream house grew ever darker and then just as quickly half imploded, glass and chairs and chicken and people flying, swirling, shearing up and away in an awful locomotion of grotesque spectacle.

Emmy heard the stairs behind her creak, and she turned to see Jim.

"Anything out of the ordinary?" he asked.

"There's plenty of food," she said, wiping the corner of one eye with her coat sleeve. "He didn't come here to live, he came here to die. To stop the pain."

"Then that's the story," Jim said softly. "Survivor Starves in Destroyed Home One Year Later."

"You're not very good at headlines," she said, poking through the shelves and picking up a jar of pickled radishes that bore the label 6-20-57, the very day of the tornado. Emmy held it out to Jim. "I guess we know how Mrs. Acevedo spent part of her day."

"Hot weather for canning," he said, taking the jar and returning it to the shelf, where it would likely sit until the entire contents of the place were unceremoniously loaded and hauled to the dump. "To think that they would have all lived if they'd come down here."

Emmy passed the makeshift bed and pointed to the picture of the little prince. "Who's that?" she asked Jim.

"The Infant of Prague," he replied. "Baby Jesus."

Emmy studied the innocent picture until she couldn't bear the idea of a god who would stand idle over so much destruction. "I guess Mrs. Acevedo was Czech."

Jim swept his hat from his head and rubbed his neck as though trying to conjure a memory. "Let's get out of here," he finally said. "You've got what you need to write a good piece."

Emmy's heart raced, and she grew quiet, contemplating whether Jim had just assigned the story to her. If so, it would be her first article, a chance to prove that she wanted to be a reporter. She climbed rapidly out of the cellar ahead of Jim, and as she placed first one foot and then the other on the crunchy dried grass, she heard a whistle from the street. She jumped, half expecting another surprise appearance from Ambrose, but was relieved to see Bobby. She cocked her head at him and then looked around at Jim closing up the cellar doors.

"I can't give you a full byline," Jim said, not noticing Bobby. "But if you do a good job, I can tell Gordon you're ready for a cub position. I know it's your day off, but if you come back to the office I can give you some pointers."

"Can I meet you there?" Emmy asked, and Jim finally saw Bobby. Jim slung his hands into his pockets and smiled, tipping his chin in Bobby's direction.

"Sure," Jim said shortly, and headed off to his car. "I'll see you there."

"I've been looking for you all afternoon," Bobby said as she got into the truck. He jerked the pickup away from the curb.

"I'm so sorry about Jesse," Emmy said, surprised by the angry tone in his voice. "I've been at the paper trying to write his story."

"Your car wasn't downtown," Bobby said. "Pete finally told me you might be here, that he saw you here this morning with that man."

"I work with 'that man,'" Emmy said through closed teeth. "Though I'm sure Pete tells it differently."

Bobby braked hard at the stop sign and glared at her. "What's that supposed to mean? Should he tell it *differently*? What are you thinking, Emmy, going around town at that hour with a stranger?"

"Jim's clearly not a stranger," Emmy said, looking out the passenger window to view Jim's car in the side mirror, directly behind theirs, waiting to move beyond the stalled conversation.

Bobby threw the truck into gear and loudly ground the clutch, glancing in the rearview mirror and scowling. "Clearly."

"There's nothing to be upset about," she said, slipping on her gloves. "Please take me back to work."

"What work, Emmy?" Bobby asked, his voice strained. "You're a switchboard operator, and it's your day off."

"I want to be a reporter," she said, pushing the words out against the strong wind of his disapproval. "Jim thinks I've got what it takes."

"'*Jim thinks*'?" Bobby spat. "Just listen to you. 'I want, I've got.' What about me, and us? What the heck are you doing, Emmy?"

"My job," she said defiantly, realizing that after all the time they had spent talking about his work over the phone, he had really never seemed very interested in what she did during the day. It was almost as though he wanted her to live one life for now, and then wake up wrapped in the marital sheets of his expectations. She roped in her frustration just enough to try to make him understand. "I've never had a boyfriend," she said, taking Bobby's hand. "I don't know very well how to talk to you in a way that helps you see how I feel, but I really do need to take this next step at work. For *us*."

Bobby pinched the bridge of his nose and squeezed his eyes shut. "My mother's preparing for the wake," he said, his voice cracking. "You're expected."

Emmy stilled her temper. "I really do need to get back to the paper," she said, feeling trapped by the idea that she was being required to make a choice. "I want— I think I can do right by Jesse, by telling his story."

"Damn it, Emmy, Jesse's dead," Bobby said, smacking the steering wheel with an open hand. "Nothing can do right by that."

Emmy felt the weight of Bobby's sorrow heavy on her heart, but she couldn't budge. "I only have a couple of hours before deadline."

"Fine," Bobby said, and made a sudden sharp U-turn in the middle of North Terrace. They rode in silence until he pulled the truck over at the curb in front of the employee entrance to *The Fargo Forum*.

"I'm sorry," Emmy said, keeping her hand from reaching for the door handle too quickly.

"Pete said this would happen," he muttered.

She touched his hand; he jerked it away.

"Your *boss* is waiting," he said. "Better hurry along and write your story."

Emmy began to combust along the rough edge of her dual desires. "Don't say that," she asked, pained by the harshness of his words. "I don't want to leave it like this."

"Then don't leave." Bobby's voice broke completely and he started to silently cry, fighting the emotion with a stiff jaw. Emmy slid across the wide seat and wrapped her arms around him.

"Don't make me choose," she whispered. "You know I love you." She felt him nod against her shoulder and she held him more tightly. "Tell you what, I'll get this done as quickly as I can, and then I'll come straight to your house. I've already written the first half, so the rest should be simple enough."

Bobby placed his hands on either side of her waist and rested his forehead against hers. "I just can't stop thinking of him, down in that cellar, alone."

"I think he just wanted his mother," Emmy said. "He's with her now."

Bobby's eyes glistened in the last light of the day. He kissed her tenderly on the lips and then pressed her across the seat. "I'll come back for you in an hour."

Emmy stepped out onto the curb and watched Bobby drive off, her damp eyes alighting on a different, familiar truck stopped at the red light across the street and down a half block. She took one step in that direction as the engine revved, the tires squealed, and Ambrose drove up, parking in front of her.

He rolled down the window. "There you are," he said. "I've been looking for you."

"I'm certainly very popular today," she replied, glancing past Ambrose's stern face into the cab. There sat John Hansen, his features as small as a rabbit's and similarly lacking expression apart from the occasional twitch. Emmy closed her coat more firmly at the neck. On the far side was Frank Halsey, glowering at her as he drew a red ember to the end of his cigarette.

"Have you seen Svenja?" Ambrose asked. His voice sounded more angry than concerned. Emmy took a step closer and met his eye.

"Why? Has something happened?" Emmy said, careful not to betray her friend's confidence.

Ambrose turned his head to the others and said something that Emmy couldn't hear. She stamped the cold from the bottom of each foot as she waited for his reply.

"John says you're the only person she ever talks about, that she must have come to you."

"You're wasting your time," Frank said, leaning in front of John, who remained silent but seemed scared. "She's halfway to the cities by now."

Emmy blinked and Frank threw his cigarette through the window, narrowly missing Emmy's cheek as she sidestepped.

"See," he said. "Never trust a Catholic. You're all a bunch of liars."

"Stop," Ambrose said to Frank as he pressed the younger man back into his seat with a stiff arm. He turned to Emmy. "Be careful." A glint of something flashed in his expression, but whether it was shame or pity, Emmy couldn't tell. He ground the clutch and shifted into gear. "And if you see Svenja, tell her to get on back home." He rolled up the window and drove off.

Emmy caught at her hat as though the motion of the departing truck had caused it to come loose, and once the taillights had disappeared around the next corner, she turned quickly toward the entrance of the building, feeling justified for having helped Svenja and yet afraid that she'd pointed the men in the right direction. She wished there were a way to track Svenja down to warn her, but knew any questions would only compromise the situation more. Emmy could only hope that the aunt in Saint Paul was hard for Ambrose to find.

Eighteen

The Start of the New

The seasons slipped from the crispness of autumn straight into the snowy chase of winter shortly after Halloween. It was the earliest snowfall anyone could seem to remember, and all the talk was about how miserable the coming months were sure to be. Not even the *Old Farmer's Almanac* would disagree with this foreboding drop in temperature, this gray sky that would not lift. Emmy barely noticed the weather, so consumed was she with her newly elevated role as cub reporter. The job wasn't exactly fun, since she was assigned to the obituary editor and spent much of her day phoning bereaved families and fact-checking birth and death dates with local courthouses. Still, her hours had shifted to daytime, her pay had improved by ten cents an hour, and she was able to maintain her copy-routing responsibilities as well as fill in for the new switchboard girl whenever necessary.

Other than church on Sundays, she hadn't seen Bobby since Jesse's funeral, as the work on the interstate was now moving around the clock in a feverish pitch to beat the pace of the earth's freezing in deepening inches. Before long, digging would be impossible. At least she and Bobby had come to an understanding about her work during frequent telephone conversations about everything and nothing—the murmuring sound of Bobby's voice sparking in Emmy an old-fashioned longing she found comforting on the coldly elongating nights. Still, she had found it useful to diminish her growing ambitions at the newspaper in response to a nagging voice of doubt that whispered in her heart, the sweet nothings of Bobby's encouragement too flimsy to mute their wistful melody. Emmy understood both her aunt's and her father's solitary lives to be wanting of intimacy, and yet she couldn't help being drawn by the sense of freedom she perceived each of them to embrace, the lack of incorporating the needs of others an accidental boon for their occupations.

Emmy stood at the stove of her father's house, staring down into the simmering water as it cooked potatoes she had dug that morning out of Josephine's frost-riddled garden. Her aunt had entered a whorl of novelistic fecundity, and due to Emmy's shift to daytime hours, their overlap in the house had vanished. A speck of water splattered out of the pot and stung Emmy's hand. She rubbed it and switched her gaze momentarily to the large black dog tapping the back of her knee with her warm wet nose. Coffee had rapidly grown into a sizable dog, but if her front paws were any indication, she had a bit yet to grow. She reminded Emmy of one of her grandfather's blue heelers—Babe—who from birth had no use with being treated as a puppy and so acted like a mature dog.

"You are the best girl ever," she said to Coffee, offering a hand to lick before returning her attention to the vat of boiling, steaming water, as though somehow she would find her future foretold in its starchy depths. Going to college seemed increasingly unappealing, even though she had opened up a savings account to that end. The more time she spent watching the seasoned reporters, the more excited she became about recording the daily dramas of human storytelling. How Josephine could be compelled to spend her time alone in a room making up tales when so many real things were happening struck Emmy as odd. Jim called this being a "natural reporter," which emboldened Emmy to want to see the world and be charged with bringing what she learned back to those who were wed to the safety of a small town.

"Oh, cook already," she said into the pot, which set Coffee to whimpering. "Sorry, girl." Emmy stroked the dog's head and kissed her on the nose.

Coffee swirled in a circle that brushed her warm, muscled flank against Emmy's skirt and sent sparks of static electricity crackling in the small room as she bolted through the house. Emmy heard the front door open, and she quickly drained the potatoes into a bowl and scraped a large chunk of butter into the middle, placing them on the table—which she had set with a new cheerful cloth of her own making—and swiftly pulled the roast out of the oven as she listened to her father groan lightly as he hung his coat, and the muffled greeting between man and dog.

"Hello, there," she called out merrily as she began to make gravy out of the pan drippings.

"Hello, Emmy," her father called back, a familiar weariness in his voice. She'd begun spending Friday nights with Christian, making him a hot meal and bringing Coffee along to cheer him up. Since Lida had died, Christian had grown even slighter in his gray work clothes, and Emmy could no longer deny that he was beginning to waste away. She would arrive at the house, loaded down with food to cook and put up for him to eat the following week. He was grateful, Emmy knew, but each Saturday she'd find much of the food still in the refrigerator, as though he was barely eating anything. She had no idea where he found the strength to keep up the pace at work, what with the end of the sugar beet harvest keeping the plant open all days and hours, requiring seasoned mechanics like Christian to pull countless shifts fixing endless broken belts, slipped gears, truck engines, and whatever else needed tending and tinkering. Emmy could only hope that there was food at work, or that he perhaps frequented Irv's for more than a glass of ginger ale.

Emmy finished placing the food on the table and stripped off her apron, entering the living room in time to see Christian ease himself into the old armchair, Coffee's sweet face cupped between his hands, the dog's long tail thumping manically on the rug and sending up little puffs of dust with each blow. Emmy stopped short, worried by how tired her father seemed.

"Hello there, old man." She squeezed his arm. "Long day?"

"Smells good in here, Emmy," he said, moving his fingers from where they scratched the dog's left ear in order to give her hand a light press in return. His skin felt papery and not exactly cold, but completely devoid of heat. Emmy could feel the bones collect neatly together as she held on to his grasp. She knelt at the side of his chair and looked him in the eye, allowing Coffee to bumble her great-pawed way into Emmy's lap, where she hugged the dog's warmth and nuzzled her fleecy neck.

"Pot roast special," Emmy said to Christian. "Hope you're hungry."

"Smells good." He leaned his head against the chair and closed his eyes, relaxing his grip on Emmy. A tiny arrow of worry entered her heart and sunk into her stomach. This is how he would look in his coffin, she thought, shaking her head hard against the gloomy notion.

She patted his arm and stood. "How about I get out some trays and we can eat in here while we listen to the radio?"

He nodded. Emmy went back into the kitchen, expecting Coffee to follow her as usual, but wasn't completely surprised when she didn't—she'd developed a keen attachment to Christian, or at least to the way that he would generously scratch and rub the dog all over and for a lot longer than anyone else had the inclination to do. Emmy started to hum as she tried not to hold her breath, waiting for the sound of her father rising from his chair to dial in a program of interest. She plated the food and placed it on trays, carrying his into the living room first. He was asleep, Coffee spread against his stocking-clad feet like the bearskin rug out at the lake cabin.

Emmy retied her apron and placed the hot plates in the still-warm oven, and then she went to the radio and turned the old worn plastic dial until the scratching stopped and some music without words cut through her father's snoring. She looked at the clock: seven. She looked at her watch, also seven. Sitting down in her mother's straight-backed chair, Emmy picked up her crocheting and waited for Christian to wake up.

❧

An hour later, Emmy sat across from her still-sleeping father, working on another square of yarn. The music on the radio swelled and stopped, the announcer murmuring about *Scheherazade*, Rimsky-Korsakov, Vienna State Opera Orchestra, and as Emmy waited for the next piece to start she gazed about the room from the discomfort of her mother's chair. All other touches of Karin were long gone, taken back out to the farmhouse as a way of telegraphing their owner's intention of never returning, though she wouldn't say as much to Christian. There were lighter-colored rectangles on the walls where pictures of Jesus had once hung. Even the doily on the radio had been removed, leaving a permanently darker circle of wood where the slight piece of lace had blocked the effects of the sun. Yet even with the absence of what could be called a feminine touch, the room felt somehow warmer and better used, welcoming. Coffee lifted her head as a car drove past on the street outside. She sniffed the air, but detecting no move on Emmy's part toward the kitchen and the promise of food scraps, Coffee lowered her muzzle onto her elegantly outstretched foreleg, keeping her eyes slightly open and her nose twitching at the yarn that Emmy pulled up out of the basket next to her feet.

Christian opened his eyes.

"Still here?" he asked.

Emmy nodded. "Hungry?"

"I reckon I could eat a little." He shifted in his chair, possibly in pain, but not showing any signs of it. Maybe he's just tired, Emmy thought, maybe he's just sad. Maybe this is what it looked like to grieve your last parent, to bury your mother before your children had all grown. Perhaps the freedom of the solitary life was less appealing to those actually living it. Coffee leaped onto all four feet and led the way into the kitchen ahead of Emmy, who stopped at Christian's chair to help him up with both hands. It was like lifting a boy.

"Great," she said, trying to cover her concern with a soft smile. "I kept everything warm, just like the good old days."

❧

By the time they finished their meal Christian had renewed color in his face, which cheered Emmy considerably. She could almost convince herself that his drawn appearance was merely the result of long work hours and poor appetite, though something else kept gnawing at her as she pretended not to notice his fumbling attempts to sneak food from his plate and into his co-conspirator's mouth, which rested dutifully on Christian's knee under the table. No wonder Coffee prefers him, Emmy thought, and it gave her an idea.

"Dad," she said as she rose to pour him a cup of coffee from the pot she'd put up while he had slept, "I wonder if I could drop Coffee by on the nights

I cover the switchboard? She gets so lonely when I'm not home, and I can't expect Aunt Josephine to always mind her." At the mention of her name, the dog sloped out from under the table and ran a quick circle around Emmy's legs, nearly tripping her return to the table. Christian smiled at the antics and nodded.

"We wouldn't mind it, would we, girl?" He poured a small amount of sugar into the cup and began his ritual slow stir, the sound of the spoon scraping up the sweetness at the bottom of the hard plastic the only noise other than the ticking of the clock out in the entryway. She wondered how he could bear the sight of sugar, considering how much he must see in a day's work.

"I'm glad you're here," he finally said, wiping his mouth with a napkin. "It can get so quiet."

"Me too," she said, and patted his hand. He placed his other hand on top of hers and caught her eye.

"I'm proud of you, little sister," he said. "I really am."

Emmy smiled. "That means a lot."

Christian blew on the surface of his coffee and took a tentative sip just as the phone rang two short bursts. Emmy jumped to her feet, the insistent tone of the seldom used bell drawing her quickly toward it in order to make it stop, if nothing else.

"Hello?" she asked, remembering the last time she'd answered this same phone, all those months ago, to find Bev on the other end.

"Emmy?" Birdie's unmistakable voice sounded odd to Emmy.

"What is it?" Emmy asked, alarmed by the strained tone. "Is Mother okay?"

"She's fine, she's here," Birdie whispered with a tremble. "A terrible thing's happened out at the Hansen farm; it's all over the radio."

"Just tell me." Emmy said. Christian walked through the living room, his hand extended for the phone. Emmy held up a flat palm. "Birdie? Speak up. What's happened?"

"It's just awful." Birdie started to sniff through her words. "John's been so lost since Svenja left . . . his parents have . . . and, oh, God." Birdie's tears became muffled and Emmy heard the phone clatter to the floor and other voices in the background.

"Emmaline." Ambrose's voice cut through the noise. "This is not your concern. Birdie was mistaken to call." The phone clicked off at the other end and Emmy set the receiver into the cradle.

"Turn the radio to WDAY," she said to Christian. "Something's wrong."

He carefully worked the dial from one end of the radio to the other, stopping wherever the scratch of words compelled, but nothing more than the usual assortment of disc jockeys, sermons, and advertising could be found. Emmy went back to the phone and dialed rapidly a number she knew better than any other.

"Carole?" Emmy said. "It's Emmy. Get me Jim." In the moment it took for the call to be connected, she waved her father closer and held the receiver between their ears.

"I tried your house," Jim said, sounding concerned. "Where are you?"

"At Dad's," Emmy said, glancing at her father. "He's on the line with me."

"Good evening, Mr. Nelson," Jim said, and then cleared his throat. "I assume you've heard about the murder out in Glyndon. Hansen farm."

Emmy's fingers felt cold as the blood drained away from her extremities in order to better protect her heart from what she didn't want to hear. "Is it John?"

"I figured you knew them," Jim said.

"They go to my church," Emmy said, thinking of the fear on Svenja's beautiful face. She could feel her father's breath as he listened. "My mother's church," she amended.

"Well, there aren't many details," Jim said. "But there's word a Mexican might be responsible. He's run off, and some men have gone after him, led by something called the"—Emmy heard the sound of Jim flipping through his notebook—"the Citizens' Council. I talked to their chief—"

"Stephen Davidson," Christian said, cutting Jim off.

"No, sir," Jim replied. "His name was Curtis. He was very helpful."

"Whatever he calls himself," Christian said, an unusual sarcasm spiking his words. "That's him. Helpful."

"I take it you don't care much for him," Jim said. Emmy handed the receiver to her father but stayed within listening distance, less confused by the mix-up with Mr. Davidson's name that she would have liked, her grandmother's words flowing into her head: *I loved Stephen, but he loved Josie, and she loved Ray.*

Christian grimaced. "Let me just say that anything he tells you is probably a lie."

"Good to know," Jim said. "What else?"

"Look," Christian said, covering his forehead with the palm of his hand as though checking for fever. "It doesn't matter what I know, but if the police don't find that migrant first, you'll be reporting a whole different story."

"Got it," Jim said. "Emmy, stay clear of this, okay?"

Emmy shook her head. "But what's happened?" she asked again.

"John Hansen's dead," Jim said without softening his voice or the blow of his words. "Shot in the back with his own gun."

Emmy sat down on the chair next to the telephone table and heard her father ask Jim to call Irv Randall and send him over. The shock roiled through her body and settled in her ears, hot and unrelenting, until she felt her father's hands on her arms, easing her up and into the kitchen, where he placed her in a chair. The glare of the overhead light did nothing to improve upon Emmy's sense of being in a cruel new world, one where people die at the point of a gun while dreaming of better things.

"Svenja came to me last month," Emmy said. "She was scared. I gave her money for the bus to Saint Paul."

"You did good." Christian squeezed Emmy's shoulder. She shook her head, trying to make the axis of her childhood tilt back to where it had always been.

"I can't just sit here," she finally said, hushing her voice in an attempt to calm her nerves. "We should go out there, help."

Christian made a sound deep in his throat, a strangled gasp of air that could have been a mirthless laugh. "It's not safe for you."

Emmy widened her eyes, taking on as much light as possible to fight the dark thoughts swimming in her head. "Do you think the Mexican is still out there?"

"No." Christian folded a hand over his mouth and pulled down on his stubbled cheeks until his fingertips rested lightly on his chin. "I hope not."

"But Jim said they think he did it."

"Jim doesn't know these people." Christian took a neatly folded handkerchief from his front pants pocket and mopped his damp brow. "Any of them."

"You don't mean the Mexicans, do you?" Emmy asked, the spent rush of adrenaline leaving sorrow aching in her joints.

"There's something I need to tell you," Christian said, and Emmy's body started to hum as though she might catch fire from the dismay his voice instilled. "A very long time ago, well before you were born, back when I was a boy." He began to cough and covered his mouth with the handkerchief. Emmy fetched a glass of water from the tap, pausing as it ran cold enough over her wrist to revive her stunned senses. She screwed the tap closed and took the glass to Christian, who drank it between racks of coughing.

"It's okay, whatever it is," Emmy said in an effort to calm her father. He held up his hand and shook his head, and as Emmy purposefully set aside the ugly imaginings of John Hansen's death, she focused on her father's words. Without pause, he told her about her grandfather's profound faith, his love of the land, his service to his country—all things that Emmy knew well, but she found this new telling tinged with confession rather than soaring with pride for a man who fought in the Great War and returned with hardened notions about true patriotism.

"He'd seen things, I suppose," Christian said. "Things that to him were un-American, and he found plenty of other men who shared his views." Christian scratched Coffee's muzzle and the dog licked at the droplets of water that had clung to his hand as he told Emmy of a preacher in Grand Forks who drew men like her grandfather in with his rhetoric—the fire of angels on his tongue—named Frederick Ambrose Halsey.

"Ambrose?" Emmy asked. "Halsey?"

"Reckon that's where they got the name," Christian said. "I went with my parents to meetings, and then to rallies, and even marched in parades. Around the time I was sixteen we went to a big gathering where I first saw Davidson speak."

"Curtis?" Emmy asked. "Or is it Stephen?"

"It's Stephen Curtis Davidson." Christian blinked and then closed his eyes as though he were describing from a picture in his mind, painting for Emmy the details of how Mr. Davidson had arrived from Indiana as the mouthpiece of this poisonous patriotism, talking of the Negro diaspora from the South, and how they were headed north to take over the land, the guns, and the women. Mr. Davidson had preached about how the local government was being infiltrated by papists and Jews, and that the good God-fearing Christians needed to form an army of the Lord to defend what was rightfully theirs. Lida, in particular, had sparked to Davidson's notions of liquor prohibition, and saw him as some sort of savior.

"And there, in the front row, was your mother," Christian said. "Looking up at Davidson as he spoke about God, country, and the sanctity of womanhood." He frowned. "She couldn't have been more than fourteen."

"Where was she from?" Emmy asked, eager to know more of history he'd never before shared.

"Down toward Fergus Falls," he replied. "Her mother had run off with a sewing machine salesman." Christian pressed his lips together in debate. "Her father took it out on Karin. My mother found out and hired Karin as a maid to make it stop."

Emmy swallowed the dryness in her mouth and touched her father's shaking hand. "I always thought you'd met at church."

"She prefers that story," he said.

"Yes." Emmy thought about her mother's words, *This is what happens,* on the night of Ambrose's assault. Karin's response suddenly seemed less cruel.

Christian cleared his throat and spit something into the handkerchief before carefully folding it away beneath the table. "Davidson came and went, and when he wasn't around, my father was in charge, holding secret meetings in the middle of the night, sometimes leaving the house and not coming back until daylight. I don't know what all they did back then, but there is nothing good about the Klan."

Emmy felt a new pounding in her ears, as though her brain were trying desperately to keep this last word from entering any more deeply. "I once saw him in a robe," she volunteered, in an attempt to share her father's burden. "The day he yelled at me and I went up the tree."

A light tapping on the kitchen door—almost the scratch of a leafless branch—startled the two of them. Coffee barked harshly, a throaty attempt at a growl sounding more puppyish than possibly intended. Christian went to the door as though he expected Irv on the other side, though he couldn't have possibly arrived so quickly. Emmy stood, gripping the top of the chair in one hand.

"Good," Christian said as he ushered three heavily bundled people into the small space. They were all somewhat slight in stature, and as a white bun of hair emerged from the unwrapped scarf of the first, Emmy instantly recognized Maria Gonzales from the Brann house. "You were right to come here. What happened?"

"It's bad, señor," Maria said to Christian. He turned to Emmy as he bolted the door behind the two men, one of whom was Maria's son Pedro, and the other Emmy had never seen before. His eyes were trained on the floor, his hands buried in the pockets of his brown cotton coat.

"Go call Dot and make sure Irv's on the way," Christian said to Emmy. "But not why." She could hear the scraping of chairs against the linoleum as she quickly executed her task, returning to the kitchen and pouring out coffee for everyone.

"What happened?" her father asked Pedro, who squeezed his cap as he talked.

"Carlos didn't do nothing," Pedro said in heavily accented English, his closely cropped dark hair making him look a great deal younger than his mother. "Milked the cows and heard noises out behind the barn, and then he hear a gun. When he goes out there, young Mr. Hansen is on the ground, not moving. So Carlos, he turn him over, and there's blood on his back."

Carlos started coughing from where he still stood near the door, a rasping sound that made Emmy jump. She stared at his hands for a moment, realizing that they were speckled with dried blood. Instinctively, she went to the sink and turned on the faucets, gesturing for Carlos to place his hands under the tap, but he didn't move.

"This is his first year in Minnesota," Maria said, her usual lilting accent hoarsely grating. "My sister's grandson."

"Hush now, *cielito*," Pedro whispered to Maria. "Mr. Nelson will help us."

"Was there a gun?" Christian asked Carlos directly. He looked at Pedro, who nodded.

"He pick it up," Pedro said, and Maria started to cry.

"Did anyone see him?" Christian asked. Pedro nodded once more, as though through a noose.

"Mr. Davidson was there."

Emmy heard the distinct sound of a car door shutting from the driveway beside the house. She turned off the faucet and brushed past Carlos and out the door. Relief flooded her as she saw Irv headed her way. As quickly as the three Mexicans had arrived, they were smuggled into the back of Irv's car, their destination known to all but Emmy. She cleared the untouched coffee cups as Christian paced a figure eight around her.

"I should have known," he said, his voice matching his contorted expression. He flattened his hand, letting it hover an inch above the counter next to the sink, lightly patting the edge as he spoke. "When my father first took me to hear Davidson speak—I couldn't have been more than fifteen—it was in a church down near Sabin. That's what they did, they used the pulpit to sow fear, talking about the Negroes coming north to rob our homes and defile our women." Emmy couldn't move from her father's stare as he continued. "There were picnics and rallies and parades, and over time more people joined up, all in the name of patriotism. Then it stopped, all of it, almost in the night. Until he came back last winter and started over with this new group—"

"The Citizens' Council?" Emmy asked.

Christian shook his head. "It doesn't matter what they call it. He's gathered a new group of impressionable men to share his message of hatred and fear. Last time it was the riots in Chicago we had to worry about, now it's the Mexicans who have worked hard and lived peacefully here for decades."

"I've heard Mr. Davidson speak," Emmy said. "Against low-rent housing in Fargo."

"Low-rent," Christian scoffed. "He showed up at the beet plant last week, demanding the union deny jobs to out-of-state workers—Mexicans. We'd have to close the plant without them."

Emmy pulled at a loose string along the hem of the tablecloth, trying to think of something she could do that would help. "What if I talk to Jim about this?" she said. "He could do a story on Mr. Davidson, expose the council."

"There were stories in the twenties and it didn't matter," Christian said, halfway between defiance and defeat. "They still managed to get their people elected to local offices. They don't do anything *illegal*, see, at least not that anyone can ever prove. They burn all the evidence."

Maybe not all, Emmy thought. "There's a green metal box in the cellar of the farmhouse," she said, her jaw aching from being clenched. "Grandfather might have kept something."

"It's worth a look," Christian said. "But I doubt there's anything there. They were very careful." He eased himself up to standing, a hand pressing at his lower back as though to force it straight like a rusty hinge. Emmy followed him to the front hall, where he took his coat from the hook.

"Where are you going?" she asked.

"To move your sister." He knotted a thick red scarf around his neck. "She can stay with your mother for the time being."

Emmy hugged her father tightly, a thing she hadn't done since she was twelve and Karin had told her that it was improper for girls to be so close to their fathers. In this moment it felt as though those nearly seven years had never passed. She leaned her head against his and felt his voice rumble in her ear the way it used to do.

"I should have done something when they burned that cross in Arthur."

"The police covered it up," she whispered, feeling his head shaking against her own. "It was lit by Frank Halsey. And now he's joined the council." Emmy thought back past the terrible night to her own innocent run around a snowy schoolyard with a sack of potatoes, and saw how her stupidity had been appropriated to explain away a far less innocent deed. Everything mattered, she realized. There was no such thing as harmless in a world that was impervious to the slaughter of lambs. "I want to go with you," she said, collecting her things and clucking for Coffee to heel.

"I'll walk you to your car," he said, leaving no room for argument. Coffee clattered across the living room with her clumsy paws and shuddered with the stretch of finding her way upright, then shook in a half spiral from the tip of her white-specked nose to the down of her tail. "By the way," Christian said as he settled the earflaps of his flannel hat over his large ears. Emmy turned. "Your boy came to see me."

"Bobby?" she asked, completely unprepared for this sudden change of topic. His name sounded as though it were from a long-ago place of innocence, and it took Emmy a moment to understand what it was that Christian was trying to tell her.

"Did he ask for my hand?" she asked without decoration.

"I want you to go directly home now, little sister," Christian said, helping her straighten the back of her collar as if she were on the verge of no longer needing that sort of parental help. "I'll take care of Birdie and call you in the morning." He nodded at Emmy to open the door. She hesitated as Christian passed her and cleared the threshold, taking the small, single step in stride. Coffee stood with her nose in the air, shivering, already at the curbside, waiting to leap into the back of the Crestliner. As Christian glanced over his shoulder at Emmy, she hurried to catch up, tilting her head downward, out of the wind. She wrapped her surging heart in the assurance that her father knew exactly what needed to be done, and so she set about doing as he had asked, without hesitation.

Nineteen

Darkness Illuminated

When dawn broke on Sunday, Emmy felt as though she had not shut her eyes firmly all night, having spent much of the time contemplating the horrible circumstances on the Hansen farm and the slim variables of who might have killed John. When Emmy had arrived home, the house was quiet and the Jeep house was dark, adding to her jumpy unease. Emmy stared at the ceiling and listened intently for any sounds of morning movement. There were none, and she had to assume that her aunt had slept out in the smaller cabin.

Emmy's racing thoughts picked up the loop where it had stalled during sleep, skidding along recklessly between whether the police had yet determined what had happened on the Hansen farm, whether Christian and Birdie were safe, and whether the contents of her grandfather's box could reveal anything useful, until she forced her thinking down the murky road of this last one, feeling her way along carefully as she tried once more to remember what she had seen all those years ago. Maybe there were just a few scraps of the past, trinkets and ticket stubs, and the objects she had actually touched. In the center of her open palm she could still conjure the weight of the large silver ring sunk down into her skin. Rolling it between her thumb and finger, she imagined holding it in front of her eyes, just as she had when she was nine, her mind filling in the time-gapped blanks. The embossed surface with its knighted prince sitting astride a silver horse was clearly something much less pure and innocent than she had once assumed. The words *Ku Klux Klan* ricocheted around in her head like three ball bearings, bruising her memories wherever they landed, but she could derive no more meaning from the discovery than she had the night before. No matter how she tried, Emmy could not reconcile the ruthlessness she knew to be the methodology of the Klan with her stern but loving grandfather.

It was still a couple of hours before Emmy was due to join Bobby at church, but there was no use trying to sleep with so much pounding against her skull. The Doyles had welcomed her into their pew every Sunday since she and Bobby had started going together, and Emmy had come to look forward to the routine of the sedate Mass followed by the chaos of the Doyle family dinner. Her father's revelation the night before about Bobby's visit trickled into Emmy's jumbled thoughts, a distraction that promised something more, and very soon. The idea of an imminent shift in her relationship with Bobby catapulted her out of bed. Was it giddy expectation or the opposite? She wasn't certain, but all Emmy could think about was whether she would have time before church to drive past work and learn more about the Hansen investigation. Emmy rose and dressed, fussed with her hair, and hurried down through the cold house and into the warm kitchen, where Coffee lay curled around Flossie, next to the coal burner. They lifted their heads at Emmy's entry, then laid them back down with the satisfaction of having already been fed and walked.

"Aren't you the lazy girl," Emmy said, scratching the dog across her withers. She gave Emmy's hand a slight comforting lick and went back to snoozing.

The coffee was on the stove, but Josephine's dishes had long been used and washed. As Emmy stood at the sink, looking out at the warm lights from the Jeep house piercing the dark gray morning, she attempted to eat a piece of dry toast with her cup of coffee going cold on the counter. It was snowing again beyond the window, the kind of flakes that Emmy had always thought of as angel wings. How could it be so beautiful outside, she thought, when so much of the world felt harsh? Realizing exactly how cold the air would be based on the size of the flakes, she shivered and decided to put a pair of wool stretch pants on under her skirt, tucking them firmly into her snow boots, and slipping her dress shoes into the pockets of her heavily burled coat.

"See you after church," she said to the animals, and opened the front door to the howl of a preblizzard wind. There, on the small stoop, was an object so out of place that it made Emmy gasp. At the same time both smaller and bigger than she remembered, the green metal box looked as though it had been frosted for a special occasion, the white of the scant half inch of snow making the muddy olive paint look even duller in the dim daylight. When she dusted it off, she found a small folded note affixed with a dot of rubber cement, her name scrawled upon the white paper in Christian's cramped script. Emmy surveyed the yard, but there were neither footprints nor tire tracks anywhere. Her father had clearly come and gone well before dawn.

Pocketing the note first, Emmy then sprinted to the car and got the engine running before she scraped the icy clotted snow off the windshield, opened the trunk, and hurried back to fetch the box, placing it between the spare tire and a small, empty gasoline can. She paused for a moment—her arms stretched up to the edge of the trunk's lid—and fought off the temptation to open the box and rifle through the contents quickly. No, she thought, better to do it methodically and in a safe, dry place, with an objective witness beside her. She sat in the frigid car and unfolded the slip of paper.

Dear Emmaline,

Your sister is staying with your mother at the farm. I'm going to help Irv deliver three off-sale kegs to a wedding. Until they are safely tapped later this week, it would be best you not mention the trip to your friends.

Whatever may come of today, know that I approve, and wish I could be there for you.

Love,
Dad

Christian was clearly Lida's son, closing and opening doors without moving any real information over any threshold. Pondering the note,

Emmy opened the car door and took a matchbook from her pocket, held the letter by one corner, and lit another. As she watched the black line of fire advance across the page like a well-positioned army, a smile pulled at her lips. Kegs. They were taking the Gonzales family away from harm. Christian's reticence revealed fresh depths of meaning to Emmy, and she dropped the last piece of smoldering paper into the snow, knowing that he was right—no matter what came of the day, he would approve of her actions because they had been guided by his steady moral compass all along. He was more true to his given name than any person Emmy had ever met. She would strive to be worthy of the gifts he'd given her.

The drive into Fargo was painfully beautiful. An overnight fog had descended and frozen into crystalline outlines on every branch of every tree, painting the evergreens and bare oaks alike with a sugary hoarfrost. This happened only once or twice a season, and as the sun rose invisibly up behind the white sky of steady snow, Emmy began to feel a glimmer of strength inside of her grow along with the swell of confidence she would need to tackle whatever might come her way. Regardless of the malevolence she had been exposed to in the past twenty-four hours, there was so much magic in the world, so much good and beauty, and she felt it in this wonderland of grace. It started to sink in that she was in a position to dig the light of truth out of the past and shine it on the shadowy goings-on in the present out in Glyndon. Maybe this was the very thing she'd been hoping for to prove her instincts right—she could uncover this darkness and write about it in a way that would reveal its malignant growth and dilute Mr. Davidson's influence. Then, finally, she would be able to show Bobby why her work was important, why she felt so compelled to seek the truth, no matter how close to home it might live.

Emmy drove straight past the church and directly to the *Fargo Forum* building a few blocks south, wondering what kind of future she would have if she decided not to join Bobby at Mass. Only once had she gone against Bobby's wishes in order to pursue her goals, and though he had allowed it, many days had passed after where she could feel he wasn't pleased by her choice. There were a handful of cars in the lot, and she swung hers in next to Jim's and turned off the engine, buzzing with the energy inspired to chart the new materials in her trunk. If she chose to heed her gut and go upstairs, pop the lid from the box, and begin the excavation right away, she knew that there would be no Sunday dinner at the Doyles' and no opportunity for Bobby to propose—for even if Christian hadn't confirmed her suspicions, there was no point in denying that Bobby's visit was for anything other than asking for her hand. If she didn't see Bobby, she wouldn't have to spin that particular wheel just yet, the one that offered happy dull days of creating and nurturing a family. There had been a time—and not long passed—that Emmy could think of nothing else. Faced with a table set for another kind of banquet, she couldn't help wanting to taste the sweet solace of coming home at the end of the day. Maybe there was a way. Her stomach growled against the black-coffee-soaked bread and Emmy looked at her watch, shocked to see that it was almost nine. A lifetime of Sunday pew sitting simmered up in her, and the decision to head in that direction suddenly felt calming, the sanctity of the Mass a dulcet lure that offered her an hour's respite from thought or action. For as much as she had seemed to rebel against her own religious upbringing, Emmy loved the things it had taught her—above all, that there was a place she could go to find peace, however temporary.

Emmy's breath fogged out of her mouth as she restarted the car and slid the gearshift into reverse. Just as quickly a knock came at the steamed-up window. She rubbed the surface somewhat clear and saw Jim's face through the streaked circle. The snow had eased, and a halo of white sky surrounded his hat-clad head. Emmy felt a swelling in her chest, a further settling of order and calm. A welcome rightness. Jim opened the door and leaned his body somewhat into the fresh warmth of the heater, keeping his arms on the roof and doorframe.

"Late for church?" he asked, smiling.

"You could say that." She smiled back.

"I just did."

"So you did."

He bit his index finger and glanced around before lowering his voice. "D.A. says the Mexican's prints are on the gun."

"Did they find him?" she asked, concerned for all the parties involved in Carlos's flight, but most of all for her father.

"No, but they pulled some prints from the shack he lived in," Jim replied.

"Curtis Davidson's breathing down my neck to write his sentence without a trial."

"To what end?"

"He seems to think that the boy was having an affair with Hansen's wife before she ran off." Jim shrugged. "He may be right."

"That day in the archives," Emmy said, blinking up at Jim and catching a snowflake on a bottom lash. "That was her, John Hansen's wife. That was Svenja."

"Do you know where she is?"

Emmy shook her head. "I haven't heard a thing." Her mind quick-fire bounced back in time to the Crystal Ballroom, Mr. Davidson's proprietary gaze on Svenja as she walked toward the Hansens' table. "But she sure was scared of someone," Emmy said, her voice sounding remote to her own ears. If Mr. Davidson was trying hard to pin the murder on Carlos, Emmy thought, then he must have had something to do with it. She touched Jim's coat. "I need your help with something."

Jim leaned an inch deeper into the car.

"There's a box of my grandfather's things in the trunk," she said, glancing in that direction. "He was involved in . . . some things. It may be nothing, but if you'll take it upstairs for me and promise not to open it, I'll come back this afternoon and we can sort through it together."

Jim studied her expression for a moment and then nodded, going to the back of the car and hefting the crate before the slam of the closing trunk caused Emmy to jump, even though she had watched his movements in the rearview mirror.

"I promise," he said, returning to the window. "See you back here around four?"

"Four." She looked at her watch, trying to figure out how long it would take Christian to reach his destination with the fugitives, wherever they might be headed. "Jim?" she asked, causing him to turn toward her, the box partially obscuring his face from her view. "Carlos didn't do this," she whispered. "Try to keep his name out of the story for now, if you can."

"Okay," he said with a wink, and walked away. A rabble of imaginary butterflies swarmed through Emmy as she put the car into gear and drove off toward Mass, so many emotions swirling with the delicately beating wings that she had to flap a hand at the empty air around her, chasing away any more questions until she could properly sit and focus on one at a time.

❧

Emmy arrived at Saint Mary's Cathedral just as the doors were closing. She rushed downstairs to the coatroom and removed her boots, coat, and trousers, smoothed down her skirt, switched her woolen cloche to her lacy little white church hat, slipped on her low heels, and tried not to make too much noise on the stairs as she ran back up to the foyer, where she was led into the nave by an usher. The organ was still in full swell, and the priests had not yet entered, so Emmy slowed her pace and took in the beautifully decorated room, from the row of carved and painted saints affixed above the altar to the stained-glass windows depicting the many apostles. Her favorite part was the soaring sky blue color of the ceiling and the host of angels that were painted high up in the middle, their harps aloft and mouths open in praise. She figured that the entirety of her old church would fit inside the front half of this one, with room to spare. Part of her did miss the paneled simplicity of the other building, and in particular, the words carved on a wooden beam above the altar—GRACE ALONE, FAITH ALONE, THE WORD ALONE—which she had read so many times they felt like something rooted inside of her heart.

The moment Bobby turned and looked at her, it was clear from his sweat-beaded brow what his intentions were that day. All the various heights of Doyle heads swiveled in her direction, shiny, smiling weirdly compassionate grins that could mean only one thing: They were all in on a secret that was soon to be made very public. Emmy's breath stuck in a way that wasn't pleasant, and she took it to be a bad omen.

The music stopped and so did she, alone now in the aisle as the usher hurried to his own seat. Emmy panicked, the pressure of moving forward into the fold of this tightly knit family distressing her far beyond a mere blush. Just as she pictured herself turning on a heel, Bobby's smile faded and he took her hand, guiding her to the seat next to his at the end of the pew. She sat and glanced shyly at him as her hand warmed against his palm. Reassurance steadied her skittish heart. This was a good place to be, Emmy thought, with these fine people in their welcoming community, far from the scratch of cold fear that was gnawing at her imagination. If she was to open this door, then she could turn away from the onerous task that lay sleeping ten blocks away—leave her thoughts of unraveling long-entwined secrets and lies, leave any thoughts of being more than a cub reporter where they perhaps belonged, for a girl with no other options. She could go to her father, tell him that she wanted no part in dealing with the past—or better yet, let Jim have the box and all that was bound to go with it. Maybe, just maybe, marrying Bobby was more than a good choice; maybe his whittling away at her ambition was for the ultimate salvation of them both. His scrubbed-up beauty shone in the brightly lit room. She smiled tentatively at him. He winked.

As the priest entered and the service began, Emmy tried to imagine what it would all look like. The wedding would be here, of course, and she'd probably have to convert to Catholicism. She'd walk down this aisle, in a beautiful white gown with long lace sleeves and tiny buttons up the bodice like the one she'd seen in a picture of Princess Grace of Monaco. Afterward, a party in the hall below with sugar-coated butter mints shaped like leaves and rosebuds, bowls of salty peanuts, and a crystal bowl of punch. A long table displaying the gifts: toaster, china, silver, pots and pans, maybe some hand-embroidered linens and a woman to write everything down for Emmy so she could personalize her thank-you notes on a rainy day in June. Cutting the cake, taking the pictures, throwing the bouquet, ducking the pelleting of rice on the way to a car that would take them to the honeymoon . . . and then what? A blank white space filled the frame, as though the projector had stuck long enough for the happy film to melt from the center out, the loose end of the beginning of life with Bobby flapping with each turn of the reel. More of this, more of this, more of this. Her fingers began to tingle from being held too tightly, and she removed them from his grasp. Up into the void of her imaginings floated her grandfather's box, the robe, the ring . . . John Hansen arguing, fighting for the gun, turning, running, falling. Emmy pressed her hand to her eyes until circles of light ringed her vision, but it couldn't stop the pool of blood from flooding her thoughts. She realized that everything she knew about John—his quietness and simplicity—pointed away from a man who could provoke another man to do such a thing.

"Emmy," Bobby whispered from somewhere above her head. She opened her eyes and realized that the whole congregation was standing and that Bobby's father had crossed the aisle with his hand extended in greeting. She stood quickly, bruising both ankles against the dropped kneeling bench, and nearly sat right back down with the pain.

"God bless you," Mr. Doyle said, his youthful face, in particular his wind-chapped lips, mirroring only shards of Bobby.

"And you," Emmy replied as she turned and offered the same handshake a dozen more times as the music changed, signaling the end of Mass and sweeping her attention into a rhythm that allowed her to shut down the grim thoughts that were trying to consume her.

Once the music ended, and the kneelers were tipped back against the pews, the Doyles surrounded her and moved out of the church in a maelstrom of freckles and curls while Bobby fetched their coats from the basement. As they cleared the front doors Bobby took her by the hand and pulled her away from the crowd.

"Where'd you park?" he asked.

"Over there," she said, slowing her pace as they reached the car.

"I have a surprise for you," he said as he slipped behind the wheel of the Crestliner.

"Something terrible happened last night," Emmy said. She moved next to him as he backed out of the lot and pulled the car onto Broadway. Her father's note about not telling her friends leaped to mind and she quieted.

"You mean that shooting?" Bobby asked. "Rough business, these Mexicans." After a few blocks he turned the car onto a side street and down a lane she'd never seen.

"They're not," she countered, annoyed at the way he jumped to the conclusion that she couldn't openly defend. "I know his aunt."

"Well, they'll get him, I suppose, and figure it out." A couple of more turns led them onto a small curved road.

"Why do you do that?" Emmy looked out the window and saw a street sign that read PLUM CIRCLE. There were about eight houses arrayed along the short street: modest two-story affairs with tidy shrubs and fresh paint.

"Do what?" The car stopped in front of an oversized lot, in the middle of which stood an odd-looking gray cement structure with an arched doorway and many arched windows with boards where panes should be.

"Why do you let other people worry about things?" she asked as he turned off the car.

"Look," he said with a sigh. "Everyone has a job, a purpose, in society. Worrying about someone I don't know being shot by another person I don't know isn't mine. My job is to build things, to make roads smoother for drivers and houses where people can safely raise their families. Priests and nuns have a calling to do good, bankers are drawn to money. It's the job of the police to take care of this, just like I wouldn't know the first thing about putting out a fire—that's Pete's job. See?"

"But I worry," she said. "And I know the people involved."

"That's what makes you great." He opened the door. "You care. It's probably what makes you good at your job, too."

"Thanks," she said, surprised by the compliment. He'd never directly referred to her work in a favorable way.

"Wait here," he said, and dashed up the sidewalk, disappearing into the unfinished house. Though she assumed it was new construction, the house could just as easily have been in the process of being torn down. In the open part of the lot next to the house on the snow-coated lawn, Emmy noticed the makings of a child's fort and a recently abandoned headless snowman with a scarf and only one stick arm. She thought about people having a purpose and how smart that seemed. At the very least, it helped her to ease up on her thinking about John Hansen. Bobby was right; there were people far better suited to figuring out what happened. They didn't need an eighteen-year-old cub reporter applying her scant experience to the conversation.

Emmy stepped out of the car as she saw Bobby reappear, waving at her to follow. "Well, what do you think?" he shouted.

"I think it's cold," she yelled from the curb.

"It's ours," he shouted back.

Emmy stood very still. It was impossible for her to imagine what the hulking gray building was supposed to look like. She tried to smile. *"Ours?"*

"Isn't it something?" he asked, running over to her and wrapping an arm around her shoulder. "I know it looks terrible right now, but wait until you see the drawings back at the house." He walked her up to the tarp of heavy canvas that covered the front door, pushing it aside and picking up a large metal flashlight from next to the wall inside. It was slightly warmer out of the wind, and as Bobby shone the wide beam around the first floor, her trepidation receded slightly.

"This is the living room, and over here's where we'll put the davenport and a couple of chairs—if that's okay—and here's the dining room and the kitchen is right off of it, and there's a back staircase. Come on, I want to show you all the bedrooms." He sprang up the set of bare plank stairs and Emmy grew winded trying to maintain the pace while absorbing the import of what he was saying. "Of course, you'll have plenty of time to decorate and stuff when you quit your job." Emmy flinched at the words, following so quickly after his praise of her abilities. She tried to convince herself that they were nothing more than typical sentiment, a thing a boy says when he's showing a girl their house. Once they reached the part of a hallway that had recently been framed and plastered, Bobby stopped at the final doorway. He turned and searched her eyes. "What do you think?"

"It's definitely something, Bobby," she said, the cold air drafting through the unpaned window at the end of the hallway. "And a little overwhelming."

"Maybe this will help," he said, tucking the flashlight under his arm and taking a small box bearing the words ROYAL JEWELERS out of his pocket. She took a step closer as he opened the dark blue square and withdrew a dainty diamond ring. "Emmaline Nelson," he said as he took her left hand. "Will you do me the honor of becoming my wife?"

The silence hung in the cold air between them as Emmy closed the box with a sudden snap that echoed off of the hard concrete floor. "It *would* be an honor," she said, her voice faltering. "But isn't this all a little fast? We're so young, we don't really know what we feel yet."

Bobby stared at the box and spoke to it. "I'm nineteen next month," he said as though he'd rehearsed the words in front of his bathroom mirror. "My mother was seventeen, and Dad was eighteen. My grandparents were just as young, and they're still married. When you know, you know, right?" He glanced at her, dismay creasing his brow. She took a finger and smoothed the lines there.

"That's very sweet," she said, resting her palm on his hot cheek. "I'm just in no rush, is all." A thin line of water collected at the rim of Bobby's eyes, and when he blinked, a drop landed on her hand.

"There's no rush," he whispered. "I'm just tired of not being with you all the time." Emmy couldn't explain, even to herself, why everything in her kept saying no, so instead, she gathered her courage and pushed against the resistance.

"If we can promise to take our time, then yes," she answered, the swelling in her chest telling her that the words were all in the right order, her deliberation nothing more than fear of the unknown. "I will wear your ring."

Bobby exhaled into a huge sigh as he fumbled with the box and placed the ring on her finger. The modest diamond in the center of the setting caught a sparkle from the flashlight before sliding loosely around Emmy's finger. "I guess I need to have it sized," she said, spinning the setting right again. The elated lift she'd felt by saying yes evaporated just as quickly. She closed her eyes, attempting to recapture it. Something was wrong. She only felt empty.

"You had me worried there for a second," he said, suddenly lifting her up and opening the only door on any room in the half-finished house. Candles glowed here, and a newly lit fire crackled in a hearth at the foot of a small blanket-covered army cot.

"So this is why you made me wait in the car," she gently chided as Bobby set her down in the middle of the makeshift bed and knelt before her. He pulled off one of her shoes, then the other, and when he reached up to her waist he drew her close and laid his head on her knee. For a moment she thought he might be crying, so she lifted his head and kissed him. Bobby returned the heat of her kiss and began unbuttoning her blouse, slipping his hands clumsily around her bare back and working at the multiple hooks of her bra. They inched ever closer to the thing she had desired for a year, only to find fear creeping up her skin, telling her to stop before it was too late to turn back. Her body once again betrayed her, though, urging him forward with small moans and uncontrollable thrusts. When he peeled down her stockings and began to kiss the naked flesh around the edges of her underwear, the resistance won, and she stilled his hands, drawing him up and pressing her forehead damply against his. She whispered, "I can't."

Bobby nuzzled against her neck, whispering harshly in return, "Please, Emmy."

Keeping her eyes closed, she said the small word again. "No. I want to wait. For everything."

He stopped kissing her and refastened her clothes as she felt the moment of passion die away. His calm movements were disappointing; the way he gave in to her wishes with such obedient respect caused her to wonder if the tone she had chosen was one she would regret forever. She leaned forward and slipped her tongue into his mouth, searching for his ardor. He responded, but weakly, and after a few seconds of tepid necking Emmy relented, her suppressed thoughts of the outside world worming steadily back in and demanding she do something more than sit in a half-finished house, making halfhearted love.

"We should get going," Bobby said, passing the back of his hand across his mouth. "They're all waiting to celebrate us." He stood and quickly extinguished the candles, throwing sand from a bucket on the fire in the grate. Emmy spun the new ring around her finger with a thumb and then stepped into her shoes, following the beam of Bobby's flashlight down the stairs and under the tarp-draped front door. She glanced back at the house, and a rush of relief to be outside of it passed through her as she gained her momentum and turned away from its blank façade.

"And it's made entirely out of concrete," Bob Doyle Sr. proclaimed as he showed Emmy a page torn from *Ladies' Home Journal.* He had led her and Bobby to his den moments after they had walked in the front door to a gathered collection of Doyles and O'Neills—Peggy Doyle's family—shouts of hearty congratulations hurled at their heads as Mr. Doyle had escorted them through the throng and down the basement stairs. A number of boys could be heard playing floor hockey in the other room, and above Emmy's head echoed the sound of countless feet moving with purpose around the kitchen. The house was much fuller than a typical Sunday, and Emmy realized this day had been planned well in advance of her acceptance. She tried to focus on her future, laid out as it was in the house plans in front of her, but where some girls would feel enlarged by the rapid change in fortune, she fought the urge to press against the paneled walls of the den or to pick up a pencil and add extra windows and doors to the drawing. At the top of the page that Mr. Doyle held out to Emmy was a picture of an unusual, large house—white stucco paint, light red roof made out of some sort of curved tiles, and the arched doorways and windows she'd seen on Plum Circle. It seemed much grander and imposing than the little street could bear.

"It's what you call a casa Mediterraneo," Mr. Doyle continued. "No wood, no rot, no termites. Warm in the winter and cool in the summer, like living in Italy."

"Well, it's certainly exotic looking," she replied. "I've never seen anything like it."

"Exactly." He rapped a knuckle on the page. "Didn't I tell you, Bobby. *Exotic.* Modern. Nothing will mess with these houses. Not a tornado, not a fire, nothing. Look, it says so right here: 'A Fireproof Home for the Bride.' The minute Peg showed this to me in her July *Better Homes*, I knew we could figure out how to build it. How about that fireplace in the bedroom? She like that, son?"

"Yes, sir," Bobby answered, slipping his hand into Emmy's. "It was one of her favorite features." Emmy grew hot with embarrassment, seeing the look that passed between father and son. Everyone was in on the joke, it seemed, but her.

A broad smile creased Mr. Doyle's face. At thirty-seven, he was six years older than Jim, Emmy thought, and one of the more handsome men she had met. His dark black hair curled the same way Bobby's did, but gave an eerie glow to the identical blue eyes by the contrast. She had trouble looking directly at Mr. Doyle without her discomfort increasing.

"I hope you don't mind my generosity," he said as he surveyed the plans. "It just makes sense that my son would have the first house I built."

"I have to say I'm not used to it," Emmy said. "The generosity, that is." Mr. Doyle glanced at her and Emmy realized he wanted her to be more effusive. "So, tell me, how is it that the walls are made?"

Bobby gave her hand an approving squeeze, and Mr. Doyle's eyes lit up as he moved his stocky frame around the desk to her other side. He flipped the plans back a page and revealed the basement. "Well, we broke ground back in September, and then in October we poured the basement, capped it, and built the wooden molds we used to pour the concrete into." He held his hands apart. "One-foot walls. No need for insulation or framing."

"September, you say." Emmy glanced at Bobby. "I guess you've been planning things for a while."

"Oh, not at all," Mr. Doyle bellowed, his face brightening. "I started this baby on a whim, with the overflow from the Golden Ridge project."

"Golden Ridge?" Emmy asked. Her memory snapped back to Jesse in the cellar, lost and alone. "I thought you were building the interstate."

"That too," he replied. "With a government loan I bought up a few parcels of land over there—helped out some of the victims so they could start new elsewheres. Who'd want to live there, after all that?"

"Victims like Mr. Acevedo?" Emmy said, keeping her voice even so she wouldn't reveal her confusion. "Did you help him?"

Bobby dropped Emmy's hand as Mr. Doyle clucked his tongue. "Terrible thing, all that." His voice sounded thin and coppery to Emmy, like a penny trying to pass itself off as a dime. "Acevedo worked on one of my crews, you know."

"Yes," she said. "Bobby mentioned that."

"I'll always look after his needs," Mr. Doyle said. "I'm still sick about finding Jesse like that, all snuggled up like a baby." He wiped at his nose with a handkerchief. "There was no way of knowing he'd run away. I'd driven him up to his aunt myself. He seemed happy enough to be there when I left him."

"It's okay, Dad," Bobby said. An awkward moment of silence was broken by the crash of the door flying open.

"Hey," Michael said, leaning his red head into the room. "Mom says five-minute warning."

Emmy's eyes strayed across the top of another set of plans that lay slightly askew under the two-dimensional fireproof house, and snagged on the words *Robertson Ridge*. "What're those?" she asked Mr. Doyle as Michael disappeared more quickly than he'd come.

"Phase two out in Golden Ridge," he said, expertly rolling the house plans away to reveal a diagram of a well-ordered neighborhood with curving streets and a mixture of small square houses and long rectangular buildings. "We'll make some low-income apartments teamed with smaller versions of the Plum Circle house. Someday this'll all belong to my sons—and grandsons, starting with this boy right here." He reached around Emmy in order to slap Bobby in the middle of his back.

"Absolutely," Bobby said, aglow in the light of his father's approval.

"Robertson Ridge?" Emmy asked, running her finger across the letters as if trying to smudge the way it all was making her feel like an accomplice to a crime.

Mr. Doyle's smile widened. "Robert and son, me and my boy. Only a matter of time before we can fully erase the negative association of tragedy and make this a real community again with affordable housing."

"Erase?" Emmy asked. "But what about the people who still live there?"

"I know this is all a little fast," Mr. Doyle said, carefully adjusting the papers until the open magazine and the casa were once again on top of the pile. "Why don't I just leave you two alone for a minute."

"Thank you very much, Mr. Doyle," Emmy said, eager to have him out of the room so she could talk to Bobby alone. "For everything. This is incredibly generous and entirely unexpected."

"Bobby's our first." He squeezed her shoulders. "Our best. My greatest hope for the future of our business. You're a good addition to the Doyle family, Emmy. I hope you think so, too."

"Of course," she murmured as he left the room, though she couldn't help thinking that she was no less a piece of doing good business than a vacant lot in Golden Ridge. "I don't get it," she said to Bobby. "Why are they giving us so much?"

"Are you kidding?" He laughed and smacked his forehead with the flat of his palm. "My folks are nuts about you." He drew her into a hug and rubbed his nose against hers. She tried not to sneeze.

"Yes, but this all seems beyond generous."

"Not for my girl." He kissed at her lips. "Besides, it's you or the priesthood."

Emmy pressed him slightly away. "What's that mean?"

"It's a joke, honey," Bobby said, but his face twitched with a hint of truth. "In an Irish family, the first son is expected to become a priest. I'm afraid that you've ruined me."

"I didn't mean to," Emmy said, sensing something more painful behind his teasing. "If that's what you want?"

His face sobered as he took her hand, gazing down at the ring. "This is right, Emmy," he said. "It has to be."

A tremor in the bedrock of Bobby's love rattled Emmy's perception. If it was constant, it allowed her to pluck at the seam of her own doubts. If it wasn't, she would be overpowered by them. "Why?"

"So much depends—" he began, but another knock came at the door. Bobby told Michael to get upstairs and then lowered his voice. "Please just tell me that you love me?" he asked Emmy. His eyes filled again with the same kind of tears she'd seen earlier that day—though this time she thought there was a caul of deception that she'd been blind to before.

"I do," she said, painful tears of her own beginning to gather like spring rain on a frozen windshield. "I love you."

He squeezed his eyes shut and held her hand to his lips, a return of confidence sparkling through his dewy lashes. Emmy stilled the chaos inside of her long enough to realize that she hadn't looked into his eyes in a very long time, and by withholding her gaze she had been denying him the intimacy she had once so freely shared. "I'm sorry," she said, looking back down at the desk. "But I can't seem to make sense of all of this."

"Growing up happens fast," he agreed, and turned to the door. "It can make your head spin, I know."

"Yes, but . . ."

"Sheesh," he interrupted. "You sure do think a lot, don't you? There's plenty of time to work out any details you don't like, okay?"

Emmy nodded, even though she couldn't shake the feeling that there would never be time enough. He led her through the empty basement and up the stairs. The noise from the crowd had reached an excited pitch, and Emmy tried to catch the loose thread that would tie her to the moment and fasten her jangling nerves. She was beginning to understand the meaning of what she and Bobby were entering together by presenting themselves before the chattering well-wishers. The paper shamrocks hanging from the ceiling that she'd found so charming on the way in the door now felt gaudy, alien. And yet they were all so willing to accept Emmy, invite her to become one of them, that she couldn't help wanting to be drawn into their enveloping embrace.

As she cleared the top of the stairs, Bobby put his arm around her waist.

The group that was packed around the dining room table and lined along the living room fell silent and then burst into applause. As the couple walked slowly into the space made for them, it seemed to Emmy that everyone moved an inch away, or that the walls were receding and absorbing all the giddy faces, the teary-eyed aunties, the squirming children, the red-faced men. There was a full assortment of neighbors, siblings, relatives, and friends, including a very elderly and frail woman snoozing in an armchair by the fire, as well as Sister Clare, Father Munsch, and in the middle of them all, Peggy and Bob Doyle. As Bobby's father quieted the cheers and began to talk about how much this day meant to him—to all of them—Emmy caught sight of a familiar face at the back of the crowd, but she couldn't quite place how she knew this slightly older woman. Her hair was a brilliant blond, her features smooth and fine. She was tall and well dressed, with profound color on her high cheekbones. For a small sad moment, as she saw smiling faces filled with tears and joy, Emmy thought maybe it was her own mother in the back of the room. When Mr. Doyle finished his speech, everyone cheered, and Emmy was jostled by congratulants to her place at the table. The woman moved toward her and it wasn't until Emmy sat down and the apparition vanished that Emmy realized she had only been looking at herself in the breakfront mirror all along. Growing up happens fast, indeed.

❧

"Emmy, this is Father Finney," Peggy Doyle said, seating an elderly priest to the right of Emmy. "He's going to help with your studies for conversion, and Sister Clare has offered to sponsor you."

"Conversion?" Emmy asked. She had barely begun to think about becoming a Doyle, and here she was, pressed into the chute out of which she would emerge a Catholic.

"Yes, my child," Father Finney said. "We know from Peggy about the beauty of your spirit, and are happy to invite you to join our faith. Jesus takes all comers." He laughed and tapped her knee with his frail hand. "First we'll get you into the current Rite of Initiation class, and by Easter, you'll be confirmed in the faith."

Emmy forced her lips into a smile. "I'm sorry, but I haven't really—"

"It's okay, Emmy," Bobby said from across the table. "Father Finney doesn't bite."

"I barely have the teeth in me anymore," the priest exclaimed, showing his missing teeth in a grin.

"That's a relief," Emmy said, realizing that it would be disrespectful to voice her concerns at the table of her hosts. She respectfully turned toward the priest. "I would love to hear all about the process, if you don't mind."

"I don't mind in the least," Father Finney said, buttering a slice of white bread and using it to soak up the glaze from the ham on his plate. "Of course you've been baptized." There was butter on his chin. "And never married."

"Of course," she replied, and silently fell to eating as the priest talked endlessly about the mysteries of faith.

Emmy found her voice less and less accessible as dinner wore on into the early afternoon, and her itch to be at work intensified. The switching of chairs next to her became dizzying, with every guest paying court—commenting on the ring, giving bits of marital advice, or showing her some sort of boyhood treasure that included a Roger Maris baseball card. At least when a Doyle sibling engaged her she was able to find something to say, but eventually the amount of food and the calamity of the noise, and the clattering of the coffee cups and the cakes plates, and the "little bit of sherry," and the endless questions took their toll as the clock struck three and Emmy's newly fitted bit strained against the grinding of her molars. It struck her that even with all of the obvious improvements, this dinner wasn't all that much different from a typical Sunday at the Branns' for how it made her feel invisible even as she was the one being celebrated. None of these people were interested in *her*. They were curious, sure, but apart from how her pieces fit into the Doyle architecture, no one attempted to discover any details of her life.

She noted the time and excused herself from the table. Once she reached the muffled peace of the upstairs bathroom, she opened the window and contemplated leaving to meet Jim early. Never in her life had she been the center of any kind of attention, and she had already had more than enough. The thought of venturing back into the fray for another round of dream dress or embarrassing ribbing about child-making was too unbearable. She lit a cigarette and tried to calm down, blowing the smoke out of the house like a detention-seeking schoolgirl.

A car door slammed somewhere down the block and Emmy glanced in its direction. In the middle of steadily falling snow stood Pete, wildly gesturing at the house as he talked; whatever he was saying was frequently punctuated with finger poking at Bobby's snow-dusted chest. When had he left? Emmy backed away from the view and held her breath for a second, nearly catching the delicate lace curtain on fire with the end of her forgotten smoke.

"Oh, dear," she whispered, dropping the cigarette into the toilet.

The men's argument drifted toward the window, but she could not hear them clearly. From the tone of Pete's voice, though, she could tell it was some sort of disappointment—even though Bobby didn't seem to be doing any apologizing. He stood there with his arms across his chest, stoically taking whatever anger Pete was throwing at him.

"Hello in there," a woman called against the closed door, rattling the doorknob.

"Just a minute," Emmy said, quickly collecting her things.

"Oh, Emmy," the unknown woman said. "Take your time, dear. I'll use the one downstairs."

"Thank you," Emmy said, and then turned back to the window in time to see Bobby getting into Pete's car. She checked her watch. It was three fifteen. Disappointment bubbled in her as she watched the car pull away from the curb. Here she was, worried about leaving early, and yet Bobby was gone without notice. Her dismay turned to anger, and Emmy eased out of the bathroom, grabbed her coat off the bed across the hall, scurried down the stairs, and slipped out the front door. She sprinted across the thickly blanketed front yard to where Bobby had parked her car. Hearing an engine rev down the block, Emmy immediately ducked into the Crestliner just as Pete sped off down North Terrace. She grabbed her windshield brush and quickly dusted the front and back windows clean of the powdery snow.

"Please just start," she whispered to the cold car, coaxing the engine once, and then it turned over and began to purr. As she threw it into first gear and let up on the clutch, she glanced at the Doyle house in the rearview mirror and felt a pang of guilt over how relieved she was to be driving away.

The streetlamps came on as she turned north on Elm, following Pete's car at a distance. The fading of the light and onslaught of thicker snow slowed her pace to a conflicted crawl. She switched on the wipers as the heavy flakes began to clump and blur her view. It was then she realized that she was shaking uncontrollably in the freezing cold car, her teeth chattering over the noise of the full-blowing heater. The red dots of Pete's taillights brightened as he turned onto a treeless road on the edge of town, just beyond Hector Airport. Emmy downshifted into second to maintain her cautious pace behind as she watched the white-and-red lights of his car trace slowly down the horizontal expanse, her many memories of parking with Bobby along that same road raising an alarm in her that she couldn't quite hear or understand. She took the turn and just as soon saw Pete's car roll into a spot a ways down. As she carefully bumped along the dirt road, following the double brown tracks Pete's tires had made in the whitened gravel, her vision blurred with the rising feeling of having been left behind.

Emmy stopped the Crestliner and backed into a spot between two other cars, their windows opaque with the fog of necking, and she waited there for Pete's car to pass on its way back out of the area. Nobody came here to talk, she knew all too well. Clearly Pete was interfering again, telling Bobby that Emmy wasn't good enough, and whittling away at Bobby the same way he'd done with her. Fighting against the desire to weep, Emmy opened her eyes as wide as she could, and tried to imagine going to Pete's car, knocking on the window, and demanding of Bobby that he make a choice between Pete's friendship and hers. But what if he chose Pete? Then again, what if he didn't? Was Emmy really so in love with Bobby that she could say for certain the wound she was nursing had been cut by anything other than her own pride?

Resting the back of her head against the top of the seat, she stared at the car's ceiling in the dark, letting the tears streak down her temples and pool in her ears until she finally wrenched from her heart the bittersweet truth she no longer had any reason to deny: She didn't want to go to the other car; she didn't care what they were doing. Pete had been right that hot summer night: She was the kind of girl who broke hearts. It just so happened that the heart she was breaking this time was her own. There was no point in denying that she had to end things before her love for Bobby strangled her ambition to grow and learn. Being his wife would mean kids and cleaning, cooking, and smiling. A vision of her wearing one of Mrs. Doyle's housedresses and a head scarf appeared in Emmy's mind, a child glued to each hip, a glint of whom she'd once been dying away in the light of her eyes. It wasn't what she wanted.

More than anything else, Emmy wanted to go to the office and sit at a table with Jim, digging into her dead grandfather's possessions. Being Bobby's girl had become a part of a routine that filled the hours between leaving work and going back again. The hum of the printing presses called to her from miles away; the way the paper was rolled around and cut and stacked and folded by the many well-oiled machines created a rhythm in her heart that nothing else could match. It was where she belonged—a cog in those clockworks—neatly turning in the service of a greater hour. I don't have to do this, she thought, and the ringing of reason quieted her panic. I don't have to do this, I can do what I want.

Emmy slowed her breathing and wiped her face with a handkerchief from her purse, rolling the damp cloth into a rope before taking off the ill-fitting ring and tying the two objects together. She dropped the entire mess into the small bag and threw it into the backseat, knowing that she would eventually have to return the diamond, and all it promised, to Bobby. The car eased back onto the dirt road as Emmy drove away from the sparkling disappointments of the day and off into the alluring gloom of the falling night.

Twenty

A Collection of Order

When Emmy arrived in the newsroom, she expected to see more people still at work. Instead, she was surprised to find only Jim and a handful of others, most of whom had already donned their coats and were headed for the door.

"You're late," Jim said without looking up as Emmy approached his desk. She checked the large clock on the far wall.

"By only thirty minutes," she said, brushing the snow from her hair with the tips of her fingers.

"Gordon's sending everyone home ahead of the storm." Jim picked up a pencil and stuck the blunt end between his teeth. "Though I doubt we'll get more than another inch."

"You want coffee?" she asked, somewhat enervated by her time spent thinking in the car.

He studied the bottom of an empty mug on his desk and shook his head. "Your crate's in the morgue."

"Thanks." Emmy walked over to the vacant switchboard and dialed the Doyle house.

"Hello?" a young boy's voice asked.

"Thomas?" Emmy said, her heart suddenly beating faster due to the nature of placing the call.

"Mike," the boy answered. Emmy could hear the soft rumble of the party in the background.

"It's Emmy," she said, coughing into her hand. She thought for a second of lying, blaming illness for her ungracious departure, but felt the Doyles deserved better from her. "Would you tell your mother that I'm sorry to have left, but I needed to be at work?"

"Okay," Michael said, and hung up the phone, clearly absent the concern of an adult.

Emmy hung the headset over its hook, and as she moved through the newsroom and down the narrow hallway to the break room, the events of the day scattered like field mice behind her, all of the emotion spent and gone, the talk of house building, converting, and marrying of no more interest to her than which cup on the counter would hold enough coffee for the night in front of her. Here, in this sanctuary, Emmy felt safe to explore the truth. Truth. Such a childish concept, she thought, clearly created by adults in order to make children believe that innocence has a home in the world. As far as Emmy could see, innocence was the biggest lie of all.

Mug in hand, Emmy went quickly to the archive room, where she found the box set squarely in the middle of the long table. She sat in one of the barrel-shaped wooden chairs and took a careful sip of the blistering coffee. Jim had placed a notepad and pencil next to the box. Emmy smiled at his thoughtfulness, picked up the pencil, and wrote the date at the top of the page before carefully listing the characteristics of the box itself, noting in particular her grandfather's stenciled name on the top.

This time the lid swung open without effort, flipping out of Emmy's hands from the force she had expected to exert. It groaned on its hinges, and the stale odor of old papers and mothballed fabric rose from inside. Neatly folded and laid across the top like a protective blanket was the white cotton robe Emmy remembered, a circle of red surrounding a white cross carefully sewn over the left breast. The material was thinner than she would have thought, more like a bedsheet and quite possibly made from one. She placed it at the far right corner of the big oak table, wanting the robe to be safely out of reach.

Under the robe was another article of clothing that unfolded into a cape, then a pointed hat with a long train that would hang halfway down a tall man's back, tied off by a black tassel at the tip. A white cord with fringe that might have served as a belt completed the uniform. Emmy shaped the objects into the facsimile of a man and tried to imagine a young version of her grandfather filling out these clothes. She trembled as the wind howled outside the window, rattling the thick panes against their heavy wooden frames. The lights dimmed once overhead and Emmy went to the window and looked out at the raging storm. She could see her car next to Jim's down in the lot, a slight drift of snow like a giant's finger caressing the front fender of the Crestliner. An updraft blew a flurry across her view, blinding in its force and breathtaking in its rapid falling away. In the shift, her reflection sharpened next to a man standing behind her.

"Oh!" she exclaimed, whirling around to find Jim at the table. He whistled low and widened his eyes. The robe lay there as though the spirit of Emmy's grandfather had just slipped out of the costume, the dingy fabric glowing in the dim yellow lighting.

Jim took a step toward the robe, laying just the fingertips of one hand on a sleeve. "I've never seen one of these. Was it in there?" he said, gesturing toward the box and trying to look over the lip from where he stood.

"It was my grandfather's," she said. "All of this. He was a member of the Klan." She said it plain and fast, prodding at the fragile balloon of her associated guilt with blunt observation. Her shaking hands belied the calm she was trying to display to Jim, and she wrung them together until they stopped. "Maybe we can find something in here that we can use to expose the council's real agenda. Some kind of link back to the Klan through my grandfather's relationship with Mr. Davidson."

"What makes you think there's a link?" Jim asked, making room for her to pass between him and the table.

"My father told me," she said, taking a chance that Jim would be on her side if she told him everything. "Right before he helped Carlos leave the state."

"Okay," he said, his expression unchanged. "Tell me more."

"There was a pastor in Grand Forks in the twenties," Emmy said, plunging into the pertinent details as she lifted the next item from the box: a large, folded piece of green satin.

"I've heard a bit about all that." Jim took hold of one end of the rectangle between his fingertips, as though trying not to leave his prints upon the cloth, or in some way not wanting to touch it at all. Emmy noticed how clean and closely cut his nails were, how on the middle finger of his left hand there was a knobby callus from where his pen pressed while he wrote.

"He started a group up there, with the help of Davidson." She took a step back, and the cloth unfolded between them like a sheet fresh from the line, revealing a large white shield in the center of a four-foot-long banner. "And then Davidson came here and started one with my grandfather." In the middle of the shield was a bloodred cross, and above it were the words GOLDEN LAMB KLAN NO. 16; below it, WKKK TROBORG, MINNESOTA.

"The Golden Lamb Klan, apparently," Jim said.

"Where's Troborg?" Emmy asked as they placed the banner on the table next to the robe. Jim went to the bookshelf and pulled down a local atlas, flipping to the city index and furrowing his brow. He replaced the book and took down another from the same section, but five books to the left.

"There you are." He tapped on the open page, then flipped open a map of Clay County. "Look at that."

Emmy leaned over his bent shoulder, her neck brushing the soft wool of his cardigan sweater as she followed his gaze and registered with shock what he was pinning under his finger. "That's our farm," she whispered. Jim turned his head, bringing his face within inches of hers. She could hardly breathe. "Good Lord."

"Why don't I get you more coffee," he said, pulling up a chair and easing her into it before picking up their mugs and leaving her alone with her thoughts. Emmy gazed at the familiar bend of the creek, the straight line of the old dirt road that intersected it, the light hash marks showing the original railroad tracks, the ones that had been long abandoned when she was a girl, and pulled up and plowed under when she was a little more than that. They'd had a stack of the old wooden ties out behind the barn that her grandfather had used for posting fences; she supposed the rails themselves went back to the shipping companies to be used on other tracks. She closed her eyes, the flood of memory bending her thoughts into a painful reverie that ended with the burning cross in Arthur. She could see it plainly etched against her eyelids now, how the wood was square and carefully mitered together in a way that showed a love of craft, dedication to the dark art of hatred. Wood that taken apart looked exactly like railroad ties.

Jim returned with fresh coffee, and they wordlessly continued the excavation together, side by side, as the wind howled louder outside the archive room, pelting filthy bits of snow and dirt against the windowpanes. The cold early evening wore on into the night, and they bent to the objective of separating the contents into three discrete areas on the large table: objects, photos, and printed materials. There were black-leather bound journals and three large ledgers with some information spelled out in her grandfather's tight script, and yet other information in an unidentifiable language.

"Code," Jim said. "I saw some of this in the war. It's a pretty basic one, but it'll still take some time to unscramble."

Emmy neatly stacked the books together on top of the collected Klan newspapers from around the country, with names like *Call of the North*, *The Protestant*, and *MN Fiery Cross*. In one they'd pored over a map of the country, showing the number of Klan members in each state in 1924—from the low number of 417 in Minnesota, to the shockingly high 70,999 in Indiana. Emmy had been taught in school that the Klan was a problem in the South, but from the look at the map, she could tell that during the twenties, the South was hardly involved at all.

In another they found a list of Klan qualifying characteristics: "Am I a Real American? The Test Is Simple. Do You . . . ?"

Believe in God and in the tenets of the Christian religion and that a godless nation cannot long prosper.

Believe that a church that is not founded on the principles of morality and justice is a mockery to God and man.

Believe that a church that does not have the welfare of the common people at heart is unworthy.

Believe in the eternal separation of church and state.

Hold no allegiance to the Stars and Stripes next to your allegiance to God alone.

Believe in just laws and liberty.

Believe that our free public school is the cornerstone of good government and that those who are seeking to destroy it are enemies of our republic and are unworthy of citizenship.
Believe in the upholding of the Constitution of these United States.
Believe in freedom of speech.
Believe in a free press uncontrolled by political parties or by religious sects.
Believe in law and order.
Believe in the protection of pure womanhood.
Believe that laws should be enacted to prevent the causes of mob violence.
Believe in a closer relationship of capital and labor.
Believe in the prevention of unwarranted strikes by foreign labor agitators.
Believe in the limitation of foreign immigration.
Believe your rights in this country are superior to those of foreigners.

Jim tapped the top of the list. "This right here is about Catholics—see how carefully worded the *Christian* religion distinction is?"

Emmy nodded. "But why single them out?"

"Because the pope is bigger than the president, if you hew to the faith. It's unpatriotic to put the requirements of a foreign—in this case Italian—head of church or state before the needs of this country."

"You believe that?" Emmy said, confused by what she herself believed.

"Look, kid," Jim said. "It's not about what you believe with these people, it's about what they think you believe, and how they word it in a way that you can't *disagree*. Look at this one, about 'a free press uncontrolled by political parties or by religious sects.' This is specifically about Jews and the paranoid belief that all the newspapers in this country are controlled by us."

"By you?" Emmy said. "You're a Jew?"

"Wanna see my horns?" He smirked.

"I'm sorry," Emmy said. She'd never met a Jew, and had considered them something that existed only in the Bible or in Nazi Germany. The thought made her cringe at her own stupidity. "I didn't mean . . ."

Jim picked up the paper and shook it, glossing over Emmy's blunder. "Now how could that be true if I'm the only Jew at the *Forum*—other than the society columnist, and I assure you, Esther is no more controlling the comings and goings of polite Fargo society than I'm slanting the good kind opinions of our community by reporting on a movie theater fire. It's hate talk dressed as patriotism." He held up the paper in front of Emmy's wide eyes. "Look here, is this the preacher?"

Emmy studied the black-and-white photo of a minister behind a pulpit, with a weasel-sharp profile and wavy black hair. Her eyes dropped to the caption even as her brain pushed out the word *Halsey*: "Rev. Ambrose Halsey, delivering a sermon on God, Country, and Patriotism." "That looks like Frank," she said, the conclusion snapping together on its own. "I'm beginning to think he's capable of quite a lot."

"Probably," Jim said, carefully folding the old newspaper with the photo showing and laying it aside from everything else. "But we can't just jump to conclusions." He tapped an advertisement below the photo. "Check this out: Karl's Kustom Kars. Look at the way the *K*s line up." Jim leaned closer to the page and put his finger under the fine print, which Emmy read aloud over his shoulder.

"Proprietor, Karl Hansen." Emmy flinched. "That's John's grandfather." She held still, thinking about old Mr. Hansen and his crippled right hand—caught in a thresher belt when he was a teen. How he would wave that claw at hospitality hour in the church basement, railing against the German prisoners of war that had been brought to Clay County in the forties to do the field work of American farm men fighting abroad. His seething words about two in particular who'd had the nerve to stay once the war was over and who were granted citizenship. She folded back the memory and found another, hazier one, something to do with two local men and their wives having to move to Ohio after the barn they shared burned to the ground, animals, machinery, and all.

"The sins of the grandfathers?" Jim pondered.

"There you go again with your clichés," Emmy said, trying to find humor somewhere in the situation.

"It's a proverb, not a cliché." He smiled and they stood there for a moment, looking at each other.

"I wonder," she said, taking a step back in order to try to assemble a bigger picture out of the pieces they had so far pulled out of the box. "The theaters." As soon as the idea was in the air, Jim snapped his fingers and hurried out of the room. Emmy shone this new light over the Moorhead fire, how Ambrose had been there, without explanation, and any doubt left in her as to just how far Ambrose would go to please Mr. Davidson disappeared.

Jim returned. "I can't believe this didn't occur to me," he said, studying the clippings of the two separate fires that Emmy had given him months before. "Your nose was right after all. There are glaring similarities: both Easter fires, both theaters owned by Jews. The Strand burned in 1923 . . ." Jim selected the encoded ledger and opened it, running his index finger down a column of dates, flipping pages until he found what he was looking for. "April 2, 1923. I'm guessing this entry translates into something interesting."

"Poor Cindy," Emmy said. "It could have been anyone's cigarette." As Jim set to work cracking the encryption, Emmy returned to the half-empty box, pulling more newspapers and other memorabilia out and adding them to the various stacks. She began to think that the only real evidence linking the past to the present might be found in one of the ledgers, but even if it were something as stunning as recorded proof of arson, she doubted it would be enough to implicate a man as deceptive as Mr. Davidson. The ease with which a man with his charisma could gather fresh patriots frightened her, yet it also sharpened her desire to get to the bottom of the box, to find evidence that could stem his influence. In all the materials they had examined so far, there wasn't a single mention of the man. Not a picture, not a note, not even an entry in the ledger. It was as though he were a ghost in the white robes, pulling the strings of bigotry from a lofty, invisible platform.

Emmy fished the next document from its depth, unprepared for the horrible image that confronted her. The photo was small, in amber tones, of a tight group of white men circled around a lamppost from which hung two half-naked Negroes; a third lay at their feet. By her estimation there were about thirty men gathered for the event—many of them smiling. Her eyes stopped at one of the faces and darted to the next. She felt a bubble of acrid bile rise in her throat, and the picture fell to the table as she clamped both hands over her mouth in order not to vomit. Jim picked up the image and flipped it over.

"It's a postcard," he said grimly. "Professionally printed. 'Duluth, June 16, 1920.'"

Emmy dropped her face into her hands and slowly shook her head from side to side. "That's my grandfather," she said. "He's *smiling*." All pretense of Benjamin Nelson's having been a good man drained from her along with the wish that the blood that tied her to him could go with it. She slumped in her chair, immobilized. "I can't look at any more," she said. "Not tonight."

"It's up to you," Jim said. "But I'd like to take this home with me if you don't mind. Try to figure out what they're hiding behind this code. I'll call the *Trib* tomorrow about this, see what they know." He closed the ledger and lifted it by the spine, causing a folded piece of paper to fall out of it and onto the floor. Emmy regarded it without moving until Jim leaned over and picked it up, unfolding it to find two sheets instead of one. "Huh," he said. "That's strange."

Emmy sat up. "What is?"

"Birth certificates." He laid them side by side on the table, smoothing the creases and sliding them in tandem in front of Emmy. The one on the right had barely any writing on it; the other was completely filled in and stamped with the word *duplicate* in smudged black ink. Emmy's eyes darted between them, until everything clicked into place.

"It's my father," she said, placing a finger where his name was fully and clearly written on the official form. "Christian Forrest Nelson, born March 5, 1915. Father, Olafur Benjamin Nelson. Mother, Adelaide Randall Nelson. Attended by Michael Jensen." Emmy pushed the paper aside and squinted at the odd bits of information on the other certificate. "Baby boy, born March 5, 1915," she slowed her speech. "Father, unknown. Mother, Josephine Catherine Randall. Illegitimate. That's my aunt."

"Does your father have a cousin?" Jim asked, his voice restrained but kind.

"No," Emmy said, not even trying to pretend there might have been two babies born to sisters on the same day. She stood as though the revelation had no effect, or that her act of wishing away her grandfather's claim on her could have no other result than a granting of her whimsy. "I wish I could say I'm surprised," she finally said, handing the records to Jim. "But I'm not. My aunt was in love with her cousin, and they weren't allowed to be together."

"It wouldn't be the first time a baby was privately adopted and the records changed," Jim said. Emmy smiled ruefully.

"Or the last," she said. "I think I need to go home now."

"Let's put everything away," he said, handing the birth certificates back to her and looking at the window. "The storm's let up."

"Oh, no," she said as she felt a slight tremor break through her shock. "I doubt the storm's even begun. There's so much here." Her voice cracked with the strain of trying to sound normal. Absolutely nothing inside of Emmy felt the same as it had twenty-four hours before.

"Listen," Jim said, and placed a firm hand on each of her arms. "You need to let this all sink in. Now go home and get some sleep. We'll start again tomorrow, and I'll help you figure out what to do about it."

Emmy looked where he held her. "You should be getting home," she said, barely above a whisper. "Elise will be worried."

He frowned and dropped his hands. "I'm surprised she didn't call. She's not good in storms."

Emmy laughed, trying to numb the thrill she had felt in his slight embrace. "I guess none of us are after last year."

Jim nodded, the distraction of Elise's name floating between them. He raised a hand in Emmy's direction but stilled it just short of her shoulder, then let it drop again. "You're . . . different," he said.

"Than Elise?" Emmy asked, rubbing her palms together and crossing her arms over her chest.

"Than anyone." He looked at her from the top of her head down to her toes, measuring something within her that she could guess at but dearly wanted to fit. He suddenly turned toward the table. "We need to pack this up."

"Oh, of course." Emmy nodded as a bright needlepoint of hope pricked the darkness that had settled over the day. She turned to repacking the materials, closed her notebook, and pulled on her coat, placing the birth certificates in her pocket. All the while a heightened awareness of Jim's quietly synchronized movements made her heart race a beat faster. She was *different.* The sound of Jim saying that one word had given her fresh purpose. As she went through the door he held for her and into the night, she ducked her head down against the brittle wind, pressing forward with all her resolve.

Part III

A Child of Solitude

Twenty-one

A Cold Day Gone Hot

The wind howled all night, but Emmy heard it only the one time she awoke, parched and confused as to her whereabouts. At first she thought she was at the farm and fumbled the wrong direction in the darkness, searching for the glass of water she always left beside her bed. When she realized her mistake, she dropped back onto the pillow, chasing away the demons that had plagued her as she had drifted off, poked by their pitchforks and the pointed tail of her grandfather's sins, until sleep once again found her.

The sun rose directly through the window and fell cruelly upon her closed eyes. She threw her crooked arm over the bridge of her nose and listened to the marked silence of the house.

"I'm not him," she said aloud as she sat up and pressed a finger to her breastbone, where a sharp pain had come and gone ever since she had left the office, particularly whenever she thought about her grandfather and tried to remember him as kind. Far worse, though, were the tormenting moments when she would play out the way her life would have been had the marriage to Ambrose gone through—and how desperately she wanted to go to Birdie and fix the mess that had collected at her feet instead. The sun crept an inch higher in the sky and Emmy squinted at it. This is what I need, she thought: light. Clarity. She gingerly placed her stocking-clad feet on the cold floor and rubbed the flannel sleeves of her nightdress, hearing the clink of silver in the sink downstairs, followed by the swift creak of the front door opening and closing. Emmy went to the window, hand to brow, in time to see Josephine walk briskly up the road toward the open field past the tree line. The temperature had risen overnight, and the snow was mostly gone, or blown into dingy striated heaps along the sides of the outbuildings. Emmy noticed how the edges of the drifts were already seeping down into puddles before disappearing altogether, returning the dirt that had become airborne during the gusts back to the ground.

Emmy dressed quickly in the clothes she had kept from her days on the farm, covering herself in a layer of familiarity. Her red plaid shirt smelled of hay, and her heavy denim overalls still carried a slight stain from the night she'd helped deliver the calf. What kind of girl was I then? she thought as she pulled on her work boots and laced them as swiftly as her fingers would go. She retrieved the birth documents from her coat pocket and folded them small enough to stick into the breast pocket of the shirt, secured by the bib of her overalls. Without pausing for a cup of coffee, she bolted through the kitchen, drawing the barn jacket from the rack and double-clucking her tongue at Coffee to heel. Out the door they went together, noses pointed high in the crisp air. The long strides Emmy took set the pace of her thoughts as her determination to eradicate all of the mysteries rose up in her and created an almost canny stillness in her soul. The time for listening had finally come to an end, and a new phase needed to begin. She knew by now who would help and who would hinder, and so she cut through the line of nearly bare apple trees, pausing only long enough to snatch a low-hanging fruit from a gnarled branch, and marched off in search of her aunt's slight figure, stooped toward the earth a dozen yards across from the main road. Glancing in both directions but without slowing, Emmy crested the median of the highway and loped down the ditch on the other side, taking in the landscape while best measuring her approach. To the far left, a boy helped his father stack baskets of gourds around the front of the small white building that bore the words TRAIL MARKET in severe red letters. To the far right, Josephine plucked her way through the tangled dying vines of pumpkins and squash, pushing away the exhausted vegetation and lifting out the fruit. She then stacked the green, orange, and buff orbs onto a flatbed wagon that sat parked along one of the remaining proliferative rows. Coffee looked up at Emmy, and she nodded at the dog to run ahead and alert Josephine to their presence. Emmy rubbed the small apple against the soft cotton of her coat sleeve and took a crisp bite as she slowed her pace in order to give her aunt time to straighten and stretch. As Josephine caught Emmy's face, her smile fell flat but then pulled tightly upward again, as though preparing to catch some unknown piece of bad news waiting to besmirch the oddly warm day. She pressed a palm to her brow and walked over to the flatbed with an acorn squash coddled in the other hand as though she were offering it to Emmy as a sign of peace, or trinket of trade.

"You look like you woke up on the wrong side of the bed," Josephine said, the squash still suspended between them. Emmy looked at it, and then away at the horizon, surprised by the narrowing of her own eyelids as she fought to suppress unexpected tears.

"I know something," Emmy said, clearing the emotion from her throat. "I'm sorry."

Josephine set the fruit on the wagon, keeping it from rolling by leaning it carefully between a pale white cheese pumpkin and a tan-colored, elongated nutter butter. "About what?" she said more than asked. There was a shortness to Josephine's speech, a sigh steeped in a soupy mixture of expectation and evasion.

"It's this," Emmy said. She drew the two birth certificates from her pocket and handed the folded papers to her aunt. Emmy studied Josephine's face as she unfolded the sheets and separated them, looking from one to the other as though trying to translate what she was seeing. A tiny ripple of relief started at her bottom lip and moved slowly to her eyelids, which fluttered and lifted as she stood straight and met Emmy's gaze dead-on, the papers clutched in her right hand, which she let fall to her side. "I've never actually seen these," Josephine said sadly. "Where?"

"In a box from the farm," Emmy replied, the mix of confusion and anticipation she'd had bottled up inside her suddenly pouring out into simple compassion. "I'm your granddaughter."

Josephine nodded and handed the papers back to Emmy. "I know."

"And Raymond was my grandfather?" Emmy asked, the last piece of the first puzzle within her reach.

Josephine turned away sharply without an answer, and bent back to her harvest. Coffee licked at her cheek, which Emmy could see was damp with tears.

"I'm sorry he died," Emmy said, and stuffed the documents into her coat pocket. "I wish I'd had the chance to meet him."

Josephine stood and walked away from Emmy, wiping at her face with both hands. She made it to the far end of the row, where she stopped, a solitary figure against the severe blue sky. Emmy stayed frozen in the untilled black soil of mid-row, waiting for her aunt's sorrow to pass through her and bring her around to the happy coincidence that had comforted Emmy. Instead, Josephine turned to her left and walked deeper into the next field, Coffee close at her heels. A net of wild imaginings rapidly descended over Emmy's brain, and she broke into a diagonal run across the field as Lida's words chased after her.

"Tell me," Emmy said, arriving at her aunt's side and taking her hand. "I want to know."

"It happened so fast," Josephine said, still staring at the horizon but grasping Emmy's hand harder. "So long ago . . ."

"It's okay," Emmy said, certain that it wasn't.

"He was a charmer." The word was harsh in Josephine's tear-strained voice. "'Pastor Davidson's perfect for you,' Lida told me, 'a man of God.' It all happened *so fast*." Josephine blinked a tear down her cheek and brushed at it angrily, her shoulders quivering as she told Emmy about the summer of the third Chautauqua, after their mother had died. "Lida couldn't have imagined what would happen, of course," Josephine said, her voice rising in that curious way it always did when she talked about the past, as though she needed to take on helium to sail above the sadder memories. "We all got along so well those handful of days, and I had taken a liking to Stephen. The last afternoon, we had a beautiful picnic by the lake and had our picture taken." She stopped and looked down at Emmy's hand trapped by her own.

"He forced you," Emmy said, finishing the story before it had to fully begin, the details of lightning bugs and a moonlit stroll too beautiful a beginning for the obvious turn the birth certificates had foretold. Anger flooded Emmy, as much for her aunt as it was for the stupid girl she had also once been. Josephine was right in her onetime assessment; this was not original.

"Yes," Josephine whispered. "Though it wasn't rough, and I can't say I didn't lay down willingly at first. His voice was sweet, his hands warm and soft. Ray had been sent away, and my heart was tender, easily taken by someone as determined as Stephen." She paused, her head slowly nodding as though she were silently counting up the details. "I woke up alone in that tent, in the dark, scared he would come back. By the time I found my way to my uncle's cabin, it was obvious what had happened."

"How horrible for you," Emmy said, controlling the disgust rising inside of her. She tried to believe that Bobby's gentle caresses were different, that his restraint was noble. Of these two poles, Emmy decided she wanted neither. "Did Grandmother help you?"

Josephine laughed, a once-harsh sound weathered by the paucity of time. "She called me *schlottern* and blamed me for chasing Stephen away. I sat on the bed in my soiled dress as she packed my bags and lectured me on my indecency."

Silence hung on the last word as Emmy pressed against her stomach, the knot of revelation therein unraveling so swiftly she thought it might knock her to the ground once unfurled. "My father?" she finally asked.

"A miracle," Josephine said firmly, releasing Emmy's hand and taking her by the elbow. "Though clearly not at first." They began to walk back to the pumpkin field as Josephine explained how she had refused to tell Stephen about the baby, even though Lida insisted he was a good man and would marry her. "Imagine," Josephine said. "Marrying someone you didn't love, after that."

"I couldn't," Emmy admitted.

Josephine paused and gazed into Emmy's eyes. "Of course," her aunt said, before resuming her steady pace through the furrows, describing how she arranged with Lida to stay at the farm until the baby came, and how, in order to save everyone from shame, they'd pretended it was Lida who was with child, and she who had given birth. Josephine had gone back to the estate to live with her aunt—Ray's mother—and Lida cut all ties to the family, unable to forgive Josephine's transgression, even as Lida benefited from its outcome. "It was for the best," Josephine said, pushing her sleeves up her arms as though she were preparing to wash her hands of the conversation. "Christian is a very good man."

"He is," Emmy said, her love for him resetting a small part of her disrupted soul. She remembered a time when she was very small, asking her grandmother why she'd only ever had one child, and Lida telling her that Christian was so perfect, she didn't need to have any more. Another memory, later still, of Karin telling Emmy that her grandmother had been very sick after having Christian, and unable after that fever to bear more children. Emmy's ire spiked again at the layers of deception she'd based her life story upon. She no longer knew what to believe, but with every new speck of truth she began to construct the narrative she would carry forward. "Does he know?"

"I wanted to tell him when Lida died, but I couldn't." Josephine stared up at the sky, her face pale as a cloud against the brilliant blue. "I'm afraid he wouldn't understand."

"I think he would," Emmy said. "I do."

"Don't try to lie," Josephine said, gratitude marking her scold. "It doesn't suit you."

She picked up a small pumpkin. "These are sugar dumplings," she added, a softer shade of pink beginning to tint her face. "Ray brought the seeds from a trip to Long Island, New York. Selected the sweetest each year for reseeding." She held one as tenderly as she would a baby's head. "This was our life, this right here." She smiled wanly at Emmy. "Go get the Jubilee. Careful not to flood her, she likes an open throttle and little or no choke. Wait for the idle."

Emmy collected as many squash as she could carry, and went back to where the flatbed sat connected to the small red-and-white field tractor, unloading her bounty into the wagon as she tried not to cry. She climbed up on the cold metal seat and did as instructed until the engine revved to cantankerous life, the noise of it covering the sound of Emmy's sharp inhales. Using the small wooden spool attached to the oversized steering wheel to turn the tractor in Josephine's direction, Emmy eased the Jubilee down the row and succeeded in suppressing her rising tide of self-pity. It was clear to Emmy that her aunt was unaware of Mr. Davidson's current proximity, and Emmy determined to maintain that fragile distance until she could find a way to render it permanent.

Only then, as her resilience spread into untested territory, did Emmy finally allow that she had traded a flawed grandparent for one who was made of far more hideous material. Her heart pinched at the thought of Mr. Davidson's fine blond hair and that of her own bearing more than a passing resemblance; the way she had found her own likeness in Josephine's high swept brow when they had first met. There was no denying that Josephine's story was true, and Emmy clearly understood that not only was she right to have chosen her destiny, but in so doing she could take it a giant leap further. She could expose the past.

The two women passed an hour working in necessary silence, their violent experiences creating a deeper bond between them than the revelation of ancestry ever could have. Emmy marked the time by looking at her watch every five minutes, feeling the intensifying draw of her grandfather's—she couldn't think of him as anything else—box still at the office, and how eager she was to get back to it. The sun had already peaked low on the horizon and set its course for the waning of the day, having imparted much more heat than typically expected in early November. Emmy took a moment to survey the wagon full of tiny Jack Be Little squash, a variety new to the farm. Somehow the cheerful quality of the teacup-sized pumpkins slightly buoyed Emmy's spirits as she whistled to Coffee and headed toward the house and a hot, mind-clearing shower.

She'd barely reached the road when Bobby's truck swung ahead of her into the drive. Coffee barked twice, and Emmy felt her finger for the missing ring, knowing it wasn't there. She raced across the road, panic spiraling up from her empty stomach with the acid pooling there—she hadn't had five minutes to think about what she wanted to say or how she would say it. By the time she caught up with him, Bobby was standing beside his truck, a grim scowl on his face.

"Get your work done?" he asked, as frank as a coin flip. Emmy stopped.

"No," she said, trying to gauge his irritation. "I'm sorry I left the party without saying anything."

Bobby kicked a pebble away from the truck's front tire. "Mom was sore," he said. "You could have told me."

"You weren't there to tell," Emmy said, flipping her own coin. "I saw you leave with Pete."

Bobby puffed his cheeks into a blowing sigh. "We went to get more beer."

"Please don't lie to me," she said. "Not today."

Bobby blinked rapidly, a sign of discomfort that made Emmy regret her bluntness.

"He had an issue . . ." Bobby began.

"Please don't," she repeated. This was not the investigation she was interested in, and playing out the petty questions made her anxious to get to the point. She shook her head. "It doesn't matter where you went. You left, so I left."

"You ran off," he countered, picking up the thread of confrontation the moment she let it dangle. "Sister Clare saw you rush out."

Emmy held her arms out in a guilty shrug. "Look, I saw you fighting with Pete, and I got upset." The childishness of the conversation grated against her desire to be done with it, into the shower, and back on the track she preferred. Emmy sighed. "This isn't right." She licked her dry lips. "We're not right."

Bobby's face blanched as he caught sight of her bare left hand. "Where's your ring?" he asked, looking as though he might cry.

"I took it off," she said, the first waves of the sadness that come with letting go of a lover—any lover—lapping at her. She touched his cheek. "You don't love me," she said. "Not the way you want to."

"I gotta go." Bobby shook his head in complete repudiation; his shoulders hunched low as he backed toward the truck's door. "We should talk about this later."

Pity overcame pride, and Emmy relented. "Yes," she said with all the compassion she felt. "We should."

"I do love you." Bobby's voice became increasingly softer yet more pained. "The best I can."

Emmy felt a small crack grow wider in her heart. "I will call you in a few days," she said, her words slow and full of purpose. "I have to take care of something."

He opened the truck's door. "Okay," he murmured, the sound of a penny dropping into a well. "I'll be at our house tonight, working, if you want to find me."

"Okay." Emmy stood in the drive as he pulled away, and the first sob of seeing him go burst from her, blinding in its unexpected force. *Don't leave me*, her head yelled as her heart whispered *Let him go*. It was hard to reconcile the vastness of this new freedom with the heartache it was inflicting. I'm sorry, she thought as she opened the door. I'm so very sorry. Coffee bolted into the kitchen and spun in a tail-chasing circle before settling. Maybe in time it would make sense to Emmy how a greatly felt love could come to so little.

"I can't think about it now," she said aloud, shocked by the calmness of her voice. Emmy folded a slice of bread and stuffed it into her mouth, chewing with the sole purpose of moving on with the day. She poured the cold remains of the morning's coffee into a glass and chugged it down black. The bitterness felt right to her, a refreshingly honest representation of a thing not trying to be any more or less than it was.

❧

Emmy arrived at the *Fargo Forum* building a full hour before her shift normally began. She wasted little time on pleasantries, weaving her way through the reporters' desks and straight back to the morgue, where the sight of Jim's wide shoulders and tousled brown hair made her tingle as she moved forward and looked over his shoulder. He'd once again laid out the objects and papers in the order from the night before, and had the encrypted ledger open before him, a notepad full of scribbling by its side.

"Hey there," he said, rubbing his hands together and standing. "I thought I'd get a jump on things." He moved the chair next to his away from the table and gestured for Emmy to sit. She flung her coat on the rack by the door and sat in the offered chair, Jim's proximity a welcome comfort.

"Anything worthwhile?" she asked as he returned to his seat and picked up a pencil.

"Plenty," he said excitedly. "Though there's still a few keys missing. I was up most of the night trying to crack the code in the ledgers, but it switches between them, and the last one is beyond defiant." He moved his chair an inch closer to hers and used the pencil to point at a column in the ledger. "This one I've got: Here's a list of all of the townships in Clay County." He turned a page. "Each of these pages begins with the name of a township, alphabetically ordered, followed by a list of names—inhabitants. Sort of like a census." He licked a finger and turned a number of pages until it fell open to a decoded sheet with the heading of the township most familiar to Emmy: Moland, where she'd grown up. She scanned the printed list ahead of his finger, her eye drawn to the familiar names: Nelson, Brann, Gunderson, Hansen, Svenson.

"This is where it gets interesting," Jim said, picking up a dark-blue-covered book with gold script across the front which read *Plat Map of Clay County Minnesota.*

"What's a plat map?" Emmy asked as he fanned open the oversized pages.

"An official surveyor's map of land ownership," Jim said. "In this case, by township. Aren't they pretty?" He turned each page and smoothed over the hand-lettered squares with his fingertips. "Quite a labor of love, creating this kind of map. You really don't see this degree of craftsmanship anymore."

Emmy drew her chair closer for a better look at the elegant depiction of the view of subdivided Clay County from above, including minuscule churches and country schoolhouses. "Where's Moland?" she asked, and Jim ran a fingernail across the top of the pages, locating a bookmark he'd clearly inserted earlier. Emmy immediately saw the name Benjamin Nelson inked along the Buffalo River on the #6 quarter section of land. The rest of the section bore the name Emmaline Brann, Ambrose's mother. A strange sensation seized Emmy, an icy liquid melting. She looked at the section to the right: E. Brann.

"Why is it in *her* name?" Emmy asked as she laid more fingers on the Branns' substantial holdings.

"It would have been her property." Jim drew his right index finger across his lips and Emmy could sense him staring at her.

"He may have married her for it," Emmy said.

"This was drawn in 1919," Jim said, turning the book slightly. "After the war. There were a lot of widows."

Emmy bit at a thumbnail. "I've always been told they married late, had Ambrose later. I have no idea what's true and what's not anymore."

"I'd say you're officially a journalist, then," Jim said, commiseration mixed with mirth in his voice. "Not that I'd wish that on anyone else."

The coldness that had flowed through her was replaced by a current of heat that started in the space between them and spread to the bone. She fought away the urge to smile by refocusing on the evidence before them, and noticed light pencil marks on each square of labeled land—small symbols that had no correlating key. "What's that?" she asked.

"Exactly my question." Jim put one finger on a tiny star and the other hand on the ledger. "O. E. Gunderson, one star here, and one star there." He moved his hands in concert. "Alias Hummel, two *X*s. Ben Nelson, two stars. E. Brann, two stars, and three tiny *M*s."

Emmy stopped his left hand in the middle of the plat. "Okay, so there's a code within the code. But what do you think it means?"

"It means that your grandfather was a meticulously paranoid man." Jim turned another page in the ledger, revealing a table of simple information, headed by the labeled columns *Bet*, *I*, and *M*. "I think it has something to do with this." Running down the left side of the page were the numbers one through thirty-six. Under the *Bet* column were initials, and after that a small, tidy check mark in either the *I* or the *M* line. Next to this, running down the right side was a series of dates, and at the very bottom of the page was a number with a circle around it. Emmy's eyes ran over all the information, her vision blurred slightly where it focused just off the page and back onto the map of Moland Township.

"There are thirty-six sections," she said, once again sourcing the square she knew best. "Three *M*s here, and look, after the number six in the ledger, the checks are in the *M* column, not the *I*." She then looked at the corresponding *Bet* column, and the chill she felt earlier came back in a rush at the sight of what was there:

M.G.

J.G.

R.G.

"Migrant workers," she said, pointing at the checks in the *M* column. "The Gonzales family. They've worked for the Branns as long as I can remember. The *R* is Ramon, Pedro's father, and those must be his parents."

"He didn't bother to fix the code." Jim made a note of the names. "What's curious is the dates—they're all three the same: May 4, 1924."

"Maybe it's when they arrived in the spring," Emmy conjectured. "For seeding."

Jim pushed his chair away from the table and stretched his arms over his head. "All these dates are on or before May 4," he said. "Why?"

"Have you looked at the other ledgers?" she asked, pulling the box closer to see inside of it. "Maybe there's another clue somewhere."

Jim nodded, and then shook his head. "One of them is an indecipherable collection of entries and dates that have my head hurting. The other is a detailed list of members and dues for the entire state, written in poorly imagined cipher so the names don't match what's in this book, but are easy enough to decode. But these names are real, from the survey maps, paired with initials—apparently of *betabeleros*. Why *M* and *I*, though?" He laced his fingers together and used his hands as a hammock for the back of his head to rest as he gazed up at the ceiling. "Unless . . . *I* stands for immigrant . . ."

"Still, they all had working papers," Emmy said, feeling oddly defensive of people she didn't really know that much about. "Do you think it was some way of keeping track of Mexicans?"

"No," Jim said. "I don't. I'm not sure what I think it is." He moved forward again and drew the box nearer, standing up in order to reach into its depths and lift out the remaining contents: newspapers, pamphlets, and other propaganda from a failed movement, but no other ledgers. "This is going to take a while to sift through, but it looks like mostly more of the same." Jim ran a hand through his hair and scratched his scalp. "Do you think your grandfather had any other journals, boxes of things, anywhere in the house?"

Emmy thought for a moment with her eyes closed, picturing the desk where she had done her homework in the fall. The image of an Indian popped up into her mind. "I think so," she said. "But I don't think I'm too welcome out there."

Jim cocked his head to the left, a pose that reminded her of Coffee. He squinted. "One of the things you will learn the longer you do this job is the only thing that matters is the discovery of truth. Lead with that, and you'll stop thinking about welcome mats. Use that nose."

"Do you mind if I borrow your satchel?" she asked, standing suddenly, his faith in her abilities trumping her hesitation. "I left mine at home."

"You're going now?" he asked, with more than a hint of pride. He stood and followed her to the door, reaching an arm in front of her in order to open it as she strode through to the hallway.

She nodded. "I shouldn't be long."

Twenty-two

Life with God Forever

Enveloped by the blue gloaming of early evening, Emmy headed east. As dusty snow began to scatter in its headlight beams, the Crestliner rumbled over the Second Avenue Bridge, through the barren streets of Moorhead, and out past the town limits. Dilworth came and went without Emmy so much as noticing the hulking gas station on one end of town, nor the smattering of blank-eyed houses as she cruised past them. Another mile, two, and then she turned onto the road that led through Moland Township, past the town hall, past the old schoolhouse, its weathered paint gray in the increasing swirl of snow. She imagined these landmarks on the plat map, their tiny representatives cartoonish and quaint. The last light of day was doused by the time she turned left again, past the cemetery, the church, the Branns' drive, over the creek bridge, and to the farm.

Emmy eased the car into the sharp left turn after the bridge and cut the engine, letting the Crestliner roll to a stop a brief distance from the farmhouse. A light was on in the kitchen, another in Lida's room. Emmy tapped a finger on the steering wheel, searching through the many pockets of possibility her mind kept emptying, sorting the reasons she had for showing up unexpected. Ultimately, she knew that none of them mattered until she saw Karin's reaction, and so Emmy took a deep breath and stepped a foot into the snowy gravel. The kitchen door opened, casting a yellow slant of light onto the powdered yard, and there stood Karin in one of Lida's old black dresses.

"Who's out there?" she asked plainly, and took one step forward.

"It's me, Emmy," Emmy said, her voice unintentionally sweet and small. She was overcome by her desire to embrace her mother, yet held in place by the fear of seeking something that would not be there. That had never been there.

Karin moved into the shaft of light. "Emmy?" she whispered, as if to a person she had thought long dead, only to find alive.

"Yes," Emmy said, encouraged by the echo of longing, and fumbling for more.

"Come inside, child," Karin said in a slightly sterner tone while nodding toward the house. The rush of yearning Emmy had felt dissipated like bees caught in a strong wind.

"Thank you," Emmy said, following her mother into the warm kitchen. The smells hit her like a wall built out of memories: the pungency of boiling cabbage slightly muted by the more seductive sizzling of roasting chicken and potatoes shot through with the hot vinegar of sautéed pickled beets. Over these, Emmy could detect the ammonia of the spotless floor and the faintest whiff of an odor she'd always related to her grandmother without having considered it before—one that she was incapable of identifying as created by any object in the room. It just smelled like Lida, a pillowy combination of flour, coffee, vanilla, wool, and roses that made Emmy's eyes water as though she were cutting onions instead of simply standing in the middle of the room, not knowing where to turn in order to restrain the press of nostalgia. The table was set for two, as though her mother had been waiting seven months for this dinner, maybe even preparing it every night in case her prodigal daughter should return. But Emmy knew better. "Is Birdie okay?"

"She's upstairs, lying down," Karin said, casting her eyes to the floor between her and Emmy, focusing on it as though she had missed a spot of grime and was considering rushing to the sink to fetch a rag.

"Oh," Emmy said, and took a step back. "Is it the baby?"

"She's fine." Karin's voice cut through the room. "She just needs time."

The clock ticked into the awkward silence that draped between them, neither seeming to know how to put down the first stone of the bridge that needed to be rebuilt. Karin sighed and turned away to the stove, and picking up a wooden spoon, she first stirred the cabbage, then the beets, and swiftly opened the oven with a thick cloth. She jerked the roasting pan from the interior, lifting it with one hand to the open burner, where it slammed to a rest. Emmy observed the wiry diligence of Karin's form, wondering if perhaps her mother had been living solely on coffee and air. Nothing about the meal seemed to give Karin any appearance of appetite.

"Marriage is never easy," Karin said without turning her head. Emmy studied her mother's profile. Deep lines had etched themselves along the sides of Karin's mouth, and her skin was stretched up across her sharp cheekbones to where it dipped into a hollow at the brow. It was equally tight and translucent at her jawline, where a blue vein meandered down to her neck and disappeared at the collar of the dark dress. It was almost as though the skull bones were patiently asserting their push toward revelation and after, the grave.

"I suppose it isn't," Emmy said, having only been a witness to two marriages up close, neither of which had seemed to her filled with joy or ease. It occurred to her that this might be a piece of her disillusion with Bobby. Perhaps she needed a better example on which to build a married life. "Will she stay here through the birth?"

Karin pressed the hand holding the dish towel to her lower back and hip, closing her eyes against whatever pain was surfacing there. "God willing. The baby will come and she'll go back. I'm praying for them." Karin went to the table and sat, lifting the family Bible into her lap and opening it, casting her eyes along a passage.

Emmy held quiet, gazing at her mother's sunken eyelids. The world kills us through our children, Emmy thought, draining a mother's love through a sieve of constant concern.

"I'm sorry," Emmy said, surprised by how compulsively the words came out of her, and the great relief she felt upon saying them. "I disappointed you, and Father, and I know that."

Karin's eyes glistened as she folded her hands together on top of the

Good Book. "I prayed for you, too, Emmaline," she said, and Emmy glimpsed in her mother's fixed gaze the depths to which all the loss had trenched inside of her, the gaping wound of it raw but dry. "The Lord has His ways."

"I'm just sorry if I caused you pain," Emmy said, fighting against the pangs of guilt that gathered into a thick clump in her throat, making it hard to talk.

Karin smiled, a slight turning up of the corners of her narrow mouth. "Rejoice with me," she said, holding a liver-spotted hand out to Emmy. "For I have found my sheep."

Emmy took the hand and folded it into both of hers, hoping some of her warmth might seep into Karin and shore her up. "Let me help you with dinner," she offered. "Like I used to do."

Karin smiled a bit wider, releasing Emmy's hand and smoothing the pages of the Bible. "I forgive you," she said plainly. "As God directs."

Emmy slung Jim's satchel onto a chair, unbuttoned her coat, and moved to the cupboards, instinctively locating a platter for the chicken and bowls for the vegetables, setting about her work as though the months since Easter hadn't passed. Even so, a kaleidoscope of images crowded into her head piecemeal: Svenja's tearstained face; Lida's last words; Christian's confession; Josephine's story; John Hansen's murder; Jesse's death.

"He was so young," Karin said, as though reading the tail end of Emmy's thoughts. A beet slipped off the wooden spoon and onto the floor, where it splattered its scarlet stain against the pale linoleum, the white cabinets, and Karin's light blue apron. Karin moved to the sink for a damp rag to swipe up the trailing stain.

Emmy knelt beside her. "Who?" she asked quietly.

"Daniel." Without physical alteration, Karin's smile turned sad. "I know that Jesus needed him in Heaven. I'm just sorry that He didn't give me back my heart. It's the one thing I'll never have, no matter how much I pray or how much good I try to do. He gave me you, and then Birdie, and you were both as beautiful, but I just didn't . . . have anything for you other than ordinary affection. I did my best, though, didn't I?"

"Yes, you certainly did," Emmy said, and wrapped her mother in a firm embrace, feeling Karin's hands flutter against her back like small birds lost in the wrong hemisphere, in the wrong season. "I have enough heart for us both," Emmy whispered in her mother's ear. When the awkward hug ended, Emmy was moved to see her mother's eyes were still dry. How broken must a person be not to mourn the thing that did the breaking? Emmy lifted Karin's hand to her own cheek. The phone rang, startling them both into standing.

"Please answer that?" Karin asked as she returned the beet-red rag to the sink. "It's probably your father."

Emmy grabbed Jim's satchel from the chair and reached the telephone table in the living room on the fourth shrill ring, lifted the heavy handset, and said hello.

"Emmy?" Jim asked.

"Yes."

"Look." His voice stopped and then rushed. "I want you to come back here right away."

Emmy turned away from the kitchen. "I haven't gone upstairs yet. What is it?"

"I talked to Stan Lewis down at the *Trib* in Chicago," Jim said, the urgency in his voice thinning Emmy's blood. He cleared his throat and continued, "In 1929, Davidson kidnapped his secretary, and it gets worse from there."

"Just tell me," Emmy whispered. She wound the phone's cord tightly around her free hand.

"He allegedly drugged her. Bit her numerous times. Raped her. Left her body on her parents' doorstep." Jim cleared his throat again. "She died before they could get a statement, and he claimed that anti-Klan socialists within the Cleveland government framed him. But there were teeth marks."

Emmy pressed a hand to her mouth and swallowed hard. She thought she heard a car in the yard, and she lifted the phone from its small table and moved to the window with it while Jim continued.

"By the time they arrested him, he'd had all of his teeth pulled, and they couldn't find his dentist." Jim cleared his throat. "Served some time for obstruction of justice, but nothing else. His supporters never faltered in their faith in him."

The memory of Mr. Davidson's perfectly aligned smile made Emmy flinch as she looked out the window. Her car sat where she'd left it next to

Karin's in the snow-blown yard. There were no other vehicles in the yard. Still, Emmy couldn't shake the feeling of another presence on the farm.

"I'll be there as soon as I can," she said, placing the phone's base back on the table and slinging the strap of Jim's bag over her head. The weight of the worn leather pressed on her shoulder like a steady hand, giving Emmy renewed confidence to complete her assignment. Jim's urgent voice had rattled her.

"Good," Jim said. "I don't want you anywhere near the council."

"Okay," Emmy said, cradling the phone and heading to the stairs. "I'm going up to see Birdie," she said to her mother. Emmy glanced through the open kitchen door as she swiftly made her way to and up the stairs, down the hallway on quiet feet, and into her grandmother's bedroom, closing the door carefully behind her. The lumpy shape of her sister's form lay still on the bed. Emmy tiptoed over to the edge and looked at Birdie's flushed face in the low light of the lamp. The carefree innocence was still there in sleep, though Emmy suspected it to be merely a slumbering mask that would fall away upon waking. Checking her watch, Emmy hurried over to the rolltop desk and lifted the wooden shutter front up noiselessly, searching the little drawers and pockets for any usable clues in the dim light, but finding only random collections of coins, tacks, ink bottles, and other casual inhabitants of the desk's warrens. She opened the flap of Jim's satchel and quickly tucked a couple of rubber stamps and a tiny black address book—the only items of interest—into the bag. After another minute of investigation, she grasped the handle of the drawer where she knew the cigar boxes to be. As before, the wood was stuck, and she had to jiggle, lift, and jerk the drawer while sweat began to dampen her brow. The drawer flew open on the third, more rigorous attempt, leaving its rails entirely and crashing to the floor, the contents tipping and scattering across the rug.

"Emmy?" Birdie said, the bed groaning under her shifting weight. "What are you doing? Why are you here?"

"I'm looking for something I left here," Emmy said, rifling through the drawer. She had no idea what she could possibly find that could help them write a story that would put an end to Mr. Davidson's influence, but a quick inventory of the mess in front of her revealed six boxes, the inside lid of each scrawled with a different year, and containing the same types of square pieces of yellowed paper slips. Emmy heard Karin's feet on the stairs. Emmy looked at the paper on top of the stack, raking it for information that might mean something. It was a driver's license, in the name of Julio Alvarez. Emmy frowned.

"Everything okay?" Karin called out.

"We're fine," Emmy said toward the door. "I just dropped something. We'll be right down." The footsteps retreated, and Emmy pushed the boxes and cards back together as neatly as she could, stowing a handful of the small papers in the satchel before lifting the drawer onto its runners and pushing it closed. She turned to see her sister sitting up, her bare legs dangling over the edge of the bed. There were a number of small dark marks on her shins, and tiny red lines on her arms. Birdie followed Emmy's stare with her own, and flinched, throwing the chenille bedcover over her exposed bruises.

"The belly makes me clumsy," she said, her eyes turned to the floor. "I keep bumping into the furniture."

Emmy approached the bed slowly. "And your arms?" she asked.

Birdie rubbed at the marks and laughed nervously. "Ambrose was trying to teach me how to whittle, and I slipped a few times."

"Did he hurt you?" Emmy asked, dismay sharpening her vision. Birdie's face registered shock at the suggestion.

"Oh, God, no," she said, with her hands shaking. "He would *never*." The girl's sweet mask crumbled, leaving the map of heartbreak etched underneath. Emmy drew her sister into an embrace, stroking her soft hair and shushing.

"I've missed you so much," Birdie said through her heaving. "I'm so alone now."

Emmy withdrew from the hug but held her sister's face between her hands. "Hush," Emmy said, wiping away a tear with one of her thumbs. "It's okay, I'm here."

Birdie's eyes crinkled shut, and a line of water leaked from her nose. "He doesn't love me," she cried, as much plaintive as befuddled. "I've done everything I can, but he still loves you."

"I'm sure you have," Emmy said, knowing it was true but incapable of adding to her sister's misery by agreeing with her assessment. "Who wouldn't love you more?"

Birdie clasped Emmy's wrists. "He follows you. Everywhere."

Emmy glanced at the window, darkened by the lamp. "Nonsense," she said. "You're mistaken."

"He's convinced himself that he's not the father." Birdie shook her headful of limp, matted hair and pulled Emmy's hands together. "He goes on and on about John Hansen, but it isn't true," she said. "None of it."

"But John's dead," Emmy said.

Birdie's round eyes went wider, and Emmy thought she detected a hint of knowledge too terrible to share.

"I'm glad Dad brought me here," Birdie said.

"Why, what happened?"

The sound of a truck door slamming cut through the quiet in the yard. Emmy jumped and went to the window in time enough to see Ambrose approaching the house. She patted at the satchel, making sure it was closed.

"Nothing," Birdie said. "He said he forgave me, but there's nothing to forgive."

"Maybe it's just nerves about the baby," Emmy soothed, eager now to be done with the emotional ramblings of her sister and back to the abandoned exhumation. "Marriage isn't easy." Karin's words were thin syrup in her mouth, but she had none that were better. "He'll come around."

"No, he won't," Birdie said sharply. She pulled a flannel robe around her shaking shoulders and drew her feet up into the covers. "He's so wrapped up in the council and Mr. Davidson. And you. There isn't time for me." The kitchen door opened and closed downstairs, causing the air pressure in the room to expand and contract. Emmy swallowed the lump of anxiety rising in her throat. She honed her last bit of focus on Birdie's claims.

"What do they do?" Emmy asked in a whisper. "This council?"

"I'm not allowed at the meetings," Birdie said, glancing at the door as though it might spring open. She picked absently at one of the scratches on her arm, reopening the cut with a ragged fingernail. "But I've seen them training in the Branns' backyard, and they've got a press in the kitchen where they make the election flyers, and other things. Ambrose is running for the township board."

"So I've heard," Emmy said. "What kind of training?"

"Like the army," Birdie said. "With guns. And sometimes they stack up piles of wood and then blow them up."

"Emmy?" Karin's voice traveled up the stairs. "Birdie? Ambrose is here."

The girls looked at each other for a suspended moment in which Emmy ardently wished to be back in their room in the small house. She sensed her sister was wishing the same. "Stay here," Emmy said, moving toward the door. "I'll tell him you're too tired to come down."

Birdie wrapped her arms around her belly under the covers and grimaced. "It's true," she said. "Be careful."

Emmy stopped short. "Careful?"

Birdie nodded. "They've been meeting a lot. At odd hours." Her eyes widened as though seeing something in her memory loom larger. "And I've heard strange sounds since John died."

"The wind's been howling lately," Emmy said, her hand on the doorknob.

"Not like that," Birdie said. "Like an animal in pain."

The door opened into Emmy's side and she stumbled slightly before turning to see her mother in the frame.

"What are you girls doing?" Karin whispered as she crossed to Birdie's bedside and placed the back of her hand against the girl's forehead.

"I have to go," Emmy said, hoping that Karin had sent Ambrose away. "But I'll be back soon."

A look of calculation stacked the lines at Karin's brow, as though she were thinking her way through the situation for the best way forward. "Maybe you should wait here until he leaves."

"Why would I do that?" Emmy asked. "I'm not afraid of Ambrose."

"He won't like that you're here," Birdie said. Her voice sounded smaller.

"I can handle him." Emmy crossed to the door, turned back. "Besides, my car is here."

Karin studied Emmy's face. "Then please tell Ambrose I'll be right down," she said, settling Birdie into the bed and tucking the sheet along the mattress. "You can handle yourself."

Emmy could neither fully read the subtext of her mother's words, nor did she consider them longer than was necessary to get down the stairs and into the kitchen in order to retrieve her coat. Ambrose stood next to the stove, a man so transformed by great ideas that he looked as if he had grown an inch. The hair lifted on Emmy's arms, but she wasn't afraid of his polished aspect, nor of what he might say to her. Their childhood friendship nagged at her core even as she brushed its innocence behind her impatiently. Too much had happened, too much still lay ahead.

"Emmaline," he said, the light behind his eyes sparking on her name. "Your mother said you were here." He seemed to have more hair, and his suit had the cut and flair of cloth that had been tailored.

"I was just leaving," she said, putting down the satchel and buttoning her coat. "Birdie's got a fever and can't come down."

Ambrose lifted his gaze from Emmy's face to just above the crown of her head. It seemed to her that there was relief, not disappointment, there.

"I'll walk you to your car," he said, and drew on his long camel hair overcoat. The imperious cocoon of it unnerved Emmy more than the ostentatious suit. She could only imagine what all of Mr. Davidson's polishing had done to Ambrose's interior, if this is how he looked on the outside, though the way he had stuffed objects in the pockets ruined the effect just enough for the awkward man he really was to show through.

Emmy slung the bag on her shoulder and passed through the kitchen door. She sensed Ambrose close behind her, a feeling that was familiar, if unnerving. *He follows you.* Birdie's words echoed. *Everywhere.* Emmy gathered the collar of her coat more tightly around her neck and walked briskly through the thickly accumulated damp snow, shocked by how much had fallen in the brief time she'd been at the farm. No matter how many years she had lived in this place, the rapid onslaught of winter caught her unprepared every November. As she approached the Crestliner, something about it seemed amiss in the yellow haze of the pole lamp: The nose pointed slightly down and to the left. She kicked the sticky snow away from the tire, unnerved to see that it was flat.

"I'll change that for you," Ambrose said. His face was shadowed, but his voice kind.

"This is the last thing I need," Emmy said as she went to the back of the car and popped open the trunk, causing all the snow that was stacked on it to dump soddenly onto the spare. "I don't even know if there's air in this one," she said, hefting it on her own and bouncing it to the ground. It too was flat. Ambrose took it from her and put it back in the trunk, closing the lid.

"I'll give you a ride," he said. "I'm headed to town."

Emmy stepped a foot away. "It's all right," she said. "Mother can run me in after dinner."

Ambrose looked up at the second floor of the house. "She should stay with Birdie, in case."

At the mention of her sister's name, Emmy's temper rose, and she broke the fragile shell that had held back her hostility toward Ambrose, toward them all. "What did you do to her?" she snapped at him. "Why is she so scared?"

"It's been hard," he said, tipping his head down in a way that caused the snow that had already collected on the brim of his hat to fall back into a sweep of wind. "I've tried."

"Not hard enough." Emmy started toward the house.

"Wait," he said loudly. "Let me give you a ride, please. I can explain."

She didn't turn. "I'd rather not."

"Don't you trust me?" he asked, a boyish note of disappointment in his voice. "Have you really gone that far away from us all?"

Emmy thought about the cards in her bag. Whatever they might hold, her instincts told her she needed to get back to the office quickly and show them to Jim. It wasn't a matter of trusting Ambrose but of expedience. She balanced her weight between one foot and the other, an aerialist with no wire, not even a net. She pivoted toward his truck on her heel, confident that stepping up into the cab held no more portent than any other vehicle in the yard. He slid behind the wheel and engaged the engine, his costume suddenly at odds with everything else. Only the round segment of his face that glowed in the faint light of the dashboard struck Emmy as familiar, and even that changed as he put the truck into gear and drove slowly out of the yard. Emmy's nerves inexplicably started firing with fright, her right hand clutching at the door handle in an attempt to remain calm. The acrid familiarity of the interior sparked images that flashed like a magician's card trick through her mind, even as she refused to take in the sleight of hand of any of them. The truck bumped up onto the county road and Emmy bit her tongue—no blood, just pain.

"Do you have a cigarette?" she asked in order to break the maddening spell his silence had thrust her into.

"I gave it up," he said proudly. "The council stands against any sort of vice."

Emmy moved her sore tongue against the offending tooth, thankful for the distraction of the pain. She gazed into the swirl of snow that shot at the windshield, and contemplated the council's definition of vice. From the little she knew, it was obvious to her that hypocrisy was not on the list.

"It's looking pretty good for me next week," Ambrose continued. "The election."

"Township board?" she prodded. His smile grew wider in the scant light.

"Curtis says it's the first step toward mayor. I know there are plenty of steps in between . . . and I'm willing to make them in order to serve my country." He absently fidgeted with the radio, but finding only static, he turned it off completely and tapped out a rhythm of his own on the steering wheel. "It's everything we dreamed of, Emmy."

"It is?" she asked, her pulse doubling.

"Remember?" He glanced at her. "At the basketball game. You said you'd like to live in town, have a big house. Well, if all goes right, we'll have that before you know it."

Emmy pursed her lips and sipped in a thin stream of air. *We'll.* "Yes," she said. "I remember."

"It's not too late for us," he said, turning the truck onto the highway toward Moorhead. "You don't know everything about Bobby Doyle, but once you do, you'll see that we're meant to be."

"You're married to my sister," she said quietly, but with enough calculated tenderness to placate a child on the verge of a tantrum.

He slowed the truck and turned onto a side road. Emmy's hopes dropped with the confirmation of his instability. She settled her bag on the seat between them and laid a gloved hand on his arm as a sign of peace. "I need to go to work," she said. "Now. At *The Fargo Forum*."

"I know where you work," he said, a slightly lower note in his voice as he shrugged off her touch. "And I'll get you there, in time."

Emmy's temper rapidly shot above her fear. "You'll get me there now," she said as sternly as she could manage.

"Hold on, and hear me out." He raised a flat hand up into the space between them. "There are a few things you need to understand. One, I'm not the father of that child. John Hansen took advantage of Birdie, and I did what was right to protect your family by marrying her. If I hadn't, they would have lost the farm to us and been destitute."

Emmy leaned forward, close to the dashboard, and tried to make out any landmark along the gravel road. Not once in all the years that she had known her sister had Birdie ever even shaded a truth. A series of calculations began to work their way through Emmy's head so swiftly that they instantly added up to one clear thought: She needed to get out of the truck, and soon.

"If you turn left up here, you can drop me off at my aunt's," she said, unable to stop the quaver in her voice. "She's expecting me for dinner."

"Two," Ambrose continued without heed. "You've strayed far enough for long enough. I know that none of this would have ever happened if I hadn't given in to the Devil's temptation and drank his poison. But I've made my amends by taking care of your sister, and now I can't let you fall any deeper into his clutches due to my sins." He slowed the truck at a stop sign and turned left. Emmy bit at a ragged thumbnail, restraining herself from saying anything that would turn them away from the lights of Moorhead, which she could barely make out through the driving snow. If they could just get into the town limits, she could slip out of the vehicle the first time he stopped, run to the nearest lit house.

Ambrose held the face of his watch at an angle to the speedometer's light. Whatever he saw caused him to make the truck go faster, grinding the engine into fourth gear. "I'm late," he said. "You'll have to come with me."

"Where are you going?" she asked without challenge, changing her tactics. If she could get her shaking under control enough to play into his fantasy of having a chance to save her, perhaps he'd take her home.

"To do His work," Ambrose said. "The council is a beacon of truth, light, and liberty. We must stop the evil knocking at our doors, in the misshapen form of papists and perverts, Semites and communists. I need to save you, Emmy, from all of them."

A numbing cold crept up from Emmy's toes even though the heat blowing in the cab had become stifling. The truck slowed but didn't stop as they entered the Moorhead city limits, and Emmy realized they were on Twelfth Avenue, headed for the bridge.

"The council has grown with God's careful tending," Ambrose said, a methodical surety fueling his speech, as though he were standing at a pulpit. "We've even started our own church, adhering strictly to the Good Book. With Curtis's guidance I've been preaching, just like Pastor Erickson always said I should. I've found my voice, Emmy. People listen to me, they *follow* me. Don't you see, they'll understand when I let Birdie free because she's sinned against us and God. You and I can stand together against the whores and blasphemers. The road to Heaven is paved with forgiveness. Walk with me down that road, and the Kingdom will be ours."

Emmy lowered the window slightly to let in enough air to combat her nausea. He's gone mad, she thought. She was desperate to get away, but the truck was still moving too fast. She moved her hand from the window crank and back to the door handle. She knew the route well from her daily trip to work, knew that once they crossed the river they would be at Elm Street, a few blocks from the house Mr. Doyle was building for her and Bobby. Where Bobby was right now, polishing the banisters of their abandoned future. The thought of her second failed engagement sapped at what remained of her patience. Emmy focused on a plan: She would throw open the door at Elm and take the back alleys to Plum Circle. There she would find Bobby and ask him to take her to *The Fargo Forum.* Two more blocks to the bridge, she counted, as Ambrose filled the air with increasingly unhinged words. He clutched her arm.

"I should have never let you go, it was my mistake alone," he said, one block from the bridge. "You can't keep running away. You'll see. I'll take care of your mother and Birdie, we'll give them the farm. It can all work out if you just trust in God's plan."

The front tire bumped up onto the Moorhead edge of the bridge, and

Emmy whistled low as they reached the center, her fondness for Jim's strange habit lending her courage. She looked out across the surface of the river and briefly thought how cold it must be in that soupy ice-flecked pool. Moving her body slowly forward so as to block Ambrose's view of her grip on the door handle, she steadied her breath and counted down the seconds as they approached the red sign.

Ambrose released her arm in order to downshift into a carefully glided full stop, and as he looked to the left for any oncoming cars, she threw open the door and bolted from the truck, finding her footing sure and swift. She cut through the yard on the corner and skirted around to the alley through a stand of poplars. The snow was unplowed here, as she had hoped, and thick enough to keep a vehicle from gaining easy purchase along the narrow utility road. As she passed by the backs of houses, their warmly lit interiors beckoned.

By the end of the second block, she stopped and listened for the truck's engine, suddenly realizing that if he had been following her for months, then he would have figured out where she was headed. She needed to rethink her plan, find a phone, call Jim. The satchel! She'd left it in the truck. Thunder sounded off in the near distance, something she had heard only once before during a blizzard. She swiveled her head, trying to decide which house to approach, and whether it was less crazy to knock on a kitchen door than a front door, and what words would she use to explain her dilemma?

Pressing forward another block, Emmy thought she could hear muffled footsteps approaching from behind, and she turned to see only the two tracks made by her own boots. The snow-fogged air crackled in her ears as she stood there, frozen by the emergence of a new, more frightening sound: a cacophony of sirens began to wail, seemingly from all around, and moving toward her specifically.

The white night sky was newly rosy to the northeast, lit by the swirling lights that had converged no more than two blocks beyond. Emmy broke into a clumsy run in that direction, led as much by the sirens as the pull to see what new disaster lay ahead. There, at the intersection of Fifteenth Street and Plum Circle, Emmy watched in horror as the flames shot through the collapsed roof of the concrete house and high into the snow-speckled sky. She moved closer slowly, stunned.

"There's another one in here!" a fireman shouted as he carried a limp body over his shoulder toward an ambulance.

Emmy felt everything around her slow to a crawl as she recognized Pete's lanky brown hair. She tried to run in his direction but couldn't move when she realized he wasn't wearing a shirt. Why was he there, and not Bobby? She ran ten steps closer and saw another fireman carrying Bobby from the house, limp. Greater confusion gripped her and she spun around, fleeing in no direction other than *away.*

People from the neighborhood had begun to gather: a woman in a man's coat hastily thrown over her housedress, a rabble of young boys, eyes agleam with the thrill of explosions and fire, a handful of men looking as though they wanted to help but didn't know how. Emmy wove past them, her breath jagged and raw in the cold wind. Clearing the main cluster of gawkers, she stopped when she saw three men standing at the curb, effectively blocking her way. Ambrose ran up from behind them and stood tall in the center, next to the much shorter Curtis Davidson. To Ambrose's right, Frank Halsey stood, a malicious glow lighting his pointed face. Emmy bunched her fists and sprang forward, a pain suddenly shooting through her temples. She doubled over, bracing her head with one hand as she fell to her knees.

"That's not necessary," Mr. Davidson said to Frank. "Put her in the car."

"I've got her," Ambrose said, and Emmy could tell by his expression that he hadn't thought things through enough to know how to handle this turn of events. He wrapped an arm around her and whispered, "It'll be okay, just stay quiet."

"I thought you said the house would be empty," Mr. Davidson snarled at Ambrose as they passed, "This ruins everything."

"It should have been," Ambrose replied. All of his earlier hubris was gone—subservient groveling had taken its place. He bundled Emmy into the backseat of the car, moving her across the leather bench to make room for Mr. Davidson on his other side. She reached for the door handle; Ambrose stopped her. "Don't," he whispered. *"Please."*

"I've misplaced my faith," Mr. Davidson said as he settled into the car and slammed the door.

"I keep telling you he's weak." Frank smirked as he started the car.

"Shut up and drive," Mr. Davidson said.

Emmy panicked as the car pulled away from the curb, and responded to her fear by taking in every detail she possibly could—if she was to escape, she would need to remember what had happened. Jim's voice from the phone echoed in her ear: *Kidnapped his secretary. I don't want you anywhere near the council.* As the car made a U-turn in the middle of Plum Circle, Emmy caught sight of a large sign that stood proudly in front of the burning house, proclaiming *ROBERTSON DEVELOPERS* as its builder. "Low-income housing," she murmured, following the clumsy logic of her thoughts past the ambitious plans for Golden Ridge on Mr. Doyle's desk, the rally held by Mr. Davidson's mayoral candidate, the evidence in John Hansen's murder pointing toward the wrong man—a Mexican.

"Look at that baby burn!" Frank exclaimed. "That'll show 'em."

Mr. Davidson grunted, but Emmy could see on his face that he was proud of the handiwork. "Take the other bridge!" he yelled. "This road is too slow."

"What happened to John?" Emmy asked directly into Ambrose's ear, hoping Mr. Davidson was too busy directing Frank to hear her. The snow slowed their progress to a pace unsatisfactory to him, but for Emmy, it was time she needed to recover from her shock.

Ambrose pressed his lips into a hard, small line and minutely shook his head. Something about the gesture told Emmy that Ambrose had been there, possibly held the gun himself. "Birdie?" She said the name so softly that only the harder sounds of it were audible. Ambrose winced.

Mr. Davidson leaned forward to see around Ambrose. Emmy met the old man's eye; she was defiant now, ready to match her inherited wits against his. "How dare you," she spat. "Take me home now."

He scowled. "Did you bring the ether?" he calmly asked Ambrose, who on command reached into his coat pocket and withdrew a small can and a white cloth.

"Ambrose?" Emmy gasped, realizing that this had been part of his plan all along—the flattened tires, the offered ride, the incendiary display of power—clearly his goal to win her back was to be achieved by either persuasion or coercion, whatever it took. His hands shook, and he bit his bottom lip as he opened the top and spilled a few drops into the cotton. Emmy tried to pull away, to open the door, to scramble up and away from him in her seat, but the sickly sweet smell of the gas seeped into her nose and mouth as he pressed it firmly against her face. As she sunk into the oddly welcome abyss, from a million miles away she heard the words *I'm sorry.* Then nothing more.

Twenty-three

Grace Alone

The familiar odor of oil-packed earth slipped into the darkness of her dreams. Emmy knew the smell, felt the dirt cold against her cheek, the black ink of the room liquid against her open eyes. A board creaked overhead, where she could barely see a speck of light like a pinprick in the heavy wool of sky. There were voices as well, but they were distant, muddled. Emmy tried to lift a hand to her face but found her arms were linked behind her back. The pain was everywhere: in her temples, the backs of her eyes, the roughness of her throat as she tried to swallow, the interior of her right shoulder, which, given how it felt, had been pressing into the dirt floor for a good long while. Her ankles—yes, these were bound as well, and it occurred to her to be grateful that she had put on trousers at some point during that day. Logic was not there at first, but as shards of memory began to cut at her consciousness, a deep, rattling cough overtook her to the point of nearly vomiting. She rolled over onto her stomach and did as best as she could without covering herself in the mess. The sight of Bobby slung over the shoulder of a fireman was the worst of it. The noises above stilled. Screaming is not an option, she thought as she rolled as far away from the sour smell now permeating the dark. Three rolls in, she came up against something soft and warm, solid, yet quivering. Emmy curled into a ball and pulled away from the thing—the animal—envisioning in her delirium a giant rat, or a number of them perhaps.

Footsteps again now, swiftly across the floor, and a door creaking open someplace above. Emmy rolled back to where she knew the pool of vomit must be and stopped just short of it, lying on her shrieking shoulder and tipping her head aside, eyes pinned shut. A light passed over her eyelids and she fought the urge to open them, to see exactly where she was and what else was there with her. Cautious, quiet steps down a few stairs—planks—then the prickling feeling of some sort of presence in the room as the light at first moved away from her face but then stayed steadily on it.

"Emmy, wake up." It was Ambrose. He gave her a careful shake on her painful shoulder, but she resisted the urge to open her eyes. A low grunt sounded in his throat, the sound of a man holding back fear. "Curtis is preparing to move you. I don't know where." Emmy squinted her eyes open a small amount. Ambrose's face was completely in shadow behind the beam of the flashlight.

The door at the top of the stairs swung open, slamming against the shelves that lined the wall behind it. Emmy squeezed her eyes shut again but had seen enough to know that she was in the Branns' cellar.

"Well?" Mr. Davidson yelled gruffly from above. "Are they ready?" Emmy heard the squealing sound start again, this time more urgent and pain-pitched. It wasn't an animal; it was the mewling of a woman. Was it Birdie?

Ambrose stood, his legs shielding Emmy's face from Mr. Davidson's view. "She's still out," he said. "I think she needs a doctor." His voice carried away from Emmy now, back toward the stairs and then up, clearly following the stranger's withdrawal. "We can't move her in this condition."

Emmy heard a sharp slap, followed by the sound of something falling a few stairs onto the floor. Then a harsh rebuke: "You are some kind of ignorant fool. I need them ready to move before dawn. If she dies on the road, it's God's plan, not mine."

"But they'll look for her here." Ambrose gathered courage in his voice. "We need to throw them off."

Mr. Davidson remained silent for a moment. "Take her watch," he growled. "And her boots. Leave the boots on a bridge and throw the watch in the river."

Emmy felt Ambrose roll her onto her back, lift her right arm, and remove her watch, letting her arm drop limply to the floor.

"On second thought, give them both more ether before you leave," Mr. Davidson said. "I don't want any trouble while you're gone." His footsteps continued up the stairs, where the door swung closed.

A small whimper came from Ambrose. He rubbed Emmy's arm and squeezed her hand, the flashlight pointed toward the ceiling joists. "God forgive me, Emmy," he whispered, anguish permeating his voice. "It was just supposed to be another cross."

Emmy opened her eyes and tried to sit up, but a fierce pain in the back of her head forced her to lie down again. "Did you?" she asked, but her throat was too raw to say more.

"Just the theater." He sniffed, sounding both twelve and ninety. He took the can and the white cloth from his pocket. "When Frank joined the council, Curtis gave operations to him and preaching to me." He moved his mouth so close to her ear that she could feel the drops of moisture on his breath as he spoke below a whisper.

"Did he shoot John?" she asked.

"No, the Mexican did."

Emmy shook her head slightly and ribbons of pain laced her vision. "Were you there?"

"No, but Curtis was."

The door slammed open again, and Ambrose pressed the cloth to Emmy's face as she closed her eyes, expecting the downward tumble of fractured dreams to reclaim her, but only scant traces of the drug remained. He hadn't even opened the can.

"Now!" Mr. Davidson yelled, switching on the overhead.

"One more minute," Ambrose said, sounding far calmer than his shaking body indicated. He slipped something hard and cold under Emmy's side, whispering, "The coal door is open." Emmy felt him move away. "Go quickly," he added before pulling off her boots and leaving the room.

The light clicked off and the wash of darkness made Emmy start to shiver in the dank room, but she wasted no time before rolling in the direction of the other person in the room.

"Hello?" she whispered, her tongue feeling large and heavy in her mouth. "Are you okay?"

The woman mewled so softly that Emmy could barely hear her. "I want to die," she murmured with a sound of defeat that struck Emmy with fresh dread.

"Svenja?" Emmy said sharply. She counted the months since the beautiful girl had shown up bruised and scared at the office. "Oh, no."

"I want to die," Svenja squeaked, the noise forcing Emmy to wriggle into an upright position and keep her voice low and calm.

"Shhh, don't talk like that." A searing pain spiraled through Emmy's head, the dizzying aftereffects of the sedative throbbing throughout her body. "Are your hands tied?"

"No," Svenja mumbled. How beaten must she be, Emmy thought, if they don't even bother to stop her from fleeing?

"Untie mine," Emmy said as forcefully as she could in an attempt to focus her energy and also to bring Svenja around. Emmy maneuvered her arms to where Svenja could untangle the coarse bale twine.

"I'll try," Svenja whispered, and the girls set about their tasks in silence and darkness, loosening the poorly tied knots and slipping out of the bindings. Emmy rubbed her sore wrists and arms, realizing through her haze that Ambrose hadn't tied them as tightly as he could have. She reached in front of her and felt for Svenja's shoulders, lifting her friend into a standing position. Svenja responded by hugging Emmy tightly. Through a flimsy layer of silk, Emmy felt the heaviness of Svenja's belly push hard against her own.

"I made it to Saint Paul," Svenja whispered, her stale breath warm on Emmy's cheek. "They found me and locked me up at John's. I had to tell him." Svenja's voice cracked. "It's all my fault. If I hadn't told him . . ."

"Told him what?" Emmy said, as desperate to start moving as she was to know what had happened to John Hansen.

"About Mr. Davidson," Svenja said, releasing Emmy and sinking into the chair. "I want to die."

Emmy leaned forward to where she thought Svenja's face to be, and laid her hands on her belly. "Is it his?" Svenja clutched Emmy's hands, and the baby moved within as a low groan funneled up from Svenja's lungs. Emmy moved her hand to Svenja's mouth, but the sound was too primal to stop.

"Shhh," Emmy warned as they waited for the moment to pass, waited for the sound of men moving to the basement door. No one did. "They must be busy," Emmy whispered, fresh hope mixing with new fear. She remembered the hard object on the floor, and quickly crawled back to where she had lain, feeling in front of her until her hand landed on the cool ivory of her grandfather's bowie knife, the leather scabbard smoothly familiar in her hand. Emboldened, she conjured a mental picture of the Branns' cellar—a place where she had frequently played hide-and-seek as a child, often in the dark. She stood slowly and felt along the wall until her leg bumped into a workbench. Every time a noise sounded overhead, Emmy held her breath, ready to fall on the floor and resume her possum play. She stealthily made her way back to Svenja.

"Ready?" Emmy asked.

"Go without me," Svenja said, resignation coloring her stilted speech. "I can't . . ."

"You will," Emmy insisted, taking off her coat and slipping it over the flimsy nightgown, buttoning the woolen garment across Svenja's belly as best she could. "Now listen—there's storm cellar stairs behind the coal bin that go out the back of the house. It's only a quarter mile to the church, and another few hundred yards to our farm—we'll call the police from there. Okay?"

Svenja didn't answer, but Emmy could feel her cowering. "Is there a blanket?" She felt around the floor near Svenja's chair, finding a small quilt. "That'll do," Emmy said, trying to be positive even as she knew that without boots her own odds against freezing weren't much better than Svenja's.

"We'll just have to keep moving, right?" Svenja asked shakily, placing her sweaty hand in Emmy's.

"Exactly." Emmy stuck the leather-holstered knife in her waistband and gathered the quilt under her arm, leading Svenja along the wall to the back of the room and behind the boiler. It was as hot in the corner as it would be cold outside, which Emmy knew was a fortunate thing, as any snow that might have fallen on the cellar doors would have melted away. She placed her stocking foot on the middle step and reached up to feel along the rough wooden door, the oval-shaped metal handle slipping into her hand as it had so many times before. Svenja released Emmy as the girl began that low, ugly groan again.

"Be strong," Emmy whispered, sensing that pain in this sort of interval indicated a greater challenge looming.

"Oh, dear God, please take me," Svenja said through her gritted teeth.

"How long has this been happening?"

Svenja ground her teeth. It sounded like gravel thrown at a brick wall. "Since this morning? I think."

"Listen," Emmy replied, a demand. "This is nothing. Keep telling yourself that. *This is nothing.*" Emmy knew the alternative was too grim to consider, so she turned back to the large flat door overhead and simply pushed hard at it until one half of it gave a bit and then after more pressure flew all the way open to the perfectly still and starry night. A bank of snow between the door and the house buffered the sound as the two women scrambled up and out into the backyard. A light was on in the kitchen, showing through the window three coffee mugs on the table and nothing else.

"Stay here a second," Emmy whispered, grateful for the advantage of having her vision return in the moonlight. She crept around the corner of the large farmhouse and observed two cars and the pickup truck in the yard. The trunk of one of the cars gaped open and Mr. Davidson was there, pushing various bags into the maw. Ambrose appeared from the house and Emmy jerked a bit farther into the shadows cast by the pole light's blue haze.

"I'll be right back," he said to Mr. Davidson. Emmy could see her boots in his hand.

"Make sure no one sees you," Mr. Davidson barked.

Ambrose ducked his head as if struck again, and climbed into his truck. Emmy used the noise of it rattling down the drive to cover her swift movements back around the house to where Svenja stood, grimacing and trembling. Emmy handed her the quilt.

"I can't," Svenja said, pushing it away. "I feel hot." The word sent a shock through Emmy. She wrapped herself in the quilt.

"We need to go now, and fast," she said, turning from her friend and marching on her already stinging feet through the deep snow toward a bank of trees. The moon was bright, and the temperature near freezing, the only two elements in her favor all night. They made it all the way to the tree line fifty yards from the house before she heard Svenja stumble and cry out.

"I'm wet!" she gasped. "Everywhere!"

Emmy spun to see what Svenja was talking about and was pinned in place by the vision of this folly: There the once beautiful girl stood, disheveled auburn hair about her head in a dirty cloud of moonlight, a puddle of dark-streaked fluid coloring the snow at her bare calves. Svenja's eyes went as wild as the heifer's once had, and Emmy knew the girl couldn't make it a mile, much less another hundred yards in this condition. The baby wasn't about to wait. Emmy tilted her head up to the sky, searching for some sort of solution. One star was brighter than the rest, and it occurred to her that a barn was as good a place as any to welcome a child.

"We need to work our way through the trees and to the other side of the barn," she said, taking Svenja's arm and leading her in that direction. "You won't make it otherwise."

Svenja pulled away and her coat fell open, revealing moon-shaped scars where her pale cleavage showed. "You go," she hissed. "I don't care what happens to me."

Emmy grabbed her by the arms and pulled her close, whispering just as harshly in her ear, "Well, I do. Now calm yourself and come."

It took five contractions to reach the soft hay in the upper loft. Svenja's labor intensified, a contraction starting nearly as soon as the one before it had finished, and Emmy alternated between holding the girl's hand and pacing the dusty room. She listened to the falsely comforting sounds of the animals below, knowing that it was only a matter of time before the men in the house made their discovery, followed the tracks out the back, through the woods, and right into the barn. She really hadn't had the time to try to trick them with deeper tracks in the opposite direction—not that she could have. As she tried to think of what she would need to help Svenja, the girl cried out in shrill pain. She sounded like a rabid cat. Emmy pulled off her sweater and wedged it under Svenja as she arched up with the contraction, the quilt falling away, the coat open and useless. Focus, Emmy, she said to herself. Watch and wait. She grabbed the quilt from the floor and shook it hard, placing it under Svenja's legs, and then with a flick of the knife, she opened the seam on Svenja's underpants, ripping them out of the way. A much darker patch of hair showed between her thighs, and Emmy felt a brief moment of gratitude that she wasn't seeing tiny feet.

"This next time, go," Emmy said, laying a gentle hand on the mounded stomach, the other against the right inner thigh. In the dim moonlight through the one window, Emmy moved a hand to the dark center and felt the hard-soft flesh of the infant's head there, pliant, ready. Inhaling once deeply and exhaling completely, Emmy readied for the moment when her breath would catch. A rumbling started under the hand on Svenja's stomach, then a sharp tightening, and Emmy could feel the child's knee strike out at the flesh that would constrict it even as the circle in her other hand grew into a dome. "Go now, hard," she commanded, and Svenja propped her body up with her hands behind her on the coat she had shed, her bruised body visibly determined to move beyond the torture, through the demands of birth, and into some sort of relief. Emmy held her friend's gaze as Svenja's face contorted, and just as quickly as the small head was out, a look of complete peace swept away her grimace. Emmy inhaled. Exhaled. Svenja mirrored the breathing, and within seconds started the next push, triumph and anger mixing in her expression, making her look as wild as a cornered raccoon and as strong as a lion.

The baby was out, and Emmy looped a piece of bale twine tightly around the cord that still connected her to her mother, laying the tiny girl on Svenja's chest. As the new mother wept, Emmy attended first to the umbilical cord, and then to the afterbirth, folding the quilt and cautiously pressing it against Svenja, and covering her and the baby with the coat. Emmy pulled her sweater over her head before swiftly crossing to the window in order to consider their next move. The sky hadn't lightened in the least; perhaps a half hour had passed, probably less.

Ambrose had not returned. Emmy felt a jolt of borrowed time course through her, and she turned back to attend Svenja, only to find Mr. Davidson standing in the loft doorway. Every hair on Emmy's body fired to attention, her hearing sharpened on the protective rush of anger she felt starting at her toes.

"Thank you, sister Emmaline," Mr. Davidson said, looking at the baby. "You've saved me one piece of trouble."

"She needs an ambulance," Emmy said. "Now."

Svenja's whimpering started anew but deeper in tone as Emmy walked sideways along the loft wall toward the pair, keeping her head low so the roofing nails that stuck through the slanted ceiling wouldn't catch on her scalp. She dared not look for the knife, sensing in Mr. Davidson a man on the prowl for any evidence of danger.

"Why don't you bring me the baby," he said, keeping his distance at the doorway. "And we'll go make that call." Emmy locked on Svenja's eyes, nodding slightly at the girl as she knelt below her, feeling the knife at her knees where it had dropped with the afterbirth.

"No!" Svenja cried, holding the child more tightly.

Emmy shot her eyes to Mr. Davidson, who turned his head toward the stairs, yelling, "Frank, go get the ether!"

It was just the slice of time that Emmy needed to pick up the knife and slip it under the coat-swaddled child. "Trust me," she whispered under Svenja's cries, and the girl suddenly stilled, her eyes wide.

"That's a good girl," Mr. Davidson said to Emmy as she walked to him with the baby, gazing down into the tiny-featured face. Emmy took a deep breath, counting to sixty on the exhale.

"It's a boy," she lied, somehow sensing this would be important to Mr. Davidson, and his face lit as he reached his empty hands toward the bundle.

"A son," he said.

Emmy leaned closer, supporting the child with her left arm as she drove the knife with her right deeply, quickly, into the soft pillow of Mr. Davidson's belly, his face not entirely registering the shock of pain in time to stop her from pulling up just as smoothly with the blade, tipping the edge slightly, as Ambrose had taught her. If it hadn't been for the child between them, Emmy would have continued until his sternum cracked.

Mr. Davidson stumbled backward, away from Emmy, fury bubbling red spit at his mouth before he sat down hard on a bale, gazing at the white hilt, the tiny red-circled cross in his useless palm.

The sirens started from far-off, a sound that brought Emmy back to the window, where she saw Mr. Brann, Frank, and two other men scurry to the loaded car in an attempt to drive away. Emmy's body started to convulse, and fearing that she would drop the baby, she made her way over to Svenja and settled the child into her arms before sinking down to the hay next to them.

Twenty-four

I Will Overturn, Overturn, Overturn It, and It Shall Be No More

The calm repose of the pale wood paneling lining the walls of the small chapel belied the activities elsewhere in the building—the births, the deaths, the sickness, the healing—and the small plaster statue of Mary at the front of the room offered Emmy no fresh comfort. For three days in a row, she had come to Saint John's Hospital, requested Bobby's room, and been told the same: Only immediate family were allowed on the ward. The first day, she'd felt guilty relief, too exhausted to make much sense of what had happened. But as the days went by and her inability to reach the Doyle family left her imagination to dwell on the worst possibilities, Emmy had found this a tiny haven.

Time had passed in an unending blur of repeated storytelling. After the initial gruesome regurgitation of facts had been completed, the distant piecing together of salient details began, only to loop doggedly around to the barn, the baby, the knife. For Emmy, it had begun to feel like she was merely reciting lines in a play—or telling the intricate twists of a movie viewed only once—and as quickly as the firm aspects of the plot loosened, new, uncertain ones would mysteriously appear to frustrate her. Had she put the baby in the coat or the quilt? Had she been given the ether before or after the car left the scene of the fire? Had she heard Frank Halsey admit to having set the blaze? How could she be certain of anything? Or certain enough to be the ultimate source upon whose word the punishments would be determined?

Emmy had been asked by the prosecutor not to talk to any of the other witnesses, including Svenja, who was healing with her daughter in her own room upstairs. And yet Emmy had felt compelled to drive here each day, to try to make some sort of peace with Bobby before the hearings began and she would have to sit in front of a preliminary jury, relive the moments for complete strangers to judge. She would never be the one on trial, that had been made clear, but unless Svenja grew strong enough to testify, much of the fact telling would fall to Emmy.

Emmy picked at the starched bobbin lace on the edge of her handkerchief and contemplated prayer, realizing that even when she had been faithful, prayer had come hard to her. She would fold her hands and close her eyes and string together words that she guessed at being what she was supposed to be thinking, but there was never any feeling other than a voice that whispered *How much longer*, and that voice clearly wasn't God's. Unwinding the square cloth, she let the tiny ring tied to its middle drop onto her plaid woolen lap, delicately parachuting the hankie over the hollow gold eye. How long had she worn it? Three, four, maybe five hours? Not even long enough to dull the metal with life's small accidents, much less the larger ones that had happened in the wake of the removal. Emmy closed her eyes, leaned her ear toward the distant sounds of people coming in and out of the hospital, passing the open chapel door, shoes squeaking, the sister at the desk greeting fresh faces full of concern with her hushed church voice.

Emmy thought about her father, and how he'd shown up at the Brann farm with Jim, the two of them gathered and delivered by Ambrose in a return to clarity. Christian had bundled her up and taken her to their farm, where her mother sat up in a chair while Emmy slept, cooked food for her when she awoke. They had temporarily reunited as a family under that roof, as quietly as they had splintered apart. She had not seen Jim in the days that followed, and his absence had created in her a drive to have the investigation over and the arraignment issued so she could return to work.

"Emmaline?" a woman asked from the hallway of the hospital.

This voice was closer, more familiar. Emmy opened her eyes and gazed at her lap, tears watering a meadow that had lain fallow for far too long. She felt Mrs. Doyle slide into the pew next to her and lay a hand on Emmy's leg, where the first drop splashed full and soundless.

"I'm trying to pray," Emmy said, her voice like a mouse caught in her throat. "He's going to be all right, isn't he?"

"He is," Mrs. Doyle replied with her usual cast-iron resolve.

Emmy lifted the hankie and wiped at her damp cheek.

"He wants you to keep it," Mrs. Doyle said, and Emmy glanced down at the guilty, deserted object. "Have the jewels reset in a necklace, maybe a cross. That's what he said."

Emmy's heart jittered as she laid a hand on top of the ring. "May I see him?" She looked at Mrs. Doyle, who seemed to have new lines etched around her green eyes, which crinkled together in a painful half smile.

"I think it's best that you don't."

"Then may I write him a note?"

"Rather you didn't," Mrs. Doyle said, adjusting a deep red lank of misplaced bangs away from her face with a hand that stopped along the way to scratch at a cheekbone, darting behind the ear and back again to pat Emmy on the leg. "He's in enough pain as it is."

Emmy caught the flighty hand and held it still. "Please tell me," she said, seeing in Mrs. Doyle's averted eyes a common understanding, willfully unshared.

"He's badly burned," she said, her façade of strength momentarily slipping. "And his father blames himself. God willing, they will both heal."

"What about Pete?" Emmy asked, not letting Mrs. Doyle pull her hand away.

"Pete's fine." She inhaled. "He knows his way around a fire, after all."

Emmy loosened her grip. "I haven't said anything to the police. Not that I have anything to say."

Mrs. Doyle pinched her eyes shut for a few moments, and Emmy watched her chest move up and down rapidly under her white woolen coat.

"They were there working," she finally said, leveling her eyes at the Virgin. "That's all there is to tell." It seemed to Emmy that the cause of the fire hadn't yet been assessed, and that Mrs. Doyle's absence of anger was blessed calm before an as-yet-uninformed storm. The news would be out soon enough. There was no point in Emmy being the one who broke it.

Emmy nodded, and they sat in the silence of the chapel until Mrs. Doyle suddenly stood and looked down at Emmy.

"He's going to take the vows when he's well," Mrs. Doyle said. "It's for the best."

"I can see that," Emmy said, the last of her girlish infatuation leaving her as she stood. She put the ring into Mrs. Doyle's hand. "Please donate this to the sisters," she said. "I don't think I could bear to keep it."

"Of course you couldn't, my dear, sweet child," Mrs. Doyle said, and caressed Emmy's cheek. "Nobody expected you to."

Emmy took the long way to the estate, even though the Main Avenue Bridge was two blocks from Saint John's Hospital. She was eager to return to the estate for a quiet lunch with Josephine, if for no other reason than to escape from the visitors who had come to the farm in a steady flow pocked with detectives and attorneys. There had been plenty of food delivered and countless well-meaning questions asked, but no matter how Christian and Karin had tried to protect Emmy, she knew that the best way through to the place where it would stop was to satisfy all curiosity.

Instead of driving straight up Elm, Emmy diverted, slowing as she passed the *Fargo Forum* parking lot, even though she didn't expect to see Jim's car this early in the day. And what if he was there? She wasn't allowed by the court to return to work until after the preliminary hearings were finished, and the district attorney had insisted that she not speak to a single reporter—including those she felt she could trust. The story had broken across the front fold all the same, and Emmy had pored over the meticulously accurate, if scant, articles. Most of the stories were written by Jim about Curtis Davidson and his previous crimes. Her blood had run cold enough that night to do what she had needed to do, but now that she knew more about him, it ran brisker still, a tiny part of her wishing the harm she had done could have been more permanent, and spared them all of it.

In time the story would certainly bud and unfurl as people packed the courtrooms and ate up every grotesque morsel of Curtis Davidson's past, every twisted hue of the evidence, as his lawyer was sure to paint a different picture than what Emmy had drawn. As she drove past the turn to Bobby's house, she couldn't help worrying that the defense would try to find a way to exploit his relationship with Pete in order to mitigate the information Emmy had been able to dredge up. No one would tell her about Ambrose—what he was saying, whose side he was on, as if there could be sides in such an undertaking. She didn't even know whether they had drawn together the burning cross out in Arthur, or if the Moorhead Theatre fire was still considered an accident, which she knew for certain it was not.

"Oh, why," she whispered in the quiet car, the sound of the words mildly startling her as she made the last turn that would take her home. Why did all of it have to happen? She vowed for what must have been the hundredth time to stop dwelling, to let go and not have to be the one who made everything turn out right. There was no happily-ever-after for any of them, not yet, and that would have to be okay until the disease that Curtis Davidson had brought into their community was gone for good.

The sight of Jim's car in the yard was not unexpected. In fact, she had been dreaming of seeing it out at the farm for days. What wasn't expected was the sheer thrill of excitement that closed up her split heart like a zipper, the teeth of her loose emotions congregating neatly into a fastened line. She let the Crestliner cruise to a stop at an angle, barely taking the time to shift into park and pull the brake before flying out of the car and rushing up the slippery walkway and through the front door. There he was. Laughing, turning slowly, settling a cup with a small click against the saucer in the other hand. Smiling. Emmy flashed her eyes from his to Josephine's and back again, pulling off her hat, coat, and gloves in a disordered hive of movement that almost felt like life had returned at last. In the momentary stillness she remembered Elise, and part of Emmy halted while the rest sped forward.

"Hi," she said, attempting composure. Failing.

"How high?" her aunt asked, laughing. She rose from the table and moved her teacup to the sink. "Jim, can I trust you?" she asked as she crossed to the coatrack, Coffee running a small circle between her two mistresses until choosing the direction of the elder one. "I need to go out for a while."

"I thought we were having lunch," Emmy said, though she could see that her aunt had carefully planned this meeting.

"I'm having lunch with your father," Josephine said, lifting her chin.

"Tell him I said hello," Emmy replied, even though she'd seen him at breakfast that morning. She knew that by suppertime they'd have quite a lot to discuss. "And that I'll be home later."

Josephine righted her collar and nodded before looking at their guest. "Jim, take good care of her."

"Scout's honor," he said, not taking his eyes from Emmy's. She saw warmth there, but behind that, something more electrifying. She slid into the chair facing his, folded her hands, and rested them on the table.

"I was so worried," he said, his face unusually open and soft. "Are you okay?"

"As can be expected," she said. A new kind of heat began at her core and scorched everything in its path as it moved upward, making her head swim, her armpits damp. She studied his face, then laughed. "Why, Jim Klein, I do believe you are at a loss for clichés."

His smile was almost demure. "I don't know what I would have done if something had happened to you."

The sentiment was so pure that Emmy grappled with her composure. "How's Elise?" she stammered.

Jim squinted and whistled low. "Why do you always ask about my sister when things get serious?" he asked. "It's a strange habit."

Emmy burst into startled, laughing tears. She put her hand over her mouth to hide her joy. "She's not your wife?" she asked with a small squeal.

"She's not my wife," Jim replied, laughing along. "She's my twin, in fact."

"Your *twin*?" Emmy dabbed at the tip of her nose with a napkin. "Oh, I'm such a *fool*!"

"Not at all the word I'd use," he said, his face once again calm. "I can see why you'd think that, grown children so close and all." He spooned some sugar into his tea and stirred once, leaving the cup untouched. "When my mother died I promised her I'd take care of Elise." He looked out the window. "She's not like most girls."

"She's *different*?" Emmy asked, conjuring up the magical word.

Jim slid the cup and saucer out of the way and reached across the table. He took Emmy's hands. "All the best girls are."

The tears came to Emmy's eyes quickly, making the room sparkle as she tried to blink them away. "I have to warn you," she said, barely able to raise her voice above a whisper. "I'm the kind of girl who breaks hearts."

"I know," he said, letting go of her hands and picking up his satchel from the floor. The moment ended as quickly as it had begun, but the promise of more hung in the air like a cottony cloud in a sunny blue sky. Jim slung open the top of the bag, the two leather straps slapping against the wooden table. "I brought you this."

"I forgot all about it," she said as Jim drew out the contents, including the things she had gathered from her grandfather's desk.

"Your friend Ambrose gave it to me. He's cooperating with the police." Jim scooted the little leather address book across the table toward her. "This is the key piece," he said. "All the codes are in here." Emmy flipped quickly through the pages and saw clusters of numbers and letters that meant nothing to her. The rush of discovery began to flow and she instantly knew she never wanted to be anywhere else, doing anything else.

"And this," he said, holding the varnished wooden handle of the small wooden stamp in the air, "is what Benjamin Nelson used to falsify these." Jim scattered the handful of yellowed cards on the table and Emmy sifted through them.

"Driver's licenses?" she asked, still not putting it all together.

"Proof of citizenship," he said. "For all the *betabeleros* in the county at the time, regardless of their nationality. So they could vote. Your grandfather was county auditor from 1920 until 1928. County auditors oversee elections." Jim squinted at her, waiting for her to puzzle it through. She couldn't.

"I still don't get it," she said, embarrassed by how much she wanted to impress him. To kiss him.

"The Klan fixed the elections on the local level by forcing the migrants to vote for their candidates." He put the papers back into a neat little stack.

"The Citizens' Council was preparing to do something similar this time around."

Emmy shook her head. "Not much of a smoking gun," she said.

"Oh, that's just the iceberg," Jim said, his smile widening into a full grin as he pulled the encoded journals out of the satchel. "Now that we have the ciphers, this here's the *Titanic*."

"Well then," Emmy said, playfully snatching a spiral notebook out of Jim's hand, a fierce ambition struck from the glow between them. "Let's get cracking, shall we?"

Acknowledgments

Let me start with undying thanks to my mother, Catherine Jents Scheibe. Without her encouragement, experience, feminism, and humor, this book would not exist. Beside her stand all the fantastic women of Probstfield blood, living and dead, whose stories helped shape my sensibility and built the sod house within which all that happens to Emmy Nelson is contained. In particular are the sisters: Edris, Helen, June, and Evie, the ghosts of whom inspire the spirit of Josephine Randall. Had I only known Phyllis, I'm sure there would be one more shade added.

If it weren't for Sarah Burnes, this book would not be worth reading. She's my gold standard, my all-in-all, my naysayer, my angel. A thousand years ago she said, "A love story about the KKK in '50s North Dakota? Okay!" I'm still not sure she meant it, but with hard work and pressure, she got the diamond she was looking for in the coal of those first few conversations.

Elizabeth Beier. The fabulous, dauntless, heroic, loyal lover of my pen. I feel like a contract player: blind, absolute, keep me by your side forever.

My rabbi, William Goldman, and his co-conspirator, Susan Burden, have lit my path on the darkest days with their support. They have read this in so many versions, and I will never be able to repay their generosity and love.

I owe an apology as much as thanks to my early readers, first sharp-eyed Cynthia Sweeney, and then Lauri Del Commune, Mindy Marin, Tina Constable, Kendra Harpster, Sloane Tanen, Susan Lauinger, Rick Monteith, and Judith Shulevitz. Everything you hated then is now gone. Jenny McPhee, Portia Racasi, Linda Greene, Jackie Maas, Jenny Blagen, Jen Strozier, Rebecca Odes, Jill Soloway, Bernie Boscoe, Jessica Gibbons, Anne Sansevero, Catherine Tangney, Karyn Gooden, Yuki Kimura, Sophie Terrisse, Jen Walther, Tristana Nesvig Trani, Natasha Lehrer, Ashley McDermott, and Holly Peterson—thank you for listening to me talk about "my novel" without rolling your eyes. All the members of the Scheibe-Flynn families for keeping me real. And also eternal thanks to my darling David Rakoff, whose words, though stopped, will always prod me forward.

To the everyday saints at the Gernert Company, in particular Logan Garrison, Anna Worrell, Rebecca Gardner, Stephanie Cabot, and Will Roberts. I thank my stars every time I think of how lucky Sarah and I are to have landed in your laps.

My home team away from home, St. Martin's Press, who took one look at this book and said, "Yes," and have been saying yes ever since: George Witte, Sally Richardson, Michelle Richter, Anya Lichtenstein, Frances Sayers, Emily Walters, Cheryl Mamaril, Jessica Lawrence, Ivan Lett, Kathryn Parise, and Laura Clark.

If I had three more pages, I would thank by name all the wonderful sales people and booksellers who still believe that the book is king. In their hands my hopes rest. Special thanks to Ruth Liebmann and Heather McCormack, because they know how to love books.

Many inspirations have sparked the writing of this book, first of which was an article in *Real Simple* by Liz Welch. Thanks to Brianna McNelly for digging in all the archives that the Internet still fails to reach, primarily those at North Dakota State University. *North for the Harvest* by Jim Norris is a fascinating look at the Mexican migrants working the sugar fields of the upper Midwest. *Behind the Mask of Chivalry* by Nancy MacLean helped guide me late in the game, verifying much of what was found in the archives at NDSU. The Minnesota Historical Society and the Clay County

Historical Society were likewise wonderful resources. Many other books and articles were inspiring, but none more so than *Candles in the Wind*, a novel written and self-published decades ago by my late great-aunt Edris Probstfield Hack.

My kids are now old enough to get their own line: thank you, Bo, and thank you, Hedda, for letting me squirrel away and play with my imaginary friends while you are at school every day.

And you, Brian: *As you wish.*